The Legend of Alfhildr

The Legend of Alfhildr

by
H.W. Coyle
and
Jennifer Ellis

Stephanie Castle Publications

an imprint of
Castle Carrington Publishing Group
Victoria, BC
Canada

2020

The Legend of Alfhildr

Copyright © H.W. Coyle and Jennifer Ellis

All rights reserved. No part of this publication may be reprinted, reproduced, stored in a retrieval system, or transmitted in any form or by any means, electronic, mechanical, photocopying and recording, or otherwise, now known or hereafter invented without the express prior written permission of the author, except for brief passages quoted by a reviewer in a newspaper or magazine. To perform any of the above is an infringement of copyright law.

This is a work of fiction. Names, characters, places, events, locales, and incidents are either the products of the author's imagination or used in a fictitious manner. Any resemblance to actual persons, living or dead, or actual events is purely coincidental.

First published in paperback in 2020
Previously published in Kindle e-book 2013

Cover Art: Jennifer Ellis
Cover Design: Margot Wilson

ISBN: 978-1-990096-00-6 (paperback)
ISBN: 978-1-990096-01-3 (Kindle-book)
ISBN: 978-1-990096-02-0 (Smashwords e-book)

Published in Canada by
Stephanie Castle Publications
www.stephaniecastle.ca

an imprint of
Castle Carrington Publishing
www.castlecarringtonpublishing.ca
Victoria BC
Canada

Contents

GLOSSARY ix
Editor's Comment xiii
PROLOGUE 1
    Present Day England, "The Dig"
    England, 1012 AD

PART ONE
VERDA (BECOMING)
  Chapter One
  THE OLD WOMAN 8
    The Saga of the Wolf's Child

  Chapter Two
  VIA EX OBSCURUM 17
    The Road out of Darkness

  Chapter Three
  BLOOD PROPHECY 26

  Chapter Four
  INTO THE GREY MIST 35
    Present Day England, "The Dig"
    England, 1012 AD
    The Saga of the Huntsman

  Chapter Five
  GIFTS OF THE GODS 51

PART TWO
THE SHIELD MAIDEN
  Chapter Six
  AN ALLIANCE OF LOST SOULS 63
    Present Day England, "The Dig"
    England, 1012 AD

  Chapter Seven
  BAYING FOR BLOOD 74
    Present Day England, "The Dig"
    The Saga of the Shield Maiden

England, 1012 AD
Chapter Eight
THE BLOOD MOON 84
Chapter Nine
THE MAGIC OF THE WHITE CHRIST 96
Present Day England, "The Dig"
England, 1012 AD

PART THREE
THE SAXON GIRL
Chapter Ten
THE WILL OF THE GODS 112
Present Day England, "The Dig"
Chapter Eleven
THE SAXON MAID 122
The Saga of the Saxon Maid
Chapter Twelve
A PROPHESY REVISTED 135
Present Day England, "The Dig" 135
England, 1012 AD 136
Chapter Thirteen
THE COURT OF SHADOWS 148
The Saga of the Old King
Chapter Fourteen
THE REIGNS OF KINGS 162
Present Day England, "The Dig"
The Saga of Two Kings

PART FOUR
SWORD ARM OF THE GODS
Chapter Fifteen
THE QUEST FOR SANCTUARY 175
Present Day England, "The Dig"
The Saga of the Quest for Sanctuary

Contents | **vii**

Chapter Sixteen
A PAUSE, A SECRET, A PLEDGE 192
   Present Day England, "The Dig"
   England, 1012 AD

Chapter Seventeen
UNHEALED WOUNDS..204
   Present Day England, "The Dig"

The Saga of the Heartless Homecoming

Chapter Eighteen
THE SPIDER'S WEBS 218
   The Saga of the Three Armies

Chapter Nineteen
THE BOAR SNOUT 233
   Present Day England, "The Dig"
   England, 1012 AD
   The Saga of the Boar Snout 234

PART FIVE
THE PEACE WEAVER
  Chapter Twenty
THE GOLD-CHASED ARMOR...251
   Present Day England, "The Dig"
   England, 1012 AD
   The Saga of the Gold-chased Armor

Chapter Twenty-one
"HER FINAL VICTORY..."
   Present Day England, "The Dig"
   England, 1012 AD
   The Saga of Alfhildr's Final Victory

Chapter Twenty-two
PASSING INTO LEGEND 278
   Present Day England, "The Dig"

England, 1012 AD
EPILOGUE **290**
England, 1012 AD

Present Day England, "The Dig"
AFTERWORD **294**
ABOUT THE AUTHORS **309**
H. W. Coyle

Jennifer Ellis
OTHER PUBLICATIONS **312**

GLOSSARY[1]

Æ	A grapheme formed from the letters "a" and "e" and a letter in the alphabets of some languages such as Norwegian. In Old English it as called "æsc" ("ash tree") after the Anglo-Saxon futhorc rune, which it transliterates. Its traditional name in English is still "Ash."
Æsir	One of the two Norse tribes of Gods, the other being the Vanir. Odin and Thor were Æsir (literally—from the East).
Banewort	Also known as deadly nightshade or belladonna, poisonous in quite small doses, but it also has medicinal purposes.
Boar Snout	A wedge formation used in battle to break an enemy's shield wall.
Bloodwort	See Yarrow
Bryd-ale	Wedding feast. The precursor to the modern word "bridal."
Brýdgifu	The bride's gift to the groom.
Burh	A defended Saxon town or site, such as a hill fort. Many were founded on pre-existing Roman sites. Some defined modern urban borough limits.
Byrnie	An old term for a short chainmail shirt—usually with half sleeves and only reaching the waist.
Ceorls	Ordinary freemen (OE).
Danelaw	That part of England over which the Danes (Vikings) held sway and started to settle beginning in 865 AD. This is generally defined by what is now known as the East Midlands.
Dimma	"Dark" or "grey" in Old Norse.
Eorl/Eoldermen	A high nobleman (OE).
Fylgja	In Norse mythology, a *fylgja* is a supernatural being or creature which accompanies a person in connection to their fate or fortune. *Fylgja* usually appear in the form of an animal.
Fyrd	Anglo-Saxon shire militia in which all freemen had to serve.
Geburs	Neither a freeman nor a slave, working the land with no pay (OE).
Hel	The daughter of Loki. To "go to Hel" is to die. In the Prose Edda book *Gylfanginning*, Hel is described as having been appointed by the god Odin as ruler of a realm of the same name, located in Niflheim.

---

[1] Note: (ON)=Old Norse, (OE)=Old English

Handfasting	In the British Isles, handfasting was the old pagan ritual of marriage. The word handfasting got its origin in the wedding custom of tying the bride and groom's hands (wrists) together. In some versions, this is only done for as long as the ceremony lasts, but in others, the cord is not untied until the marriage was physically consummated.
Handgeld	The dowry in a marriage (ON).
Hirdmen	Warriors who make up a royal retinue (ON).
Huscarl	A warrior who is part of the household troop in personal service of a lord or king (OE).
Kotsetlas	In Saxon culture, the better off peasants who owned their own small holdings.
Lovsigemann	Old Norse, the man who remembers and recites the laws that govern the community whenever the freemen gather for a common meeting.
Middle Earth	Where man lived, literally between heaven and the nether world.
Morgengifu	Old English, literally "morning gift." The day after a wedding, the groom presented his new wife a gift, or *morgengifu*.
Norns	Norns are a kind of *Dísír*, female beings who rule the fates of the various races of Norse mythology. The three most important norns, Urðr (Wyrd), Verðandi and Skuld come out from a hall standing at the Well of Urðr (well of fate). They draw water from the well and take sand that lies around it, which they pour over a tree called Yggrasill, so that its branches will not rot. In the play *Macbeth*, the three Weird Sisters are a Shakespearean representation of these Norns. In *Lord of the Rings*, Yggrasill is represented by the White Tree of Gondor.
Peace weaver	A woman who is given in marriage to join two formerly hostile tribes or kingdoms. The term presumably originates in Beowulf, where Queen Wealtheow is married to an enemy as a "peace-pledge between nations." The Old English word is *fríþwebba*.
Ragnarök	Old Norse mythological end of days, which includes Odin leading all the slain warriors chosen by the Valkyrie from Valhalla into a final battle.
Rod	A unit of length, equal to 11 cubits, 5.0292 meters or 16.5 feet.
Runes	A Germanic/Scandinavian alphabet used before the adoption of the Latin alphabet. Also known as *futhark* by the Old Norse people.
Runestone	Old Norse memorials to the dead with a runic inscription.

Glossary | **xi**

Shieldmaiden	A woman who had chosen to fight as a warrior. Shield maidens mentioned by name in Norse sagas include: Brynhild, in the Volsunga saga; Hervor, in the Hervarar saga; Thornbjörg, in Hrólfs saga; as well as Hed, Visna, and Veborg in Gesta Danorum. According to Saxo Grammaticus, 300 shield maidens fought on the Danish side at the Battle of Bravalla in 750 AD. In Anglo-Saxon England, Ethelfleda (also spelled Æthelfleda), who was the daughter of Alfred the Great, succeeded her husband, the King of Mercia, in 911 AD. She was a skilled military leader and tactician who defended Mercia against its enemies. These women were the inspiration for J.R.R. Tolkien's Éowyn.
Seiðr	Witchcraft. Can also mean Witch (ON). Generally considered the darker arts, including illusion and control over beasts.
Shieldwall	A multi-rank linear battle formation in which the men in the front rank "lock" their overlapping shields together.
Skald	A poet or storyteller (ON).
Skuld	One of the three norns that determine a person's fate. Skuld is the future, or that which shall become.
Spá	Another form of witchcraft (ON). More commonly associated with divination. Occasional references include magical healing.
Steading	Property, such as a farm, owned by a freeman.
Thegn	An aristocratic retainer of a king or nobleman.
Theow	Slave (OE).
Torcs	Also spelled torq or torque, a rigid piece of personal adornment made from twisted metal worn as an arm or neck ring.
Vættir	Wights or nature spirits in the Old Norse religion.
Valhalla	In Old Norse mythology, it is an enormous hall in Asgard ruled over by Odin where the Valkyrie take chosen warriors who die in battle.
Valkyrie	In Old Norse mythology, they decide which warriors killed in battle will join Odin in Valhalla and whisk them off the battlefield.
Verða	"Becoming" or "happening" (ON).
Viking	In Old Norse, it literally means "to go on an expedition." A Viking was a seaman or warrior who went on an expedition. Western Europeans used the term to define the Scandinavians of what is known as "the Viking era," which coincided with the Medieval warming period, 800-1300 AD.
Weregild	The compensation paid for death or injury (OE).

Whale Road	A kenning or metaphoric expression used to describe the seas.
White Christ	In Norse pagan society, during this period, Christ was referred to as "the White Chris'" or *Hvítakristr*. There were derogatory connotations in calling a man *Hvitr* (white or fair) as it implied cowardice or effeminacy. The current term "lily livered" stems from this. Thus, the "White Christ" was considered unmanly compared to Red Thor, who was a warrior's god.
Yarrow	Also known as Bloodwort, Woundwort, and Soldiers Friend. It has astringent properties used in managing blood loss. Often borne on the helmets of Saxon warriors as a token.

Editor's Comment

The Legend of Alfhildr is a work of historical fiction, a genre of literature that:

transports readers to another time and place, either real or imagined...requires a balance of research and creativity, and while it often includes real people and events...offers a fiction writer many opportunities to tell a wholly unique story.[2]

At the Associated Writing Programs annual conference in March of 2002, Sarah Johnson posed the following question: "What are the rules for historical fiction?" In response, she argues,

In my opinion...the goal of literary historical fiction is not to show readers exactly what life was like in a historical time period, although it may have that effect. Rather, authors...center their tales not on the historical setting but on the plot, which may help us better understand the differences (or parallels) between then and now, and on characters who manage to transcend time and speak to us from their own perspective in a way that we, today, can understand. One definition of literary historical fiction is "fiction set in the past, but which emphasizes themes that pertain back to the present.[3]

There is no question that *The Legend of Alfhildr* fulfils these mandates to a significant degree. Set in the early medieval period, when Danes and Saxons were at odds over land and resources in the place that would later become known as England, the pledge of two young women from opposite sides of the conflict secure peace for both communities. In the Afterword, H.W. Coyle carefully delineates various aspects of the historical period, customs, culture, medical treatments, beliefs, and social conduct that underlie the story. Moreover, Jennifer Ellis has written original poetic sagas, using Icelandic sagas as examples, which appear throughout. These provide historical authenticity, figurative imagery, and vivid sensory context for the story.

The portrayal of the primary character as an intersex person[4,5] is a

---

[2] https://www.masterclass.com/articles/what-is-historical-fiction-definition-of-the-historical-fiction-genre-and-tips-for-writing-your-historical-novel.

[3] https://historicalnovelsociety.org/guides/defining-the-genre-what-are-the-rules-for-historical-fiction/.

[4] Intersex: "a general term used for a variety of conditions in which a person is born with a reproductive or sexual anatomy that doesn't seem to fit the typical definitions of female or male," see https://isna.org/faq/what_is_intersex/, http://aisdsd.org/.

[5] interACT, (formerly the Intersex Society of North America,

meaningful story element. Although the narrative does not use this term specifically, that Alfhildr is intersex establishes an underlying premise that supports the broader arc of the story, sets our heroine on the path of adventure, and underpins much of her inner dialogue, as well as her interaction with other characters and the valiant decision-making that ultimately wins peace for Danes and Saxons alike. It authenticates her early training as a Viking warrior and her ostracism from her family following an accident that reveals her "true nature": in the end, it affirms her ultimate responsibilities as shield maiden and peace weaver.

Alfhildr is a fictional character. Nevertheless, remains of an ancient, high-status, Viking warrior, originally excavated in Birka, Sweden, in 1878, buried with a sword, axe, fighting knife, lances, 25 armor-piercing arrows, and two horses—and long assumed to be male—have been recently (2017) identified as female.[6] This discovery along with other burials, including a find in Solør, Norway, of a woman interred with deadly weaponry, a shield, and a significant battle injury,[7] substantiate long-held mythological claims for the existence of warrior women, or shield maidens (*skjaldmær* in Old Norse).

Dr. Leszek Gardeła, an archeologist and Viking Age specialist from the University of Bergen, Norway, offers interesting insights.

> *We find women who have a lot to do and a lot to say in the wider public arena. Women who travel to very distant locations. Women who engage in cross-cultural-contacts in trade… So, I think, both women and men had largely equal roles in the Viking society… This is the image that emerges from archaeology combined with textual sources…*
>
> *For a woman to actively participate in war, to become a warrior on the battlefield, she would have had to acquire a somewhat masculine role or masculine appearance. And when we read the sagas, it is often mentioned that those women who engaged in military activities changed their appearance to look more manly, or even changed their*

---

https://interactadvocates.org/) an organization based in the US that "advocates for intersex youth," estimates that approximately 1.7% of people are born intersex.
[6] https://www.livescience.com/64816-woman-viking-warrior-burial.html, https://www.cambridge.org/core/journals/antiquity/article/viking-warrior-women-reassessing-birka-chamber-grave-bj581/7CC691F69FAE51DDE905D27E049FADCD
[7] https://www.dailymail.co.uk/news/article-7642565/Scientists-reconstruct-face-1-000-year-old-Viking-warrior-woman.html.

names for male names...
I think it also depends on the status of that woman. If she was a member of the elite, someone from the royal household, perhaps this would have been easier and, indeed, several warrior women that we know of...are members of the elite... I suppose she would have had to prove herself, prove her ability in wielding weapons and using them. She would have had to become part of a group, accepted as an individual, as a woman, and as a warrior... [but] this is something we can only speculate about.[8]

The *Legend of Alfhildr* is an epic tale of heroism, friendship, loyalty, and community, a quintessential hero(ine)'s journey.[9] The portrayal of Alfhildr as an intersex shield maiden is a literary device that draws attention to issues beyond the immediate storyline. The intent is to imbue deeper meaning to the plot and evoke reader reflection on broader themes of bias, inclusion/exclusion, and what it means to be human. Readers are cautioned that the language used to describe intersex conditions, as well as social perspectives and the appropriateness of medical interventions, have changed substantially over time. Accordingly, the words, attitudes, and actions that may have been acceptable at one point in time may have become less so at another. The representation of Alfhildr's experience, as offered here, is intended to be respectful and thought-provoking, although not necessarily representative of the experiences of others who are intersex. With that in mind, the editor notes that only minor editorial changes have been made to the depiction of intersex in the narrative and Afterword. Interested readers are encouraged to consult more recent discussions of this issue. [10]

Margot Wilson, PhD
October 2020

---

[8] https://podcasts.google.com/feed/aHR0cHM6Ly9mZWVkcy5jYXB0aXZhdGUuZm0vdGhlaGlzdG9yeW9mdmlraW5ncy8/episode/NWQ0MTY0ZGYtNDZjZS00NzUwLTg0MWItYjNlOGY2MWE2ZWJm?hl=pl-DE&ep=6&at=1576584134493&fbclid=IwAR35NDp1-IEtGrVyr_TGGWM909cHXdtiYSN8RliRFQbLqhdrmYBpINvrBII See also https://www.youtube.com/watch?v=RdeMmkBXqHQ&feature=emb_title.
[9] https://blog.reedsy.com/heros-journey/, https://www.well-storied.com/blog/heros-journey/
[10] Some reliable sources for information on intersex include: interACT (https://interactadvocates.org/), AIS-DSD, Support Group and the Canadian Centre for Gender+Sexual Diversity (https://ccgsd-ccdgs.org/intersex-awareness-and-allyship/).

Figure 1: England circa 850 AD

PROLOGUE

Present Day England
"The Dig"

The young students watched in silence as Professor Thomas Bannon and a trusted graduate student reverently brushed away the last of the dirt from the mortal remains of a warrior. The anticipation was palpable. After years of careful research and months of arduous labor, the figure everyone suspected had built what locals called The Great Keep would see the light of day for the first time in a thousand years. Only when he was satisfied that he'd cleared as much away from the armor-encased skeletal remains as he dared did Bannon rise off his knees and step back in an effort to take in the whole.

"That certainly doesn't look like what we were expecting," a student behind him observed as the breeze gently tugged at the stray strands of copper red hair that fanned out from the gold trimmed helmet. "All the accounts said Godric had fair hair."

"Perhaps the accounts were wrong. I mean, who else would it be?" Professor Bannon murmured as he tried to make his response sound like a statement but failed as all detected a note of uncertainty in his voice.

The lean young woman who had diligently worked under Bannon on this project from its very beginning said nothing at first as she too examined the peaceful figure laid out before them. The remains they'd labored so long to unearth lay clutching a sword resting upon a frame that was anything but imposing. Were it not for the pronounced hips, it could easily have been mistaken for a youth and not a mighty warrior deserving of the sort of funeral that had been given. With a sweep of her hand, the graduate student pushed a strand of her own red hair back behind her ear as she mustered up the courage to put forth a theory that, if true, would undo her professor's preconceived notions.

"Have you ever heard of the legend of Alfhildr?" she finally whispered.

Wide-eyed, Bannon looked over at the girl beside him, then back at the fragile remains that had rested in solitude and peace for centuries.

"No," he muttered without hesitation as he shook his head in disbelief. "It couldn't be."

Yet, even as he was uttering those words, deep down inside a feeling began to stir as it slowly dawned upon him that perhaps, just maybe, the discovery he had hoped would save his position at the university would, instead, become the sort of find that occurred but once in a lifetime. Ever so slowly, the elderly professor looked back over at the young girl at his side, almost afraid to ask the question that was now on everyone's mind.

"Just how familiar are you with that myth, Elva?" Bannon asked carefully.

Dropping to one knee, the girl reached out with feather soft fingers to gently touch the warrior's red hair, still vibrant after a thousand years. As the late afternoon sun turned her own locks to glorious flame, she smiled. In a voice no one save the legendary warrior before her could hear, she muttered.

"I daresay more than you could ever imagine."

Æ

England
1012 AD

Struggling to hold back his tears as he walked away, the willowy youth did his best to ignore the taunts hurled at him by those who should have been his peers but would never see him as such. The thought of going to his father's side was dismissed out of hand. Like the other men of the small village nestled in the lee of the Great Keep, the boy's father was honing his skills with sword and shield before the watchful eye of their lord in the hope he would be chosen to join the lord's huscarls. Any thought of seeking out his mother and sister at the market, where farmers from far afield were hawking their goods, was also dismissed. To do so would only have provided his enemies with even more reason to mock him. With no one else to turn to, the shy, red-haired child turned toward home in search of his grandmother, the only person who seemed to accept him for what he was and not what others thought he should be.

Upon reaching the modest wattle and daub hut where his family lived, the boy hesitated. For the longest time, he simply stood in the entrance, silently watching his grandmother kneading dough as she hummed a familiar melody to herself. It wasn't until she reached over to snatch a pinch of salt from a bowl at the edge of the table that she saw him there. Startled, the old woman drew back, bringing her hand to her chest as she did so.

"Dear God, child, you frightened me."

Looking down at the beaten earth floor, the boy shuffled his feet as long strands of fiery red hair cascaded down about his shoulders.

"I didn't mean to."

The old woman was about to admonish him but stopped when she noticed the fresh bruise, not yet fully blossomed on his cheek. Instead, she stepped away from the table and went over to where he stood, wiping her hands on her apron as she did so.

"You've been fighting again," she muttered sadly without needing to ask how he'd come by it.

"I didn't start it," the boy mumbled.

Drawing her grandson into her arms, the old woman fought back the urge to cry.

"No, I don't expect you did."

After several long minutes, the boy finally found the strength to look up into his grandmother's eyes. He didn't bother asking her the question to which he already knew the answer. He knew why the other boys, led by his own brothers, found it necessary to torment him. Instead, he asked her why God had chosen to curse him as He had.

Surprised, the old woman drew back without letting go of the boy.

"What makes you think you are cursed?"

Having gone this far, the boy saw no point in holding back any longer. Stepping away from his grandmother, he stood in the middle of the room where the women of his family gathered to cook, sew, and chatter. With his feet planted shoulder-width apart and his arms held out to his side, he fixed his grandmother in a steady gaze.

"Look at me. I am almost as old as Oswin, but still I look like a child. And Godric, who is younger than I am, has begun to sprout the beginnings of a beard. Even my little sister, Hilda, is more stoutly built."

Reaching out, the old woman took the boy's outstretched hands in hers before leading him to a bench set close to the hearth. Even after they'd both taken a seat, the boy's grandmother didn't answer. As she turned her gaze toward the open hearth, focusing her attention on the flames as they wrapped about the logs, she took to considering an issue she believed they had put off for far too long. Only when she was ready did she turn toward the boy.

"You mustn't concern yourself with what others think of you. You have many God-given gifts that far outshine the growing of a beard."

"What good is it being the best bowman in the village when everyone laughs at you whenever you try to enter a contest?" the boy shot back as his anger enflamed his high, delicate cheeks.

"I wasn't talking about your skills with bow or sword," the old woman replied, placing her hand upon the soft cheek of a boy who would never know true manhood. "You've a lovely voice, you know," she mused as she gazed into his shimmering blue eyes, partly hidden by long dark lashes many women in the village thought were wasted on a boy.

At the moment, those eyes were looking back into hers through angry, narrowed slits.

"It is a curse, not a blessing," the boy hissed. "I sing like a girl."

Unable to stand the scornful glare with which the boy held her, the old woman looked away.

"I always knew this day would come," she muttered to herself, once more struggling to hold back her tears as she stared at the fire, this time using the awkward pause to steel herself for what she needed to do.

"What are you talking about?" the boy asked, confused by his grandmother's sudden change in demeanor and seemingly off-hand remark.

Rather than answering him, she stood up.

"Come with me," she commanded. "It is time you and I took a journey."

Baffled, the boy remained seated. "To where?"

With a heavy heart, the grandmother looked down at her grandson, who, even at his age, stood half a head shorter than she.

"I am taking you to the only person who can answer your questions."

"The village priest?" the boy cried out in a high-pitched voice. "He has no answers. I asked him during confession why God has cursed me, and he told me nothing. 'It is God's will'," the boy spat, cruelly mimicking their priest's querulous, reedy voice. "'It is God's will'—he kept repeating it as if that justified what the Lord has done to me."

"We are not going to the priest. The help you need is beyond his purview."

"Then who? Who can explain to me why I have been cursed?" the boy demanded harshly as his frustration at his grandmother's refusal to provide him with a reasonable answer began to evolve into anger.

Reaching out with both hands, the old woman once more took her grandson's hands into hers and pulled him up off the bench.

"Come, I will tell you as we go."

"Go? Go where? Why can't you tell me here?"

"As I said, I am not the person who can answer all your questions," the grandmother replied sadly. "There is only one person who can help you, a wise, old woman who lives alone in the forest. They say that she is older than my own mother, that she has always been there, and, some believe, always will be."

"Does she live far from here?" the boy asked as he was led out of the hut, through the thriving village, past the Great Keep built by Godric, the Wise, and out into the forest along a trail he had never taken.

The old woman sighed as she gazed ahead into the gloom of the forest.

"Not far."

"Shouldn't we tell mother where we are going?"

"She already knows."

"How?"

Once more the old woman found herself unable to look down at the delicate young boy at her side as she answered.

"We have discussed this matter often. Though she would have preferred to wait a little longer in the hope we would not have to take this journey. I fear we have waited too long already."

"Waited? Waited for what?"

Rather than answer the boy's question outright, the old woman looked down at him out of the corner of her eye.

"Are you familiar with the legend of Alfhildr?"

"Yes, of course."

"What do you know about Alfhildr? I mean the real Alfhildr," the old woman asked.

With furrowed brow, the boy regarded his grandmother, trying to decide if she was attempting to play some sort of trick on him. When he saw by her expression that she was serious, he decided to call her bluff.

"The Legend of Alfhildr is just a myth, a story that old men tell children about a girl raised by wolves. It is said it has been passed down to us from the pagans who settled here long ago."

The old woman allowed herself a hint of a smile.

"Most legends are based on real people and their adventures," she informed the boy. "This is especially true of Alfhildr, the shield maiden who roamed these very woods before Godric's keep was here to protect us. It was only through her efforts that the terrible wars between the people of this island and our ancestors, who came from across the sea, were brought to an end."

"That is what the legend tells us," the boy announced knowingly. "But is it true?"

The old woman nodded as they travelled deeper into the forest to where the trees grew so tall that they blocked the late morning sun.

"Yes, it is true. But before she could do so, first she had to take a journey, one very much like the one you must take."

"There is no mention of a journey in the legend," the boy informed his grandmother.

"That is because the monks who recorded the legend did not bother to remember it as it was passed down to us from our ancestors, people who not only shared Alfhildr's life journey, but were of the same blood that links her to both you and I."

The ease with which his grandmother announced this fact caused the boy to wonder if he had heard right.

"Our ancestors are related to Alfhildr?"

"Yes," the old woman admitted with pride as she squeezed the boy's hand. "They are. My great grandmother was a direct descendant of Alfhildr. The women of our line not only carry traces of Alfhildr's blood, we have been left with the responsibility of keeping her story alive and true. It is our duty to do so. By remembering the terrible trials she had to endure in order to bring peace and prosperity to the very people who once cast her out, just as your friends do to you, we can take heart as we go forth to meet the challenges each generation must face."

Awed by this revelation and drawn in by the solemn tone with which his grandmother spoke, the boy continued along for the longest time in silence. Finally, after giving the matter some thought as they made their way along a path that was barely discernable to the naked eye, he looked back up at his grandmother.

"Will you tell me of Alfhildr's journey?" he asked hesitantly.

Once more, the old woman squeezed her grandchild's hand.

"Yes, of course, I will" she replied in an almost reverend tone. "It is time

I told you of Alfhildr, so that one day you can pass the story of her journey down to your granddaughters."

PART ONE
VERDA (BECOMING)

Chapter One
THE OLD WOMAN

The Saga of the Wolf's Child[11]

Before our grandfathers, and their grandfathers,
There was no peace 'tween Saxon and Dane.
Hot blood spilt demanded blood price or vengeance,
And only the crows and wolves grew fat.

No man could sow his fields in the spring,
Safe knowing he would see the harvest in.
Not those whose forefathers called this island home,
Nor the men of the North who came for land and plunder.

Then came the shield maiden, Alfhildr, brave and fair,
Bearing a sword forged by the mighty Thor himself.
Accompanied by Skadi, the she-wolf, and Hoenir, the crow.
She came with the grey mist, dire and vengeful to her foes.

Red was the hair of Alfhildr, red as the blood on her blade,
She brought our folk from terrible darkness,
Through the blood of usurpers and reavers,
And guarded all to share equally the riches of peace.

Alfhildr's brave father was Gunnar, the noble son of wise Folkmar he,
Each year Gunnar led his hirdmen from their hearths
To defend their folk from wild reavers,
Men who defied the will of the gods and the laws of men.

The Valkyrie claimed Gunnar 'fore Alfhildr's first moon
In grief, to the forest her mother fled.
Maddened by sorrow and loss,
She cast Alfhildr off, to the mercy of the gods.

Were it not for the kindness of Skadi, a she-wolf,
Alfhildr would have perished alone.
Long years Skadi nursed Alfhildr,
Teaching the young girl the ways of the hunt.

---

[11] This poetic saga (and the ones that follow) that precede each major section of *The Legend of Alfhildr* are original creations written by Jennifer Ellis using Icelandic sagas as examples.

*In time the gods took pity on the forgotten girl.
In honor of the service her father had rendered,
They sent Hoenir in the form of a black crow,
Wise counsel and gifts he brought.*

*The sword was Durthfang, sister to Naegling she,
And the bow, Falissar, unlike any had seen.
With Skadi at her side, and Hoenir circling above,
The red-haired maid ventured forth, sword arm of the gods.*

Æ

As he was gathering his father's hirdmen, Gunnar, son of Folkmar, felt a tugging on his leg. Looking behind him, his eyes lit upon the shimmering, green eyes of a red-haired child gazing up at him.

"I want to go," the child announced in a firm, even tone.

Despite the grim work that lay ahead, Gunnar could not help but set aside all else in order to take his son in his hands and hoist him up until he held the boy at eye level.

"You may come with me when you can stand on your own two feet and stare me in the eye like this. And..." he added as he studied the boy's fair complexion, "when you have a beard as full as mine."

Gunnvor, son of Gunnar, did not hear the laughter of the other men. He was too busy trying to gauge how much he would need to grow and burned into his memory the exact length of his father's beard. Fulfilling the tasks set before him would not be easy, the small boy thought as his father placed his small feet back on the ground before turning once more to his assembled warband. And though he could not fight off the same forlorn feeling that came upon him every time he saw his father head off to battle, at least the small, green-eyed son of a Dane warrior and leader of his grandfather's hirdmen now had a clear understanding of just what it would take to one day lead men such as these into battle just as his grandfather, Folkmar, had, and his father did.

When the men were no longer in sight, Gunnvor ran off to find Urthr, his grandmother. He wished to tell her of his father's declaration as well as hear one of her wondrous sagas, lyrical accounts of gods and heroes of old that he so loved. He particularly enjoyed those that spoke of the Valkyrie, the choosers of the slain. It would be many weeks before the small boy learned they had taken his father. It would be even longer before Gunnvor came to appreciate that he would never be able to measure up to the criteria his father had established for him.

Æ

As was all too often the case, Ragna's heart sank whenever she watched her oldest son prepare to go out to where the other boys gathered to hone their skills with sword, spear, and bow when they weren't otherwise busy tending to the mundane chores needed to sustain life in the land to which their forefathers had laid claim. Neither bid the other farewell.

Instead, when Gunnvor, son of Gunnar, was ready, he simply left the hut without a word. As the oldest grandchild of Folkmar, it was expected, in the fullness of time, that Gunnvor would take up the duties his father should have assumed long ago, responsibilities that had belonged to his family since before Kraki, Folkmar's father, decided his people would not return to their native Denmark but, instead, settle on the land he and his warband had wrested away from the Saxons.

From across the room, Urthr, Folkmar's wife, watched the sad little scene between her daughter-in-law and Gunnvor play out.

"I worry too," she finally muttered without the need for a preamble. "But there are some things that cannot be rushed. Give him time," Urthr advised. "He will soon come into his own and I expect surpass the other boys, just as my Gunnar did."

Though unconvinced, Ragna said nothing. There was no longer any point. Everything that could be said had been said. All she could do now was wait, wait until nature, and the gods, saw fit to bestow upon Gunnvor the promise of manhood, hinted at but not yet seen fit to confer. With each passing day, she found herself wishing that Snurre, her second son, was the older of the two. She feared the day when Snurre would come to realize what everyone in the village was already beginning to suspect, that he, and not Gunnvor, was better suited to take his grandfather's place. Heaving a great sigh, the widowed daughter-in-law of a Dane chieftain set aside the concerns that were rightfully those of men, turning her attention back to tending to the chores that filled the days of the women of the village.

Æ

Upon seeing Gunnvor approaching, Varin smirked as he shouted out to Snurre, who was crossing swords with another boy.

"I see your mother has let your sister out to play," Varin called out loud enough that all, including Gunnvor, could hear.

Without needing to look Snurre knew Varin was speaking of Gunnvor and not his younger sister, a girl who already stood half a head taller than the boy who birth alone had marked as the one who would take their grandfather's place as chieftain of their people. Instead, Snurre brought his sword up to the ready as he prepared to take out his frustrations and anger by laying into the boy with whom he'd been sparring before the interruption.

Ignoring the other boys, Gunnvor made his way over to where the men of the village practiced with the bow. Though he could handle a sword well enough to hold his own against any boy his age, despite being handicapped by a physique that was pitiful at best, it was with the bow that Gunnvor excelled. No one, not even the best of Folkmar's hirdmen could match him when it came to hitting the mark with an arrow, at any range, on foot or mounted.

Ignoring Varin's remarks and the laughter it evoked, Gunnvor strung his bow and took up a good stance. When he was ready, he loosed arrow after arrow with an unerring accuracy that silenced most of his critics. But not all. Once more, Varin took it upon himself to mock Gunnvor by hassling his brother.

"While it is true Snurre's sister is a fair shot with a bow, I doubt she has the strength to pick up a sword, much less wield it," the dark-haired boy proclaimed in a loud voice, pretending to be talking to a companion.

Though he had been trying his best to ignore the comments being made about his brother, Snurre was unable to do so any longer, causing him to miss what should have been an easy parry. Instead, he found himself in the embarrassing position of having his own sword flicked out of his hand by his opponent. With the sound of cheering for the victor and the jeers hurled at him ringing in his ears, Snurre walked over to where his sword lay and picked it up before marching up to Varin.

"Here!" Snurre growled, offering his tormentor the hilt of his sword. "Take it and see just how good my brother is with the sword."

Unfazed by Snurre's menacing expression, Varin did not take the sword. Grinning mischievously, he glanced, for but a moment, over to where Gunnvor continued to send arrow after arrow into his target with an accuracy that gave him pause before turning back toward Snurre and staring intently into his eyes.

"I cannot," Varin finally proclaimed.

"Unlike some, I have a father who has taught me well. He would whip me like a Saxon dog were I to cross swords with a girl."

In and of itself, having others mock his brother was more than enough to irritate Snurre. However, to be cruelly reminded that his father was dead—a man of whom he had no living memory—was akin to a slap in the face. Though tempted to challenge Varin, Snurre decided it would be best if he were the one who showed the others Gunnvor could wield a sword as adeptly as he handled a bow. Besides, Snurre knew his brother all too well. He couldn't count on Gunnvor keeping his anger from getting the better of him and injuring his opponent if he were to cross swords with another. Having spent countless hours sparring with his brother, Snurre was confident that he could keep things from getting out of hand, even if their peers used the occasion to mock a boy who's temper was as fiery as his red hair.

After borrowing the sword from the boy with whom he had been practicing, Snurre called his older brother over.

"Put aside your bow, Gunnvor. We already know there is not a man alive, Dane or Saxon, within ten leagues who can match you with that weapon."

Snurre shouted out as he held up the second sword.

"Here. Come practice with me."

Practicing with the sword with his brother was something Gunnvor did not enjoy, especially when the other boys were watching. As the younger of the two, Snurre took great delight every time he bested him, which wasn't often. On those rare occasions, when he did manage to score a particularly notable coup, Snurre enjoyed turning away in the middle of their match in order to acknowledge the cheers of his friends, cheers that came at his expense.

While the idea of demurring was tempting, to have done so would only encourage Varin to become even more vocal in his mockery. With a sigh, Gunnvor signaled his assent with little more than a wave of his hand.

"First, I must retrieve my arrows," he called out, hoping beyond hope that the gods would intervene by unleashing a great storm while he was doing so. Or perhaps a rider with word the Saxons were coming would suddenly appear; anything that would allow him to gracefully bow out. Spring was upon them, a time when the Saxon warlords sent their men to harry and harass the smaller Dane farmsteads that separated Saxon holdings from Danelaw.

No such reprieve came, however. When he was finished drawing his arrows from the target and with a heavy heart, Gunnvor made for where the other boys of his village were gathered, patiently waiting for another opportunity to mock him.

Æ

At first, the two brothers were hesitant, as much to provide the other with an opportunity to rest from their former labors as to gauge just how aggressive each would need to be in order to make a good show of this, without losing sight of the fact that this was nothing more than sword drill, practice meant to sharpen their skills and nothing more. Unfortunately, when two brothers are involved and one has something he must prove, nothing is ever as simple or clean cut as it seems. This was especially true when the two are engaged in the most highly prized activity in which two Dane males can participate—fighting.

In no time, the brothers were coming at each other with all they had, swinging and thrusting in a manner that would have caused a serious wound if any of their blows did, by chance, strike home. It was in the midst of one such exchange that Gunnvor lunged at Snurre with all his might. Only luck, two steps back and quick twisting of his body allowed Snurre to avoid Gunnvor's wild thrust, causing the older boy to fly stumbling past him as he went. Unable to resist the opportunity to have a bit of fun at Gunnvor's expense, Snurre quickly pivoted about on one foot and, with the other, gave his brother a swift kick in the hindquarters.

Amused and delighted by this feat, the other boys watching the mock battle between the brothers clapped and howled in delight, encouraging an overconfident Snurre to look away from Gunnvor in order to bow to his appreciative audience.

Already enraged by the taunts heaped upon him by those who were said to be his peers, Gunnvor came about after regaining his balance. Without pausing to catch his breath or collect his wits, the red-haired lad once more hoisted his sword up over his head. With a rage reserved for mortal foes, Gunnvor hurled himself at Snurre.

The glint of Gunnvor's raised blade caught the eye of one of the cheering boys.

"Snurre! Behind you!"

Spinning about, Snurre saw an anger no words or gesture would check. Once more, stepping back in an effort to avoid his brother's blade, the younger of Folkmar's grandsons lost his footing, sending him tumbling over backward. With all hope of escape gone, Snurre brought his sword up before him in a desperate bid to parry the oncoming attack. He had not intended to draw blood, but that was what happened as the tip of Snurre's sword neatly severed the seam where Gunnvor's trouser legs were joined, biting into the flesh beneath.

Momentum did the rest, as Gunnvor staggered onward, no longer conscious of anything save the pain coursing through his body from a glancing wound, a wound that was to prove fatal to the dreams of a boy who had been destined by birth to be a chieftain.

Æ

Long before she saw them, the Old Woman knew of their approach. The shrieks of a widow-to-be was an all too familiar sound to a woman who was always the last resort of a people who chose to ignore her, except when they were in need of her special skills and herbs. From the door of her hut, tucked deep in the forest, she watched as an older woman led another who was clutching a red-haired child to her breast. Wide-eyed and wailing, the pair staggered breathlessly toward her.

"Come in, come in," the Old Woman calmly called out, stepping aside as she did so.

"Lay the child there," she commanded as she pointed to a table already stained with the blood of those who had come before.

"Then, step away."

In haste, Ragna obeyed, laying Gunnvor on a wooden table worn smooth by many years of use. Quickly backing away, she watched as the Old Woman took her place. For the longest time, she examined the unconscious child's wounds without flinching. In her eyes, this was but a scratch.

"Give me a moment," the Old Woman muttered softly as she took to carefully pealing back the hastily applied bandages soaked through with fresh blood.

"I need to have a sense of things before I can begin to undo the harm others have done."

Not knowing what else to do, Ragna retreated into the waiting arms of her mother-in-law. Together, the two watched anxiously as the Old Woman went about her work. With hands long practiced in tending wounds made by man and beast alike, the healer gently probed and prodded until she had a full measure of the severity of Gunnvor's injuries. When she had completed a full examination, but before she began the tedious work of mending, the Old Woman glanced up at Ragna.

"Why have you waited so long before you brought this child to me?" she asked.

"Had you delayed much longer, I would have been unable to save her."

Distraught and confused, Ragna blurted out in protest through her tears.

"There was no delay, Old Woman. We brought the boy to you as quickly as our legs could carry us."

Now, it was the Old Woman's turn to regard the mother with a puzzled look.

"Boy?" she intoned quizzically.

"This is no boy," she announced with a certainty that would brook no argument.

"Though there is, or was, what may have seemed to you to be the makings of a man between this child's thighs, beneath the jumble of flesh that should never have been there is all any young girl needs, save the portal from which life emerges."

Æ

When she was finished and Gunnvor had been moved to a raised bed where many a warrior had rested while recovering from his wounds, the Old Woman turned to Ragna.

"There's nothing more I can do for her now," she stated in an even tone.

"If she survives the next few days, she will recover and finally be ready to lead the life for which she was meant. Though it will not be the one for which she may have wished, I expect she will, one day, make you proud: for if your child can overcome this, there will be nothing she will not be able to do. Now go, leave me to tend to her. I expect you have other children who will soon be calling for your attention."

Badly shaken by the events of the day and what she had just witnessed, Ragna took one final look at Gunnvor before turning her back on him and leaving the hut. Urthr, exhausted and drained of tears, lingered a moment over her daughter-in-law's oldest child, placing a hand upon Gunnvor's smooth cheek and planting a soft kiss upon the matted, sweat-soaked mane of fiery red hair.

For the first time that day, the Old Woman allowed her own emotions to show through as she placed a hand upon Urthr's shoulder.

"A spirit resides within this frail frame before us unlike any I have felt before," the Old Woman murmured in a reassuring tone.

"Though I am mistaken about such things from time to time, I believe this is anything but the end for this child."

Taking heart from the Old Woman's words, Urthr turned toward her.

"Will you cast the runes?" she blurted out.

Something resembling a smile crossed the Old Woman's lips.

"It was my intention to do so," she replied.

But then, as quickly as it had come, the smile was gone as her face once more took on an expression that betrayed neither emotion nor mortal thought.

"You do know that I cannot pass onto you what they tell me, for only those to whom the runes speak can hear their message."

Sensing it would be unwise to demand more of the Old Woman than she already had, Urthr nodded.

"I understand," she whispered.

After thanking Gunnvor's savior and caretaker once more, Urthr hastened from the hut.

Æ

In the gathering gloom of early evening, in stunned silence, Ragna swiftly retraced the steps that had taken her to the Old Woman's hut. Upon catching up to her daughter-in-law, Urthr began to recite what the Old Woman had told her. Gunnvor's mother did not allow the older woman to finish. Without taking her eyes off the trail ahead, a trail that was barely visible as such, Ragna spoke with a voice as cold as a long winter's night.

"My son is dead."

Stunned by Ragna's statement, Urthr came to an abrupt halt, staring in disbelief for several long moments at her daughter-in-law before she was able to find the ability to reply.

"Gunnvor is far from dead," she ventured cautiously.

Stopping, Ragna turned to face her mother-in-law, wearing an expression that was as unfeeling as her words.

"That creature back there, whatever it is, is not my son. Gunnvor is gone. I have other children who I need to tend to and another son who I must prepare to step forward when Folkmar is no longer able to lead our people. How can Snurre do so with that *thing* lurking in the shadows?" Ragna proclaimed haughtily as she pointed back toward the Old Woman's hut.

"Our people will see it as a curse, as a constant reminder of Snurre's childish misstep, not only causing them to question his every decision and command but leading them to wonder if Snurre has been forsaken by the gods."

"No," Ragna concluded in a tone that told Urthr she would tolerate no discussion on the matter,

"Gunnvor is dead. From this moment on, we shall speak no more of this. Nor shall we look back. Like all dead, we shall bury the memory of what we saw and heard in the Old Woman's hut and turn instead to tending to the needs of the living, as is our duty."

Confused, emotionally wrung out, and unable to mount an effective counter argument, Urthr dropped her gaze. Sensing she had carried the day, Ragna turned away and, once more, headed back toward her village.

As she had so often done in the past, Urthr hesitated, looking back in the direction of the Old Woman's hut. For the longest time, she simply stood there, torn between her love of a still-living grandchild and her duty as the wife of a Dane chieftain and the grandson who, one day, would replace him. With heavy heart and fresh tears in her eyes, she too turned her back on the red-haired child who was teetering on the edge of death, the first of many challenges the young girl was destined to face.

Chapter Two
VIA EX OBSCURUM

The Road out of Darkness

Gunnvor's skin was slippery with sweat and white as milk as the wound fever held him. His breathing came in erratic, quick, shallow gasps as the Old Woman sat quietly beside him, watching his lips, while she passed the time by gently teasing out the wool on her distaff. Every so often, she would lean forward and lift the rough blanket, sniffing carefully at the child's wound in an effort to catch the first foul odor of putrefaction before it took hold. The only time she left the child's side was when she needed to go outside and tend to her goats or gather wood for the fire. Occasionally, she went further afield to seek out the barks, leaves, roots, and berries for her medicines. But whenever she returned, she always took a moment to lean down and sniff, testing for the first signs of corruption in the ragged sword wound.

Snurre's wild stroke had ripped Gunnvor's malformed genitals apart. The dull blade had torn, rather than cut the soft tissue from the boy's slight frame. In doing so, it had revealed something no one could have imagined, not even the mother who had given him life. The Old Woman squinted closely in the half light as she prodded the inflamed edges of her handiwork to ensure the fat yellow sutures of catgut held and the maiden's channel still lay open and clear. At the head of the wound, she had stitched back what little remained of the near useless stump that all had mistaken for a penis. Though she had been extremely careful, using all the skills she possessed, it was only after Gunnvor had managed to pass a few drops of urine that the Old Woman breathed a sigh of relief. When she had done all she could to undo the mistake either the boy's gods or nature had made when he had been conceived, the Old Woman gently daubed the lines of the sutures with thick honey and placed a fresh poultice of dried and shredded yarrow over the wound.

Gunnvor knew little of this as he drifted in and out of consciousness, existing in a world of pain and dreams that fused together, wavering back and forth between near consciousness and blessed darkness. Sick, exhausted, and near death, he felt himself caught in a trap from which there was no escape. One moment, he found himself desperately trying to escape Snurre as his brother came closer and closer, a bloody sword in his hands. In the next instant, he imagined he could see his mother in the distance with her back to him. Though he cried out to her, she could not hear him. She just stood there, oblivious to his cries, as she fondly watched Snurre. Merging with these images was that of an old crone dressed in black leaning over him, pressing a bowl containing a foul brew that she forced him to drink. He would watch muzzily as she leaned close and sniffed him like a wolf snuffling a carcass before feasting. Unable to make sense of any of these images and dreams, Gunnvor closed his eyes as darkness mercifully claimed him once more.

On the third day, when the Old Woman sniffed, she frowned. Leaning closer, she sniffed again. Hidden beneath the sweet scent of the honey, the first sickly notes of rotten flesh caught in her nose, causing her to sigh. She had been ready for this. With great care, she uncovered the wound and softly wiped away the coating of honey she had daubed on the raw flesh to protect it from the Dark One's corruption. The child moaned and tried to move, but she gently held Gunnvor still with one hand while she continued to mop away the thick yellow honey. When she was satisfied that the wound was clean enough, she fetched the little stone crock that had been sitting outside for the last three days. Within it was a small piece of rotten meat now buried under a layer of wriggling maggots. Ever so carefully, she tipped the maggots into the palm of her hand before gently pouring them onto the festering wound. Again, she sat back as her helpers took to feasting on the rotten flesh of the girl's wound. When the child stirred, she sought to calm her by softly singing a lullaby in an ancient language.

"*Lalla, Lalla, Lalla, aut dormi, aut lacte*," the Old Woman crooned, half to the sick child and half to herself.

The gentle song took her back to a decaying hall in Dumnonia, a kingdom long vanished and far to the west where her father had held her on his knee and showed her the ancient sheepskin scrolls, stained and brittle with age.

"And this is the work of the surgeon Galen, and this is the first book of Meditations of the Emperor Marcus Aurelius," he had informed his ever attentive daughter as he held her on his lap, watching as she struggled to read aloud the scripts he so revered.

"From my grandfather, Verus, I...learned good...morals and the...the..." Pausing, she pointed to a word. "What is this word Daddy?"

"'Government,' my dear little Virgilia...'government'. Something we sorely lack in these days of barbarity."

The Old Woman shook her head to clear the memory before turning once more to gaze down at the pallid young child. Here was a grandchild of a Dane raider who had burnt, slaughtered, and enslaved Saxons, descendants of the same barbarians who had murdered her parents and burnt the decaying hall with all its priceless scrolls. They had been like animals dragging everything down into their filth around them. They had dragged her away to be used like an animal. She knew she should have felt rancor and hatred. But time and toil had leached all her bitterness away. All she saw before her was a sick child.

Leaning forward, she gently teased the child's beautiful red hair from her eyes. She knew that out of such innocence both good and evil sprang. What path this child would follow was not within her power to determine. All the Old Woman could do was to help the frail, red-haired Dane cling to the slender thread of life onto which she was struggling to hold.

Æ

Four more days were to pass before Gunnvor was finally able to emerge from the world of dreams and nightmares. He tried not to flinch as he watched the Old Woman repack the wound with a fresh poultice of dried yarrow.

A warrior does not flinch at his wounds, he told himself.

"So. How soon will I be fit?" he barked brusquely in imitation of the way he had heard men speak.

"I must be up and training, else the youngsters will think me a shirker."

The Old Woman smiled sadly to herself, wondering how to tell her. Gunnvor's mother had not returned. With each passing day, it became clear to her that she never would. Looking into Gunnvor's flashing green eyes, the Old Woman could not help but notice how they were framed by long, delicate lashes.

So pretty, she thought.

"Child, your strength will come when the gods will it. You have come back from the bridge of swords and the gates of the underworld. Such a journey is enough to tire the greatest warrior."

Gunnvor thought long on what she had said. He liked the idea of a hero's journey as he allowed her to help him drink a soothing concoction of goat's milk and honey. Upon finishing it, there was something of a smile on his lips as he laid back and once more drifted off into a deep sleep.

Æ

Over the next few days, Gunnvor's strength slowly returned. When the time came to clean away the maggots, poultice, and honey from his groin, the pain of the Old Woman's efforts caused Gunnvor to press himself into the straw-filled mattress and grasp the side of the rough-hewn bed's frame until his knuckles were white. After finishing, the Old Woman took a moment to carefully inspect the wound. Only when she was satisfied that the angry redness had receded and the wound's edges were beginning to knit together did she gently replace the blanket as Gunnvor slowly unclenched his fists, letting out a deep rattling sigh as he did so.

"Do you think my mother will come today?" he asked when he was finally able to speak, making no effort to hide the plaintive edge that tinged his voice as he did so.

The Old Woman turned away to hide her face. Not a word had come from Folkmar's village since the fateful day. She knew she would have to tell the child the bitter truth of her abandonment: but, on this day, her courage failed her.

"No, not today."

"Perhaps tomorrow?" the child shot back, betraying a hint of desperation.

"We will have to wait and see," the Old Woman murmured as her eyes stung with her lie and the thought of the pain to come.

Gunnvor remained silent. He had dreamt his mother had been here, he knew she had. But, in his dream, he had been unable to reach out to her. She had stood with her back to him, watching as Snurre approached. He shivered. She was coming back. She had to!

The following day broke dry and bright, the late summer sunshine casting sharp patterns on the beaten earthen floor of the hovel with the smell of the forest clean and crisp in the air. Gunnvor *knew* today was the day. Today, his mother would come to take him home.

"You will be glad to see the back of me," he announced as he grinned at the Old Woman.

"I shall make sure my grandfather, mighty Folkmar, rewards you. He is a generous man to those who serve him well."

In good spirits, Gunnvor settled himself to wait, idly considering how best to repay Snurre for his stray blade and his taunts.

I will show him. I've been to the gates of death itself and returned! Now, he will have to show the respect due me.

The day wore on, morning turning to afternoon as Gunnvor waited for his mother.

Of course, she would do her woman's work first, he concluded when she did not appear. *And it is a long walk through the forest.*

The Old Woman watched the child staring eagerly at the door until the shadows slowly began to lengthen. As the darkness gathered, she lit the evening fire before pouring a bowl of milk and honey into which she crumbled a small handful of dried herbs. When she was finished, she took a deep breath to steel herself before facing the nervous child.

"You need to drink this, child."

Gunnvor frowned, irritated by the way she insisted on calling him a child. He was no mere child. He was Gunnvor, son of Gunnar. But mindful of the debt his family owed her and still unsure of the Old Woman, he said nothing as he took the bowl and drank deep without complaint. When he was finished, he looked up into the Old Woman's eyes.

"My mother is late coming. Does she not know it is foolish to roam the forest at night?"

"Gunnvor, she is not coming."

"Don't be foolish. I'm her son and Folkmar's heir. Of course, she will come for me."

"Gunnvor, please forgive me, but you are no longer her son."

He stared at her as she drew a ragged breath, willing herself to go on.

"The sword that cut deep between your legs was more than near fatal. At first, your mother feared that your manhood was lost. But, as I tended the wound, what I found told us otherwise."

As she spoke, Gunnvor felt an icy, leaden weight in his guts. Dreading to hear, yet desperate to know, he asked in a low, ominous growl.

"What did you find, Old Woman?"

"The blade stole much but revealed more. Between your thighs, I found your secret self, hidden behind a flap of flesh."

She sighed, "You are no man but a woman, child, complete and whole."

Instinctively, Gunnvor snapped as anger and fear rose like bile in his breast.

"You lie! What magic have you done to me?"

"No magic of mine save to keep you alive. It is the gods who made you as you are."

His voice rose to a shrill scream, "You witch! I am Gunnvor, son of Gunnar, son of Folkmar. I am my father's son. My hirdmen will come, and you will be burned. I am Gunnvor, son of Gunnar, son of Folkmar. I am…I am Gunnvor son of….son of…"

As the child ranted and screamed abuse, the sleeping draught she had given him slowly took effect until, at last, the peaceful dark of sleep finally muffled her cries.

Æ

As if to taunt Gunnvor in his dark misery, the next day again dawned bright and sharp. He tried to cling to the last shreds of sleep and the escape from reality it offered, but to no avail. Keeping his eyes closed, he slipped a hand stealthily under the coarse blanket, tentatively exploring the ruin of his manhood. He could not, would not, believe the foolish nonsense the Old Woman had spouted the previous night.

She was lying, he told himself angrily, while doing his best to bury an icy fear that would not let go of him.

When his fingers touched the raw edges of the wound, he flinched, pausing to catch his breath before continuing to carefully probe. He could feel the rough knots of the catgut edging his wounds as he found the channel the Old Woman had opened within. He jerked his hand away, afraid to find the proof of what he knew to be impossible. On the other side of the hovel, he heard the Old Woman scraping up the ashes from the fire as his mother used to do.

"She hasn't been here, has she?" he asked in a dull, lifeless voice.

"I'm sorry, child, but no." She could think of nothing else to say.

Gunnvor remembered his dream. He remembered seeing his mother, calling for her. But she never heard. No matter how loud he had cried out, his mother made no effort to respond.

"How long have I been here?"

"Four weeks this day, child," the Old Woman replied as she came across to the bed carrying a horn beaker of water and a fresh griddlecake.

"Eat, you need your strength."

Gunnvor had no desire to eat but took the hot cake and slumped back onto the bed.

"They say you are a witch, skilled in powerful magic. I have heard you know the arts of *seiðr* as well as the runes and the healing *spá-kona*."

He paused and glanced down at his body, his voice little more than a whisper.

"Make me whole again. Make it grow back."

The Old Woman's tears came unbidden as she heard the desperate, quiet plea. She reached out and took the child's hand and held it close.

"With all my heart, if I had such powers, I would do as you ask but…"

The Old Woman's voice tailed off, and Gunnvor heard the refusal in her tone.

Yanking his hand free, he turned his face to the wall, letting the hot cake roll to the floor. The Old Woman quietly stood and left him to his grief, sadly watching as his shoulders silently shook under the threadbare blanket.

Æ

The next morning, Gunnvor reluctantly allowed the Old Woman to examine his wound. Hot bitter shame coursed through his soul as she prodded and poked his mutilation. At length, she nodded to herself and turned to him.

"You can get up if you feel able, child."

As he nodded his assent, the Old Woman placed her hand behind Gunnvor's head, slowly easing him into a sitting position before pausing. When he was ready, they struggled together to shift legs too long unused onto the floor. Gunnvor clenched his jaw tight against the wave of nausea bubbling up from his stomach as he tried to pull himself upright. Their first attempt proved to be too much, causing Gunnvor to fall backward and leaving him breathless and dizzy. He lay still for several minutes as he struggled to catch his breath and gather the courage needed to try again.

"It's too soon. I shouldn't have made you try," the Old Woman muttered.

"No! I shall get up. I am a warrior, not some feeble child," Gunnvor declared.

Again, he tried to force his body upright. Gunnvor staggered, grabbing hard onto the Old Woman's shoulder, causing her to gasp. His legs felt like pudding, but he was standing.

Over the next few days, Gunnvor's strength slowly returned until he no longer needed to clutch tight to the hovel's walls or the Old Woman as he rose and shuffled about. At last, he felt ready to go outside and escape the dark prison of the hovel.

With nothing more than a blanket draped about his shoulders, Gunnvor leaned against the doorframe, drinking in the bright summer sun.

"I need clothes," he announced without bothering to look back at the Old Woman.

Behind him, he heard her rummaging through the battered old clothespress. When he did turn around, he was shocked to find a rough homespun gown laid out on his bed.

Fixing the Old Woman with a hard, steely glare, he gave way to his long-checked anger.

"Are you mocking me?" he raged.

"Because I am injured, you would turn me into a useless female? Well, listen close. Before the gods, I, Gunnvor, son of Gunnar, son of Folkmar, swear that I shall never wear a woman's gown or girdle," he thundered, breathing heavily as his green eyes flashed in anger.

The Old Woman looked carefully at the furious child but for a moment before setting aside her arguments that a gown would be easier on the wound. With a shrug, she returned it to the chest before pulling out a baggy jerkin and breeches.

Gunnvor struggled into the rough clothes. His rage masked the pain as the material chafed the still raw wound. He fought his way into the jerkin and forced himself out of the door. The Old Woman said nothing as she watched him go, turning back to her hearth instead.

Æ

In time, the jagged wound healed cleanly. When she judged Gunnvor to be ready, the Old Woman took to giving him small tasks to do around her holding, such as tending the goats and chickens, gathering firewood, scouring the cauldron, and baking flatbread.

Some of the tasks she put to him were ignored, chores no man would bother with, such as teasing and carding wool. Nor would he spin or sew. Yet, for all his stubbornness, the youth found himself drawn into her lore of herbs. He discovered that the yarrow, also known as bloodwort, and its poultice had helped heal his wounds. He also learned of the healing powers of honey and the uses of lavender, dandelion, nettles, and banewort.

Under the Old Woman's guidance, Gunnvor started to wash and groom himself using a sweet-smelling soap. Despite his best efforts to pretend otherwise, he began to delight in the feeling of cleanliness, wrinkling his nose at his own body's odor after only a few days. He also began to take pride in his luxuriant red hair, combing it daily until it shone. The Old Woman smiled secretly to herself as, every day, the child took pains over his appearance, carefully teasing out knots and flicking the unbound tresses from his eyes.

As autumn approached, and the evenings drew in, the Old Woman slowly took to telling Gunnvor a little of herself. He learned her name was Virgilia, a child of one of the last Roman British families living in far off Dumnonia, amid the decaying splendor of a villa near Exeter, or as her father used to call it, Isca Dumnoniarum. Gunnvor had heard of Dumnonia, a fabled land rich in cattle and dark, fertile soil where the sun shone strong all year. Not sure if he believed the Old Woman, he asked her how she had come to live here.

The Old Woman smiled sadly as the memories, still painful after all these years, came flooding back.

"We had a little farm where we grew all kinds of wonderful things to eat," she started slowly, as if gazing upon images of the past as they flashed before her mind's eye.

"Home was a hall built by the ancients. On the floor, you could still see the remains of beautiful pictures of men and animals made up of tiny little colored stones set in wonderful patterns. I was playing on that floor when the raiders came. I heard the shouts and screams of my people. I remember how I tried to hide under a table, or perhaps it was a bench. But a warrior, his face hidden behind a grinning iron mask, found me. He had heard my whimpering."

Pausing, the Old Woman closed her eyes and shuddered.

"I tried to flee, but he hit me on the side of the head with the flat of his sword. When I woke up, I was with the other children. We were all tied together with a coarse rope looped tightly about our necks."

Once more, she hesitated, unconsciously bringing a hand up to her neck as she took to gently feeling her throat as if checking to see if the rope were still there.

When she continued, her voice took on an unnatural, almost wraithlike quality.

"Everything about us was in flames. All lay in ruin. Nothing of my world or the world of the ancients who came before us remained whole. Not building. Not family. Not spirit. As we were dragged away, I could hear my mother screaming as the flames took her."

She stopped as silent tears ran down her face. A lump rose in Gunnvor's throat when he saw her distress, causing tears to form in his own eyes.

"I'm sorry," he whispered.

"Why? You weren't there," the Old Woman suddenly snapped as she gave her head a quick shake as if to erase the unseen images that were still as vivid and painful as the day it had been burned upon her memory.

"Anyway, I became a slave to a Saxon huscarl. He gambled me away in a drunken wager with another warrior when the great king held a gathering at Staeth Forda. Osfrid was my new master's name. He took me north where I served his woman, Eanfled, for many years. Then, your people came. Osfrid was killed and I had yet another master, Aðalvaldr. One day, he was brought back from a raid, wounded many times and as near to death as one can go without crossing over. I nursed him to health, just as I did with you. For this, he gave me my freedom."

"Don't you ever want to go home?"

"I have no home, child. Isca is gone forever. My family has been taken from me. All dead. I have come to accept that I am the last of my people. All that is left for me here on Middle Earth is to help those who still live and keep alive, in my own little way, some small memory of the days of peace."

As she spoke, Gunnvor felt the first stirrings of sympathy for the Old Woman. He had thought only of the joy and glory of battle and the rich plunder he would win. For the first time in his life, a small secret shame at such desires began to awaken within him.

Chapter Three
BLOOD PROPHECY

Autumn slowly fell upon the forest and still Gunnvor's mother did not come. With every passing day, his hope slowly drained away as the bitter truth of his abandonment seeped into his soul. Each evening, the old woman watched in silence as he prayed for magic from his gods and, each morning, he checked between his legs. This sad ritual continued until one day, as he was stripping in order to wash himself in the wide earthenware basin, his nails scraped across his chest. The old woman came quickly when she heard his yelp, one that betrayed more surprise than pain.

"What's wrong, child?"

Tears of pain ran down Gunnvor's smooth, elfin face.

"My chest! It's sore."

Ever so gently, the old woman lifted his hands away to see a slight puffiness around each nipple. With the tips of her fingers, she felt the tender skin, eliciting a sharp gasp from a child who made no effort to hide her fear. Only when she was sure did the Old Woman stop and look up deep into the child's emerald green eyes.

"It is time we spoke of your future."

With that, she led the unresisting child back into her hovel where the two settled on a bench before the hearth.

"We are so alike, the two of us," she stated as she stared into the fire.

"We have both suffered loss and pain. Even the gods have cast us loose upon the seas of fate." Ever so slowly, she turned to face Gunnvor.

"Neither of us can go back to what we were," the Old Woman muttered in a voice that still spoke of her own suffering as she gently squeezed the girl's hand.

After taking a moment to set aside her own bitter memories, the Old Woman gazed intently into Gunnvor's eyes.

"Do you now accept that your mother is not coming for you?" Before Gunnvor could answer, the Old Woman continued.

"Even if she did, do you think you could go back? How do you think you would be received in Folkmar's steading?"

The girl looked away, unwilling to admit what she had known for some time but had kept hidden deep within herself.

The Old Woman sighed before pressing on.

"My dear child, if we have no direction back to what was, then where must we go?"

Gunnvor sucked in a ragged breath. Her voice was no more than a whisper when she finally answered.

"Forward."

"Now that you feel your breasts quickening beneath your hand, do you accept you are no longer the wounded boy who was carried to my door? Do you now believe the truth of my words, no matter how painful they may be?"

Again, the young girl could not trust herself to speak but merely gave a tiny nod.

"The time has come to start you on your new journey. As is the way with all beginnings, there must be a naming. I believe you are a child of the gods and that it was their will that you were brought to me. They also gave you beauty."

Upon hearing this, Gunnvor flinched in denial. But the Old Woman would not let this pass, catching her hand until she once more had the child's full attention.

"Do not shake your head. It is true for all who see, just as it is true you were born in battle."

She paused in thought for a few moments, then smiled.

"I name you Alfhildr, the elfin warrior."

For a long time, the only sound was the harsh snap, grumble, and hiss of the logs on the fire and the quiet wind as it swept through the dark trees outside. At last, the girl looked up, her face stark.

"My mother has cast me aside, declaring by so doing that I am no longer Gunnvor, son of Gunnar."

She paused as she struggled to hold back the emotions this thought brought to the fore.

"I am no one's son," the frail young girl whispered as a single tear broke through her defenses, coursing its way down the smooth, silken, white skin of her cheek.

When she had managed to regain her composure, the girl looked back at the Old Woman.

"Though you did not give me birth, you have given me life. So, it is only proper that you give that life a name. It shall be Alfhildr," the girl declared as she tried, but failed, to find a smile with which to thank the Old Woman.

"It is, after all, a name better suiting the fate to which the gods have condemned me than that which I leave behind, much in the same way my people left me."

Æ

Days passed as autumn turned to winter. With it went any hopes the Old Woman had of Alfhildr accepting her sex and her place as easily as she had her name. The young girl continued to insist on wearing the breeches and jerkin, pointedly ignoring the gown the old woman laid out for her from time to time. To be fair, Alfhildr did start to help more around the holding, accepting she could no longer arrogantly insist some of the tasks set before her were solely women's work. This admission, however, did have its limits. She continued to refuse to touch the loom or the distaff, turning her attentions instead to fashioning a hunting bow that she used to seek what sparse game there was in the deep forest. In some ways, the Old Woman was thankful for Alfhildr's efforts to augment her meager stores: for without the meat the girl brought home, both would have gone hungry long before spring.

As they sat by the fire one dark and chilly afternoon, the old woman went to her chest and carefully took out a battered old parchment scroll, spreading it before her and tilting it ever so carefully until it caught the light from the fire. Alfhildr, curious as to what the old woman was doing, set aside the arrow she had been fletching and looked over her shoulder at the little marks and squiggles.

"Are those magic runes?"

The old woman looked up at the girl and chuckled.

"No, not runes. They are letters that make words used to tell stories like the skalds do. They also record ideas and thoughts, ideas and thoughts that can be passed on to others, both the living and those yet unborn."

Furrowing her brow, Alfhildr tried to understand if what the Old Woman was saying could be true.

"Show me," she demanded in the tone of voice Alfhildr always used when she was vainly trying to affect the manner of a man. Then, a thought occurred to the girl.

"What would my name look like in letters?"

A smile crept across the Old Woman's lips as she plucked a small charred branch from the edge of the hearth and took to drawing on the wall of the hovel.

"A…l…f…h…i…l…d…r. There, now you try."

When she went to hand the stick to Alfhildr, the girl drew back aghast.

"That's magic," she all but gasped. "The art of the *seiðr*."

The girl's eyes were wide as she stared at the simple stick as if it were a poisonous adder.

"No, child," the Old Woman sighed heavily. "No magic here. Just a way to remember words. You saw your grandfather's tally sticks of his farmers' taxes, did you not?"

Alfhildr nodded.

"That is a way of remembering numbers, no different from how letters remember words."

After giving the matter much serious thought, Alfhildr picked up the stick. With shaky hand and the need to pause every so often to look over at how the Old Woman had made her letters, Alfhildr carefully traced her name on the wall. When she was finished, she stepped back and studied her efforts for a moment before whispering to herself, "Alfhildr."

Æ

The shortening days left Alfhildr with little to do after dark. When they weren't talking, the Old Woman would sit with her scrolls and her one precious book or would quietly tend to the preparation of her remedies. Occasionally, Alfhildr would help, but largely she was bored. At last, she dragged in a thick tree limb as fat and as long as her leg. The Old Woman looked quizzically at her as Alfhildr took up a sharp dagger and set to trimming and shaping the wood.

"I need to do something, Virgilia, else I will go mad," the young girl explained.

With that, she went back to whittling and shaping the wood, the shavings scattering across the beaten earth floor. It was three days before the Old Woman recognized what Alfhildr was making. A heavy pommel and cross guard stood proud at the end of the long straight wooden blade. She watched as Alfhildr chewed her lip in concentration as she carefully carved the likeness of a dragon into the blade.

"What are you going to do with that?"

As Alfhildr looked up sporting a broad smile on her lips, the Old Woman caught a flash of the girl's exceptional beauty.

"Practice."

Thereafter, every day would find Alfhildr outdoors, swinging the heavy wooden blade as she skipped forward and danced back, fighting with an invisible opponent. As she did, her color would slowly rise so her cheeks glowed while her eyes flashed like bright emeralds. The Old Woman frowned as she watched. She had hoped that time and quiet would slowly gentle the girl to accept her place in the world, if not here, then in some other steading or burgh. But the dancing blade left no doubt in the woman's mind: Alfhildr's warrior spirit remained unbroken.

When not tending to chores or practicing with her wooden sword, the girl ventured deep into the forest armed with her hunting bow. It was a rare day when she did not come back with something for the pot, most often a hare, but occasionally a small roe deer that the Old Woman helped to skin and gut. Together, they would strip the meat from the bones and hang the strips over the hearth, built up with damp hazelwood to smoke the meat for the coming months. One evening, as they were doing so, Virgilia noticed Alfhildr rubbing at her breasts.

"Is something wrong? Have they become sore again?"

Alfhildr grimaced as she rubbed the tender area.

"The bow string caught on my chest as I let fly."

"Let me see."

Alfhildr blushed as she peeled off her baggy jerkin under the Old Woman's eye, revealing two breasts, the size of small apples that stood out proud and firm. Across the right breast and nipple, there was a livid red graze. Virgilia grunted before turning to her medicine chest, pulling out a small crock, which she handed to Alfhildr.

"What is it?"

"You helped me make it. You tell me."

Alfhildr sniffed the pot and tipped it to study its greyish contents by the fading light.

"Goose fat, yarrow, and lavender?"

The Old Woman laughed.

"So, you did remember something. It will ease the tenderness and help it heal."

"But what about next time I hunt?"

"You must learn to shoot around your breast," the Old Woman ventured, causing Alfhildr to snort when she realized the Old Woman knew nothing of hunting.

"Either that, or you must protect them."

As she spoke, she pulled a length of linen bandage from the chest.

"Raise your arms and we shall see what we can do."

Alfhildr stood still, her arms above her head as the Old Woman started to wrap the long bandage around her torso, squashing her breasts against her small frame. It was the first time in weeks Virgilia had looked this closely at Alfhildr. Much was changing, she told herself as she made note of the subtle changes in the girl's body. The breeches now hung low despite the tight-pulled rope belt, revealing a slim waist and spreading hips. As Alfhildr held her cascade of flame-red hair up to keep it from being trapped in the bandage, the Old Woman glanced enviously at the sinewy arms and graceful neck of the young girl, remembering she too had once been beautiful.

Yes, the Old Woman thought to herself. *And she had paid a terrible price for that beauty. The men who had admired her had had their way with her, leaving her in the dirt once they had taken their pleasure.*

Unable to help herself, Virgilia scowled at the memory.

Perhaps it was no bad thing this young girl hones her skill with blade and bow. No man could then force himself on her without thought or care.

Æ

The chilly rain turned to sleet as the year turned. More and more Alfhildr and the Old Woman huddled close to the small hearth as smoke eddied around the hovel. They had no skald, or storyteller, to pass the long evenings, but, prodded on by the young girl's eager curiosity, Virgilia began to remember stories buried from long ago. She told the attentive young girl tales of an ancient word of peace and prosperity that her father had in turn recounted on the long cold evenings in Isca with his family close around. She spoke of the legendary heroes, such as Arturios, Dux Bellorum, who had kept the Saxon hordes at bay and won a mighty victory at Mons Badonicus. She described the marvels left by the ancients, beautiful buildings alive with light and color, hot springs gushing from the earth where men and women took their ease in baths the length of a longboat.

"That's silly!" Alfhildr derided scornfully.

"No one would build a room just to have a wash in."

The Old Woman chafed at both the interruption and the girl's tone.

"It is true. My father had business in the old city of Aquae Sulis. Without fail, when he came home, he told us all of what he had seen and heard. He claimed he had even sat in one of the hot baths."

Alfhildr held her tongue, still disbelieving, but unwilling to call the Old Woman a liar.

Perhaps it was like the sagas of the skalds? She would remind herself. *Everyone knew they weren't really true, but that didn't make them less enjoyable.*

The two women, young and old, grew closer. Virgilia remembered more and more of her childhood under the young girl's boundless interest. Not just the bad, but also the good times, memories she had held locked away for so long. She recounted her grandfather's tales of the mighty Roman legions and the great roads they had built across the world.

She talked of the law courts to which her father had once taken her when a neighbor had tried to move the boundary stones. But most of all, she spoke with a wistful voice of a time when men lived together without sword and flame, fear, and theft.

"The Saxons left us alone so long as we paid their tribute and never thought to threaten them," the Old Woman recounted wistfully.

"I never found out why they attacked when they did. My father just wanted to be left alone to farm."

As bitter memories once more washed over the Old Woman, her voice became harsh and angry.

"Now, all that is left is violence, Saxon against Dane, the strong over the weak. Men take rather than share and steal rather than work. They kill and call it glory; rob but call it the spoils of war."

Once again, Alfhildr felt sharp pangs of guilt. She had yearned to be such a hero, a mighty warrior feared by all, rich on the plunder of Saxon enemies. Now, she was not sure what she was, or wanted to be. Instinctively, she knew the world held no neat place for one such as her. Her hand reached across and sought the Old Woman. Together, they sat silently, hand in hand, remembering the past, even as they pondered an uncertain future.

Æ

The first snows turned the ground to icy slush, often leaving Alfhildr and the Old Woman trapped within the little hovel for days with little to do. The bitter cold and hard frosts also made it difficult for Alfhildr to hunt in the surrounding forests, causing her to become more and more irritable with the enforced idleness. One morning, she woke feeling bloated and annoyed. Angry with herself and the world, an innocent comment from the Old Woman about breakfast was answered with a nasty retort thrown sharply back as Alfhildr stomped out into the slush to check on the goats. After feeding them, she made her way to the deep pit she had dug as a privy before the ground had frozen.

The sharp scream shocked the Old Woman to her core. For an instant, the brutal images of her childhood flashed before her, causing her heart to leap to her throat. She rushed to the low door and stared out, her eyes darting about wildly in search of the raiders. There were none, of course. The little glade was deathly quiet. Cautiously, she stepped out to see what was wrong. She had gone but a few steps when she saw Alfhildr at the forests edge, her breeches around her ankles, staring down as a trickle of blood ran down the inside of her thighs. The Old Woman grabbed her chest and let out a heartfelt sigh of relief, then quickly turned to her medicine box to grab a linen bandage before making her way to the terrified young girl.

When she saw the Old Woman coming toward her, Alfhildr cried out in anguish.

"The wound! It's opened again! Virgilia, stop it. Please!"

Kneeling in the mud before the frightened girl, the Old Woman looked carefully between Alfhildr's thighs. Satisfied it was what she had thought, she nodded to herself and tore a length from the bandage, dabbing up the fresh blood.

"If you've finished, pull up your breeches and come inside, my girl. You and I need to talk, and I need to show you what to do."

Æ

Alfhildr was wide-eyed and fearful as the Old Woman explained about the woman's curse that came with each moon. She looked down in repugnance at her own body as Virgilia showed her how to place and secure the linen bandage.

"It's horrible."

"No," the Old Woman countered patiently.

"It is what proves you are a woman. Every moon you will bleed so, unless you are with child."

"I shall never be with child. *Never!*"

Though Alfhildr vehemently spat the words out, the Old Woman smiled quietly to herself.

"Never is a long time. Perhaps, we should see what your future does hold?"

Alfhildr turned quickly at the tone of Virgilia's words.

"What do you mean?" as uncertainty began to creep into her voice.

"You have watched my small skill with herbs and the lesser magicks of the healing *spá-kona*, have you not?"

Alfhildr nodded as her eyes grew round. The Old Woman held up the bloody rag with which she had wiped Alfhildr's thighs earlier.

"This is your first maiden blood, fresh and powerful. Perhaps now is an auspicious time to attempt the arts of *seiðr* and rune."

She paused a moment, glancing quizzically at the wide-eyed young girl.

"Unless, of course, you are afraid?"

Æ

Alfhildr was sent out into the forest with strict instructions not to return before the sun was no more than a hand's breadth above the horizon.

"But I can help," she had ventured when told to go.

"You are still but a child and are not yet ready to enter the mysteries of the Woman's goddess."

"You mean Freya?"

"She has had many names through the years, child. Freya, Selene, Isis, Aphrodite. All different. All the same. Now, leave me and do not return until the appointed time."

The Old Woman's voice was kindly but now held a note of command Alfhildr could not disobey.

The young girl wandered aimlessly through the snow-capped forest, her head a swirl with a thousand and one thoughts. A silence beyond the muffle of the snow wrapped itself about her. In the trees, a crow watched her with bright sharp eyes, hopping from branch to branch as it kept track of her wanderings. Both fear and curiosity raged within Alfhildr. She feared the Old Woman's magic. She feared to hear her fate. But most of all, she feared not knowing the truth. At last, she looked up in response to a sharp croak from the crow to see the sun slowly setting. When, at the appointed time, she finally did turn back toward the hovel, tendrils of grey mist were beginning to rise from the ground to meet the lengthening shadows of the trees, causing Alfhildr to shiver.

Flickering, ruby light danced in the entrance to the hovel as she approached. She paused uncertainly before the entrance, willing herself to go in though her fear grew tenfold. At last, the girl hunched her shoulders and lunged across the threshold. As she entered, she coughed as the sickly, sweet smell of burning herbs caught in her throat.

Before her, the Old Woman crouched over the hearth, rocking to and fro and sucking in great lungfuls of the pungent fumes. She made no sign that she saw the girl enter: but, at once, pulled out the bloody rag in one hand and a small leather pouch in the other. Blindly, she thrust her fingers into the bag, pulling out a carved, flat token, then another and another. For an eternity, the soiled cloth was rubbed with indecent tenderness against the pieces of bone while the Old Woman rhythmically rocked backward and forward, backward and forward.

Alfhildr jumped in fright when the Old Woman's eyes suddenly sprang open, revealing only their whites. A long-drawn-out hiss froze the young girl's blood, pinning her to the spot. At last, the Old Woman spoke, her voice sibilant and sharp, while the words cut deep into Alfhildr's soul.

> *Girl child is she, though no mother or father has she.*
> *Huntress is she, who brings down prey with fang and claw.*
> *Shield maiden is she, but her shield the grey mist.*
> *Strong allies has she, though all are unlikely.*
> *No man shall defeat her, but her final victory will be to yield.*
> *Safe lands shall she make with an enemy at her side.*

Chapter Four
INTO THE GREY MIST

Present Day England
"The Dig"

Day by day, Professor Bannon and his students laboured away, carefully teasing away the soil that had both hidden and preserved the stone funeral ship they had discovered. On one occasion, when an undergrad uncovered the outline of what remained of a small casket, he drew back.

"Hey! Look what I found," the student shouted out, unable to contain his excitement before quickly going back to work with a small brush.

Though eager to find out what he had stumbled upon, he took his time as he swept off the last traces of dirt still covering the skeletal remains of a medium-sized animal contained within an ornate box.

Another student dropped what he had been doing to see what his companion had unearthed. Looking over his friend's shoulder at the new find, the second undergrad waited until he was confident enough about his conclusion.

"It looks like a dog."

Without looking up from what she was doing, Elva muttered.

"It's a wolf."

Æ

England
1012 AD

The two continued along the path in silence as the young boy mulled something over in his mind. Finally, he looked up at his grandmother.

"But where did the she-wolf come from?" he asked. "The one who found Alfhildr and raised her?"

The grandmother gave the boy's hand a squeeze as she smiled to herself.

"Patience. In time, in time," she muttered, pleased she now had the boy's full attention.

Determined to keep his mind off where they were going, she continued to pass onto him the story of Alfhildr exactly as her grandmother had passed it onto her, word for word.

Æ

The Saga of the Huntsman

Through winter forests Alfhildr rode.
Her steed, Dimma, grey as the mist she was named for.
No man's voice the shield maiden heard,
To answer her questions of the gods.

Long nights, she sat before a hunter's fire
Her teachers wily Skadi, farseeing Hoenir.
They taught her the gifts of kindness,
Showed her the blessings of friendship.

Long grew the maiden's hair,
A river of fire upon her shoulders
To match the flames in her breast,
A forge within which the sword arm of the gods was fashioned.

Each day, Alfhildr sought her answers
Like mist, she passed through the forest,
Her eyes the farseeing raven,
Her ears the quick, silent wolf.

From the depth of the forest, a hunter was drawn to her fire
The Saxon came like a thief in the night,
Determined to take that to which he had no right.
For Osgar, the Saxon, feared no man.

With Hoenir upon her shoulder and quiet Skadi at her side,
The shield maiden boldly stood her ground,
For within her heart, Alfhildr was a warrior,
That rebelled against the elfin frame in which it resided.

Durthfang did not taste blood that night,
For Alfhildr's kind words defeated Osgar.
A smiling offer of meat and the warmth of her hearth
Were enough to disarm a man who bore the scars of many a battle.

He saw the sharp-eyed Hoenir, and Skadi by her side
The fierce hunter saw a huntress, no Viking reaver she.
Harsh winter had been their enemy, with no pity for Viking and Saxon alike.
Together, he saw that through kindness that dire foe could be defeated.

Thus, the scarred and cunning Osgar, rode at Alfhildr's side.
Saxon and Viking together, sharing meat and the lore of the hunt.
Each night, they would tell the tales of their peoples,
Defeating the loneliness of the wilds.

Æ

Words by themselves were harmless. The Old Woman knew this. It was what people did with them that created problems, which was why she was always so careful when she divulged a prophecy. Some took her words to heart, believing once a prophecy concerning them had been revealed, their future was unalterable. For them, it was as if the gods had spoken and nothing the recipient of the prophecy, or any other mortal, did could change what was to become of them. Others believed the Old Woman's words were a warning, a prediction of what might be, causing them to alter their behavior or avoid certain people or a journey. Then, there were those who twisted her words to fit a preconceived notion or ambition. Unsure how Alfhildr would react to what she had been told, the Old Woman left the troubled young girl alone for several days, allowing her to reflect upon what she had heard and to decide for herself what to do with the prophecy.

That Alfhildr was giving the matter serious thought was obvious. For three days, she said nothing outside what was needed to carry out her chores. When she did speak, her tone of voice was halting and barely above a whisper. Even then, Alfhildr seldom lifted her eyes up from what was before her. It was as if there was a great weight bearing down upon her, one with which she was struggling. Fearing Alfhildr was once more withdrawing from the reality about her, the Old Woman watched her carefully, prepared to intervene with an herbal remedy that had the effect of shocking those who took it back into the reality of the here and now, should such a radical step prove necessary.

Thus, when the girl finally did break her silence, it came as something of a relief, though it was short-lived. It was on the evening of the third day, when the two of them were seated across from each other at the table where Alfhildr had been placed on the day she had been brought to the Old Woman's hut. As she had on the previous evening, Alfhildr was staring down into her bowl, mechanically lifting each spoonful of broth to her lips.

The Old Woman was doing likewise when Alfhildr suddenly looked up and across the table at her. For several long seconds, the young girl did nothing as she stared into the Old Woman's eyes with an intensity she had not seen in days. Setting aside her spoon, the Old Woman waited for the girl to speak.

"I have no future here," Alfhildr stated calmly.

When the girl said nothing more, the Old Woman nodded.

"No, you don't. There is nothing here but the past, my past. It is one you cannot share."

"Then, it is decided. I must go."

Once more the Old Woman nodded. When she spoke, there was a tinge of sadness in her voice.

"Yes, you must go."

There followed another long pause during which Alfhildr looked away as if weighing the consequences of her decision. Finally, the girl looked back at the Old Woman. The expression on her face betrayed the apprehension all children experience when it comes time to sever the ties with everything they've known and to venture out into the world beyond their childhood. Drawing in a deep breath, Alfhildr slowly let it out before asking the question the Old Woman had been expecting for a long time.

"But where do I belong?"

"I cannot answer that for you, child, for I do not know what is in your heart. I do know you are most fortunate," the Old Woman declared without a hint of irony in her voice.

Confused, Alfhildr shook her head, tilting it to one side as she regarded the Old Woman out of the corner of her eye for a moment. A small smile slowly appeared as the Old Woman reached across the table and took both of Alfhildr's hands in hers.

"You are fortunate because you are free, free of the expectations of others, free of the obligations that once bound you to a future for which you were ill-prepared. Your fate, your future, your life is in your hands, these hands," she stated, turning Alfhildr's hands over until their palms were exposed and open.

"You are free to make of yourself what you will, provided you have the strength and courage to do so."

In the silence that followed, the two sat looking into each other's eyes. Finally, Alfhildr broke the silence, confessing something to the Old Woman she had never imagined she would ever have admitted to another living soul. Turning her hands back over, Alfhildr grasped the Old Woman's hands, again drawing in a deep breath before speaking.

"I know what you say is true," she stated hesitantly.

"I know I must venture forth and discover what the gods have in store for me. It's just that I'm, well…"

After hearing the girl's voice trail off and waiting patiently for her to continue but without her doing so, the Old Woman squeezed Alfhildr's hands.

"Only those who have lost touch with their sense are never afraid. Fear is a great barrier, one that serves to keep a person from rushing off and doing foolish things. It takes courage, skill, determination, and, on occasion, a bit of luck to overcome that obstacle, to conquer fear. It is not a sign of weakness to acknowledge your fears. It only becomes a weakness when you allow them to keep you from doing what you know needs to be done."

With her emotions roiling within her, Alfhildr found herself unable to hold back as a single tear ran down her cheek. After taking a moment to compose herself, the young girl managed to return the Old Woman's smile as she gave her care-worn hands a gentle squeeze as a means of thanking her, both for her understanding and the wisdom she had shared.

Æ

Having come to a decision, Alfhildr eagerly set out to follow through on it. It was as if she feared any delay would cause her to reconsider her chosen course, to put off the journey she needed to make. When the Old Woman mentioned to Alfhildr that it might be best if she waited until spring had once more returned to the land, the girl shook her head. No longer fearful of being thought weak if she admitted her apprehension, Alfhildr confessed that she feared if she waited any longer, if she tarried and allowed the warmth of a new spring to settle upon her where she was, she might never leave.

"I feel the tides are right. If I do not cast off from this haven now, I may never again find the courage to do so."

Suspecting this to be the case, the Old Woman said no more on the subject. Instead, she did all she could to help the girl prepare for her journey into an uncertain future.

The next several days were taken up with the preparations necessary for a journey both knew would take Alfhildr far afield. There was much discussion and debate over what she should and should not take. It went without saying Alfhildr's first order of business was to assemble a small, but useful, arsenal for herself, consisting of the bow she had fashioned, a dagger someone had left as payment for services the Old Woman had rendered, and a small ax that had once belonged to a Dane who had been left with her but had died from his wounds.

The efforts of the Old Woman, on the other hand, turned to more practical matters, such as preparing dried meats and hard biscuits that would provide Alfhildr with a source of sustenance if wild game proved to be difficult to find. She also spent a considerable amount of time preparing a number of potions and ointments. When tending to this chore, the Old Woman insisted Alfhildr assist. Though the girl objected, at first, to being taken away from fashioning arrows to fill her quiver, the Old Woman scoffed.

"When these have been used up or they have lost their potency, you'll thank the gods you took the time to learn how to prepare them for yourself."

Having already borne witness to the power of the Old Woman's concoctions, Alfhildr said no more.

At night, when both were tired from their labours but not yet ready for bed, Alfhildr insisted the Old Woman teach her more about the words and letters she so enjoyed or tell her more about the legends of her people. When the Old Woman asked why this sudden curiosity, Alfhildr presented her with what amounted to a utilitarian explanation.

"I expect my travels will bring me in contact with many people, people of whom I have no knowledge. If I can learn something from your scrolls as you have, or glean some wisdom from your stories, I will be far better prepared to deal with them."

And while the Old Woman accepted this explanation at face value, she could not be fooled, for she never failed to miss the way the girl's eyes sparkled and a smile tugged at the corners of her lips as she listened attentively to the stories or succeeded in deciphering a new word.

On the day before Alfhildr was set to leave, the Old Woman opened an old chest, the one where she kept the female gown, she had once tried to talk Alfhildr into wearing. Alarmed, the girl drew back.

"I already have far too much to carry to be weighed down by useless clothing I shall never wear."

The Old Woman ignored her as she rummaged about in the chest until she found what she was looking for. With a touch of drama, she pulled out a heavy, grey, woolen cloak.

"Then, I imagine you won't be needing this," she muttered.

Embarrassed by her presumptions, Alfhildr dropped her chin, but kept her eye on the cloak.

"Well, perhaps there are a few things I could use," she muttered sheepishly.

Stepping forward, the young girl took the cloak from the Old Woman.

As she was draping it about her shoulders, the Old Woman explained how she had come by it.

"One of your kinsmen who had been wounded was brought here wrapped in this cloak. His companions said it was taken from the body of a dead Frankish noble, a man who the stricken warrior had killed in battle before being wounded himself. When it came time for him to leave, he gave it to me as payment."

Ignoring the stains left by the blood of a Frank and a Dane, Alfhildr gathered the cloak up under her chin. After ensuring it was not too long, she took to looking about the room in an effort to see if there was something she could use to secure the cloak. Guessing this was what the girl was doing, the Old Woman once more turned to her chest.

"I think I have something that will help hold the cloak closed."

Upon finding what she had been searching for, the Old Woman straightened up and turned to Alfhildr. Ever so carefully, she untied the string securing a small pouch from which she fished out a gold brooch studded with small stones the color of Alfhildr's eyes.

In the light of the fire, the stones shimmered like tiny stars, causing Alfhildr's eyes to sparkle as well.

"I cannot accept such a wondrous gift from you, not after all you have done for me," she whispered in awed reverence. "I should be the one showering you with riches for saving me."

The Old Woman brushed aside Alfhildr's objections as she stepped forward and fastened the brooch to the grey cloak.

"Don't be foolish, child. I am an old woman with no use for such treasures. Besides," she added when she was done and had stepped back to admire the way the cloak set off the flaming red of the girl's hair, "how do you expect to hunt if you need to use one hand to keep your cloak from falling away all the time?"

Unable to help herself, Alfhildr reached up, took the brooch between her fingers and turned it so she could admire it. Of all the gifts the Old Woman had bestowed upon her, this was the one she cherished above all others. And while she did thank the Old Woman, Alfhildr took great care to hide her love for this item, least the old hag suspect she was right about her, that the gods had always intended her to be a female.

Æ

It was long before dawn, when the hut was lit only by the light of a few dying embers, that Alfhildr concluded there was little point in laying there, tossing and turning in a vain effort to go back to sleep. The time had come to cast off, to put behind her the hovel that had been both sanctuary and crucible. Thus galvanized, Alfhildr rose from a bed that would no longer keep her warm and snug as she turned her attention to her final preparations for the ordeals that lay just beyond the door across the room from her.

Once up and about, Alfhildr made her way to where she had piled dry wood for the fire the night before. Taking her time, she carefully selected some of the smaller pieces with loose bark hanging on them, stacking them neatly across the glowing embers. When she had enough, she lowered her head until she was at eyelevel with the raised platform where the fire was kept, blowing into the mixed pile of dying embers and fresh fuel, breathing life into the pile. When she was satisfied that enough of the newly added wood had caught, she added more substantial bits of firewood before turning her attention to her preparations.

There wasn't really all that much to do. Everything she would be taking was already packed and waiting or neatly laid out on the table. Ever so carefully, she went over everything, item by item, arranged in the order she would carry them. First off, there was the wide, leather belt on which a small pouch with a silver clasp was attached. In it were a few silver coins the old woman had given to her and several phials filled with potions she herself had prepared. A dagger tucked securely into a wooden sheath hung on the left side of the belt. It would serve her as a tool, one she could use for gutting wild game as well as a weapon in a tight situation. The same was also true of the small axe the Old Woman had given her. It was stuck into her belt, where it would be near at hand whenever needed.

The next item on the table was an oversized leather pouch that would be slung over her left shoulder. It contained enough food to last for four to five days, more if she were careful, a length of cloth she could use for a number of things, including as a bandage if that became necessary, a small cooking pot, and a number of personal items. Most precious of all, in the last category, was a comb made of bone decorated with a carved dragon's head. Secured to the outside of this shoulder bag was a bedroll consisting of a blanket and a rectangular hide with the fur on one side that Alfhildr could put between herself and the cold, winter ground as she slept. Suspended from her other shoulder, she would carry a leather waterskin that could be refilled from a clear, running stream or melted snow if need be.

The one item Alfhildr had no intention of taking was the gown the Old Woman had left neatly folded at the end of the table. Already weighed down by weapons, equipment, and food, Alfhildr saw little need to burden herself with something she would never use. So, it was left where the old woman had placed it. Perhaps, Alfhildr snickered to herself as she moved onto other things, the next unfortunate lad who was laid on this table wouldn't be as pigheaded as she.

From her bed, the Old Woman silently watched the red-haired girl as she made her solemn preparations to leave. Like Alfhildr, there were things she left unsaid, lest she change the course of the future. The Old Woman would miss the child she had helped mend. Never having had a child of her own that lived past infancy, she had come to view the Dane girl as a last, final chance to fulfill her obligation as a woman by serving as a mother. The only regret she had on this matter was that her opportunity to enjoy the experience of nurturing a weanling had been much too short. With this thought in mind, she threw off her blanket and rose from her own bed, determined to seize one final opportunity to play mother to this most unusual child.

"You were not planning on leaving without putting some warm food in your stomach, were you?"

Sheepishly, Alfhildr turned to face the Old Woman, bowing her head ever so slightly.

"I must get an early start," she muttered, looking up at her mentor and guardian like a child who had been caught sneaking about.

"Yes, this is true," the old woman agreed as she set about preparing their last meal together. "It is also true that it is far easier to carry a meal in your stomach than on your back. Now, set aside your tools of war, fetch some more wood, and see to the goats. They will miss you when you are gone."

Alfhildr smiled as she set about doing as she was told. *Yes, they will miss me, Old Woman*, the girl thought to herself, *just as you will miss me, and I you.*

Æ

The grey morning fog still clung to the trees surrounding the small hut as Alfhildr gave the Old Woman a final hug. She did not go far at first, only a few steps. Stopping in the center of the small glade in which the hut sat, Alfhildr looked about, going over in her mind the paths that lay open to her. To the east, the whale road, over which her ancestors had traveled to reach this island, lay behind her. In her mind, to go in that direction would be akin to going backward, into the past. Traveling north, where her kinsmen were, was rejected out of hand. Having been cast aside by them once, Alfhildr did not wish to provide them with another opportunity to do so. To her left were the lands to which the Saxons clung with a tenacity that had once stunned the proud Danes. No doubt, they would be even less accommodating than her own kind, which ruled out that path. This left only the west and the ancient kingdoms of which the Old Woman had so often spoken in fond, reverent tones. Perhaps she was wrong, Alfhildr found herself thinking.

Perhaps, there were others like her, kinsmen of the Old Woman, who had survived the devastation that had claimed her family. The idea of finding such people, alive and once more rebuilding a world in which people were free to farm their lands in peace was too tempting a quest to put off. Drawing herself up, Alfhildr shifted her load about her lean frame as she gazed ahead as if trying to see past the grey morning mist that obscured her chosen path. Only when she was ready did she give the Old Woman one last smile before setting off, into the west.

Æ

Despite an early start, Alfhildr did not go far that first day, discovering as the day progressed that her stamina was not quite up to the demands for which her desires called. By early afternoon, she found herself having to make frequent stops to rest. At first, these breaks were little more than a pause, an opportunity to bend over, catch her breath, and gather up the strength needed to press on. In time, however, the pauses grew longer and longer and the intervals between them less and less. Eventually, Alfhildr decided there was little point in going any further that day. After coming across a spot that suited her needs, she dropped her burden and set about gathering wood for a fire.

On that first night, Alfhildr found herself facing a foe she had not prepared for—loneliness. As darkness closed in around her, she found herself unable to ignore the groaning and cracking sound the trees make as they gently swayed to and fro in the wind, or the noise nocturnal creatures created as they scurried about in the shadows just beyond the light of her fire. For the longest time, Alfhildr simply sat there, draped in the grey cloak, nervously running her fingers along the handle of the small axe in her lap as her eyes darted this way and that each time she heard a new sound. Before long, she found herself unable to keep from wondering if the mythical creatures in the stories her grandmother used to spin really did exist. If they did, Alfhildr hoped the spirits lurking just beyond her sight were not *vÆttir*, sent by the gods to torment her even more than they already had. That they would behave no differently than the boys in her village had toward her was something Alfhildr found she could not discount out of hand. The world, after all, could be a cruel place, a sad fact of which she was well aware.

Bit by bit, as Alfhildr sat there, tightly clutching the grey cloak under her chin with one hand while grasping the handle of her axe with the other, she pulled together the various threads of her life that had led her to this dark, lonely camp with no one to keep her company except the creatures of the forest, both real and ethereal. The curse the gods had bestowed upon her at birth, one that condemned her to a life filled with scorn and ridicule had set in motion a chain of events that had torn her from her family and home as neatly as Snurre's blade had ripped her from the feeble claim she once had had to manhood. Could what the Old Woman's prophecy foretold be true? Could her tribulations be little more than trials, challenges placed before her by the gods to see if she were worthy enough to serve them?

The sound of a branch breaking off and crashing to the ground caused Alfhildr to jump. After calming herself, she once more took to pondering the strange journey upon which she had embarked. If everything that had occurred up to this point were challenges fashioned by the gods to test her mettle, then Alfhildr was determined to prove she was worthy of their trust by not only meeting them, but overcoming them with the same courage her father had shown in his efforts to protect his kinsmen.

From out of the darkness the hoot of an owl once more distracted Alfhildr. Having renewed her resolve to go on, she set her mind to dealing with the loneliness that held her in its chilly grip. Softly, she began to hum a lullaby she had enjoyed as a child. In time, she was singing out loud in a desperate bid to banish both the spirits lurking all about her and the loneliness of the long winter night.

Æ

The bowshot Alfhildr was preparing to make was not particularly demanding. It was well within the range of her skills. Unfortunately, the strain she needed to place on the bow she had crafted at the Old Woman's hut exceeded its capacity. With a sickening crack, the bow snapped in two, alerting the stag, on which Alfhildr had been drawing a bead, of her presence long before the infuriated, red-haired girl took to muttering a string of vile oaths.

It had been five days since she'd set out on her strange journey. Five days of stumbling about in the forest on legs that had long forgotten how to hold up under the demands she was placing on them. Five days filled with futile efforts to track and bring down wild game that mocked her by lurking just outside the range of her bow or fled with ease whenever she attempted to pursue them. Five days that were always followed by long, cold nights with nothing more than her small axe and the sound of her own voice softly singing the songs of her people to keep herself company and ward off the *vÆttir* who lingered all about her in the flickering shadows beyond her lonely campfire.

On the morning of the sixth day, after tossing what remained of the wood she had gathered the night before into the fire, Alfhildr took to rummaging about in the pouch in which she kept her food. There was not much left, perhaps enough for that day and maybe, if she were careful, the next. Tomorrow, she told herself as she gnawed away on a piece of hard biscuit, she would need to find something to eat. Otherwise, she would starve.

With that thought in mind, she took up her bow and inspected her efforts of the night before to repair it. With furrowed brow, she examined the strips of leather she'd wrapped tightly about the crack before wetting them. While the leather had dried and shrunk as she had hoped, Alfhildr was not at all sure that this makeshift attempt to repair the bow would hold up when it was drawn. With a sigh, she decided this was as good a time as any to give it a try. Rising to her feet, she made sure the bottom bow string knot was securely seated before grasping the upper end of the bow and, ever so carefully, bending it down to where she was holding the upper knot.

She had just about managed to bend the bow to where she could slip the upper knot on when she heard the sickening sound of wood cracking and felt the bow give way. In a fit of anger and frustration, Alfhildr took the bow in both hands, snapped it in two over her knee and threw the pieces into the fire. As she stood there watching the flames consume the bow, her anger ever so slowly morphed into a stream of tears. Not knowing what else to do, the young girl, hungry and very much alone, stared up at the grey, lifeless winter sky.

"Why are you doing this to me?" she shouted to the heavens above. "What more do you expect of me?"

When no answer came, she crumpled into a heap on the ground and began to cry as she had never cried before, muttering to herself over and over, "Why me? Why?"

Æ

Sick at heart, almost lame from days of wandering and with hunger gnawing away at her stomach, Alfhildr found herself looking over her shoulder all morning, off in the direction from which she had come, wondering if she had the strength necessary to make it back to the Old Woman's hut.

Perhaps, the old hag had been right about her from the very beginning, Alfhildr found herself thinking. *Maybe the gods had intended her to take up the ways of women. But the Prophecy*, she told herself. *The prophecy had been so clear.*

Or had it? Had she taken the words of the Old Woman as a justification to follow her own heart and not the will of the gods? If that was so, Alfhildr reasoned, they were justified in punishing her as they were. Perhaps, she even deserved to die for the arrogance with which she had defied them. Sadly, she concluded as she looked down at the ground, if that were the case, they didn't have very long to wait.

Æ

The pale winter sun that shared none of its warmth with the earth below was well past its zenith when Alfhildr came upon a small clearing. Halting before crossing the open space, she spied what appeared to be a pit with the ends of sticks jutting up out of it.

Without having to go any further, she knew it was a trapping pit, a hole dug into soft soil and covered over with branches and vegetation designed to trap wild game or unwary humans. At once, her eyes lit up as she found herself hoping there was something in it, something that hadn't been dead too long. *Perhaps*, she thought, as she threw her cloak back and away from her right arm and before withdrawing her small axe from where she kept it tucked in her belt, *the animal that had stumbled into it was still alive*. That would mean fresh meat. When she was ready, she approached with caution.

It wasn't until Alfhildr had reached the edge of the trapping pit and was able to glimpse enough of the bottom to see luck was with her. An animal had indeed fallen into it. She was only a little disappointed that the creature was a wolf, as grey as the cloak on her back. Though she had never had wolf meat before, at the moment Alfhildr didn't much care so long as the flesh of the carcass was still fresh enough to stomach.

From where she stood, it looked as if the animal was still intact and unspoiled. She could see there were no marks or blood left behind by scavengers who had beaten her to this prize and gnawed away at the trapped creature below. Nor were there any flies about. Of course, with this being winter, Alfhildr imagined there wouldn't be any.

"Lucky for you," she muttered while staring down at the motionless carcass, as something of a smile graced her lips for the first time in days. "You don't have to worry about maggots crawling about you. It is not a pleasant experience, I can tell you."

The sound of her stomach growling, as if it had suddenly been awakened by the nearness of its next meal caused Alfhildr to cast aside any further hesitation and prepare to descend into the pit to retrieve this unexpected and most welcomed gift from the gods. Before doing so, she cast off her cloak, pouches, water bottle, and other equipment. When she was stripped down to just her jerkin and breeches, she paused a moment to judge the depth of the pit in an effort to determine if she would be able to climb back out once she'd gone down into it. Just to be sure she didn't supply the trap with a second victim, Alfhildr drew her dagger from its sheath, pounded it into the ground at the edge of the pit using the backside of the axe, and looped one end of her belt about the handle of the knife. After giving the belt a firm tug to see if the dagger would support her weight, Alfhildr set aside her axe before slowly climbing down into the pit with her back to the wolf.

With her feet firmly planted on solid ground at the bottom, Alfhildr turned to take a closer look at the dead animal. It was only then that she realized she had made a terrible mistake. Instead of finding the lifeless corpse of an unfortunate creature, Alfhildr found herself staring into the eyes of a wolf that was still very much alive. Drawing back against the side of the trapping pit, her right hand instinctively flew across her body for a dagger that wasn't there. Without taking her eyes off those of the wolf, she reached behind her and took to groping about with her hand in search of the belt as she braced herself to flee if the wolf held off his attack long enough, or to receive its attack as best she could, unarmed and alone.

Once more, luck seemed to be with her as her hand grasped the loose end of her belt before the wolf struck. Tightening her grip about it, she was just about ready to turn her back on the wolf and scramble out of the pit when she heard the creature at her feet whimper.

It was injured, Alfhildr thought to herself, *injured or weak from starvation, just like her.*

For whatever reason, rather than take advantage of this revelation, the young girl hesitated as she watched the animal stretch one of its front legs out toward her and paw at the ground as if it were trying to reach out to her.

Letting go of the belt, Alfhildr leaned a bit closer to the animal. As she did so, the wolf laid its ears back, lifted its head off the ground and, once more, let out a pathetic, almost plaintive whimper.

"Are you hurt?" Alfhildr asked as she took to examining the creature with greater care as her fear ebbed away to be replaced by the first stirrings of sympathy for another creature that, like herself, had been abandoned by her own kind. As if in response, the wolf once more whimpered while feebly pawing away at the ground.

Ever so slowly, Alfhildr eased down onto her haunches before reaching out with her left hand, watching the wolf's eyes as she did so for any sign of a sudden change in its demeanor. There was none. Instead of snapping at the hand before it, the animal simply remained still as her hand came to rest on its head. Having passed that test, Alfhildr gently moved her hand further along the wolf's head, down along its neck, then back toward her, teasing the creature's chin with her fingers: providing it with every opportunity, she dared, to turn on her.

Taking her hand away, Alfhildr rested it upon her knee as she stared into the wolf's eyes, wondering what to do now. It was during this interlude, as two forlorn hunters stared at each other in silence, that Alfhildr recalled a passage in the Old Woman's prophecy.

Strong allies has she, though all are unlikely.

Why this should have occurred to her at this moment at first seemed odd. Then, she remembered another line:

Safe lands shall she make with an enemy at her side.

Was this wolf the enemy she was meant to have at her side? she wondered.
"Well, you definitely would make for an unlikely ally," Alfhildr announced as she once more reached out and caressed the wolf's neck, this time with her right hand.

As if the wolf also sensed the danger had passed, the animal closed its eyes, relaxing as it reveled in the attention Alfhildr was giving it.

"Perhaps the gods have sent me something more valuable than food. Maybe they have given me something I have been in need of for a long time."

Easing back off her haunches and onto her bottom, Alfhildr scooted herself forward a bit until she could rest the wolf's head in her lap. With both hands, she took to rubbing the wolf's neck. When the animal responded by giving its tail a slight wag, the lonely girl smiled. Though still hungry, she suspected she had discovered something even more valuable than food in the pit. She had found a friend.

Æ

Alfhildr didn't go any further that day, devoting what was left of the pale winter daylight to hauling the wolf from the pit, building a fire, and sharing the last of her food with the animal. As darkness fell and the girl once more found herself surrounded by the strange noises that filled the darkness beyond the light of her fire, Alfhildr softly sang while the wolf, still weak from its long ordeal in the trapping pit, cuddled next to her for warmth. Rather than maintain a safe distance from a predator that was beginning to show signs of regaining its strength, Alfhildr gently caressed the wolf's neck with the tips of her fingers as she stared up at the stars in the clear winter sky and sang.

Æ

The next morning, it came as something of a surprise when Alfhildr found the wolf still with her, snuggled up close to her. Not that she minded. The warmth of the animal's body was most welcome. When she stirred, the wolf popped up its head and looked about before turning to face her.

"I thought you would be gone by now," Alfhildr announced as she raised her arms up high above her head to stretch.

Perking up its ears, the animal wagged its tail in response.

"If you are waiting for more food, I have no more to give you," Alfhildr informed the wolf. "I tarried far too long yesterday. Today is dedicated to hunting, for if I do not find anything worthy of the name 'food,' your savior may very well become your executioner."

Once more, the wolf wagged its tail, causing Alfhildr to laugh as she took to stroking both sides of the animal's neck.

"I'm serious, wolf friend. If the gods do not favor me today, tonight one of us will be gnawing on the bones of the other. Now," she announced as the two came to their feet, "we have much to do."

Once more, the wolf surprised Alfhildr as it followed her throughout the morning rather than striking off on its own to search for its pack. The idea of shooing the animal away never occurred to the girl. Whether this was because she longed for company, even if it was a mute animal, or due to a sense that this creature was meant to be with her, didn't matter. Whatever the reason, Alfhildr turned her attention to seeking out game, any game she could find and take down with the limited means she had at hand, which she believed consisted of nothing more than a dagger and a small axe. In this, she was wrong.

Shortly before noon, Alfhildr became aware of a sudden change in the wolf's behavior. Fearing trouble, she stopped as she took to watching what the animal at her side was doing while slowly drawing the small axe from her belt, just in case.

Cocking its head back, the wolf took to sniffing the air, first to the left, then to the right. When it had a better sense of where it wanted to go, the wolf fixed its gaze upon a snow-covered mound before slowly advancing toward it. Looking off in the direction the animal was headed, Alfhildr spotted the mound and recognized it for what it was, a burrow or lair of some kind. Tightening her grasp about her axe, she followed the wolf, stopping a short distance from it as the animal took to circling about the mound, seeking out an entry point. When the wolf found what it was looking for, it began to dig.

Far too hungry to stand back and wait to see what happened next, Alfhildr joined the wolf in digging, using her axe to break up the soil before scooping out the loose dirt with her hands. Both were furiously clawing away at the ground when they received a nasty surprise in the form of a badger who suddenly pushed his way through the loose dirt the two had churned up. Drawing away, Alfhildr took up her axe while the wolf, ears pinned back and teeth bared, gingerly eased back without taking its eyes off the badger.

Roused from its slumbers, the badger paused, looking to where Alfhildr stood with her axe poised to strike and at the wolf. Judging the animal to be the greater threat, the badger snapped at the wolf.

Upon seeing an opportunity, Alfhildr took a few quick steps toward the badger. That creature, however, was far too fast, turning away from the wolf in order to deal with the new threat. With short, quick strides the badger growled as it fearlessly advanced on Alfhildr. In doing so, it exposed its flank to the wolf, which lunged forward, matching the badger's fierce growl with one of its own. Once more distracted, the badger stopped before it reached Alfhildr, turning its head toward the wolf in order to snap at it.

That was all the opening Alfhildr needed. With quick strides, the girl closed the distance, bringing her axe up to the ready as she did so. Before the badger could turn once more to confront her, Alfhildr was able to strike, neatly cleaving the badger's skull in two.

Æ

The pair of predators managed to dig out and slay three badgers that day, allowing them to enjoy a feast that night as well as prepare what was not eaten for later consumption when luck would not favor them as it had this day. The she-wolf, who Alfhildr took to calling Skadi after the Norse goddess of winter and the hunt, watched attentively as the girl went about skinning and roasting the badgers over their campfire. Skadi's patience was rewarded when Alfhildr tossed bits and pieces of raw entrails over to the wolf from time to time, causing the girl to laugh as the wolf reared up on its hind legs to snatch the fresh meat while it was still in mid-air.

After both had had their fill and darkness once more descended upon them, Alfhildr sang songs of the hunt that she recalled while stroking Skadi's neck as the wolf lay by her side with its head in her lap. When exhaustion finally overcame them, they snuggled together under the blanket, with Alfhildr's arm draped about the neck of the first of many strange allies the Dane girl would find on a quest she hoped would lead her to a place she could call home but would, instead, take her on a heroic journey the likes of which no man had ever taken.

Chapter Five
GIFTS OF THE GODS

With stealth and cunning, Alfhildr moved through the early afternoon mist, her footfalls cautious as she stalked her prey. Pausing, she looked back over her shoulder at her partner, grinning to herself with approval as the grey wolf crouched low and still, sniffing the quiet air again. The fresh scent of a deer tantalized her nose. It was near. Then, off in the shadows, a shiver of dappled brown caught the she-wolf's eye, causing her ears to perk up as she took to circling warily around the thicket, flitting from shadow to shadow. At last, when she was close enough, she stopped, crouched, and looked across to Alfhildr.

Unfolding gracefully from the mist, Alfhildr quietly loped toward the thicket with her sharpened ash stick held firmly before her at the ready. Finally, aware of its mortal danger, the roe deer's ears flicked up in alarm as it quickly glanced about before turning to flee from the sudden threat. It did not get very far. The last thing the frightened animal felt were Skadi's fangs closing about its throat as the she-wolf sprang from her hiding place and took the deer down in a single, quick bound.

The two huntresses wasted little time butchering the deer and preparing to feast upon it. It had been days since their last kill, and both were ravenous. The game in this part of the forest had largely fled from the silent grey killers. Soon, they would need to move on again in search of fresh hunting grounds.

With practiced ease, Alfhildr quickly set the kindling around the feathered sticks and dried bracken she had prepared for the fire the night before. Striking dagger to firestone, she rained bright sparks down onto the pile. When some caught, she began to blow softly, ever so carefully fanning the tiny embers until the flames took hold. Skadi watched her friend with quiet amusement for a moment before going back to the still warm entrails of the deer Alfhildr had rewarded her with for her contribution to a successful hunt.

Once the fire was well alight and a small haunch was roasting, Alfhildr turned her attention to a stack of thin saplings she had gathered. She began by planting a line of twelve in the earth, each a handbreadth apart. Then, she started weaving the remaining sticks to and fro between them. She checked the roasting meat before going back to the thicket to collect more thin saplings, doing so again and again until, at last, the wattle shelter was complete. Pulling it forward to form a sloping roof in front of the small fire, she finished it by laying rough cut sods on top to keep out the threatening rain.

When darkness finally closed in about them and the rain began to fall, Alfhildr settled back into the little shelter to gnaw hungrily on the deer haunch, letting its hot juices dribble down her chin as she did so. With her stomach distended from her gorging, Skadi was barely able to waddle over to Alfhildr where she flopped down beside the young girl. The red-haired Dane smiled to herself as she reached over and caressed her friend. Over the past few weeks, the pair had slowly learned how to hunt and live together in the deep forest. They had become two quiet shadows that had made the woods their own, moving slowly west and south whenever prey in an area grew scarce.

Sated at last, and with the fire damping down under the spitting rain, Alfhildr took up the long ash spear to sharpen the tip once more before thrusting it deep into the embers in order to harden the point. With that chore taken care of, she pulled a pile of smaller lengths of wood toward her to feather them as kindling for the next night's fire.

As Alfhildr worked she started to sing. Skadi, recognizing the nightly ritual, pricked up her ears and gave her tail a quick wag before resting her head between her paws.

Alfhildr's voice rose above the gentle patter of rain, sweet and clear as she sang to the wolf, to herself, and to the quiet forest. She sang the quiet lullabies she had loved as a child as well as songs that honored the gods or told the story of her people. The singing voice she had despised as a young boy was now something to be enjoyed and shared with her ever attentive friend. Only when the rain had finally drowned their small fire and extinguished its light did Alfhildr stop, pull out the heavy grey cloak, and spread it out under the shelter. Once she had settled, Skadi snuggled up next to her. Together, this unusual pair of huntresses lapsed into a contented sleep brought on by full bellies.

Æ

The rain eased overnight and with the dawn came a mist, turning their little camp into an island in a grey sea. Alfhildr shivered as she pushed her way out of the shelter.

Ignoring a grunt of protest from the wolf, the young girl made her way to the edge of the clearing to relieve herself. *The hunting had been good here*, she thought to herself. They had found deer and badgers and hares, but now nothing moved. Alfhildr sighed. It was time to push on again. With the meat from the deer they had, she was confident they could easily go for a few days until they found better hunting. Thus resolved, upon returning to their little camp, she turned her attention to packing away their few possessions. Within the hour, the huntresses were on the move.

They traveled together quietly for several hours until Skadi abruptly froze. When she saw the way that the wolf raised her snout and sniffed the air, Alfhildr took to scanning the brush eagerly for the game her friend had found. She was, therefore, taken by surprise when Skadi began to carefully back up toward her, her hackles high and a low growl in her throat. Alarmed, Alfhildr crept forward to see what had disturbed the wolf. She had gone but a few paces when she came across a fresh boot print in the soggy forest mulch, a sight that caused Alfhildr to shiver.

For days, she had not thought of other people. She had come to think of the forest as hers and hers alone. Looking back, the red-haired girl caught sight of Skadi, crouched low with her ears laid back. This caused the girl to smile grimly to herself. Like the wolf, she too had been hurt and left for dead by people, giving both good reasons to be wary of them. With that thought in mind, Alfhildr also backed up to her friend and together made a wide detour away from the smell of man.

Æ

The weather continued wet and cold as the two hunters slowly continued westward. From time to time, snow blanketed the forest in a silent white shroud, thawing swiftly to leave a bitter chill that bit to the bone. Once again, they were hungry as game proved to be scarce and illusive. Pausing, Alfhildr ran her fingers through the greasy tangled locks of her hair as the young girl thought longingly of the Old Woman's sweet-smelling soap.

This brought a smile to her face. If anyone used soap in the forest, both Skadi and she would have been able to smell them long before they got close. A sudden cold wind sent a shiver down the girl's spine, causing her to pull the stained and ripped jerkin tighter around her before going on.

They had not gone very far when Skadi suddenly slowed, then stopped, her ears flicked forward as she took to snuffling the air. Alfhildr's head jerked up, alert and wary after coming across the hunter's tracks they had found a few days prior. She carefully watched her friend in order to get a sense of what Skadi was sniffing. The she-wolf paused only for a moment before springing to her paws and loping swiftly into the thicket ahead.

Puzzled, Alfhildr followed more cautiously, pushing her way through the thick brambles. As she broke clear of them, she froze. No more than a score of paces away a man's body lay sprawled on the blood-darkened earth, his helm hacked apart and his skull cloven wide. Terrified by the possibility there were other armed men near at hand, Alfhildr's eyes flicked about. Within her chest, her heart was pounding like a hammer.

Then she saw it. Dropped a few feet from the body was a bow. It was no simple hunting bow, but a beautifully tooled weapon of strange design, its belly banded with shimmering wire. Within Alfhildr a sudden desperate longing for the bow warred with her caution.

Surely no warrior would kill, yet leave his foe's weapons behind, she thought to herself. Straining every sense, Alfhildr edged nervously toward the bow, her eyes darting in all directions as her hand closed tightly about the handle of her axe. When she reached the bow, she snatched it from the forest floor before turning to the corpse in search of arrows.

A terrified shriek ripped from her throat. Sitting on the far side of the clearing with his back against a tree, a Saxon warrior grasping a bloody sword across his knees glared at her. Alfhildr could only stare wide-eyed at the grim warrior's steady gaze as her blood drummed in her ears.

Skadi, on the other hand, seemed totally unconcerned by the warrior's presence. When she returned to the clearing, without pausing, the wolf trotted over to the Saxon warrior where she took to snuffling around his feet. He didn't move.

Alfhildr shuffled back toward the gorse, but the warrior's eyes never followed her, remaining fixed on the body of the fallen bowman. That was when she saw the two ragged stumps of arrows sticking from his chest. She let out a juddering sigh, ashamed of her earlier frightened squeal as she struggled to tamp down her fear. When at last she was able to approach the second corpse, she stepped as carefully as if walking on thin ice.

Even in death, the warrior showed his wealth. A fine mail shirt was cinched tight with a richly tooled sword belt. The naked sword, still sticky with his foe's blood, was clutched in his hand. Even from a distance, Alfhildr could see it was a beautiful weapon, decorated with an intricate design and topped with a gold-chased pommel. Reaching out tentatively, she touched the slain warrior's cheek. The skin was cold and pallid, causing her to shiver. It was her first experience with violent death. And, while she knew from sagas what needed to be done, it took her a while to summon the courage to pry the sword from a hand locked tight in death before stripping the corpse.

As she gingerly went about this grisly task, from behind her a hoarse croak broke the eerie silence, causing her to whirl about. On the body of the bowman, a crow had settled to feast upon the bloody grey pulp still oozing out of the bowman's sundered skull.

Unable to hold back her revulsion any longer, Alfhildr threw up.

Æ

It took an hour before both bodies were stripped. Alfhildr was in the midst of doing so when she found herself looking again at the Saxon's boots. Though they were far too big to be of any use to her, a thick white scurf that coated the leather on the inside of each boot caught her attention. She paused, brow furrowed as she picked one up and sniffed it thoughtfully. Only then did she recognize the smell, one that brought a smile to her face before setting aside the boot and heading off into the nearby thicket.

As she pushed through the undergrowth, a muffled stomp and snort alerted her that she was close. While Skadi watched with interest, Alfhildr whistled softly, an effort rewarded by another snort. Hidden in a small dip, she came upon a grey mare. The animal threw back its head and rolled its eyes when it caught sight of Alfhildr approaching. Ever so carefully, the young girl came up to the shivering horse, humming softly as she did so. Slowly, the terror left the mare's eyes as Alfhildr sang until she was near enough to reach out and pet the skittish animal's neck. Across the horse's saddlebow, the carcass of a mature buck was strapped, while full saddlebags bulged on either side.

"And where did you come from, my new friend?" Alfhildr whispered as she slipped the mare's hobble and carefully led her to a small stream nearby. "Are you the daughter of Sleipnir, sent to me as a gift from Odin himself to give these tired legs of mine a rest?"

The horse lunged toward the water and drank greedily until Skadi trotted up to see what her friend was doing. The mare instantly shied away and neighed in fear as Alfhildr hung tight to the bridle.

"Calm, my grey friend. Calm, grey Dimma. You are safe. Look, Skadi is not hunting you. Shhh, little Dimma."

Again, Alfhildr sang and gentled the mare back to the stream. At length, thirst won over fear and the mare drank, though she still kept a nervous eye on the lolling wolf nearby.

Once the horse was watered, Alfhildr reset the hobble and returned to her grisly task. Ignoring her, the crow continued to feast until Alfhildr rolled the young bowman's corpse over to strip his jerkin and recover the near full quiver from beneath his body. As she was doing so, Skadi took to snuffling around the naked corpses until Alfhildr shooed her away. Undaunted, the she-wolf crept back toward the corpse, leaving Alfhildr no choice but to slice off some meat from the deer haunch and toss it to her friend.

"This is revolting enough as it is, my friend, without you adding your own grisly touch to it."

By the time darkness fell, Alfhildr was exhausted. As the ground was too hard to dig proper graves without an iron-edged spade, she had little choice but to roll the bodies into a ditch before covering them with a thin layer of earth. Too tired to build a shelter when she was finished, the red-haired girl huddled under her cloak before a small fire upwind and a little way from where the mortal remains of a Saxon and a Dane would rest side by side for eternity.

After reflecting upon the day's labors, Alfhildr hugged Skadi close.

"What madness drives men to fight to the death like that?"

Looking about, she sighed.

"These woods are vast. While not always readily at hand, the game here is sufficient for our modest needs. Why didn't they work together as we do?" Alfhildr asked aloud as she scratched between the wolf's ears.

Though she tried to sing in an effort to banish her grim thoughts, tonight the words failed to come. In the end, she just rolled up in the cloak and tried not to think of the boy and the man, their naked corpses tumbled together in a ditch but a few paces away.

Æ

In the chill morning sunshine, Alfhildr inspected her plunder more closely. The young bowman's boots, breeches, and jerkin were in better repair than her thin, ragged garb and would fit well enough once she had washed out the piss and shit where the youth's bowels had cut loose in death. Taking up the strange bow, she marveled at its construction. It was made of horn, curved deeply, and bound with fine wire unlike any hunting bow she had ever seen. She tested the draw weight and found it hard but manageable. At last, when Alfhildr slipped the bow cord she was surprised to find the two ends sprang forward. After carefully setting the bow aside, she picked through the Saxon warrior's gear. Save for the two arrow holes, his fine mail byrnie was in good repair with little rust in evidence, telling her it had recently been cleaned. She tried on the helmet but found it wobbled around on her head so much that she had no choice but to set it aside. In battle, a loose-fitting helmet would be more hindrance than protection.

Finally, she turned her attention to the sword. It was indeed a beautifully crafted weapon with few nicks and dents marring its sharp, bright blade and new leather wrapped lovingly about the handle. Reverently, she took the sword to the little stream where the mare had slaked her thirst and washed away the sticky brown crust. Rising to her feet, she swung and cut the air, marveling at the blade's perfect balance and weight. With a grin, she launched into the exercises she had practiced with the wooden foil a lifetime ago at the Old Woman's hovel. As she danced and spun in the morning light, the crow returned, settling upon the lower branches of a nearby tree from where it followed the flashing blade with its bright, sharp eyes.

At length, Alfhildr paused, breathing deeply as she admired the glittering steel, sending splinters of sunlight flashing around her as she tilted it this way and that. As if in admiration, the crow threw out its wings and cawed loudly three times. With each hoarse cry, Alfhildr felt a shiver run through her body.

"What are you?" she whispered to the crow, which answered by arrogantly returning her gaze.

"Are you my *fylgja*? Are you a messenger of the gods?"

Alfhildr could not help but be awed by both the bird and the bright blade in her hand. Closing her eyes, the hissed words of the Old Woman once more came back to her.

> *Huntress is she, who brings down prey with fang and claw*
> *Shield maiden is she, but her shield the grey mist*

She looked again at the mail byrnie and the shining blade. She thought of the beautiful bow, the grey mare, and her grey cloak.

"I do not understand this," Alfhildr muttered to the crow.

"If the gods wished that I should follow the ways of the warrior, if it truly is my fate to live by the sword just as the Old Woman said, then why this slight body?"

She shook her head as the crow looked on, its head tilted to one side as if considering her words. Once more, Alfhildr felt the weight of the prophecy settle on her shoulders, leaving her to wonder just what it was the gods wanted of her.

Alfhildr was quiet as she led the strange band of companions away from the blood-stained grove. In the deep forest, she had hidden from the prophecy: yet, even here, the gods had found her and forced her to confront her fate. She stumbled on into the late afternoon until, at last, a worried Skadi pushed against her legs and the girl stopped, mechanically setting up their simple camp while overhead the crow settled on a branch and cawed.

Æ

The weather held clear and sharp the next day, allowing Alfhildr to recover some of her spirits. She found herself looking about for the crow as they moved, scanning the sky and branches above. Occasionally, she caught a glimpse of a black wing or the glitter of a bright eye in the trees. In the late afternoon, Skadi spotted a badger foraging in a clearing too far from cover for them to sneak up on it.

As the wolf watched, Alfhildr pulled out her new bow, grinning down from her mount at her friend.

"Watch this," the girl murmured softly to her companion.

She drew and loosed in one swift motion. Hitting home with an audible Thwack! the wickedly barbed arrow bit deep into the badger's chest, bowling it over like a rag toy.

After a moment's hesitation, during which Skadi looked back and forth between Alfhildr and the stricken badger in utter confusion, the wolf leapt forward. By the time Alfhildr and the grey mare approached, the she-wolf was worrying and growling at the dead badger as if she had killed the beast, causing Alfhildr to burst out laughing.

"You will get your share. Don't worry!"

Proud of her skill, she stroked the curved bow in her hand, running her fingers across the braided wire before looking up to see a black shape circling above.

"Today, we must also make our thanks to the gods," she murmured reverently.

To that end, that evening, as she butchered the meat, Alfhildr cut out the entrails and hung them in a tree before returning to her tasks. When she next looked around, the crow was ripping at the blood dark guts and stomach.

Eventually, after girl and she-wolf had had their fill of badger and were settled by the fire, Alfhildr inspected the strange bow more closely. On the inner curve of the weapon's belly, her questing fingers lit upon a series of deep cut marks. She tilted the bow in an effort to make them out. The letters looked strange compared to the ones the Old Woman had shown her, but Alfhildr did her best to guess.

"F…L…S…R. Is that your name?" She asked the bow. "Flisarr? Falissar? I wonder what it means."

Shaking her head tiredly, the girl carefully set aside the bow, pulled the grey cloak tightly about her and curled up around the drowsing Skadi.

Armed now with a bow that was as lethal as it was handsome, the two huntresses soon found they rarely went hungry. At the conclusion of each successful hunt, Alfhildr made an offering to her *fylgja*. Over time, she grew used to having the small bright eyes of the crow watching as she hung the scraps on a branch. Still, it came as something of a shock when one evening as she was reaching up, the crow leapt neatly down onto her shoulder and snatched the meat from her hand. Alfhildr stood frozen in awe at the messenger of the gods on her shoulder.

"You are beautiful," she whispered. "But you don't say much. Perhaps you are Hoenir, sent to me from the Æsir."

The crow looked briefly at her before going back to feeding. Each evening thereafter, Hoenir took to sitting on Alfhildr's shoulder waiting to be fed, cawing loudly, and returning into the trees above when she was finished.

Æ

As Christ's birthday approached, a Saxon, who went by the name Osgar, prayed to his Lord for a miracle as he meandered his way through the forest. He hadn't eaten for two days and knew if he did not find game today, he would be reduced to grubbing for roots and worms on the morrow. His clothes hung loose about his thin frame, and his beard and hair fell in matted lank clumps, a far cry from the hard and vengeful hunter who had sworn on Christ's blood to track and kill the reaver scum who had slaughtered his family six months ago. Since that day, the harsh forest and cruel winter had leached his bitter rage and robbed him of his strength. He had killed Danes silently in the forest, never knowing as he did so if they were the ones who had murdered his beloved Wulwina and little Merwenna. Now, Osgar did nothing more than wander without purpose or home, struggling to survive from one day to the next.

With his shoulders hunched, he rode east in the chill of the late afternoon until something caught his attention. Slowing his pace, Osgar took to sniffing the breeze, stopping only when he was convinced that he was not imagining the faint scent of roasting pig. Giving his head a quick shake, he uttered an angry oath. Not even Christ and Saint Osyth could conjure that for him. But yet, there it was again. Bringing his mount about, Osgar turned into the wind and started to creep toward the tantalizing aroma, keeping his spear at the ready as he went.

Æ

Alfhildr smiled happily to herself as she ran the whetstone across the razor-sharp barbs of a hunting arrow. The finding and taking of the wild boar had been a glorious hunt.

From the moment Skadi had flushed the beast from the thicket until she had planted the third broad arrow deep into its chest, she had never felt so alive or blessed by wonderful companions. And now, to cap their victory, they would dine until they burst on fresh boar. As she turned to select another arrow, she started to sing gently to herself while Skadi and Hoenir sat quietly nearby, enjoying their share of the feast.

In the shadows, Osgar watched the girl by the small fire. He looked around seeking her man but saw no one. His stomach growled quietly, reminding him of his hunger. When she started to sing and he heard the Norse words, his expression darkened at the thought that some reaver's slut had grown fat on stolen Saxon meat while his sweet Wulwina was reduced to worm meat, left to molder away in the cold earth. Enraged, he stood abruptly and started to boldly advance on the red-haired Norse bitch.

As he closed on the girl's back, a crow took off from a nearby tree with a loud caw. Startled, the girl looked up in surprise. Turning, she took to staring straight at Osgar. The war cry in his chest died stillborn as he found himself gazing into a pair of green eyes that met his stare with a calmness that was strangely unnerving.

"May I help you?"

Her question was soft and quiet, but Osgar made no answer.

Instead, he continued to move forward, clutching his spear tight until dark wings brushed his hair, causing him to flinch. At first, Osgar ignored this as he stumbled on, coming to a halt a scarce eight paces from the girl. Only when a black crow came around and landed on the girl's shoulder and cast its eyes upon him, did his earlier rage quickly turn to doubt.

Was this some Norse witch and her familiar? he found himself wondering. *Why was it she wasn't afraid?*

"Stranger, I asked if I may help you."

This time, the girl's voice was sharper as she slowly took up a sword. Osgar started to take another step but stopped once more when he heard a long low growl behind him. Ever so slowly, he turned his head. When he saw the gleaming teeth of a wolf in the faint firelight, he realized that before this witch armed with a bright blade and surrounded by her familiars, he had no chance, no chance at all.

With his end now but a hair's breadth away, Osgar threw aside his spear, fell to his knees, and took to praying aloud, begging Christ to take him to His bosom before the Dane witch had a chance to steal his immortal soul.

Alfhildr stood perplexed as the ragged figure tightly clutched his hands together and stared skyward, furiously gibbering away as he did. She lowered her sword and stepped closer.

"Are you sick? Are you hungry?"

She spoke slowly and clearly, hoping the man could understand. When he failed to respond, she pointed toward the roasting meat.

"Hungry? Are you hungry?"

Slowly, the gabbling ceased as the man lowered his gaze and took to looking over at her through narrow slits. Alfhildr pointed again at the fire.

"Do you want food?"

"You would feed me?" Osgar asked in wonder.

"There is too much for me to eat before it spoils, and the feast of Yule is upon us. The gods look kindly on those who share," Alfhildr informed the Saxon as she stepped back and sheathed her blade.

Still unsure if his blessed Lord Jesus had sent the diminutive Dane before him to serve as his salvation or damnation, Osgar slowly came to his feet. Pausing, he cautiously looked about, searching the dark woods to see if there were any more of her unholy familiars lurking about ready to spring out at him. Only when he was satisfied that the girl's offer was sincere and he was safe, for the moment at least, did he accept Alfhildr's invitation to join her at the fire.

Æ

Osgar sprawled beside the small fire, his belly full for the first time in weeks. He looked across at the young girl as she pulled out her whetstone and began to stroke it along her sword's shining blade while the she-wolf lay curled at her feet like a hunting dog.

"How did you kill Coenred?" Alfhildr looked up surprised.

"Who?"

"Coenred, the last owner of the sword you bear. He often boasted the only way another would wield Durthfang was if a warrior better than he pried it from his lifeless fingers."

Alfhildr shivered at the memory of the day she had done so. Her voice was low as she answered.

"I did not kill him. Another claimed that honor. Still, your friend did manage to take his revenge before the Valkyrie claimed him. I buried both."

Osgar snorted, unsure if he should believe the girl. Most warriors that he knew would be proud to claim to have bested the mighty Coenred. He thought for a moment, then tried to turn the conversation to safer ground.

"So, where is your man?"

When the Dane's head jerked up, her flashing eyes provided the answer.

"I serve no man," she all but growled as she ran the whetstone across the sword.

Osgar paused as he took a moment to looked more closely at the girl whose elfin beauty shone through the grime. Dropping his gaze to the fire, the Saxon took a moment to clear his throat.

"Perhaps we might…." he started tentatively.

When he looked up again, he saw her glaring back at him with a stare that was as cold as ice. At the girl's side, the she-wolf raised her head and bared her teeth at him. Dropping his gaze, Osgar shied away from her anger.

Perhaps another time, he thought as he settled to sleep. *Perhaps another time.*

PART TWO

THE SHIELD MAIDEN

Chapter Six
AN ALLIANCE OF LOST SOULS

Present Day England
"The Dig"

In a corner of the crowded little pub, Elva and Professor Bannon sat together, poring over the geophysics results of the area around the tomb, while the young undergraduates at a nearby table focused their efforts on merely pouring. At the center of that noisy mob was a boy named Simon, a gifted rugby prop forward in the First XV. As was his wont, he was holding forth on one of his favorite subjects.

"I know they let women into the Army these days but not where it matters, not with the infantry," he loudly proclaimed. "If it's true now, it had to be true then. No girl can carry the load, let alone summon up the sheer, bloody, mindless ferocity a soldier needs to call on when it counts."

Leaning back in his chair, Simon grinned as his mates nodded sagely.

Under the table, Elva's knuckles were white as she struggled to keep her temper in check. Knowing his protégée's ability to brutally cut obnoxious gits like Simon down to size, Bannon laid a restraining hand on her arm.

"He's not worth it."

Though she knew he was right, Elva still wanted to wipe that smug grin from the arrogant young idiot's face. This thought caused her to wonder how Alfhildr would have dealt with someone like Simon. Ever so slowly, a grin took hold as the image of a rather gruesome scene played out in her mind.

Æ

England
1012 AD

"Was Durthfang beautiful?" The young boy had a wistful look in his eye as he followed his grandmother.

The boy's grandmother hesitated before answering. When she did, she chose her words carefully.

"They say it was beautifully made."

"I think it must have been beautiful."

For a moment, an old bitterness rose to the surface as the boy's grandmother remembered how the swords thought to be "beautiful" by the men and boys she had known had maimed and slaughtered them before their time.

"It was just a tool," she snapped. "A killing tool, no more. Now, come on. We still have a long way to go."

The young boy grinned as he picked up the pace, wondering what gifts the gods would bestow upon him during the journey to which his grandmother had alluded. He would so love a sword like Durthfang.

Æ

Roused from his slumber by the need to relieve himself, Osgar threw off the fur he used as a blanket and pushed himself up off the ground. As he did each morning, he looked about, as much to reacquaint himself with his surroundings as to ensure all was in order. In the half light of a new dawn, his eyes came to rest on the small mound that lay on the far side of the fire, now reduced to a pile of smoldering ash and a few pathetic embers that offered neither warmth nor light. A few strands of fiery red hair fanned out from under the edge of the blanket, reminding Osgar what was under it. A thought flitted through his mind, bringing a smile to his face and a stirring of his blood.

Coming to his feet, he took a few steps away from his bedroll before undoing the knot in the leather drawstring of his trousers. Before continuing, he paused to cup his hands before his lips and blow on them to warm his fingers. As he was standing there, tending to his business, the idea he had discarded out of hand just moments before once more wormed its way into his conscious thoughts. Looking over his shoulder, he eyed the blanket concealing the diminutive Dane girl. With the wolf, that had stayed at her side all night casting a leery eye his way every so often, no longer in sight, and his desires manifesting themselves in a way he could not ignore, Osgar pulled his trousers up without bothering to tie a knot in the draw string as he turned his attention to satisfying a requirement as compelling to a man such as he as his need for food and drink.

With the ease of a skilled hunter, Osgar silently circled round the fire to where Alfhildr lay. Once he was in position, towering over the small mound that rhythmically rose and fell with every breath the girl took, Osgar hesitated but a moment as he pondered how best to go about taking the young girl. Suspecting he ran a risk if he showed too much kindness, he decided it would be best if he simply took her in hand and forced himself upon her. While she probably would struggle, Osgar was confident his strength would be sufficient to subdue the girl, just as he was sure the pleasure he would bring her would be more than adequate to make the use of force unnecessary in the future should he decide to take her along with him. More than ready in all ways, he reached down, took hold of a corner of the Dane girl's blanket, and threw it off.

Having expected one thing, the sight of a snarling wolf, rising up onto its hunches with teeth bared, as well as the sensation of a sword point coming to rest where the legs of his trousers met, came as something of a shock. Even more unnerving was the Dane girl's expression. Rather than anger or rage, her cool, unflinching green eyes told him she was simply waiting for an excuse to thrust her sword arm forward.

Æ

Osgar kept his distance from Alfhildr as the two finished those parts of the boar she had not dried and packed away for later consumption. It was only when she was tying off her blanket roll to the back of Dimma that he approached her with great care, showing the palms of both of his hands while keeping the horse between himself and the Dane girl as an added precaution.

"What I did before, it was foolish," the proud Saxon muttered.

"Very foolish," Alfhildr replied in a casual, off-hand voice, without taking her eyes off what she was doing.

"While I did not want to geld you, had it been necessary, I would have done so."

Once more, the calm, easy manner with which she spoke of her willingness to inflict such a crippling wound sent a shiver down Osgar's spine.

"Perhaps there is something I can do to atone for my sin," he muttered, unsure what that could possibly be.

Pausing, Alfhildr looked across the saddle at him. "Sin? What do you mean by that word?"

Now, it was the Saxon's turn to gaze upon the Dane girl with a puzzled expression. "Do you not know what a sin is?"

Cocking her head to one side, Alfhildr looked away for a moment as she searched her memory in an effort to recall if she had ever come across such a word. When she concluded she hadn't, she looked back up at Osgar.

"No, I am sure I have not heard of it before. Tell me, what does it mean?"

"To sin is to do something that violates God's commandments, the ten laws He passed down to Moses," Osgar explained.

"This Moses, is he your *lovsigemann*?" Alfhildr asked.

Now, it was Osgar's turn to furrow his brow as he regarded the girl while wearing an expression that told her that he had no idea what she was talking about.

"Among my people, the *lovsigemann* recites the laws that govern the community whenever the freemen gather for a common meeting," she explained.

"No, Moses is not a person—well, not a person who is alive. He is of the Bible," Osgar explained. "You do know what the Bible is, don't you?"

"No," Alfhildr stated as she finished securing the last of her belongings. "I do wish to know, but you will need to explain that, as well as what sin is after we hunt."

Looking up at the sky, Alfhildr took a moment to study the clouds.

"It will snow soon, tonight maybe, tomorrow for sure. When it does, the creatures of the forest will go to ground, making them difficult to find until it has stopped. So, we need to be about our business if we have any hope of finding enough meat to last us until the snow stops, as well as gathering wood for our fire and building shelter before it arrives."

Osgar had never considered the idea of staying with the Dane girl much beyond a day, maybe two, and only if she didn't prove to be a nuisance. Still, there was something about her self-confidence, the certainty in her voice, and the calm surety with which she carried herself that was compelling. Without having to give the matter a whit of consideration, he turned to tend to his own horse and equipment as quickly as he could, suspecting she would wait for no man, riding off when it suited her.

"I will tell you of the Bible, and Moses, if, in return, you explain to me what your freemen do at a meeting of the commons," he called out as he was gathering up his things.

A smile crept across Alfhildr's lips. Again, she found herself recalling what the Old Woman's prophecy had said as she looked over to where Skadi was casting a leery eye in the direction of the Saxon.

"You have nothing to fear, my four-legged friend. He will not trouble us again. So long as you and I stay at each other's side, no man can defeat us."

Upon hearing the girl's voice, the wolf looked up at her, perking up her ears and wagging her tail by way of answering.

"Now," Alfhildr concluded as she took to searching the sky, "all we need to do is wait for Hoenir to return to see where the gods wish to take us today."

Æ

It did not take Osgar long to understand the wolf was more than a companion and guardian to the Dane girl. In time, he would come to wonder if the she-wolf was what Alfhildr claimed her to be, a *fylgja*, a supernatural attendant possessing unnatural powers. It was a concern that caused Osgar to fear the beast even more.

On that first day, the two slowly meandered their way westward on a course that made little sense to Osgar. Only as morning gave way to afternoon did he realize Alfhildr was following the she-wolf who gave every indication that she was following a scent that he could not detect. This more or less turned out to be the case when, with a suddenness that caught him off guard, both the she-wolf and Alfhildr stopped as one. Unprepared, Osgar's brown gelding, a sad creature that had seen better days and little care as of late, stumbled on, earning him a withering glare from Alfhildr. Only after the Saxon had managed to regain control of his mount and bring it to a complete stop did she turn away and gaze off in the direction Skadi was staring.

Before going on, the she-wolf glanced back at Alfhildr. With little more than a flick of her hand, she signaled Skadi to continue. As the wolf did so, Alfhildr ever so carefully brought the strange bow she carried on her back around to the front before drawing an arrow from her quiver. When she was ready, she lightly tapped Dimma's grey flanks with her heels and followed Skadi, applying gentle pressure with her knees to guide her mount. Not knowing what else to do, Osgar followed at a discrete distance, straining his eyes, as they went, in a vain effort to spot what it was that the strange pair of hunters were tracking.

The next time the pair stopped, the Saxon huntsman was ready to do likewise. Once more, Alfhildr waited patiently until Skadi had finished sniffing the air and listening. And, once more, the she-wolf looked back at her human consort as if seeking further guidance on how to proceed. Without taking her eye off whatever it was the two were tracking, for Osgar was still unable see a thing, Alfhildr used her arm to signal Skadi. Obediently, the animal began to make a wide, circling sweep to the left.

The temptation to move up beside the Dane girl in an effort to catch a glimpse of what it was she was after was countered by the realization that, by doing so, he might spook the prey she and her wolf sought, thus incurring the Dane girl's wrath. Of the two possibilities, it was his concern over what she would do if he did spoil the hunt that caused him to continue to hang back, for he was now convinced the red-haired girl was more than prepared to make her displeasure with him known by doing something unpleasant and painful, at the very least.

Osgar was still reflecting upon this last thought when Skadi suddenly lit off, causing Alfhildr to straighten up in the saddle and bring her bow up to the ready. From where he sat, Osgar watched her track the still unseen prey with well-practiced ease. At almost the same instant that he finally spotted the magnificent stag breaking from cover, Alfhildr let fly. As if guided by an unseen hand, the arrow hit true, biting deep into the stag's neck, causing it to snap its head about in response to the sting of Alfhildr's deadly missile.

Caught in mid-flight, the stunned and mortally wounded creature stumbled and tumbled forward as its momentum carried it onward.

Neither Alfhildr nor Skadi waited for the stricken stag to come to rest. The moment her arrow was gone, she dug her heels into Dimma, spurring the horse on. The wolf, too, was racing toward the stag.

As there was no further need to hang back, Osgar followed on Alfhildr's heels, wondering as he did so what other surprises this strange Dane girl had yet to reveal. It was clear she was someone who was not to be trifled with, as his foolish efforts to rape her that morning had established. Now, he had ample proof that she was a skilled hunter, ably assisted by a wolf that was so much more than a mere pet.

A wise man, a Godly man, Osgar thought to himself, *would turn and flee from a girl such as this. It was unnatural for a female who possessed such striking beauty to wander free, bound by no law and accompanied only by strange creatures that were wed to her in an unnatural alliance.*

There could be no other explanation. She was a witch who defied the order God had brought to the world.

And yet, when he finally brought his mount to a halt where the stag had finally come to rest, Osgar could not help but look upon the Dane girl as she went about preparing to butcher the dead animal and wonder if, perhaps, she just might be the agent of his own salvation. For too long, he had wandered these forests, first in an effort to find redemption through vengeance, then in a vain attempt to flee from memories of a past that were too painful to live with. Whether her gods had brought him to her, or his own had played a role in helping him find her campfire on the day His son was born, Osgar found himself wondering if he was meant to join this most unusual pantheon of creatures that followed the grey cloaked Dane girl.

When she paused to secure a better grip on the bloody dagger in her hand, Alfhildr looked up at the Saxon.

"Well?" she asked crisply as she held his eyes in a steady gaze. "Are you going to sit there all day and simply watch? Or are you going to help me?"

A hint of a smile crept across Osgar's face as he looked down at her before he replaced it with a frown.

"If you wish to make use of that animal's hide, you're making a mess of it, girl. Here," he snorted as he threw a leg over his horse's neck and slid off his saddle while drawing out his own knife. "Let me show you how to do it properly."

Neither said much as they worked on the dead stag. What few words did pass between them concerned how best to do something, with Osgar doing most of the talking. When he did so, it was in a tone of voice that reminded Alfhildr of the way she had heard the men of her village speak to their sons as they were instructing them on the use of weapons, the secrets of the hunt, or the intricacies of a craft they would one day be expected to master. Like them, there was a loving gruffness to the manner with which Osgar was now treating her, causing her to stop at one point and look up over the carcass of the dead stag at the Saxon, wondering as she did so if this was what it would have been like had her own father lived long enough to have a hand in how she was raised.

Glancing up from what he had been doing, Osgar took note of the strange way the Dane girl was looking at him. Despite his best efforts, he could not help but be reminded of the expression his own daughter had often worn whenever her mind was adrift, lost in thoughts she was not willing to share with another.

He was tempted to say something that would distract the Dane girl, for the memory of what had happened to his daughter was still a festering wound that refused to heal. But he didn't as it slowly dawned upon him that the same sad events in his life that had caused him to take up roaming the forest were driving the Dane girl to do likewise. If that were true, maybe it had not been witchcraft that had brought them together but, rather, a sign from God himself that it was time for him to set aside the anger and self-pity that had been driving him these past few months and, instead, embrace a new beginning, a rebirth of sorts in much the same way as Christ had experienced.

When she noticed the Saxon staring back at her, Alfhildr blushed, hoping he was not reading her thoughts. Averting her eyes, she went back to what she had been doing but stopped when Osgar told her to wait.

"That dagger of yours might be a handy weapon in a pinch, but it is not at all suited for what you are trying to do," he stated brusquely.

"Here," he continued as he reached across the dead stag, holding his own bloody knife by its blade while offering it to her handle first.

"You will find this one much better."

Alfhildr hesitated at first. Not because she didn't understand what he was saying. On the contrary, she understood perfectly well what he was doing. It was more than a knife he was offering her. It was a symbolic gesture, a way for him to inform her that he trusted her with his life, for no man would be foolish enough to yield up his only means of defending himself when face-to-face with an enemy. Once more, a faint memory of her own father flitted through her mind as her vision became blurred by tears that were coming dangerously close to overwhelming her ability to hold them back.

Osgar was not blind to the effect his offer was having on the Dane girl. Upon seeing this, after she took the knife from him, he came to his feet.

"I have another, back in my saddle pouch," he softly muttered while vaguely thrusting a thumb up over his shoulder to where their mounts were tethered.

"I'll be back."

Alfhildr was thankful for the brief interlude, for it allowed her to dry her eyes without the Saxon seeing the way she was behaving. As much as she was tempted to give into the damnable emotions that often left her weeping for no reason at all, she felt the need to maintain the impression that she was as cold and unfeeling as a stone, lest she be seen by the Saxon as weak and vulnerable.

At the moment, the idea that the gruff Saxon huntsman was also wiping away a stray tear that had managed to escape his futile efforts to keep it in check never occurred to Alfhildr. He was, after all, a man, a skilled huntsman and, by all appearances, a fearsome warrior. If there was one thing Alfhildr knew without having to be told, it was men did not wail and weep at the silliest little things. Only pathetic girls, fit only for home and hearth, did so.

Finished drying her eyes, Alfhildr looked over at Skadi.

"We must be strong," she whispered conspiratorially as the she-wolf sat at her side, watching her butcher the stag while patiently awaiting her reward for the role she had played in that day's hunt.

"We cannot let our Saxon friend suspect that I am lost in every way imaginable. Perhaps, the gods have sent him to us as well," she concluded as she looked over to where Osgar was standing with his back to her, "though I cannot imagine why they would put their trust in anyone who follows a god that allowed his own son to be nailed to a cross."

A whimper from the she-wolf distracted Alfhildr. With her ears perked up and tail wagging, Skadi stared intently at Alfhildr, causing the girl to laugh.

"All right, all right. You have waited long enough."

With that, she sliced off a piece of raw meat from the dead stag and tossed it to the she-wolf before turning her attention once more to what she had been doing before becoming distracted by the memories that haunted her.

Æ

Having been an outcast her entire life, it took time for Alfhildr to grow used to having someone never more than a bow shot away all day, every day. The Saxon was always there in the morning when she woke, just as he was there when it came time to curl up with Skadi and drift off to sleep. The fact that she always left him sitting before the fire at night, staring into it as if waiting for the flames to reveal something to him, didn't bother her. It was the time the two of them spent together, before sleep took her, that was, at first, difficult for her to deal with. Singing childhood lullabies to a wolf and a crow was one thing. Doing so in front of another person, a Saxon no less, was an entirely different matter. Again, and again, Alfhildr's perceived need to cling to a guise that was at odds with her feelings cast a chill over the long winter nights.

The first effort to push past the awkward silence that Alfhildr's little camp tended to settle into each night came from Osgar himself, two weeks after the Saxon had stumbled in from the dark. As he sat staring into the fire and without bothering to look up from the burning logs, he asked Alfhildr about her family. She attempted to brush aside his request with little more than a shrug.

"What's there to tell?" she muttered as she took to staring into the fire. "My family is…"

When she didn't finish her statement, Osgar looked up at her.

"Are they dead?"

Once more, Alfhildr shrugged as she squirmed about, disturbing Skadi who had been sleeping peacefully next to her.

"My father is," she finally whispered in a low, sorrowful tone.

"What about your mother, your kinsmen? Also dead?" Osgar asked in as gentle a manner as the rough-hewn Saxon could manage.

Slumping down, Alfhildr took to caressing Skadi's neck with her fingertips as she slowly replied.

"I suppose they could be. Not that it matters."

Appalled, Osgar regarded the Dane girl with barely concealed contempt.

"What does it matter? They are your kinsmen, your blood. How can you speak of them in this manner, as if what becomes of them is of no concern to you?"

Alfhildr didn't answer Osgar straight off. Rather, she continued to pet Skadi as she stared into the fire for several long minutes. When she finally did look up at the Saxon, he could not help but take note of the cold, almost detached expression she wore, one that matched the tone of her voice as she spoke.

"The wound caused by my brother's sword did not compare to that left by the woman who turned her back on me when I needed her the most. I would call her a mother, but to do so would be disrespectful to that esteemed title."

Looking away, Alfhildr wrapped her arm about Skadi's neck and gave the she-wolf a hug before she took her free hand and rubbed the animal's wet nose, pulling it away a bit in order to allow Skadi to lick her hand.

"This wolf is the only mother I have now," she whispered as if to herself. "And the crow, a more faithful sibling than any I ever had before I was cast aside with the same care one uses when tossing out a carcass too repulsive to be of any use to anyone."

After another brief pause, she looked over at Osgar.

"I expect you ask me these questions and look at me with that expression on your face only because you have also lost your family, though I expect it was under circumstances far different than mine. Tell me of them."

Now, it was Osgar's turn to pull away as he took to staring into the fire, wondering what he should say, if anything, to a child who once called the very people who had ripped his life to shreds kinsmen. Finally, after giving the matter much thought, he concluded that if he didn't speak of his family, if he didn't do something to keep their memory alive, they would truly be dead. After drawing a deep breath, he peeked up at Alfhildr.

"My daughter was very much like you in so many ways," he began.

And though she suspected that could never be possible, Alfhildr listened attentively as the Saxon huntsman spoke of a wife and children in a manner that reflected the love that he still had for them.

In this way, the two outcasts took to exchanging stories about their people and their ways. In time, Alfhildr once more took up her songs, songs that reminded Osgar of a time that he could never recapture but could once more enjoy, if only in his dreams.

Æ

The day's hunt was not nearly as successful as either Alfhildr or Osgar would have liked. In the end, they had only managed to snare two hares, neither of which had reached full maturity. They were enough, however, to satisfy the immediate needs of the strange hunting party that roamed the ill-defined boundary separating Danelaw from Saxon holdings.

Their routine seldom varied when it came time to settle in for the night. Alfhildr always tended to the horses, for she had a way with animals that caused Osgar to hold to his belief that there was something mystical about the Dane girl he followed. For his part, the Saxon took to gathering wood for their fire and, when the weather called for it, preparing a shelter for them. They shared the responsibility of preparing their evening's meal, for each had a particular way in which they liked their food, as did Skadi and the crow.

It was only when she had had her fill and was finished tending to her weapons, ensuring they were ready to deal with either unwelcome visitors during the night or a new day of hunting, that Alfhildr fished a comb with the intricate carving of a dragon's head from her pouch. Once settled before the fire, she would gently tease out the knots from her hair, left by a day of hard riding. Skadi, curled up at her side, listened as she hummed a gentle lullaby that never failed to weigh heavily upon Osgar's eyelids. And while the urge to give in to sleep was tempting, one night, the Saxon huntsman valiantly fought it off as he had decided the time had come to discuss a topic he had held off from raising for some time.

After shaking his head in an effort to keep from dropping off, he looked over at the red-haired Dane girl.

"You do not belong out here," he stated without preamble. "The forests of Middle Earth are not a suitable place for someone like you."

Like an arrow to the heart, Osgar's sudden pronouncement hit her. Stopping what she had been doing, Alfhildr's hands sank to her lap as she took to peering off into the dark forest beyond their campfire as if searching for a response. When she finally did reply, it was with a whispered, almost plaintive tone

"This is the only place for someone like me."

After waiting for the Dane girl to explain why she would say such a thing and without her doing so, Osgar shook his head, steadfastly rejecting her foolish claim.

"You have a way about you, little one," he assured her. "Your beauty aside, you have the strength and courage that would make any man proud to take you as a wife."

Snapping her head about, Alfhildr glared at the Saxon wearing an expression that would have caused a lesser man to tremble.

"No man born shall ever take me. And any who tries will regret it," she added as she wrapped her hands about the hilt of her dagger.

Having no doubt that the Dane girl would do as she threatened without so much as batting an eye, Osgar set off on a different tack.

"Do you imagine you can wander these woods forever?" he asked softly. "I will freely admit, you have been fortunate thus far. Whether your luck has been a gift bestowed upon you by those pagan gods you are so fond of or the habit of my Christian Savor to take pity on all sinners, you cannot expect the blessings of either to last forever. The day will come when you will meet your match, when all your skills and courage will fail to save you from a fate you are determined to avoid. What then, little one?"

Tightening her grip on her dagger, she bravely lifted her chin in the same manner she had seen the men of her village do whenever faced with a challenge to their honor.

"Then I shall meet my fate as a…"

In the silence that followed, Osgar waited for the Dane girl to finish. She didn't though. She couldn't, not as she would have wished. In the twinkling of an eye, Alfhildr lowered her gaze, first looking into the fire that was consuming all it touched, before ever so slowly turning her head away, peering off into the darkness surrounding them. Osgar assumed she was doing so in order to think of an appropriate way to end her bold declaration. The idea that the Dane girl was hiding her face from him so he would not see her struggle to hold back her tears never crossed his mind. When it finally became clear she wasn't going to finish her thought, Osgar grunted before turning his attention to settling in for a long, well-earned sleep, leaving Alfhildr alone and lost in her thoughts.

With only Skadi at her side, Alfhildr once more revisited the question that haunted her every night as she set aside the labours of the day and prepared herself for the challenges of a new day: *'What will become of me?'* With the dreams of finding Dumnonia and the people the Old Woman had spoken of so reverently fading like the last of winter's snows, Alfhildr knew without having to be told by a Saxon that she needed to find an answer to this question. Just how and when she would, was something that she was willing to leave in the hands of her gods. Thus far, neither they nor the Old Woman's prophecy had failed her.

The idea that either would was simply too much for the young girl to deal with. She would find her place. She was sure of it. It was only a matter of time.

After wiping away the last of her tears, she turned to Skadi.

"We must put our faith in the gods and our trust in each other if we are to see our way ahead," she whispered to the she-wolf as she roughly kneaded the sides of its neck. "Until then, let us rest so we will be prepared to meet the new dawn and the challenges it is sure to bring us."

As she always did whenever Alfhildr spoke to her in this manner, Skadi wagged her tail by way of response. With her mind once more free of the troubling question of what the new day would bring, Alfhildr prepared to bed down by laying her drawn sword beside her and lifting the blanket up until Skadi had finished curling up next to her. With her arm comfortably draped over the wolf's neck, Alfhildr closed her eyes, wondering what the next day's hunt would yield.

Chapter Seven
BAYING FOR BLOOD

Present Day England
"The Dig"

With painstaking care, Elva and Sarah catalogued the odd assortment of everyday items they had recovered from the richly decorated little chest. Elva watched the young undergraduate approvingly as Sarah patiently worked, her deft fingers cautiously selecting each small treasure. She was currently examining a simple brooch roughly carved from bone in the form of a bird. A green groove showed where a copper pin had been attached.

After examining it, Sarah made a face.

"You know, it really doesn't make any sense why all these simple items were kept in such a beautiful box. We all thought it held jewels or precious coin when Sandy first uncovered it."

Elva pushed a few strands of red hair behind her ear as she turned to study more closely the brooch Sarah was holding.

"To Alfhildr, they were more precious than jewels. Each item in this box represented a gift from a grateful farmer or his wife for saving their lives. While maybe not as clear as Oskar Schindler's list, everything here represents at least one life Alfhildr saved," Elva proclaimed with the same surety she used whenever she spoke of the mythical warrior.

After taking a moment to study the item she was holding, Sarah sighed.

"Oh, how I wish you could talk and tell me of your people and times," the fair-haired undergrad softly murmured to the simple brooch.

"That's what we are here to do," Elva whispered as she too stared at the brooch, wondering what had occurred on the day Alfhildr had received it.

Æ

The Saga of the Shield Maiden

Fresh young spring the dire winter overthrows,
And earth awakens to accept the farmer's grain.
Lean cattle fatten on sweet new grass,
Yet, fear returns to haunt men's hearths.

Bright bladed and bloody, the reavers return
To renew bitter strife 'tween Saxon and Dane.
Alfhildr, once carefree, now god-bound, must fight
Slaughter and pillage her duty to halt.

Sharp nosed Skadi was first on the scent
But soon, all could hear the screams of bairns.
Tho' bright flames leapt from farm's thick thatch
'Twas no match for the fury in Alfhildr's breast.

In Alfhildr's hands, Falissar sang true,
A score of reavers lay slain ere they fled.
Her mistress demanding, swift Dimma sprang forth
With Durthfang and Skadi, no reavers were spared.

In their wake, dread, fear, and pain,
Amongst the farmer folk remained.
Death and dying, children crying,
Turned vengeful shield maiden to gentle maid.

Softly singing her childhood lullabies,
Alfhildr soothed the fear-wracked young.
Sure hand with blade now soft and gentle
Mending gaping rents in flesh.

Saxon Osgar watched the shield maiden
Bring succor to bloodied folk.
His hands too hard to tend the living,
Turned he instead to serve the dead.

Thus, was born Alfhildr's legend,
The Gods bright sword to guard the weak.
No line drew she 'tween Dane and Saxon
Flame hair, flame wrath for evil men.
Æ

As the winter grudgingly gave way to the first gentle green of spring, the forest began to come alive. Birds called and flitted among the branches while the first insects started to disturb the strange pair's evening campsites. The hunting too became easier as the wary deer and hungry badgers were forced to seek fresh grass and new roots, leaving Alfhildr and Osgar free to spend more time talking about their people and their gods.

Alfhildr frowned as she listened to Osgar's explanation, her hands busy as she lovingly shaped a new handle for her dagger from a stag's antler.

"So, beneath your king there are eoldermen. And, below them, there are thegns, then freemen who can be ceorls, kotsetlas or geburs. Finally, there are the slaves." She thought for a moment, then nodded. "It is the same with us."

Osgar grunted. "My people believe every Dane is a brigand, intent only on spoiling our crops and stealing our wealth."

Alfhildr shook her head roughly. "We Danes think all Saxons only wish to burn our farms and rape our women."

The two hunters looked at each other and grimaced before Alfhildr returned to a subject that still confused her.

"Now, tell me again about your magicians, these priests of the Christ God. How do they work their magic?"

Osgar sighed. The girl's curiosity was unbounded.

Æ

Riding along, Alfhildr found herself taking pleasure in the simple beauty of the forest around her. Occasionally, she would pause to gaze upon a woodland carpet of bluebells, their heads nodding together in a gentle breeze, or would gasp for joy at a fleeting glimpse of a young fawn with his mother, both skittering into a thicket as they approached. While she found new joy in the coming of spring, both Dimma and Osgar's rangy gelding slowly began to fatten on the sweet, new grass, regaining their tone and strength after the harsh winter months. Even Skadi was not immune to the rising spring, allowing Alfhildr to laugh when she saw the she-wolf chase off after a small shrew, leaping and bounding like a young pup before looking up at her friend with an embarrassed grin when she realized she was being watched.

Yet, as the year quickened around her, Alfhildr felt the weight of her future press down more heavily upon her shoulders, and, for each moment of simple gaiety and the thrill of the hunt, there were many more spent seated by the camp fire at night, pondering again and again the words of the Old Woman's prophecy until at last Skadi would gently nudge her hand and remind her of the need to sleep.

Æ

A spring storm was brewing, and the air was close around them as they rode. Dark clouds above hung pregnant with rain and Thor's own thunder, while the forest itself grew still under the foreboding sky. On this day, they rode with no thought of hunting. Instead, Alfhildr followed the call of the crow as if mesmerized.

At dawn, Hoenir had woken the small party with a raucous racket, flitting from tree to tree as they roused themselves. Alfhildr felt a sense of unease, of portent conveyed by the bird, which her other companions soon picked up. Dimma skittered as she was saddled, making Alfhildr skip in an effort to keep her toes intact. Off to one side, Skadi prowled restlessly back and forth. Osgar had kept his own counsel and stayed quiet, his eyes flicking warily and constantly between the silent girl, the nervous wolf, and the squawking crow.

They followed the crow south and a little east into a part of the forest in which they had not travelled before. Skadi ranged ahead, as always, but kept glancing back to Alfhildr, unsure and nervous. Behind the girl, Osgar rode cautiously, his hand frequently slipping inside his jerkin to touch the rough wooden cross he wore around his neck. There was something strange, almost fey about the girl today, causing him to silently pray for the Christ God's protection from all evil spirits and witches.

Without warning, Skadi stopped dead to sniff the air. As the horses paused behind her, she sniffed again, tipping her muzzle to the sky while Alfhildr watched with rapt attention. The wolf looked around before starting forward once more, this time her pace quickening. Far to their front, a crow cawed twice. When Alfhildr heard the sound a third time, she realized it was no crow's call but a hoarse scream. Without hesitation, she set her heels to Dimma and urged the mare into a canter.

Even as she rode, Alfhildr could sense a terrible wrongness around her. The trees began to thin, and what she had at first taken for the darkening rain clouds, now reached up in thick grey coils. The scream was repeated, this time long and shrill, ending suddenly against a growling background of cries, yells, and the clash of steel.

Æ

Alfhildr pulled Dimma short just within the wood line where she stared in horror as thick, greasy smoke bellowed up from neat, thatched hovels. On the ground, a young boy, scarce Alfhildr's age, was writhing in agony as he tried to hold his guts from spilling out of his belly. Above him, a Danish warrior laughed and kicked the boy's face, causing him to lose his grip, letting the thick rope of purple intestines slither out into the filth of the yard. She watched as a farmer ran screaming at another raider, whirling a wooden spade above his head. The warrior easily parried this futile attack by holding up his shield to ward off the blow while another crept behind the maddened farmer and speared him in the small of his back. The farmer arched and convulsed on the bright point like an eel speared from the brook, his eyes betraying the shock of the blow before rolling up into his head as death took him.

Beside Alfhildr, Osgar's face had become a rictus of rage, but she was blind to all but the slaughter before her, unable to tear her eyes away. A young girl, no more than nine or ten summers old, tried to flee toward the forest across a fresh ploughed field, her breath coming in hoarse shrill gasps as she ran. Yet, before she had covered half the distance, a burly warrior caught her and threw her to the ground. As he did, an old woman hobbled toward him, shrieking curses and waving a small blade no more than a hand's breadth long. The warrior grunted and put his foot on the fallen girl's hair to hold her as he turned toward the old woman. She rushed forward across the furrows until the point of the raider's spear flicked out lazily, almost contemptuously, burying itself in her stomach. As she fell to the ground, the Saxon raider dropped his spear and turned back to the trapped girl, fumbling with the drawstring of his breeches as he prepared to take her. Across the steading, a companion laughed as the girl struggled.

"Hey Kvígr, are you making sure all the pretty ones get a taste of your spears?"

The raucous laughter of the two men snapped the spell of horror that had held Alfhildr transfixed. Without thought or pause, she swung her bow up and nocked an arrow. She drew and let fly with fluid grace. Just as easily, she selected another, fitting it calmly as if on the hunt, drawing and letting fly again without hesitation.

Osgar watched as the first shaft buried itself to the fletching in the throat of the old woman's killer. The laughing raider stared slack-jawed for a moment, watching in shock as his comrade clawed at his neck before he too fell, the second arrow piercing deep through eye and brain. And still, Alfhildr carefully nocked, aimed, drew, and loosed.

As if in a dream, Osgar stared at Alfhildr. He watched as her hands moved with elegant precision as her curved bow sang time and again. He had faced many men in battle, screaming and snarling across the shield wall, cursing and yelling and spitting as they killed and maimed and died. But he had never seen anything so terrifying as the chalk white calmness, devoid of all expression on the girl's face. Her eyes shone like emeralds while, unnoticed, silent tears ran in two thin tracks down her cheeks. And still the girl methodically slaughtered the Danish reavers like vermin.

When the raiders saw their comrades falling around them, one by one, they took to turning this way and that in a desperate effort to spot the hidden archer. In confusion, they dropped a woman and the plunder they had dragged from the burning hovels to once more take up their shields and spears. Their leader screamed for them to rally and form a shield wall while more men fell, a methodical slaughter that stopped only when Alfhildr reached down to find an empty quiver.

Within the little shield wall, the only sound to be heard was the hoarse rasp of breathing as fearful men crouched behind their linden shields, their eyes darting left and right in a desperate search for their unseen foe. For an eternity of twenty heartbeats, they waited.

A shrill screech finally ripped the silence like a jagged blade as a grey warrior on a grey horse sprang from the darkness of the forest. In her hand, a bright blade flashed high while her unbound, maiden's tresses streamed behind her like a flaming banner. Alfhildr screamed her fury as she rode toward the shield wall. By her heels, a snarling wolf leapt, followed quickly by a Saxon spearman who ran close behind. More than one man pissed himself at the sight of the raging Valkyrie bearing down upon them.

Even before she reached them, some turned and fled from the shield wall, throwing their spears aside as they ran. Alfhildr was blind to their panicked flight. With measured ease, her blade swept down toward a shivering youth, his beard still thin and straggly, neatly slicing his throat open with a single sweep of her sword. She brought Durthfang around with ease and slashed down onto a second warrior's arm as he tried to spear Skadi. The man dropped his spear and screamed in terror as the wolf's jaws locked about his throat.Shaking her head from side to side with a guttural growl, Skadi ripped his windpipe to tattered shreds.

Alfhildr rode on, her scream becoming a keening joyous yell of bloodlust and battle as her blade rose and fell among the terrified reavers. She crashed through the shattered shield wall, hacking down a snarling warrior as he tried to hamstring Dimma. Behind her, the warband leader ran toward her back with his spear held high until his attack was brought to a jarring stop by Osgar's spear slicing at his ankles. The warrior hit the ground hard, rolling onto his back in a desperate bid to fend off his attacker only to look up into the pitiless eyes of the Saxon huntsman. Osgar neither hesitated nor held back as he thrust down with savage force, skewering the reaver through his open mouth and pinning him to the dirt while he jerked and twisted in agony.

Their shield wall broken, the reavers fled in terror from the merciless flame-haired warrior. As she fought, her blood sang in her veins and her soul soared at the joy of battle and victory. Slipping from her saddle, Alfhildr stood in the middle of the farmyard, her eyes darting about in search of another foe to slaughter. But none within reach were left for her to assail. Instead, she found herself surrounded by the dead and dying. Gasping for breath, she stood there and listened for a moment to the whimpers of the wounded Danes, the snarls of Skadi as she tore at flesh, and the grunt of Osgar as he speared the wounded Danes. When she realized she had no need to go on, her arm dropped to her side as Durthfang suddenly became as heavy as a blacksmith's anvil. Unseen, Osgar loped off after a pair of fleeing reavers, still eager for blood and vengeance for his Wulwina.

Æ

As suddenly as it had come, the exquisite joy of bloodlust deserted Alfhildr. Her breath now came in harsh, burning gasps as the blood that had sung now pounded in her ears. A wave of exhaustion more profound than anything she had ever known swept over her, leaving the blood-stained girl struggling to keep her feet, staring unseeing at the wall of the largest hovel while angry, dark smoke roiled from the thatch above. As she stood transfixed, the threatening storm broke, at last, above her, unleashing its rain and turning the earthen farmyard into a slick, muddy swamp of red and brown. And still, she couldn't move.

Ever so slowly, other sounds returned to the ravaged farmstead. One by one, the survivors set aside their fear of what they would find and searched, calling out the names of their missing kinsmen. The cries of the women and children rang out as they called desperately for their loved ones, cries too often turning to shrill screams of despair whenever a woman found her man, or a mother her child, sprawled on the ground in awful stillness. Running from hovel to hovel, they slowly began to take quick, frightened glances at the dire young warrior who stood alone in the midst of the chaos, oblivious to all around her while a snarling wolf paced in short circles around her heels.

Among them, a little boy ran from adult to adult, tears streaming down his face as he begged them to come help.

"My Gamma. Please help my Gamma. She's crying and won't get up. Please, please help." The boy wailed as he ran from person to person, pulling at the women's sleeves. But they pushed past, desperate to find their own loved ones. Without thinking or looking, the boy turned to the stationary figure in the center of the yard. Though Skadi snarled, the boy came on, grabbing hold of Alfhildr's arm with frantic strength.

"Please! My Gamma! Please help. She won't get up."

The sudden tug rocked Alfhildr, causing her to stagger as she tried to keep her footing. In a daze she looked down into the pleading cornflower blue eyes of the sobbing child while he continued to tug on her bloody sleeve.

"You've got to come. She can't get up on her own and I can't lift her."

Alfhildr turned sluggishly, allowing the frantic boy to pull her across the yard and out into the fresh-ploughed field, grabbing Dimma's reins as she passed.

Æ

The old woman was lying where she had fallen, wheezing as she struggled to breathe.

The young girl, who Alfhildr had seen thrown to the ground, was kneeling at her side, cradling her grandmother's head as she stroked the iron, grey hair.

"It's all right, Gamma. Peada is getting help. You're going to be all right, Gamma." She repeated it again and again as if the desperation of her words alone were enough.

Alfhildr laid her hand on the girl's shoulder. Turning to see who had come, the girl squealed in shock at the sight of the bloody, grim warrior, throwing herself backward to escape Alfhildr's clutches. But Alfhildr wasted no time calming the girl as she took her place beside the old woman and reached out to take her hand.

"I need to see the wound if I am to help," Alfhildr murmured gently. The old woman looked up in surprise at the soft-spoken warrior girl beside her before relaxing and nodding stiffly, letting her other hand fall away from her waist. Alfhildr looked down to where the spear had entered her belly low and to one side before being twisted and yanked back. Dark blood flowed sluggishly from the wound and in its depths Alfhildr could see the smooth purple intestines. She leant forward, close to the wound, and sniffed. Her nose wrinkled as the smell of shit and bile hit her. When Alfhildr looked up, the old woman could see the truth written on her face.

"It's in the guts," the old woman muttered through clenched teeth. "I could feel it," she added while letting out a long sigh that turned into a wracking cough. When she could speak again, she stared up at the flame-haired girl.

"Who will look after my babies?" she asked sadly.

Alfhildr did not answer. Instead, she stood, turned to her horse and took to rummaging in her saddlebags, pulling out a small pouch of powdered yarrow, her water skin, and linen bandage before turning again to the old woman. With gentle hands, she eased the muddy gown away from the wound and tenderly started to wash the frightful gash as well as she could. She sprinkled on the powdered yarrow and carefully lifted the old woman in order to wrap the bandage around her stomach. As she did, the old woman hissed but uttered no other sound, her jaw clamped tight in a vain effort to check her pain. The two children stood and watched quietly, not seeing the tears of misery that ran in silent rivers down Alfhildr's cheeks. Even as she worked, she knew the old woman was doomed. No one survived a spear deep in the guts. She could only hope to make her passing more comfortable.

The old woman stared at Alfhildr all the time, her bright eyes noting the bloody sword and empty quiver as well as the tears and the girl's gentle hands.

"You were the archer, weren't you?"

Again, Alfhildr could only nod, ashamed that her voice would betray her. A rare small smile escaped through the old woman's pain.

"You saved my babies, and you have done all you can for me. Be at peace, child."

Æ

Alfhildr did what she could among the wounded farmers and their families. At first, many were afraid of the red-haired Dane witch and refused to allow her near. Ever so slowly, thanks to Osgar and the two children, she gained their grudging acceptance while protecting herself from the farmer' thirst for revenge.

It was her singing that eventually gained their trust. Night was falling on that first day as Alfhildr was cleaning a deep knife wound in a young boy's shoulder. He whimpered as she carefully picked out scraps of torn cloth before stitching the gash closed while the boy's father scowled as he held his son's arms fast. As she concentrated on the task before her, Alfhildr began to hum under her breath. The boy began to relax even as the needle bit into his flesh, causing Alfhildr to look up surprised.

"Don't stop, please." His voice was almost a whisper.

Alfhildr looked into his half-closed eyes and gently started a little lullaby. The boy still flinched as the needle threaded the wound, but a soft smile played across his face.

Alfhildr sang as she worked until the wound was clean and closed. As she finished the bandaging, she stretched her back and looked up. Huddled around the narrow door, five or six children were staring at her wide-eyed, causing her to smile for the first time that day.

"Would you like to hear more?"

The little boy who had dragged at her sleeve that morning looked up at his sister for a moment, then nodded solemnly. Alfhildr cocked her head inviting them in and started to sing. As she ended a second lullaby, the wounded boy's father staggered abruptly to his feet and, with a choke, almost ran from the hovel. He kept his face averted from Alfhildr and the children, but, in the boy's hair, Alfhildr could see the matted wetness where his father's tears had fallen.

Æ

It took two days for the old woman to die. Alfhildr had done what she could to make her comfortable and had stood silent, off to one side, apart from the woman's kinsmen, as Osgar and the surviving men had buried her under the eaves of the forest alongside the other victims of the raid. She had shown a few of the women what to do when the wounds turned bad and had listened politely to the farmer's eldest surviving son as he haltingly thanked her for her help while thrusting a meager bag of food toward her. Only when there was nothing more that could be done did Alfhildr quietly ride off with Skadi and Osgar close by, and Hoenir watching from high above.

As they entered the forest, two children waited nervously. The old woman's granddaughter held tight to her little brother's hand as she stared at Alfhildr.

"Lady?"

They were the first words Alfhildr had heard the girl say since she had knelt beside her grandmother in the field. Alfhildr drew Dimma to a halt.

"Gamma wanted you to have this. We want you to have this."

She cautiously held out something small toward the warrior. Alfhildr almost dropped the gift as the girl snatched her hand back. In her palm, lay a simple brooch of carved bone in the shape of a bird. The brooch was worn smooth with age and almost black, but Alfhildr could see it had been well-cared for and cherished as evidenced by a new copper pin that had been fitted to it. Smiling, she looked over at the two children as tears welled up inside.

"Thank you." The girl whispered, echoed by her little brother's "'hank you." Then, they both turned and ran back toward the farm.

Alfhildr stared after them as they ran, not caring if Osgar saw her tears.

She cried out of shame and guilt. Shame that men could do such things as this and guilt that she had not been able to avert the slaughter. But most of all, Alfhildr felt her own shame for the joy of the wild blood lust that had enveloped her as she had ridden down the Danish reavers.

Slowly she turned away, leading her little party back into the dark forest.

Æ

England
1012 AD

At length, the boy's grandmother finished the tale leaving the pair to walk on in thoughtful silence. The old woman dwelt on the grief of losing loved ones to the blade and spear while the young boy dreamed of gloriously riding in to save a farm and battling with evil reavers. At length, the old woman shook her head to clear the memories and turned to her grandchild.

"So, which bit did you prefer? Where Alfhildr rode down the Danish reavers or where she healed and cared for the farm folk afterward?"

The boy grinned. "The battle, of course. Anyone can look after the wounded." He said dismissively.

His grandmother stopped short and looked hard at the child. As she stared, he began to fidget uncomfortably.

"So, it's easy, is it? Tell me, was Christ a warrior or a healer?"

"Uh, a healer."

"Is it not a victory worth celebrating to drag someone back from the jaws of death?"

"I suppose."

"Were you not happy when your father recovered from the red fever?"

The boy hung his head, causing the old woman to soften her tone.

"There is a place for both warriors and healers, child. Alfhildr learned that both face hard battles, and there is joy in both. But she also learned another lesson. Now, you show me if you have also learned that lesson. Which is more important?"

"Healing."

His word was little more than a whisper, but the old woman smiled. The child was learning, allowing her to hope that the story her grandmother had passed on to her would make what was to come all the easier.

Chapter Eight
THE BLOOD MOON

Having ensured that the farmer and his family had no wounds that needed her attention, Alfhildr made her way to where Osgar sat perched upon a chopping block, watching the Danes run about gathering up the frightened chickens and goats that the Saxon raiders had not had time to slaughter.

"You were lucky," Osgar grunted when the red-haired Dane girl was close enough to hear him. "Another second and that big oaf would have cleaved you clean in two."

Grinning as she continued to approach, wiping away traces of dried blood from her face using a rag the farmer's wife had given her, Alfhildr brushed aside Osgar's comment.

"There was no luck involved," she stated dismissively. "I knew he was behind me."

"Then, why the surprised look on your face when you turned and saw him towering over you with that two-handed axe of his hoisted over his head?"

Stopping before Osgar, Alfhildr shrugged. "Well, perhaps I was a little lucky."

Reaching out, she took the arm the Saxon was favoring and turned it ever so slightly so that she could better see his wound.

"That's more than I can say for you. If that Saxon had had a better grip on his sword, I would have been picking this arm up on the other side of the yard."

Osgar grunted as he attempted to pull his arm away.

"It's nothing."

Tightening her grip, Alfhildr refused to let go.

"Today it is nothing. Tomorrow it will be red and swollen. Next week green pus will run, making it impossible for even Skadi to eat in your presence."

"Well, we wouldn't want that, would we?" Osgar snickered as he looked up into the Dane girl's eyes.

Taking the rag that she had been using to clean her face, Alfhildr used it to cover the gash on Osgar's arm.

"Now, stay here and hold this over it while I gather the horses and fetch my pouch," she commanded in a manner that reminded Osgar of the way his wife used to deal with him when he was being obstinate.

"Do I have a choice?" Osgar asked mockingly.

Mustering up a stern expression, Alfhildr scrunched her nose.

"No."

With that she turned and headed off.

Æ

Much to Osgar's surprise, Alfhildr accepted the offer made by the farmer and his wife to stay the night, sharing a meal with them. When they were alone, he asked why she had done so.

"These were no ordinary brigands," she informed her Saxon companion. "They are part of a warband, warriors in the employ of some noble."

Osgar didn't need to say a word. His expression betrayed his doubts.

"Look at their weapons. These are fine tools of war that are well cared for, not the sort of thing we have found when dealing with mere reavers. The two that managed to slip away will no doubt go back to their lord or the others belonging to their warband. Whether they return to extract vengeance for the death of their friends or simply to finish what they started doesn't matter. They will return. And when they do, we will be here," Alfhildr stated as she turned her attention to surveying the lay of the land.

"Besides," she added as her gaze dropped down to the ground at her feet, "I do not feel up to another hard ride."

Of the two reasons she gave, Osgar suspected it was the latter that was really behind her decision to stay. As tough as the Dane girl was, whenever her time of the month came, she found a reason for lingering about a camp near a stream or river for several days.

"We should tend to our filthy clothing," she would say, or use the horses as an excuse.

"This is a fine meadow. We should allow them to eat their fill of grass before moving on."

Having had a wife and a daughter who had come of age, Osgar knew of the curse women endured with the passing of each moon. He also knew it was wise not to get on the wrong side of a woman when that happened. So, he merely played along with whatever pretext Alfhildr used, giving her wide berth least he run afoul of an irritable woman, as well as providing her the privacy women seemed to crave at such times.

There was no fooling the farmer's wife. She took Alfhildr by the arm while the men were burying the dead Saxons.

"Come with me," she bid Alfhildr in the same firm, yet commanding manner Alfhildr herself used when letting Osgar know she would tolerate no argument.

"I will show you where you can clean yourself in private and tend to your needs."

Though in time, she had grown used to the way the Old Woman had dealt with her, this was different. The farmer's wife, a woman by the name of Jorunnr was looking at Alfhildr as an equal, no different than she. When Jorunnr saw the expression on Alfhildr's face, she took one of her hands and gave the reluctant girl a reassuring smile.

"There are no secrets between women like us. Though you may move about in the world of men and, therefore, must be ever so careful to keep them from sensing any weakness, there is no need to be anything more than what you are with me, a young girl in need of some quiet, a little rest, and a good scrubbing."

Alfhildr had reservations about yielding to Jorunnr's efforts to help her, fearing that the other woman would somehow discover she was not really like her, or anyone else of whom she knew. Still, Alfhildr found herself unable to deny she was in need of some time away from her grumpy companion, not to mention an opportunity to bathe. So, she allowed Jorunnr to lead her away, determined to meet this trial with the same courage she had relied on earlier in the day when she had been faced by an entirely different challenge.

Æ

Taking their time, the two Saxon warriors who had survived their first visit to the farm crept to the edge of the woods. Upon reaching it, they paused to look and listen. Only when they were sure there was no one standing watch or lurking about in the shadows did they signal their companions to join them.

"No sign of the horses," one of the scouts whispered to the huscarl who insisted upon raiding Dane holdings that bordered those of his brother's lands.

"They say the Danish witch rides off as soon as she finishes butchering the bodies and feeding the entrails to her wolf."

"I pity the poor wolf that is given any part of you to feast on," the first scout's companion muttered to his partner.

"Silence, both of you, or I'll feed you to the wolf myself," the huscarl snapped while he surveyed the lay of the land for himself.

After ensuring the pair who had taken part in the earlier attack on this farm had missed nothing, the warrior tightened his grip on his axe as he took to scanning the heavens for any sign of clouds to hide the bright, waxing moon. Seeing none in sight, he drew in a deep breath.

"Right, then, let's get on with this. Remember, no one is to be spared. We must show these pagan curs this witch of theirs is no savior."

With that, he boldly stepped out of cover and into the open field lit up by a near full moon that all but turned night into day. With his small band of thegns following behind him in a loose formation, he began to boldly advance on the small farmhouse.

Rising up from where she had been concealed not more than two rods from where she had expected the Saxons to emerge from the woods, Alfhildr cast off her grey cloak before ever so slowly bringing her bow up to the ready. After taking careful aim at the well-armed man, she took to be their leader, she let fly.

Before any of the Saxons were able to recover from the shock of seeing the huscarl struck down by an arrow, another of their small party was hit square in the neck, causing him to drop to his knees as the gurgling sound of him choking on his own blood filled the night air.

"Behind us, in the trees," one of the Saxon thegns shrieked in a panicked voice as he brought his sword up to point to where Alfhildr stood upright, drawing her bow even as he spoke. The efforts of this raider were rewarded with an arrow that struck near enough to his heart to seal his doom. While some remained rooted to the ground they stood on by fear, three turned on their assailant, rushing toward her at a dead run. One never made it anywhere near to the menacing dark silhouette, struck down by yet another arrow that sent him sprawling to the ground before Alfhildr tossed aside her bow and drew her sword.

Not content to wait for the other two to reach her, the Dane girl with flaming, red hair stepped out of the shadows and rushed to meet them, letting out a shrill war cry that was enough to cause a mortal's blood to run cold.

The fight was sharp and quick. Bringing her sword down from the high guard in a wide, sweeping motion, Durthfang's razor sharp blade bit deep into the neck of one of the Saxons where it met the shoulder, showering both the stricken warrior and Alfhildr in a fine spray of blood. Unfortunately, Alfhildr's sword had bitten into bone, preventing her from easily drawing it out of the Saxon's mortal wound. Without hesitation, she released her grip on that weapon, deftly stepped to one side so that the body of the first Saxon separated her from the second as she drew her axe.

The remaining Saxon soon found himself outnumbered as the sound of a snarling wolf rushing toward him from out of the shadows drew his attention momentarily away from Alfhildr. This unexpected distraction left him little opportunity to bring his shield back around in time to fend off the Dane girl's attack.

Once more, she lunged forward, stepping up and onto the body of the dying Saxon to gain height before leaping down upon the last of the trio that had charged her. Pushing aside his outstretched sword arm with her left hand, Alfhildr threw herself upon the Saxon's shield while bringing her small axe down with all her might, sinking it deep into her opponent's face even as the two tumbled over onto the ground.

The other Saxons, those who had remained about the corpse of the dead huscarl were not permitted the luxury of watching this gruesome fight. The moment they turned their backs on the farmhouse, Osgar and the farmer sallied out from either side of it, howling at the top of their lungs for all they were worth. The first of Osgar's prey that night was neatly skewered through and through with his spear. The second was dispatched with the sword. Even the farmer managed to strike down one of the raiders, using a Saxon spear taken from the corpse of one of the previous attackers.

Whether the two surviving Saxons dropped to their knees as a sign of submission or simply because their legs had given out from under them did not matter to Osgar.

Without hesitation, he thrust his sword into the chest of the closer of the two, while the farmer, maddened by the sickly sweet smell of warm blood, drew his spear from the stomach of his first kill and turned on the second. In the bright moon light, the Dane farmer did not see a helpless, terrified man on his knees, wide-eyed as he held his bare hands out, pleading for his life. He saw an animal intent on murder that had been caught creeping up on his wife and children under the cover of darkness. With all his strength, he sank the spear he held into the last of the Saxons, leaving the stricken man pinned to the ground, violently writhing and squirming until the last of his strength ebbed away in a futile effort to escape his fate.

Having dispatched all of their would be assailants, Alfhildr, Osgar, and the farmer stood stock still where they had finished their grim labors, looking about with their weapons at the ready, listening intently for any sign that there were others they had missed. Only when all were satisfied no more Saxon's were about did they turn to the task of ensuring their initial blows had done the job.

Not far from where his companions had left the cover of the woods, the lone Saxon thegn charged with tending to their mounts drew back in horror after witnessing the manner in which the others had been slaughtered. The last image he saw was that of a diminutive warrior with long, flowing hair advancing to where her companions were. With her sword resting on her shoulder and a wolf trailing closely behind, stopping from time to time to sniff a corpse, the fortunate Saxon knew it could only be the witch about whom he had heard so much.

Æ

For the longest time, no one spoke. It wasn't out of fear of waking the children who were all bundled up together in one corner of the farm hut. They had slept through the entire fight, such as it was, without stirring. Rather, the silence that permeated the modest hovel was due to the exhaustion that combatants often experience in the aftermath of a close-in and vicious fight. Osgar and the farmer sat hunched over at the roughhewn table, gulping down mead. Off in another corner, Jorunnr stood with her back to her husband and Osgar, holding up a blanket to screen Alfhildr as best as she could as the young Dane girl stripped away her blood-soaked clothing and washed off the Saxon blood that had splattered her face, hands, and hair.

When she was done, Jorunnr broke the strange silence when she offered the sullen shield maiden one of her gowns. Shaking her head as if awoken from a deep sleep, Alfhildr looked into Jorunnr's eyes for a moment before glancing over to where Osgar sat. Though he said nothing, Alfhildr could see by his expression that he had heard what the farmer's wife had said. For the briefest of moments, Alfhildr wavered before shaking her head. "No, I shall wrap myself in a blanket until my clothes are dry." The temptation to dissuade her never occurred to Jorunnr. In the short time she had known the painfully modest young woman with flowing, red hair, she had concluded that the girl did not yield once she had made a decision. So, she wrapped the blanket that she had been holding about Alfhildr's shoulders and led her to the table.

Once more, silence descended upon the hut as Alfhildr slowly sipped the mead Jorunnr set before her. The farmer was the first to break the silence. Looking up at Alfhildr, he stared at her until she pried her eyes off the cup before her to meet the farmer's.

"Is it always like this?" he asked haltingly. "I mean, do you always feel like this after a battle?"

"How do you feel?" Alfhildr asked softly.

The farmer shrugged. "Exhausted. I feel like I do after working all day under the hot summer sun, drained of all my strength and dazed by my labors."

"How did you expect you would feel?" she asked pointedly.

Once more, the farmer shrugged as he looked down at his cup as if he were ashamed of what he was thinking.

"I thought it would be like the legends of old, those our fathers passed down to us," he muttered.

"And you believed them?" Osgar snorted. "You heard the lies of old men, spun by those who never tasted the blood of another man on his lips and thought that they were the way things happened?"

Pausing, Osgar took a long deep gulp of his mead, staring at the cup in his hand before setting it down on the table.

"We drink until we're drunk to celebrate that we're alive, not what we have done."

"And we drink to forget," Alfhildr whispered without taking her eyes off her own cup.

Osgar nodded. "That too."

Æ

Alfhildr and her small party stayed with the farmer and his family for another day before leaving. As they were securing their belongings to their mounts, Jorunnr came up to Alfhildr.

"We have no way of repaying your courage and kindness," she stated as she stood before the red-haired female warrior. "We owe you our lives and there is nothing I can ever do to repay that. But please, take this modest offering as a token of my eternal friendship and gratitude for the lives you have given to my husband, children, and myself," she implored as she held up a neatly folded, embroidered gown.

Alfhildr gazed down at the fine needlework for the longest time before finding her voice.

"This is far too beautiful to be wasted on someone like me," Alfhildr murmured without taking her eyes off the gift.

Jorunnr smiled, suspecting the red-haired girl was simply trying to find an excuse to turn away something she wanted.

"Here," she whispered conspiratorially as she leaned closer while pressing the gown into Alfhildr's hands.

"The Saxon does not need to know anything about this. Perhaps, the day may come when you will have a need for it," Jorunnr concluded as she pulled back, wearing a knowing smile.

Though Alfhildr was sure that would never be the case, she kept the gown.

Æ

The efforts of Alfhildr and Osgar did not always meet with success. All too often, they came upon a farmstead where all they could do was bury what remained of its previous owners. On these days, neither Dane nor Saxon spoke while they went about their grim chores before retreating back into the woods where they would set up that night's camp as far from the putrid odor of death as their mounts could carry them.

From time to time, the strange party of hunters would happen upon the trail of a raiding party. On one occasion, they stumbled upon a band of Danes who were about to sally forth from the woods where they were hiding and fall upon a rich Saxon holding. Osgar was all for waiting to strike until the Norsemen were committed to the attack.

"Their attention will be on the owners of the farm," he pointed out. "They will not be expecting us to fall upon them from the rear."

"And what if our timing is off?" Alfhildr countered.

"What if they are able to divide their force on the fly, dispatching a few of their party to hold us in check while the rest fall upon the farmers?"

Osgar shrugged. "It is a chance we have to take."

"It is a chance I am not willing to take," Alfhildr thundered back as she jerked her reins and brought her mount around until it was facing the direction of the Danish raiders.

"Besides," she snapped. "Why kill many when we can accomplish the same thing by only killing one?"

Realizing what the Dane girl was about to do, Osgar rose up in his saddle in an effort to stop her. Alfhildr, however, before the Saxon could do anything, dug her heels into Dimma's flanks and took off to where her fellow Danes were gathering.

The shock of seeing Alfhildr ride into their midst, her red hair flowing and sword drawn, threw the raiders into confusion. Both Skadi and Hoenir added to this in their own special way, leaving the raiders torn between standing their ground and fleeing for their lives. Only the efforts of their leader, a man who went by the name of Sigmund, kept the raiding party from scattering to the four winds.

"Stand your ground, you worthless dogs," he thundered.

Upon determining Sigmund was the one she wanted, Alfhildr boldly rode up to him but did not strike. Instead, she brought Dimma to a halt just out of reach of the two-handed axe Sigmund was holding at the ready. With her sword resting on her shoulder, she looked at the raiders who stared at her with a mixture of awe, astonishment, and fear.

"I am Alfhildr, a Dane like you," she proclaimed boldly. "But, unlike you, I do not butcher defenseless women and children for sport."

Sigmund boldly met the girl whose hair was as red as his own by setting the head of his mighty axe down on the ground before him and resting his hands on the end of the handle. "And I am Sigmund, known to my people as 'the Just.' This is my warband, come here to extract revenge for the murder of my kinsmen."

"Do you repay the murder of the innocent by murdering those who had no hand in the crime you allege?" Alfhildr asked, now that the initial shock of her appearance had passed, and she had managed to maneuver the leader of the warband into what amounted to a parley.

"Blood demands blood," Sigmund hissed. "You know the law."

Throwing her leg over Dimma's neck, Alfhildr slid off her saddle. Once on the ground, she boldly marched up to Sigmund, ignoring as best she could the fact that he stood a full head taller than her and had shoulders that were almost as wide as Dimma's withers. After stopping, she brought her sword around, planting Durthfang's tip in the ground while cupping her hands on its pummel.

"Yes, I know the law," she replied softly. "It is under the law that govern us both that I challenge you. If I am victorious, the men of your warband will swear an oath that they will stop raiding and will return home to their own families and farms."

Though astonished by such a bold challenge from a mere girl, Sigmund gazed down at Alfhildr sporting an amused smile.

"And if I win?"

Alfhildr replied with a smile of her own.

"That is not possible. For I am Alfhildr, sword arm of the gods. No man born can defeat me."

While several of the Danes chuckled nervously among themselves, most drew back, fearing the strange girl before them just might be all that the stories they had heard claimed she was, possessing powers that no mortal could match, bestowed upon her by the gods themselves.

For the longest time, the two warriors stood staring at each other. For his part, Sigmund was attempting to decide if the waif of a girl before him was serious. When he came to the conclusion that she was, he chuckled once more before turning to his fellow Danes.

"If I accept this foolish challenge and lose, is there any man here who would be unwilling to give his oath and do as this child asks?"

When no one spoke up, Sigmund looked back at Alfhildr.

"Then, it is agreed, provided you promise not to use any of your magic, and you keep your creatures out of it."

Once more Alfhildr smirked as she replied. "I need neither magic nor assistance from others to hold my own in battle with one such as you."

"And your Saxon?" Sigmund asked as he eyed Osgar.

"I am sure he will spare some of you if you are foolish enough to cross swords with him, but don't count on it."

Amused by the boldness of the brash, red-haired girl, Sigmund roared.

"It will be a sadder place when you are dead, little one."

"Then, we shall all live happily for many years," Alfhildr quipped as she stepped back, taking a firm grip of her sword's hilt as she did so.

Though her comment caused everyone save Osgar to laugh, Alfhildr's expression quickly took on a cold, determined look that caused Sigmund to realize the red-haired girl was deadly serious.

Taking up his axe, Sigmund began to whirl the fearsome weapon over his head in great circles, slowly at first but with ever-increasing speed as its heavy blade cut through the air with a menacing whooshing sound. For her part, Alfhildr kept her sword at the charge guard, a pose that partially hid the weapon along the length of her right leg while she ever so slowly circled around the massive Dane before her. Moving to her right, she ignored the axe as it sliced through the air, concentrating instead on watching Sigmund's eyes for they would tell her when he was about to strike.

When he judged the time to be right, Sigmund took a step forward with his right foot just as his axe was beginning to slice along a downward arch to the right of his body. He had no intent of killing her, not if he didn't need to. Instead, he wished to hit the red-haired girl low, about her waist with the shaft of the axe before jerking it toward him, hooking her in the back with the lower horn of the axe head, throwing her off balance and perhaps even off her feet. Alfhildr, however, was able to dodge this assault by dancing back and away from the axe's blade as it passed within inches of her. Both this maneuver and the effort Sigmund had put into his swing left him vulnerable, a fact Alfhildr exploited by quickly shifting about to her left.

When Osgar saw her bring her sword up and across her body, he knew she had the over-confident Dane. All she needed was one swipe and she would lay her foe's back open. It, therefore, came as something of a shock when instead of striking Sigmund with the cutting edge of her sword, at the last second, she gave her wrist a quick twist and instead, smacked the Dane across the buttocks with the flat of her sword.

A mighty roar rose as all who were watching broke into laughter, all except Osgar who was perplexed by the opportunity Alfhildr had wasted to put a quick end to this fight. Sigmund also found nothing comical about the red-haired girl's antics. When he came about to face her, his face was distorted by a rage that would have caused a lesser being to quiver. Alfhildr, on the other hand, greeted this development with a smirk. She had succeeded in enraging her opponent. She knew through painful experience in a fight such as this, one needed to maintain a cool head and keen eye. Anger and rage tended to push aside caution and clear thinking, just as eyes seething with hatred blinded a combatant to the dangers to which he was leaving himself open.

Thus, in quick order Sigmund's wild, but fruitless, efforts to strike down his nimble opponent deteriorated into something of a comedy that even Osgar was eventually able to enjoy once he realized what Alfhildr was up to. In time, Sigmund's strength began to ebb, causing the momentum of the axe he was wielding to throw him off balance and leaving him stumbling about like a drunken man. After one mighty swing, he found himself unable to stay on his feet. Like a great oak, he tumbled onto the ground, losing the grip on his axe as he flailed about in a vain attempt to keep from doing so. Disarmed and winded, he lay on the ground, waiting for the red-haired fury he had tried to strike down to put him out of his misery.

Though she too was exhausted from her efforts, Alfhildr did a masterful job of keeping her composure. Once more resting her blade on her shoulder, she approached the prostrate warrior. Looking down at Sigmund with a cold, expressionless stare, Alfhildr regarded him for a moment before she spoke.

"I could end this now," she finally stated in a calm, clear voice as she slowly brought the tip of her sword down until it was resting just below Sigmund's Adam's apple.

"Or," she continued, shifting the tip a few inches off to one side, "I could accept your word as we had agreed and allow you to return to your family, whole and unharmed. The choice is yours."

A grin began to make itself evident as Sigmund realized he was being offered an honorable escape.

"A man would be a fool not to accept such a gift from someone the gods watch over, and Sigmund, the Just, is no fool."

Stepping back, Alfhildr sank the tip of her sword into the ground before placing her hands, one upon the other on its pummel. "Then, it is agreed."

Propping himself up on his left elbow, Sigmund raised his right hand, palm out toward Alfhildr.

"By my oath, it is agreed. Now," he added as his grinning men watched in amusement, "having bested me, the least you can do is to help this sorry wretch back up onto his feet."

Æ

Sigmund insisted that Alfhildr and her party share their camp and a meal that night, an offer to which Osgar was reluctant to agree but did so when Alfhildr gave him that same, cold stare she used whenever she wanted it to be known that she would tolerate no argument. It was after they had finished eating and Sigmund had told her of the Saxons he had been seeking that Alfhildr asked if their leader had a scar on his right cheek below his eye and carried a green shield with two diagonal bars of yellow that ran on either side of the boss.

"Yes," Sigmund bellowed. "He is the one. Do you know where he is?"

Dropping her gaze, Alfhildr blushed.

"Well, yes and no," she muttered in a low voice. "Though I know where he is, in the main, I have no idea where Skadi carried his right arm off to."

All the men, including Osgar broke out in laughter. As it died away, one of Sigmund's men asked why she did not chase after her wolf to see what she had done with the Saxon's arm. Alfhildr shrugged.

"We were all hungry that day. I expect she feasted upon it."

When several of the men took to muttering, Alfhildr looked up at them in surprise.

"Well, even a wolf deserves a reward for a fine day's work," she intoned defensively.

After another round of laughter, Sigmund came to his feet.

"Having done me a great service, I am obliged that when you call little one, Sigmund and his men will come," he proclaimed loudly.

As one, the men of Sigmund's warband came to their feet, shouting Alfhildr's name at the top of their lungs by way of acclamation, leaving the diminutive Dane girl blushing like a virginal bride on her wedding day.

Æ

It was when the warm summer nights were fast becoming a memory that Alfhildr and Osgar came upon a scene that left the two wanderers discouraged and wondering if all their efforts over the past few months had been for naught. Thin tendrils of smoke alerted them to the tragedy they were too late to avert. The sight of a woman clawing at the earth with her fingers in an effort to fashion a grave for the mutilated corpses of her husband and oldest son told them of the cost others paid for their efforts earlier that day to hunt down a boar. And though Alfhildr had no way of knowing if their presence would have made a difference, she still could not help but feel a pang of guilt over the way she and Osgar had laughed as they butchered and packed away the boar to be eaten later that night.

As they approached the woman, Osgar noticed a girl and a young boy standing off to one side, clutching each other as they watched their mother tend to her dead as best as she could. While Alfhildr continued toward the woman, Osgar made for the children, neither of whom moved as he approached for both were still in shock, stuck senseless and confused by the sights and sounds to which they had been witness. For once, their roles were reversed. As Osgar tended to the living, Alfhildr took care of those who were beyond suffering.

As often happened on days such as this, few words were exchanged as Dane and Saxon took to helping those who had survived pick through what remained of their hovel before erecting a shelter, preparing a meal for them and, then, after bedding them down as best they could, sitting about the camp fire, lost in their own thoughts as each stared into the flames until they themselves turned in.

The dawn of a new day seemed to make all the difference in the two small children who had escaped the raiders by hiding in the woods. Though they clung to Osgar wherever he went, they seemed no less the worse for the horror that had befallen the rest of their family. The same could not be said for their mother. Alfhildr had to take her to a nearby stream where she peeled away the blood-soaked rags in which she had slept and washed her. When she was finished, Alfhildr dressed the woman in the gown Jorunnr had given her.

"It suits you better than it would me," the Dane girl declared once they were done.

It was a comment that elicited little more than a vacant stare from the woman.

As the day wore on and the woman showed no sign of doing anything more than sitting by the mounds of dirt where her husband and oldest son were buried, Alfhildr asked Osgar what he thought they should do since it was clear to both of them that the mother was too lost in grief to tend to the children she had left. The answer he gave was not at all what she expected.

"I shall stay and care for them," he announced as he watched the girl who was no more than six and her younger brother chase Skadi who was behaving like a puppy with new-found friends.

When he looked away from them and saw the stunned expression on Alfhildr's face, he gave her a warm, friendly smile.

"I am too old to keep wandering about the forests," he announced. "Besides, the hatred that drove me to turn my back on my God and my people has played itself out. I am ready to set aside the sword and once more turn my hand to the plow."

Though saddened by Osgar's decision, she was glad he had found a place where he would be welcomed and accepted. That she would ever be able to find such a place was still a hope that Alfhildr clung to, like the last stubborn leaf clings to the tree that had given it life as summer gives way to fall.

Chapter Nine

THE MAGIC OF THE WHITE CHRIST

Present Day England
"The Dig"

"Of all the writings attributed to Archbishop Plegmund, his transcript of the legend is not only the oldest known written copy of it, it is also the only non-ecclesiastical piece he ever penned."

Elva found it nearly impossible to keep from snickering to herself as Professor Bannon unconsciously adopted his lecture theatre style as he spoke to her.

"Do you suppose there was some sort of connection between a Viking girl who never converted to Christianity, yet married a Christian, and a man who would become one of the most learned theologians in Alfred's England?"

At first, the red-haired graduate student didn't respond as she continued to scrape away a thin layer of clay from an object the ground penetrating radar had detected.

"Elva?" Bannon asked again, wondering if she had heard him.

With a sigh, she eased back on her haunches before sweeping back a strand of hair that had escaped the high ponytail jutting out from a New York Yankees' baseball cap she always wore when working at the dig. She didn't look up at her professor as she went over in her mind just how much she wished to tell him what she knew about Alfhildr or, at least, what she thought she knew. This was particularly true when it came to religion.

She had been hoping to avoid becoming entangled in any discussions on that subject since they usually took members of the team away from the evidentiary aspects of what they were trying to establish and into heated, and oftentimes contentious, theological debates that were purely a matter of belief and faith, not science.

Elva looked up at Professor Bannon as he stood there, hovering over her with his back to the hot summer sun, so that he appeared to be no more than a featureless silhouette. As appealing as it was to remain silent, given the doubts he continued to express regarding her opinion that the grave did belong to Alfhildr, holding back any aspect of the legend from her mentor would be wrong. After wiping away the sweat from her forehead with the back of her glove, she sighed.

"I could use a break right about now," she announced as she came to her feet. "Besides, this probably is a good time to get into this," she added betraying the resignation she felt before turning her back on the last few layers of clay that still concealed the fist-sized crucifix Alfhildr had once been given by a then obscure monk.

Æ

The young man nervously rubbed his hand over his freshly shaven forehead as he hurried along the forest path. When he had stood before the Abbot in Chester and declared his intention to go among the heathen Danes to bring them the love of Christ, it had all sounded so noble. Now, in the gathering darkness, on the edge of the Danelaw, Brother Plegmund was not so sure.

As a child oblate, who had grown up in the service of God, Plegmund knew little of life outside the monastery. He had thrilled at the stories of St. Augustine who had converted the Saxon kings and had marveled at the stories that told of how the old monks had gone among the heathen to save their souls. He often dreamed of venturing out into the wilderness and doing so himself. But the Abbot kept him safe within the scriptorium, learning to read and write, laboring away day after day, copying the precious scripts with a fine, careful hand that few could match. And though Plegmund knew he had to be obedient to the Rule, in his heart a tiny flicker of longing to save souls continued to burn quietly within him as he grew.

For two weeks, the young man had journeyed across Mercia, staying with village priests and small religious communities each night. Yesterday, he had broken bread with Father Alfwine in a ramshackle little steading bounded by a strong wooden stockade.

"I'll pray for you, boy, like I did for all the others," the old priest sadly intoned as Plegmund was preparing to venture into Danelaw. "Are you sure I can't persuade you to turn back?"

With more confidence than he felt, Plegmund had held his head high as he answered.

"I am safe within the Lamb's loving embrace. Even though I walk in the shadow of the valley…"

"Yes, yes, they all said that too," Father Alfwine interrupted, making little effort to rein in the dismissive tone in his voice. "But none of them ever came back either."

He looked sideways at the earnest young monk and dropped his voice.

"And now they say there is a pagan witch riding loose with the devil's own familiars at her heels. They say…"

He paused and glanced around before going on.

"They say she has hair of flame and tempts God-fearing men into carnal sin and eternal damnation, that once she has your immortal soul, she gives your body to her wolf and crow to devour."

Though Alfwine's story did not dissuade him from going on, Plegmund had shivered as he prayed long and hard that he would be spared such a fate during his one-man crusade.

With the forest shadows now beginning to lengthen, Plegmund started to look for somewhere to shelter for the night. He was sure he hadn't strayed from the path the old priest had pointed out to him: but, as dusk fell, his fear began to blossom.

"Pater noster qui es in coelis, sanctificetur nomen tuum…"

As Plegmund stumbled on, he began to pray, clutching to the familiar words like a talisman against the evil of the forest around him, words that kept him from hearing the approaching soft hoof falls.

When he finally did turn around, the young monk found himself beholding a frightful sight. Framed by the setting sun, he looked up to see a warrior astride a grey horse approaching him, her flaming red hair falling loosely about her shoulders. A choking cry burst unwillingly from his lips when he realized it was the Dane witch herself. Turning, Plegmund took to his heels, looking back over his shoulder at the mounted terror as he did so. He never saw the tree root that tripped him, sending him headfirst into the trunk of a slim ash tree.

Æ

The young monk woke to the sound of singing. For a moment, he thought he was in the monastery, listening to Matins. Then, ever so slowly, the splitting pain in his skull speared the recollection of more recent events back into his consciousness. As he lay there terrified, a soft, cool compress smelling of fresh moss was gently laid upon his brow.

Reluctantly, he opened his eyes. Rather than beholding a monster, the monk found himself staring up at a frowning young girl who was gazing down at him with caring, green eyes.

"You really ought to look where you are going. It was lucky it was only a tree. If it had been a rock, you could have killed yourself. Would you like some water?"

Ever so gently, Alfhildr cradled Plegmund's head with one hand, lifting it until he was able to sip from the water skin. He stared uncertainly at the young girl wearing a baggy chainmail shirt and unfeminine breeches.

"Thank you," the monk managed to rasp. Then he remembered what he had been told about the Danish witch and his mouth opened before his addled brain could think.

"You aren't going to tempt me into carnal sin, then feed me to your wolf, are you?"

She looked at him strangely. "What's carnal sin?"

Averting his eyes, a blush rose in Plegmund cheeks as he began to stammer. "You know…when a man and a woman…" He wasn't prepared for a matching blush to rise in the girl's cheeks.

"No!" Her tone was cold and certain.

They watched each other cautiously for a long moment, both unsure what to do.

At last Alfhildr broke the silence. "Why did you think that I would…you know…"

Plegmund had been brought up to tell the truth, so with more honesty than tact, he told the strange warrior girl everything Father Alfwine had told him. By the time he finished, she looked more annoyed than anything.

"I am not a witch. And I most certainly do not do things like…like that," she declared before taking a deep breath to calm herself.

"You are not fit enough to go anywhere tonight. I'll make a camp," the Dane announced as she stood up abruptly and started to hunt for firewood, leaving Plegmund to lay back and attempt to make sense of what had just happened.

Witches weren't supposed to blush, were they?

The next morning, the worst of Plegmund's headache and nausea had largely gone, leaving behind a fat, purpling bruise across his forehead. As he pushed himself up on his elbows, the girl came over and squatted beside him.

"So…who are you, and what are you doing wandering the forest alone?"

"I am Brother Plegmund." He paused and winced as she delicately probed the tender bruise.

"I've come to bring the word of the living God, our Lord Jesus Christ, to the unbelievers."

Even as he said it, he knew it wasn't the smartest answer he could have given.

Alfhildr snorted. "Unbelievers, are we? What of my gods? Do they not matter? Unlike yours, mine do not allow themselves to be killed off like sheep without a fight."

Tilting her head to one side, she stared at the young monk until he began to squirm.

"Hmm, if you go around saying things like that you won't last long." She paused again as if trying to make up her mind. "If I take you to a safe farm will you tell me about the White Christ and the magic you do in return?"

Plegmund slowly grinned. A real pagan actually wanted him to tell her all about the Lamb of God, the Danish witch herself no less. If by some miracle he succeeded in converting her, he would be famous. That thought had no sooner came to mind then he found the need to scold himself for such arrogant pride. Setting that thought aside, he nodded humbly to the self-assured girl, a person so unlike anyone he had ever met before.

Æ

Even though it was obvious the Dane girl was holding her mount back for his benefit, Plegmund was finding it more and more difficult to keep up with her. By late afternoon, he was exhausted enough to no longer worry about the wolf that ran ahead or the crow circling above. When she finally informed him that they would halt for the night, he sank to the ground in relief.

After she had dismounted and tied her mount off, Alfhildr walked over and stared down at him for a moment.

"If you want to eat, you can help with the camp. We need firewood, Holy Man."

Plegmund had the grace to look embarrassed at her less than subtle reprimand. With a groan and more effort than such a simple task should have required, he pushed himself back up off the ground and started hunting dry timber. Only when the fire was lit, and two rough shelters had been constructed did Plegmund reach into his scrip. He pulled out a small, round loaf and placed it to warm beside the fire. Alfhildr looked at the bread for a moment, then smiled as she placed a haunch of deer beside it.

"We'll eat well tonight. Thank you for sharing."

It wasn't long before all of the strange party had eaten their fill, although Alfhildr had to stifle a laugh as Plegmund had bowed his head and prayed over his meat. At length, they sat quietly by the fire listening to the crunching of bones as Skadi tried to get at the marrow. Plegmund watched the wolf for a moment before fetching a long straight stick. Alfhildr stared in surprise as he took the thighbone from the wolf and started to push the juicy gobbets of marrow from the end. She had expected Skadi to snarl at the very least, but the wolf just snatched up the morsels as they fell, before skipping back and waiting eagerly for more.

When he realized Alfhildr was staring at him, Plegmund looked across apologetically.

"I used to do this for my father's hunting dogs. I thought your wolf wouldn't mind."

Alfhildr was even more surprised when Skadi flopped down at the young monk's feet and continued to chew on the now empty bone. He reached down and scratched behind her ears, causing the she-wolf to stretch her neck and grunt with pleasure. Alfhildr had learned to trust Skadi's judgment and, as she watched her friend, she decided that she too liked the calm, sweet-natured young man before her, even if he was unfit and had silly ideas.

Æ

The next day, Alfhildr explained to Plegmund that she was taking him to the farm of a Danish farmer she had helped.

"Because he is so close to Saxon land, he trades with a nearby Saxon village, although that didn't stop some hunters from trying to take rather than trade."

"What happened?"

"Justice."

Plegmund shivered at the word, for he understood what pagans took to be justice. By mid-afternoon, Alfhildr was in high spirits having taken a young buck that was unlucky enough to have crossed Skadi's path. Only when she had properly dressed the buck did they push on toward the little farm with Plegmund struggling once more to keep up.

Suddenly, the girl, wolf, and horse stopped ahead of him, followed by a swift chopping hand signal that froze Plegmund to the spot. He watched as the girl carefully drew her bow and nocked an arrow as she silently slid from her mare's back. A quick glance back reinforced her signal for him to remain silent before she disappeared into the brush.

Plegmund waited uncertainly, unsure if he should flee or stay. He looked again at the placid mare and took heart from the beast's relaxed stance.

Perhaps it would be better to stay. He sat down and rested against a tree.

The young monk woke with a start to a slobbery, meaty kiss. Looking up, he found himself eye to eye with the wolf, standing over him with her wet tongue hanging out and her tail wagging.

"Skadi likes you, Holy Man," Alfhildr grinned. "It's lucky I didn't ask you to stand guard."

"Where did you go?"

"Saxon raiders."

"And did you….did you…?"

Alfhildr looked grim faced at the naïve young man.

"What would you have me do? They planned to steal, kill, and rape."

When Plegmund's head drooped at her words, she could see the pain that the thought of killing caused him.

"Don't worry. One has an arrow in the leg and the other, a bite out of his arse." She grinned and reached down to ruffle Skadi's ears. "Is that all right, Holy Man?"

It was getting dark as they approached the roughly stockaded little farm. Alfhildr nudged the young monk and pointed him to a door.

"Go on in and make your greeting. I will be along as soon as I have tended to Dimma."

With that she left him and led the mare toward a byre on the other side of the yard.

Uncertainly, Plegmund approached the door that she had indicated. He knocked tentatively on the frame and stepped across the threshold.

"May the blessings of the Lord Jesu..." His words were chopped short as the young monk was grabbed and thrown against the wall. He looked down in terror at the blade waving in front of his nose.

"And what were you going to steal, Saxon scum?" The farmer leaned close as he growled, bathing Plegmund with the full force of his rancid breath.

"I…I…nothing. My friend said…. I'm not a thief… I was told…" Plegmund stammered and stuttered desperately in the face of the hard-eyed farmer.

"Ha!" the Farmer scoffed. "Like all Saxons, you squirm when you're caught. So, why are you dressed like a woman, Saxon?"

The slur to his habit stung Plegmund into a degree of coherence.

"I am a man of God. I came to bring you news of the risen Lord, Jesus Christ."

The farmer just stared and narrowed his eyes.

"You know what I think? I think you're a lying little toad. I think you're a Saxon thief and spy. So, little spy, tell me true, now, why did you come? And if I don't like your answer your God had better be close."

Plegmund opened and closed his mouth in shock. "I was …."

"…brought here by me, Jarl," Alfhildr announced calmly as she walked in. "You can put him down if you like, he's harmless. I spotted three hunters up by the old barrow sneaking close, but he's not one of them."

The grip on Plegmund's throat loosened.

"Are they still around?"

Alfhildr laughed. "No. I persuaded them that honest hunting was more fruitful and less dangerous."

Jarl grinned and let go of the monk to stretch out a big meaty hand to the young girl.

"You have our thanks, again, Alfhildr." He turned and shouted over his shoulder to his wife. "Ho! Ragnar, we have guests."

Plegmund was surprised when Alfhildr left him with the farmer that night after they had all shared a meal together. He was about to go after her when Jarl put his hand on the young monk's shoulder.

"Leave her be, boy. She has her own way."

Together they watched quietly as the girl vanished silently out into the dark.

That evening, Plegmund's ministry started. He had thought to preach but something made him stop and he listened instead. He heard of the endless feuding and raids, he listened to Jarl tell him how their gods didn't care. Only when the Dane farmer was finished singing the praises of a girl the monk once had thought was a witch did he start to speak of his God and the salvation He brought.

The next morning, Plegmund was already up when Alfhildr returned to the farm. He smiled as she approached.

"Jarl suggested that I should go to the village of Aethel's Ham. He tells me they trade with Danes and it would be a good place to start."

Alfhildr grinned and nodded her agreement as Jarl and Ragnar came to the door.

"Jarl, my thanks for your hospitality."

"Alfhildr, you know we would offer you more." Jarl smiled sadly as the girl shook her head.

"You'll take your holy man to the Saxons' village?"

"I will."

As she started to turn away, Jarl clapped the young monk on the shoulder.

"Go on then, lad. You've given me a lot to think on. Perhaps we'll meet when I come to the village."

With that the farmer turned and headed over to his pigs, leaving the bemused Plegmund to make his way after the young Danish witch, who was not a witch, and warrior, who had stayed her hand when she could have killed.

Æ

Plegmund and Alfhildr never quite made it to the Saxon village that day. First, a Saxon smallholder's wife found the girl and begged her protection from Danish reavers. Once the warband had passed, they had moved on, only to stumble on a burned-out farm nearby. Alfhildr had watched as the young monk broke down in tears as he cradled the corpse of a little boy before tenderly laying him alongside his mother and father in the grave they had dug. Together, they shoveled the earth back in somber silence until at last he turned to Alfhildr.

"Why do men do this?" The tracks of tears were still fresh on his face as he stared at the young girl.

"Because they can."

Alfhildr's answer was brutal and stark. Even in his own grief, Plegmund felt the pain behind her words. Without realizing it, that was the moment the monk made his decision. He would stay with this warrior who fought for those who couldn't, who did God's work even though she was no Christian.

Later, as they sat companionably beside their small fire, Plegmund tried once more to interest Alfhildr in the love of Christ.

"He sent his only son among us to save us."

"But his enemies nailed him to a cross."

"In dying, he redeemed our sin and…" Plegmund paused to make sure he had her full attention as he lowered his voice. "He rose from the dead…"

"All the Gods do that!" Alfhildr snorted derisively. "Odin rose from the dead after he hanged himself from a tree. That's how you know they are a god."

Alfhildr soon found herself growing tired of the monk's efforts to win her over to his God. Eventually, when she decided she had heard enough of the monk's praises of the one he called Christ, she stopped him with a glare.

"I do not see how any man can follow a God that allows himself to be nailed to a cross, or admonishes his followers to turn the other cheek while their homes are being burned and their families slaughtered."

Alfhildr slapped the pommel of Durthfang fiercely as she spoke.

"My gods embrace those who stand up and meet their enemy eye to eye, with a sword in their hand. So, pray to yours as you see fit, Holy Man, and leave me to follow mine. In the end, we shall see who goes the furthest in this world and the next."

With that, Alfhildr turned away and quickly rolled Skadi and herself in her blanket.

Plegmund gazed upon the girl's back for a long time and quietly smiled. While the strange girl who had befriended him would probably never bring herself to accept Christ as her savior, he had already decided she was more worthy of Christ's embrace than many of his fellow Christians.

"I will pray that when your day to be judged comes, Our Lord is able to overlook your sins of pride and arrogance," he whispered to himself. "And if He is not able to do so, well, then, Heaven will be a much poorer place without you."

Then he too rolled himself up in a blanket and settled to sleep.

Æ

Alfhildr wasn't quite sure why the monk stayed with her as she travelled from farm to farm, watching for raiders and thieves. She wasn't even sure why she let him. For some reason, the farm folk, both Saxon and Dane, seemed pleased to see him and actually listened when he talked to them about his God; although Alfhildr made sure she had other chores to tend to when he started spouting his nonsense about a helpless God.

The late spring turned to summer and, even in the deep forest, the heat often became sweltering. One afternoon, Alfhildr called a halt beside a little stream. Her time of the month had come and, with it, a stink that caused her nose to wrinkle.

"Make yourself useful, Holy Man. You've seen me make shelters often enough. Today, it's your turn."

With that, she grabbed some things from her saddlebags before heading back to a sheltered little pool by the stream she remembered spotting.

Plegmund sighed and started to weave the rough shelters. He wondered why the girl had been so irritable that day. Perhaps, one of the honey cakes the last farmer's wife had thrust into his scrip would cheer her up. He smiled. She hadn't seen that, and it would be a nice surprise. He would take it to her as soon as he had finished setting up the camp.

Alfhildr quickly stripped off and plunged into the little pool. The minnows fled as she splashed happily in the chilly water. Alone and, for the moment, free of anything more pressing than enjoying this late summer day, Alfhildr reveled in the thought of being clean and fresh, if only for a short time. Thrusting her head under the surface, she took to scrubbing at her greasy hair until the cold water began to make her teeth ache. When she surfaced, Alfhildr eyes met Plegmund's at the same moment. Instinctively, she dove back into the water, leaving a dumbstruck monk standing on the bank with his mouth agape.

The next time Alfhildr surfaced, her face betrayed the rage she felt at the holy man's rudeness. She was ready to curse the monk to his hell and back, only to see him desperately scrambling away as fast as he could, his ears glowing like torches. Behind him, lying forlornly on a rock next to her clothing was a single cake.

It was nearly dusk when Alfhildr stalked angrily back to the camp. Plegmund already had the fire alight and Skadi was contentedly ripping meat from a bone. As he heard her approach, the young monk sprang to his feet, almost tripping over his robe.

"I...I...I'm so sorry. I didn't know... I just wanted to give you the cake... It was a present. I really didn't mean... I'm so sorry."

As the flustered and stammering young man gabbled on, Alfhildr saw his ears turn red once more, causing her furious outburst to die on her lips as she took in Plegmund's woebegone expression. He reminded her of a scolded puppy, so much so that she had to bite her lip to avoid smiling.

Struggling to keep a straight face, Alfhildr sniffed haughtily.

"Amongst my people, it is considered polite not to intrude when they are washing. You will do well to remember that." She sniffed again.

"You might also consider the benefit of a bath yourself, Holy Man."

She turned to make a dignified retreat to her side of the fire when she looked down to catch Skadi grinning at her.

"And that goes for you too!"

Æ

The days turned to weeks as the ill-matched pair continued to prowl the edges of the Danelaw. Farmers, who at first had grudgingly offered hearth space to the young monk because he was Alfhildr's companion, now welcomed both with equal pleasure. Yet, most nights, the monk and the girl continued to camp deep in the forest, settling into a companionable routine both seemed to enjoy.

One night, when he judged the light of the fire to be sufficient, Plegmund rummaged about in his scrip. Pulling out a small book, he turned to a page he had marked with a well-worn piece of ribbon. Alfhildr, returning to the fire, couldn't resist the urge to look over his shoulder. Upon spotting an ornate letter 'A' at the beginning of a paragraph, she grinned. Unable to contain her excitement at seeing this, she reached out and pointed to the letter.

"That is how my name starts, with that letter," she announced proudly.

Surprised, the monk glanced up at her over his shoulder.

"You know how to read?"

In an instant, Alfhildr's smile disappeared as she averted her eyes.

"No," she muttered as her cheeks began to redden. "I only know the letters of my name."

Having struggled to find a way to repay the kindness the girl had shown him, the monk hit upon an idea.

"Well, if you will not allow me to share with you the blessings of our Savior, perhaps I can earn my keep by teaching you how to read."

Looking back into the monk's eyes, Alfhildr's smile returned as her excitement at the prospect of learning to read overwhelmed the stern, warrior image she struggled to project.

"Would you?"

From then on, every evening, the campsite became a classroom, with Alfhildr eagerly looking forward to her lessons with an enthusiasm that pleased Plegmund. Their blackboard was the forest floor and her schoolbook an English translation of a Psalter. A farmer gave the monk a small piece of parchment he had been using as a window which Plegmund had carefully scraped clean. Another farm provided goose feathers while their fire and the forest furnished the soot and sap the monk needed to make ink.

Plegmund watched with quiet satisfaction as Alfhildr bent over the parchment, studiously frowning in concentration and chewing her lip as she painstakingly copied the short text that he had given her. At length, she looked up with a triumphant grin, pointing down at her efforts.

"I've done it!" she proclaimed.

Carefully picking up the parchment, Plegmund blew gently to ensure the ink was dry before tipping it toward the fire to read it, smiling to himself as he did so.

"We will make a scholar of you yet," he announced solemnly. That is nicely written. You did miss the letters L and E in this word," he informed her as he pointed to the offending word. "It should read *'the glorious titles of the king were magnificent'*."

When she realized what she had actually written, Alfhildr blushed, then burst out laughing as a lewd image came to mind.

Æ

The first gold of autumn was showing in the leaves when Alfhildr and Plegmund approached the little hamlet of Aethel's Ham. They sang quietly together as they made their way slowly among the trees, practicing a chant Plegmund thought he remembered. Alfhildr had fallen in love with the pretty hymns and chants the young monk had grown up with and insisted that he teach them to her. For his part, Plegmund felt oddly comforted to have another voice join his each evening. It was as if the whole forest became his cloister for the service of Vespers, allowing him to sleep all the better for this simple touch of the familiar.

Plegmund's voice sang sweetly in the forest. *"Laudate Dominum omnes gentes."*

When Alfhildr's hand abruptly silenced him, he looked up in surprise. The image of a young girl who had been laughing with him a moment before had been replaced by that of a hard-faced warrior staring sharply into the trees. Even the she-wolf was alert, crouching next to Plegmund, her hackles rising on her neck.

"Stay here," Alfhildr barked before she and the wolf raced off among the trees, taking up her bow as she did.

Plegmund watched as the warrior and wolf vanished from sight. Alone, he slowly dropped to his knees as he silently prayed to God to protect the young girl who had become as dear to him as his own sister. With each passing day, he grew more fearful for her safety and was dreading the day when she did not return. So, he knelt and prayed with all his heart among the dappled shade of the beech and oak around him.

When, at last, Alfhildr returned, she was accompanied by another, a stocky Saxon farmer with a russet thatch of a beard in which you could hide a badger's sett. Plegmund looked at the stranger in surprise as he stomped up and grasped the young monk's shoulders in two meaty hands.

"Thank the Lord you are safe, good brother. Father Alfwine asked us to keep watch for you."

The farmer cast a sidelong glance at the young girl as she sat quietly in the saddle nearby, then leant close and hissed in the monk's ear.

"We heard you had been taken as a slave and made to serve the Danish witch. Then, what do you know, she comes riding in and fights off her reaver friends and, bold as you like, tells me you're here."

Plegmund felt his anger growing at the farmer's words and struggled to stay calm.

"Tell me, were you glad of her assistance against the reavers?"

The farmer frowned at the monk's tone.

"Well, yes. If it were not for her, they would have made off with all our cattle and young Godwine's daughter."

"And have you seen her work magic?"

"She has the wolf and…well, it's not natural for a woman to go dressed like that and carry sword steel. She must be a witch."

Plegmund glared at the farmer as his voice rose.

"Do you know the story of the Samaritan? Though she is pagan, that girl has done more for the poor and the helpless, Christian and pagan alike, than any other I have met here."

The color rose in his cheeks as his tongue lashed the burly farmer.

"Did she demand payment from you? Has she stolen or threatened?" the monk demanded. "I tell you now, before God, she is no witch, and you would do well to offer thanks to both our Lord Jesus and this warrior for your cattle and the girl child's safety."

The farmer wilted before the young monk's fury as he glanced apologetically across at the red-haired young warrior.

"We'd best be heading back to the village, brother," he finally mumbled. "You and...your companion are welcome to break bread with us."

Æ

That night, the villagers gave thanks for Plegmund's escape from the evils of the pagans after sending a runner to Father Alfwine to let him know the prodigal had returned. While none were openly hostile to his companion, it was clear they were leery of the young girl. All were grateful when she slipped off into the woods for the night. The burly farmer, Egfrid by name, settled himself next to the young monk as they ate.

"Winter's coming, Brother."

"What do you mean?"

"Well, as I see it, you're no hunter, are you?"

Plegmund shook his head, unsure where the conversation was leading.

"'Tis hard enough to find food for one in the forest in winter. Likely you would both starve. 'Twould be unfair on both you and the girl."

As the evening wore on, Egfrid continued to gently drop hints that Plegmund would be helping the girl if he were to stay in the village.

"Course, she can come here regular, and we'll feed her too if you like. It's good land here and there are plenty of pagans who trade with us. We could even build you your own church if you want."

Doubts slowly entered the naïve, young monk's mind as the wily Egfrid oozed honeyed words with care. The village had been in need of a cleric ever since old Father Guthrun had died of the plague four winters back, and the Saxon farmer wasn't going to let this one slip through his fingers.

Out in the forest, Alfhildr was having similar thoughts. She worried about the coming winter and worried that the young monk, unlike the hardy Osgar, would not survive the harsh weather and tight belts. She sat silently by her little fire ruffling Skadi's ears. She had grown to enjoy the company of the gentle, young man and thought hard about how to persuade him to stay safe with his people. A tear ran down her cheek as she considered what to say, for whatever happened, she would miss him.

When they met the next morning, it was as if each could read what was in the other's thoughts. Alfhildr felt a wave of relief as she saw his hesitant stance and noted the secret gloating on the farmer's face. But her relief was tinged by sadness as she recognized that they were about to go their separate ways as, once more, a fragment of the little family she had built was torn away from her again.

They went out into the forest, away from the smirking face and prying eyes of Egfrid to say their farewells.

"I will miss you," Alfhildr muttered as she found herself unable to look up into the monk's moist eyes.

"Me too."

"It's for the best."

"I know. You couldn't hunt enough for both of us and this little lady too." Plegmund added as he reached down and softly stroked Skadi's flank.

"You'll come back, won't you?"

"I will try."

Shyly, the young monk reached under his robe and pulled out a silver crucifix from around his neck. Alfhildr tried to protest, but he held his hand up to still her.

"It's to protect you," he hurried on before she could start. "Not from the gods you refuse to abandon, but from good, God-fearing men who do not understand what you are trying to do. They are not bad men. I expect they are no different than the Roman soldiers who crucified Jesus. That doesn't make what they are doing right, however. So, take care and be careful."

With that the monk made the sign of the cross. "May God go with you and watch over you, little sister."

He watched as she slowly turned, took to saddle, and rode quietly away among the trees until the tears in his eyes obscured her fading image. When he could no longer see her, Plegmund dropped to his knees and prayed for the lonely young girl.

Æ

England
1012 AD

The boy went silent for a moment, looking off into the woods as they continued along.

"Do you suppose God ever forgave Alfhildr?" he finally asked in a low voice without looking back at his grandmother.

"Forgave? For what? For killing those who were raiding the farms?"

"No, Grandma, for not becoming a Christian," the boy replied looking up at her. The old woman didn't answer right off, knowing full well that she needed to be very careful in how she justified the way Alfhildr, and many of her descendants, continued to cling to the old ways, even after they claimed to have accepted Christ as their savior. When she was ready, she looked down at the boy next to her.

"If someone came to this land and demanded that we give up the way we worship and accept their beliefs, would you?"

The boy furrowed his brow as he shook his head. "No! Never."

"Why not?"

"Because we are Christians," the boy replied, wondering if his grandmother was serious.

"What if they told you that what you have been taught all your life was wrong, that the faith they followed was the only true faith, and that those who did not believe as they did were pagans and heretics? Would you still hold to what you were told?"

"Yes, of course."

"Even if they placed a sword at your neck?" the old woman asked, jabbing her bony finger against the side of the boy's throat in an effort to emphasize her point.

Though frightened and unnerved by this line of questions, the boy bravely drew himself up.

"I would never give up my faith. Not ever."

"Then, why would Alfhildr?" the grandmother suddenly asked. "Why should she turn her back on the religious beliefs and practices of her people simply because someone said she was wrong, and he was right when it came to matters of their faith?"

Unable to answer, the boy once more looked away, turning over this issue in his mind as they continued along the path, deeper into the unknown, but ever closer to their destination.

PART THREE
THE SAXON GIRL

Chapter Ten
THE WILL OF THE GODS

Present Day England
"The Dig"

"Is she trying to make us all look bad?" Simon asked as he and the other students lounged in the shade during one of the mandatory breaks on which the Professor insisted.

From where she sat, Sarah watched the wisp of a girl as she continued to scrape away at the ground with a trowel. Dressed in a loose fitting, long sleeved, sweat-soaked, white shirt that looked as if she'd borrowed it from her father and baggy khaki cargo pants, Elva continued to labor away on her own, oblivious to the noonday sun that baked the fresh layers of clay she was scraping away almost as soon as the sun hit them.

"Elva, you need to get your skinny bum over here and hydrate," Sarah called out.

Pausing, the red-haired graduate student straightened up for a moment. Stretching, she rolled her shoulders in an effort to work the knots out of her muscles before responding to her friend's admonishment with a smile.

"I'm fine," was all she said as she lifted the peak of her baseball cap and wiped the sweat from her eyes with a swipe of her sleeve.

Without another word she pulled her cap back down and went right back to what she'd been doing.

"If you were a Saxon lord who had been offered an opportunity to buy her, how much would you have paid?" Simon mused to no one in particular as they continued to watch the ginger-haired graduate student toil away.

"Well, that depends where she would fit into Saxon society," one of Simon's cohorts reflected before taking a long gulp of bottled water. "Me, I think she would probably have fetched considerably more than your average theow."

"A theow?" Sarah snapped. "You're kidding, right?"

"No, I'm not," the outspoken young student replied. "That girl is possessed. I mean, look at her. Since we've been here, Elva has been running about as if she were the professor's personal slave. She's here every morning before most of us are out of bed and she doesn't leave the site until there's not enough light left to see. Even then, Bannon the Barbarian has to all but drag her away by that ponytail of hers that she flaunts in our faces like a mare in heat."

"She does not go about flaunting anything," Sarah snapped. "Especially in your face," she added as she glared at her fellow undergrad. "She's simply dedicated," she muttered after looking back to where her friend was slaving away.

"Possessed is more like it," Simon chuckled. "So, back to Dave's original question: what's her wergild? Me, I say she'd fetch, oh, maybe 200 shillings."

"Oh, please," Sarah shot back incredulously. "If I recall correctly, according to Alfred's Doom that's the price at which a freeman was valued."

"All right, smarty pants," Simon snickered. "If Elva isn't a theow or a ceorl, what is she?"

Sarah didn't answer right off, choosing instead to gaze out to where Elva continued to work away, very much alone and, yet, happy as a clam.

"I expect Elva is like Alfhildr, something very different, something no man could ever quite figure out, much less place a value on."

Æ

Only when Hoenir's behavior became too annoying to ignore did Alfhildr drag her downcast eyes off the ground and look about.

"What is bothering you so?" the red-haired girl snapped as she watched the crow flitter about overhead. Quite naturally, the bird provided her with no answer. It was Skadi who alerted Alfhildr that something, or someone, she had yet to perceive was near at hand.

Taking care to keep from over-reacting, lest she spook the unseen menace, Alfhildr watched the she-wolf out of the corner of her eye for several seconds.

"What is it?" she whispered to Skadi as she began to surreptitiously scanned to the left, then to the right, while keeping her head bowed low as it had been before she became aware of her companions' agitation. It took all her will power to bring Dimma to a slow, almost leisurely halt when Skadi stopped suddenly and took to looking about.

The she-wolf was decidedly less subtle in her response to a danger she perceived yet could not quite pinpoint. Alfhildr watched in silence as the fur along Skadi's spine stood on end. With one of her front paws held high as if prepared to take off at a dead run, the wolf's head slowly pivoted about as she intently peered into the grey mist around them, stopping from time to time to sniff the crisp autumn air before continuing her search for the unseen threat. When Skadi did move on, she did so cautiously, keeping her ears perked and her head swiveling about from side to side, first to the left, then the right. For her part, Alfhildr did her best to continue on as she had been, pretending as best she could she was oblivious to the fact that the hunter was now the hunted.

Æ

"Where do you suppose she's off to?" the fair-haired Saxon muttered when he and his two companions came upon the grey horse, belonging to the Dane witch, tethered to a tree.

"Behind you," Alfhildr stated in a tone that was anything but menacing, but more than enough to rattle the three Saxons who had been tracking her since early dawn. Each reacted in accordance with their varied nature. Their leader, a man of obvious wealth and position wearing a fine mail shirt was the first to rise to meet this unexpected challenge. With his sword already in hand, he spun about, prepared to charge the Dane witch they had been hunting. Even when he saw her standing a full two rods from where he was, staring down the shaft of an arrow nocked and drawn, the Saxon did not hesitate. Bringing his shield up, he lunged toward her. Alfhildr didn't hesitate either.

Her first arrow flew straight and true, hitting the valiant, yet foolish, warrior in the unprotected calf of his left leg, causing him to lose his grip on both sword and shield as he pitched headlong onto the ground. For the briefest of moments, his two companions, both of whom had neither mail nor shields, hesitated, wavering between rushing the Dane witch who had so easily struck down their leader and fleeing to where their own mounts were tethered. Yet, while the sound of a she-wolf's growl and the sight of the Dane girl with flaming, red hair standing ready with another arrow nocked and drawn convinced them a vain, but gallant, defense of their honor was probably not worth their lives, it was the sight of a crow swooping down from the heavens to perch on Alfhildr's shoulder that totally unhinged them. First one, then the other, threw aside his weapons before dropping to his knees, pleading with tightly clutched hands for their lives as they nervously glanced back and forth between Alfhildr and Skadi who, like her mistress, was amused by their antics but remained poised to strike nonetheless.

Ignoring the vile oaths the wounded warrior was leveling at his fellow Saxons, Alfhildr, eventually, eased the bowstring forward, withdrew the unused arrow and returned it to the quiver, never once taking her eyes off the three men. Hoenir, roused from her perch by this, once more took to wing. Circling the small clearing once, the crow came to roost on a tree branch above the two quivering men. From there, it looked on, watching as Alfhildr set aside her bow, drew Durthfang slowly from its sheath and advanced to where the wounded Saxon sat upright, clasping his wounded leg with his hand.

"Who are you? And why do you follow me?" she finally asked.

Momentarily setting aside the pain he was in, the wounded Saxon looked up at Alfhildr, regarding her with an expression that reflected his astonishment that the Dane witch would ask such a foolish question, wondering as he did so if she was mocking them.

"I am Bowdyn, sent by my ealdorman with those worthless curs to capture you if possible, or kill you if it proved to be necessary," he thundered when he realized her question had been sincere.

Alfhildr stunned Bowdyn yet again when she asked him why. With furrowed brow, he stared at the diminutive female wearing a shirt of mail that hung loosely from her elvish frame.

"You killed Hereric, my lord's brother."

"If your lord wanted revenge, why did he not come himself as a man of honor should?" Alfhildr asked, drawing herself up as she closed the distance between herself and the stricken Saxon.

"There is no honor in hunting a witch," Bowdyn muttered.

"I am no witch," Alfhildr shot back, offended by the ease with which men branded her as one.

Before responding, Bowdyn glanced over to where Skadi stood over his sword, poised to strike should one of Bowdyn's companions decide to reclaim his honor by rushing Alfhildr while she conversed with his master. Behind him, he caught a glimpse of Hoenir resting on a low hanging branch, watching them with great interest.

"To my people, a woman who communes with creatures of the forest and conjures up the grey mist in which to hide from the sight of godly men is considered a witch."

Pained by his words, Alfhildr lowed her sword as she looked away.

"I may be many things, but I am not a witch," she muttered after giving the matter some thought. "Of that, I can assure you" she concluded as she once more turned to face Bowdyn.

"Be that as it may," Bowdyn shot back. "My lord demands justice and your head."

In the twinkling of an eye, Alfhildr went from sullen and reflective to barely contained rage.

"Justice! Your lord sends his own brother out to butcher innocent women and children, and he seeks justice for those who were slain in the act of committing murder?"

Tightening her grip on her sword, she brought it up, pointing to each of Bowdyn's companions in turn. "You two. Take to your horses and ride back to this lord of yours. Tell him if he has any sense of honor and wishes to seek justice, he will meet me, Alfhildr, on the field of battle where we will decide this matter, face to face."

The two wide-eyed Saxons didn't need to be told twice. Without a jot of hesitation, they took to their heels and fled. When they were gone and Bowdyn had used the last of his oaths to curse them and the women who had borne them, he looked back at Alfhildr.

"What do you intend to do with me?" he asked, putting up as brave and noble a front as his circumstances would permit.

After sheathing her sword, she advanced to where Bowdyn lay, taking care to scoop up his sword and toss it aside. Kneeling, she took to looking at his leg. Skadi, drawn to Alfhildr's side by the scent of fresh blood, took to sniffing Bowdyn's wound. When she saw the way the Saxon's eyes grew large at the sight of the wolf, Alfhildr found it all but impossible to keep from smirking. Doing her best to keep her laughter in check, she turned toward Skadi, pushing the wolf away with one hand.

"It is not yet time to eat, little one. Go," she commanded, pointing in the direction the other Saxons had fled. "Make sure they have gone."

Though reluctant to do so, the wolf backed away, giving Alfhildr a long, hard stare before trotting off in the direction Bowdyn's erstwhile companions had fled.

"Is that it?" Bowdyn muttered contemptuously as he surreptitiously glanced out of the corner of his eye over to where the Dane girl had thrown his sword. "You plan to feed me to your wolf?"

No longer able to keep a straight face, Alfhildr chuckled as she used her dagger to open a slit in Bowdyn's trousers on either side of the arrow.

"I cannot believe you put your faith in the legends and sagas I have heard your people are spreading about me. I am neither a witch nor a *vÆttir*. I am just me, Alfhildr."

The smile that had lit up her face disappeared as Alfhildr, once more, found herself reflecting on how she always answered that question. It was as if there still remained some doubt as to what she really was. The dream that she would one day be able to go back to the way things had been had died hard, leaving a void unfilled by one that was a better fit for what she now was, a female, as whole and pure as any she had come across. Still, in her mind, Alfhildr continued to believe she was unlike them, someone who was very different and very much alone, adrift in a hostile world that had no place for someone like her.

"And what does Alfhildr intend to do with Bowdyn?" the Saxon huscarl muttered contemptuously.

With a shake of her head, Alfhildr set aside her wandering thoughts and turned once more to examining Bowdyn's wound.

"I shall draw this arrow, for I do need the arrowhead, tend your wound and, when you are fit, send you on your way as well."

"You do know that my honor demands that I will have to come back after you?" Bowdyn informed her.

"I expect that is how it will be," Alfhildr sighed betraying the sadness she felt over the ways of the world.

"It will be a pity too," she added. "I have grown weary of killing good men, such as you, simply because your people and mine cannot share this land in peace. Now," she announced as she took to examining Bowdyn's wound. "Tell me of this lord of yours. What is his name?"

"He is called Godric."

Æ

The huscarl known as Bowdyn stayed with Alfhildr for several days, during which time she nursed the wound she had given him. At first, he was reluctant to allow her to do anything to it other than draw out the arrow and cauterize it with the flat of a hot knife.

Knowing full well she had no hope of intimidating the tough warrior, Alfhildr took to treating him as if he were a child. Whenever Bowdyn tried to stop her from looking after his wound, she would make a face or roll her eyes.

"Are all Saxon men taught by their mothers to whine like a woman?" she would ask with mock severity.

And though he bristled whenever she did so, Bowdyn always grudgingly gave in, though, in time, he too was able to make something of a show of it, muttering as if to himself but loud enough for Alfhildr to hear that no man deserved to be treated in such a manner.

If the truth be known, the Saxon huscarl found he was both fascinated and captivated by the Dane girl. By the end of the first day, any thought of trying to overpower her, which he could have done with ease, was dismissed. Far from being the monster, or witch, the stories he had heard made her out to be, the fetching young girl with flowing red hair had a gentle innocence about her that complemented her beauty. That first night, after Alfhildr and Bowdyn had settled themselves before the fire, Skadi joined her, resting her head in Alfhildr's lap. Above them, just beyond the campfire's light, the crow flitted about from branch to branch until it found one that would allow it to remain aloof, yet near enough to watch Alfhildr as she stared into the fire, caressing Skadi as the Saxon huscarl answered her questions about his ealdorman and their kinsmen. When he was finished, there was an awkward silence, which Alfhildr quickly filled by humming softly to her wolf.

It was only when Bowdyn asked her how she had come to take up the life that she was leading that Alfhildr's expression darkened, bringing an end to her humming as a chill descended upon this most unusual gathering of humans and creatures. For the longest time, she said nothing as she stared into the fire. When Alfhildr finally did speak, she did so in a mournful tone, betraying a loneliness that drained away what little hatred he still held for the diminutive Dane girl.

"The people who were once my kinsmen could not find a place about their hearth or in their hearts for me," she whispered before looking up at the Saxon seated on the far side of the fire from her.

"I would be as welcomed in the place I once called home as I would be in your ealdorman's longhouse."

Bowdyn returned Alfhildr's gaze, wondering as he did so what terrible wrong she had committed against family and kinsman. The temptation to ask her was tempered by her expression, one that told him this wound, unseen, and unhealed, was far more painful than the one her arrow had caused. Instead, he simply sat there and listened as she took to humming one final lullaby to her she-wolf, a mournful tune to match her mood.

When she was finished, and without another word, Alfhildr turned to her bedroll as she began to settle in. Looking across the fire at her, Bowdyn could not help but ask what she intended to do about him.

"Are you not going to tie me up or bind me to a tree?" he asked, making no effort to hide the confusion her baffling behavior was causing him.

Glancing back over her shoulder to where Bowdyn was still seated, Alfhildr shrugged.

"You are free to go if you wish," she replied in a casual manner that further bewildered the Saxon.

"But I would not recommend it," she quickly added as she went back to arranging her blanket and ground cloth. "Not until your wound has been given at least a few days to mend and we are sure there will be no infection."

"And what's to keep me from attacking you while you sleep?" he asked doing his best to sound menacing as he watched her settle in.

"Your desire to see a new dawn," Alfhildr replied off-handedly without bothering to offer any further explanation as she lifted her blanket high in order to allow Skadi to cuddle up next to her.

Æ

When Bowdyn finally did take his leave, he warned Alfhildr that Godric would not be pleased when he returned without assuaging his desire for revenge.

"Have no doubt, he will send me after you again. Though they seldom agreed on anything, Hereric was Godric's only brother. My lord's honor demands Hereric's death be revenged. If I do manage to find your trail once more, I will not hesitate to fulfill my obligation to my lord."

Despite Bowdyn's effort to make his warning as ominous as he could, Alfhildr gave the Saxon huscarl a charming little smile, one that lit up her face.

"If he does, then I suggest, before you do so, you find yourself a longer coat of mail." With that, she gave the reins of her mount a tug to the right, turned her back on Bowdyn, and rode off.

Æ

Bowdyn and his weak-kneed companions were not the only Saxons who had been dispatched to hunt Alfhildr as summer faded from memory, replaced in its turn by a cold, wet fall. And while the reasons for hunting the Danish witch were as varied as their size, these parties were no less determined to put an end to Alfhildr's efforts. At first, she did her best to avoid them, leaving her pursuers a confusing trail that meandered haphazardly back and forth until, when both the timing and conditions were right, Alfhildr struck off, riding hard and fast over ground or under conditions that made tracking all but impossible. On occasion, when she had the opportunity to do so, she used some of the traps and snares Osgar had shown her how to lay in an effort to slow or discourage the men who sought her out at a time when honest men were laying in the last of their crops as they prepared for the long, hard winter ahead.

Only when neither flight nor the hazards she left in her wake were enough to demoralize and turn back her pursuers, or they managed to maneuver her into a tight corner, did Alfhildr risk battle. Even then, she was often able to do so on her own terms, striking from ambush or when her opponents were themselves vulnerable, such as was the case one day when a party of four Saxons who had been doggedly nipping at her heels for days were fording a small river swollen from a recent downpour. Soaked to the bone and exhausted from a hard night's ride through pouring rain, all of the riders were taking great care as they picked their way over the partially submerged, moss-covered rocks least their mounts slip and spill them into the fast-moving water.

Alfhildr waited until the last of Saxons was carefully guiding his mount down the steep embankment and into the river before she let her first arrow fly, taking down the lead rider whose horse had just managed to gain firm footing on the far bank. Hit in the side, he tumbled from the saddle. His two companions who were in midstream and had been looking down at where their horses were stepping had no idea where the attack had come from. Panicked, they struggled to maintain control of their own mounts while, at the same time, madly looking about in an effort to determine where their assailant was. The second to fall from his saddle, struck down by an arrow, never did find out where the Dane witch was hidden.

It was his companion, who had also been caught in the middle of crossing, who finally managed to spot Alfhildr standing where there was a small break in the trees on the side of the river they were leaving. Without hesitation, he drew his sword, turned to where she was, and charged toward her. Unfortunately for him, his mount was unable to find any firm footing once they left the narrow cluster of rocks that served as a ford. Pitching forward, the horse threw its rider over his head and into the river before Alfhildr had a chance to strike. Though she tracked the unhorsed Saxon with her bow drawn and ready to shoot as he was swept away in the river, Alfhildr did not loose her arrow, choosing instead to turn her attention to the last member of this little party, the one who had not yet entered the river.

To her surprise, she could see neither hide nor hair of the fourth man belonging to the Saxon hunting party. How he had managed to remain in the saddle and where he had gone off to troubled Alfhildr until she caught sight of Skadi leaping her way from rock to rock as she crossed the river to where the first Saxon Alfhildr had taken down was struggling to crawl away from the wolf. The temptation to dispatch him with another arrow before Skadi reached the far side and tore into him was checked by her need to conserve her dwindling supply of arrows. The opportunity to fashion replacements for those she had used, like when hunting for food, had been limited due to the tenacity of this latest band of pursuers.

Perhaps, with winter fast coming on, she would have an opportunity to do both, Alfhildr thought as she watched Skadi climb up the bank on the far side.

Just as cold, wet, hungry, and exhausted as her pursuers had been, Alfhildr turned away and retreated back into the forest, ignoring as best as she could the screams of a wounded man as he struggled in vain to fight off a ravenous wolf. At the moment, the only thing that really mattered to Alfhildr was making her way back to where she had left Dimma. Though there was no food waiting for her there, the cache of dry wood she had left behind would allow the dispirited girl to build a fire and dry out some before Skadi returned.

Perhaps tonight, she found herself hoping, *she would be free to enjoy a much needed and well-deserved sleep, undisturbed by men who sought to put an end to her, one way or the other.*

Æ

A shiver caused Alfhildr to tighten the grip with which she held her rain-soaked cloak about her as she stared into a fire that did little to banish the chill coursing through her careworn body. All thought of stumbling about in the dark forest in order to gather up the material needed to erect a shelter to protect her from the rain was dismissed as little more than a waste of time, just as her quest for sanctuary was proving to be. All hope of finding someplace where she could hole up for the winter, free to hunt by day and snuggle about a warm, friendly fire with Skadi by her side during the long, cold nights were fast fading, much like the flames of the fire before her. In its place, wild, impractical schemes began to worm their way into Alfhildr's conscious thoughts. Among them was the idea of making her way back to the Old Woman's hovel, one she always dismissed out of hand. Besides being visited by warriors, both Saxon and Dane, in need of the Old Woman's care, Alfhildr knew those seeking vengeance would not stop with simply killing her. The same thought kept her from seeking shelter with one of the many farmers who had befriended her.

Even less palatable was the thought of returning to her own village. In her wildest dreams, Alfhildr could not picture her kinsmen accepting her with open arms once they discovered she had once been Gunnvor, son of Gunnar. Even if they were able to find a way to forgive her for the manner in which she had dealt with the marauding Dane warbands she had come across during the course of the past summer, like the Saxons, her fellow Danes would see her as a *seiðr*, not a child who had been cursed by the gods.

Besides, Alfhildr doubted if she could ever face the woman who had turned her back on her without unleashing the anger and scorn that she still harbored for the person she had once called mother.

The sound of a branch snapping caused Alfhildr to whip her head about.

"Skadi?" she called out, barely able to control the quiver in her voice.

When the she-wolf failed to appear, Alfhildr turned her back on the cold, dark world that surrounded her as she once more took to staring into the dying fire.

"Well," she muttered to herself mirthlessly as she recalled the way Skadi had taken off after the Saxon she had wounded earlier in the day. "At least one of us will have a full belly tonight."

Æ

Though he was tempted to rush forward now and strike down the Dane witch, the lone Saxon, who had managed to make good his escape from the ambush at the ford, held back. The reward for bringing his lord a live witch would more than make up for the misery he would need to endure as he waited for the girl to fall asleep, hoping as he did so that her she-wolf did not suddenly appear. Of course, the Saxon reasoned, that would not necessarily be a bad thing. A nice grey pelt would be a wonderful trophy that he would be free to keep and cherish for years to come. So, he settled in to wait until the rain finished quenching the fire and sleep disarmed the witch.

Chapter Eleven
THE SAXON MAID

The Saga of the Saxon Maid

The name of Alfhildr men soon learnt to fear.
Saxon Lords offered bright gold,
For the shield maiden of the grey mist,
Who stopped their raids on soft Viking farms.

Wily Olwyn made bold at the promise of gold
Hid from Alfhildr and watched 'til she slept.
In cowardice, he lay the brave shield maiden low
And dragged her in triumph to Osmund's great hall.

Osmund, the Bloody, saw wealth in his captive.
Angry Lords sought revenge for the losses she'd wrought.
As men bargained her price, in her cage she was bound.
In sadness and loneliness, the shield maiden sang.

Fair Elvina, Osmund's daughter, the singing did hear.
She crept close and spied on Alfhildr, the Dire.
No monster she found, but a young girl like her.
Trapped in a cage and clothed in rags.

Alfhildr sang softly, the lullabies of babes,
Sweet music and sorrowful, Elvina's heart it did pierce.
Fresh garb and good meat, the fair Saxon brought,
Kind softness she offered the sorrowing girl.

Before bargain was struck for Alfhildr's head,
Elvina demanded from her father a gift.
"Shield maiden no more, my handmaiden, she
And for love of his daughter cruel Osmund agreed.

A child of the wild unschooled in the hall,
Alfhildr was fearful of stronghold and burgh.
Yet, Elvina taught her kindly, the ways of women,
The loom and the spindle, over sword and sharp spear.

*An unlikely ally Alfhildr found in soft Elvina
But the wise woman's runes showed it was true.
More sister than handmaiden Alfhildr became,
As the two shared their worlds and saw each their strength.*

*Fair Elvina was bride promised to Cerdic, the Unready.
All knew the loyal Cerdic to be beloved of the king
As handmaid, Alfhildr to the royal burgh was taken
Her lady to be Queen as the gods wove their fate.*

Æ

Alfhildr regained her wits slowly. Her mouth tasted of bile and her head felt as if an axe was lodged in her skull. Keeping her eyes tight shut, she tried to roll over to reach her water skin.

"Had a nice sleep, you Danish bitch?"

This ominous greeting caused Alfhildr's eyes to snap open in shock to see a smirking Saxon huntsman squatting a few feet away, a spear held ready in his hands. Desperately, she threw herself forward, her fingers scrabbling for Durthfang. As she did, fire erupted around her throat as a noose choked tight, viciously checking her lunge at the grinning Saxon. In shock, she fell back, smacking her head hard against the tree. A blaze of azure pain speared through her skull before the blackness took her once more.

Æ

The next time she woke, Alfhildr found herself draped face first across a saddle. Inches from her nose, she could make out the scurf marked belly of a small bay pony as it ambled along. She watched blankly as flies buzzed around the girth before landing on her face and in her hair until an explosive sneeze sent a fresh wave of pain coursing through her skull, sending the flies flittering off.

Out of sight, she heard a snicker.

"Woken up, bitch?"

A rough hand loosened the rope tying the bonds around her hands and ankles under the pony, causing her to fall back in an ungainly heap on the ground. As she lay there, stunned, Alfhildr felt a blade hacking at the cord at her ankles. "Danish shit like you don't deserve to ride. Get up and walk."

Rolling onto her side, Alfhildr attempted to stagger to her feet. She got as far as her knees before the dizziness hit. She tried to take a deep breath, but the noose and her dry throat made it a hoarse rasp. The weasel-faced huntsman clutched her sword unsurely as he watched her carefully from a few yards away.

"Water…please." Even as the words passed her dried lips, anguish and despair engulfed Alfhildr, causing her to slump forward despondently.

The witch looked in a bad way, causing Olwyn to frown. Lord Osmund's orders had been clear. She had to be alive when she was brought to him. Knowing just how vicious his lord could be to those who failed him, the huntsman backed cautiously toward Dimma and hastily snatched up the water skin before throwing it at the girl. He watched from afar as she grabbed at the skin and with pathetic gratitude began to suck down the rancid water, blind to the tears of shame streaming down her cheeks.

A harsh jerk on the noose around her neck caused her to cough and splutter, sending water spraying from her nose.

"On your feet, bitch! Start walking." With that, Olwyn swung up into Dimma's saddle and circled behind Alfhildr. He reached out with Alfhildr's own sword and prodded her hard in the back before wrapping the loose end of the noose around the saddle pommel. Alfhildr stumbled forward while, behind her, Olwyn wore a self-satisfied grin as he dreamed of the rewards Lord Osmund would heap upon him. Perhaps, he would even be allowed to keep the sword.

Æ

It was full dark when Alfhildr was jerked once more to a stop before a tall, wooden wall. She had stumbled blindly through the day, scarcely seeing where she shuffled her feet. At the brief stops Olwyn had taken to rest the horses, Alfhildr had collapsed to the ground where she remained broken and motionless until the bite of the rope and the tip of her own sword forced her back up onto her feet. She had not even stirred when her bladder had loosed, releasing a stream of warm pee down her legs and into the grass.

There, standing before the gate, Alfhildr swayed on her feet while a chorus of voices called back and forth from within the earth and timber stockade.

"The witch…" someone shouted out.

"Olwyn caught the witch," another uttered in amazement.

"She doesn't look much," a woman muttered dismissively.

"Lord Osmund will shower him with gold, lucky devil," a jealous spearman opined.

At last, torches were brought, and the gate was pulled wide to allow a grinning Olwyn to drag his captive into a circle composed of the envious and curious. In their midst, Alfhildr stood alone, forlorn, and helpless, drained of all emotion and feeling, within the light of the guttering torches. A few men laughed when they saw the small-framed girl, her hair matted with filth and her breeches stained where she had wet herself. Others looked askance as if unsure, wondering if this could indeed be the Danish witch who had killed so many of their fellow Saxons. It was only when they saw the grey mare and the sword Olwyn proudly bore that they, at last, believed, causing many to cross themselves in an effort to avert her witchcraft.

At last, a loud bellow rang out.

"Bring the Danish witch here!"

Once more, Alfhildr was dragged and prodded, this time toward the great hall. Inside, her eyes began to sting from the acrid smoke that eddied and billowed from the large fire in the hall's center where a pair of servants were turning a deer carcass on a spit above it. The alluring smell of roasted meat caused the forlorn girl's stomach to knot in hunger.

With everyone's attention on him, Olwyn savored the moment as he pushed the Dane girl on, until, with one final shove, he sent her sprawling onto the rotting rushes at the feet of his lord, a man known to all as Osmund, the Bloody.

Without waiting, Olwyn pitched into the speech he had been crafting all day as he rode, reveling in the envious looks of the other warriors and the furtive glances of the servant girls.

"My Lord, as you demanded, I have fought the witch and triumphed. Before you is the red-haired murderess. By my own hand, I threw her down despite the evil she called on to slay my comrades. It was with God's grace and my skill that I was able to turn aside her witchcraft, prevailing over her after a long and vicious fight. I…"

A fist the size of a quart pot slammed down, shocking the huntsman into silence.

"Enough babbling. Are you sure this is her?"

Olwyn reluctantly drew forth Durthfang and presented it to his lord. A few moments later a strong hand grabbed Alfhildr's hair and jerked her head back. Wincing, she found herself looking into the hard-bitten face of a Saxon lord. From his perch upon a rough-hewn dais, a pair of hooded, grey eyes stared down at her. A white stripe, like a badger's, showed starkly across the cheek of his greying beard. Even through tears brought on by the way the Saxon was tugging at her hair, Alfhildr could see where the same sword blow had cut deep into his ear.

"So, how did he really defeat you, bitch?"

Surprised at the question, Alfhildr frowned and closed her eyes to think. A sharp slap snapped her eyes open.

"Answer me!"

"I…I don't know," Alfhildr stammered through her exhaustion and shock. "I was asleep. The next thing I knew, I…"

"So, Olwyn, by your own hand you threw her down, eh?" Osmund sneered though his eyes never left Alfhildr's face as he spoke.

The luckless huntsman started to stammer his denial before being cut short again.

"Enough, you little weasel!" Osmund grinned mirthlessly as he gazed into the dazed eyes of his prize. "But, for all your lies, you did bring me the witch. So, take your reward," he growled, tossing a small pouch of silver pennies in the dirt before Olwyn. "I claim her as well as all her gear and horse as wergild for the men she has slain," Osmund proclaimed loudly.

His lord's declaration caused Olwyn to release the grip he had on the Dane witch's hair as he let her fall to the floor as if she were nothing more than a rag doll.

"My Lord! But I thought…" Olwyn's voice faded as he wilted under the scornful gaze his lord and master turned upon him. "Umm, nothing my lord. They are yours, of course."

With that, the deflated warrior scrambled for the purse and quickly scurried away as he sought to escape Osmund's baleful stare.

"Confine the witch close with guards. In the morning, prepare riders to seek out Lords Godric, Oswin, and Ordgar. I shall have word for them."

Having disposed of the matter of the Dane witch for the moment, Osmund sprawled back in his chair, cradling Durthfang in one meaty fist while guards yanked Alfhildr to her feet and pushed her from the hall.

Æ

A heavy door slammed behind Alfhildr, shutting out what little light there had been from the guard's feeble torch. For a moment, she stood stock still, listening as a heavy bar was dropped across the door and the guards settled themselves outside. Only then did the young girl slowly collapse to the ground, curling into a ball among the straw and manure. Tightly hugging her knees, she began to slowly rock back and forth among the filth. At last, the thundering waves of the despair she had struggled so hard to hold back crashed down upon her bruised and battered body.

Alone and in the dark, Alfhildr sobbed, deep, racking sobs of pain. All for whom she had cared had deserted her. Her mother had spurned her like a piece of rotten offal, leaving her hovering near death in the care of a stranger, who had all but cast her out.

Even those she had saved and cared for had turned away from her. First, Osgar left for a grubby farm. Then, Plegmund, a gentle soul, but a weak man, had allowed himself to be seduced and lured away by the poison whispered in his ear by a Saxon farmer. Most damning of all, however, had been Skadi, a creature she loved and cherished above all others. At the thought of her beloved she-wolf, Alfhildr could contain herself no longer. A keening wail rose from her cracked lips as she rocked and sobbed, knowing that even her gods had deserted her.

At length, a spear butt hammered against the door.

"Shut it, bitch, or I'll come in there and give you something real to squeal about!"

Alfhildr choked and shivered at the harsh menace in the guard's voice. She reached up to rub the raw welts around her neck that Olwyn's noose had raised. As she did her fingers touched a thin chain. In the dark, her hand slowly quested down the delicate links to touch the simple gift of the monk.

"It's to protect you," he had told her. "Not from the gods you refuse to abandon, but from good, God-fearing men who do not understand what you are trying to do. They are not bad men. I expect they are no different than the Roman soldiers who crucified Jesus."

Upon recalling those words, a spark of anger rekindled, tempting Alfhildr to tear the heathen symbol from her neck. But even as she grasped the Christian relic, she found she could not. It was all she had left of her life. In time, Alfhildr retreated to a corner of her foul prison where she curled up into a ball and lay silent in the darkness until, at last, she fell asleep in the straw, her fingers still clutching the little talisman close to her chest.

Æ

The next morning, Alfhildr woke to the sound of the heavy bar on the door being withdrawn. For an instant, she struggled to remember where she was. When she did, in panic, Alfhildr shoved the little crucifix out of sight just as the door swung wide. The harsh morning light hurt her eyes until a bulky figure blocked out the sun.

"Food and water," the first man through the door barked. "Although why our lord bothers with such for a witch when you're going to be carrion fodder yourself soon enough, I've no idea," he grunted as he dumped two foul smelling buckets on the floor beside her before leaning forward and gobbing in each. Behind him, Alfhildr could see two more guards standing poised and alert with spears pointing toward her. A tiny spark of satisfaction flared within her.

They still fear me.

Then, the man was gone, and the door slammed shut once more, plunging her back into darkness.

Æ

The young girl held her richly embroidered skirts off the ground as she delicately picked her way among the discarded bones and pools of vomit littering the floor of the great hall. She wrinkled her nose at the aftermath of the previous night's feasting.

"I really must get the servants to replace the rushes today," the girl muttered to herself.

In the center of the hall, she caught sight of her father, sprawled as always on his favorite carved chair as he talked quietly to his steward. Elvina, Osmund's daughter and only child, smiled secretly to herself as she took to creeping closer in order to listen to Papa.

"They've all lost men, so they'll all want a piece of the witch, but my bet is on Godric. Word is his brother was killed by the little bitch, so I expect he will be the most eager to have her."

Osmund scratched along the snowy line in his beard as he thought for a moment.

"Make sure he is told that the other two have made offers, say four hundred shillings. Let's see what he comes up with."

Bending over, the steward whispered something in his lord's ear that Elvina wasn't able to catch.

"No, leave her be. I don't sell spoiled goods. Although scrubbed up, I imagine she could be a tasty morsel for the right man."

Osmund guffawed at his own joke, in which the steward politely joined before bowing and swiftly heading out to the waiting messengers.

Elvina quietly stepped back, but her father heard the rustle of the rushes and swung round suspiciously. When he caught the glimmer of her golden hair, his frown turned to a broad smile.

"Elvina, my little sunbeam, why are you hiding in the shadows?"

For a moment, the pretty young girl looked flustered before she managed to set her face in a frown.

"Really, Papa, you ought to have the servants beaten. Just look at the floor in here. I don't know when they last changed the rushes."

"So, you weren't sneaking close to listen to men's business, young lady?" His gentle smile belied the gruffness of his voice.

"Papa! How could you think such a thing?" Elvina chided as she approached and kissed her father on the cheek before gracing him with a sly little grin. "Well, maybe a little, but the rushes really do need changing. I don't know what the servants are thinking."

Osmund watched his daughter as she pretended to be upset about the floor. She looked so much like her mother that, all too often, the hardened old warrior's heart lurched when she unconsciously adopted a pose or a tone that reminded him of his beloved Æffe. He tried to be angry that she had eavesdropped on his orders but couldn't bring himself to tell her off.

Perhaps it's no bad thing, he thought. *If she is to be Queen, then she will need her wits and spies about her to protect her and the fool the King claims as his son.*

"So, Papa, what have you done with the little Danish witch? Do you really think she is pretty?" Elvina grinned mischievously at her father.

"She's safe under guard in the old byre where she will stay until I decide what to do with her."

Osmund looked suspiciously at his darling daughter for a moment. He knew too well her flights of fancy.

"And you're not to go poking and prying, you understand? She's as dangerous as she is evil. So, stay well clear."

Elvina lowered her head and looked demurely at her father from under her lashes.

"Yes Papa. I understand."

Osmund grunted and turned back to examining the witch's sword as his daughter carefully made her way back to the women's hall, furiously considering how she was going to get a look at the Danish witch.

Æ

Elvina waited until her father and his close retainers rode out to hunt later that morning. Once she was sure they were gone, the fair-haired Saxon girl escaped from the cloying confines of the women's hall and ambled innocently around her father's keep. By chance, her aimless wanderings took her out of sight behind the smithy. Grinning to herself, she squeezed between the back of the smithy and the stockade. It was a narrow passage, one that allowed her to sneak up on the back wall of the old cow byre unseen.

Once there, she paused to rest against the wall. Doing her best to control her fears, by closing her eyes and taking long, deep breaths, Elvina listened to the grumbling and laughter of the guards on the far side as they squatted and threw dice before turning her attention to deciding how best to get a peek inside without being caught.

At first, it was almost too soft to hear. Elvina frowned and placed her ear next to the wattle and daub wall. She heard it again, louder now but still soft. A girl's sweet voice was quietly singing. As she strained, Elvina could just make out the words of a lullaby.

"By the fire in my arms, you are wrapped safe and sound."

The words and the tone reached out to Elvina. Entranced, the young girl found herself trying to remember what it had been like to be held tight and cuddled by her own mother. As the last notes died away, Elvina shook herself and shivered as a fearful thought occurred.

Is she casting a spell on me? How did she know I was here?

The young girl gathered her skirts and was about to flee, back the way she had come when a new song began. At the first words, Elvina froze in shock.

"Regina caeli laetare, Alleluia,"

In her mind, the image of a line of cowled monks sprang forth. She had been seven summers old at the time of the king's last marriage, held tight to her nurse's hand as the solemn procession had passed, singing quietly as it went. Elvina stuffed her hand in her mouth as she listened to the wall once more.

"Quia quem meruisti portare, Alleluia."

The voice reminded her of the young boys at the back of the royal procession, their sweet, high-pitched voices singing counterpoint to the heavy chant of the older monks in their magical language. Elvina shook her head in confusion.

No witch would sing to the glory of God. No witch could learn the magical Latin. God wouldn't allow it, would he?

As she struggled with her thoughts, a boot kicked against the byre door. "Shut up bitch!"

The singing cut off abruptly with a little choke, causing Elvina's heart to go out to the imprisoned girl before she quietly headed back toward the smithy the way she had come.

Æ

It was late afternoon when Elvina spotted one of the guards heading for the kitchen. She quickly followed to see if there might be a chance for her to peek at the strange Danish girl while he was gone. She almost bumped into him as he strode jauntily back out into the yard.

"Oh, sorry, Milady. Didn't see you there."

He stepped back politely to let his lord's daughter pass as Elvina looked down into one of the buckets. On top of the congealed kitchen slops, she caught sight of a fresh dog turd. In an impetuous instant, Elvina's anger flared bright.

"How dare you! My father's orders were to feed her, not torment her."

As the young girl's fury hit him, the guard shifted uncomfortably under the lash of her tongue.

"She's a witch, Milady."

"And you know that, do you? Wait here!"

Before he could reply Elvina knocked both buckets from his hand and stormed into the kitchen. A few moments later, she returned clutching a fresh loaf and a horn beaker of water. Elvina strode swiftly across the yard as the guard struggled to keep up.

"Open the door!"

"But, Milady…"

Elvina drew herself up regally and turned on the two guards.

"Would you rather face me, or my father?"

Elvina knew she would end up in trouble with Papa over this, but right now her blood was boiling. The two guards looked at each other, wondering which of them had the grit to deny the girl passage. When it became clear neither wanted to challenge the young girl or face Lord Osmund, both shrugged before one picked up his spear as the other reached for the heavy bar.

The door swung wide, giving Elvina her first sight of the Dane so many of her father's people had come to fear. Far from being a vicious monster, a grubby young waif of a girl, blinking owlishly looked back at her. Big green eyes peered out from behind the matted filth, causing Elvina to feel ashamed of what had been done. As the two young women regarded each other, a certainty grew in Elvina's heart, one that told her this was no witch. Drawing herself up, she took a tentative step across the threshold, ignoring the guard's hissed warning as she did so. Inside the wretched, foul-smelling stall, she crouched down beside the girl, placing the bread and water before her.

"Please, you need to eat and drink."

The emerald eyes gazed up in surprise at the fair-haired young noblewoman for a long moment. Then, Elvina saw them fill with tears.

The girl's first words were little more than a whisper.

"Thank you, my lady."

Elvina smiled weakly at the forlorn creature.

"Where did you learn to sing like that?"

"Like what?"

"Like the monks."

Alfhildr sighed as she recalled sitting by the campfire with Plegmund.

"A monk taught me," she admitted as she bowed her head dejectedly.

"For a time, we traveled from farmstead to farmstead. He taught the people of his god's mercy while I…well…"

For a moment, Alfhildr looked away, almost as if she found herself unable to recount what she had done. After casting aside that awful image, she looked back at the Saxon noble woman.

"At night, when we had finished the day's work, we would sing together in the forest."

Behind her, Elvina could hear the guards stirring restlessly.

"I better go."

Coming to her feet, she once more drew herself up as her nursemaid had taught her to do when addressing those below her station.

"I shall make sure you are properly fed from now on."

Then, after once more allowing herself to set aside her role as a nobleman's daughter, she dropped her chin and smiled.

"I liked your singing. It was very nice."

With that she turned quickly and marched from the byre, her head held high to avoid the questions of the guards. Inside her thoughts were in turmoil.

Æ

The next day, Lord Osmund was in a foul temper, trying hard not to show it but failing miserably. The reply he had received from Godric was not at all what he had been expecting. Rather than offer to take the Dane witch, the man sent by his friend and fellow Eorl informed him that Godric had no desire to pursue the vengeance he had once been so keen to extract for the death of his brother. The huscarl who had personally delivered the message offered neither explanation nor apology. Though he was disappointed, almost to the point of anger, Osmund had granted Godric's man his request to see the Dane witch. To have done otherwise would have violated his obligations as a host. Besides, with his plans of ransoming his prisoner off to Godric for a small fortune now in tatters, Osmund needed to decide what to do with the little bitch.

Æ

The rumpled pile of rags huddled in the corner of the byre that Bowdyn was shown bore no resemblance to the proud young girl who had humbled, then befriended, him. Whether the Dane girl, who called herself Alfhildr, was awake or asleep didn't matter. Either way, the sight of such a magnificent warrior reduced to such a sorry state caused Bowdyn to sigh. As much as he had once wished to see his lord's nemesis laid low: now that she had been, he felt sickened. Unable to bring himself to further humiliate the Dane girl by announcing his presence, he turned and walked away. Godric would not be pleased when he heard of this.

Unfortunately, there was nothing either could do. While Godric had found it within himself to set aside the blood debt, he doubted if the other Saxon lords who were seeking vengeance would be as merciful.

Æ

As soon as Elvina heard of Godric's reply, her hopes leapt for the imprisoned girl and a plan to save her began to form. Each day, while her father was out hunting or visiting his villages, she would march to where the Dane girl was kept, demanding access to the prisoner with such arrogance that the guards assumed these visits by the strong-willed, young girl were sanctioned by their lord.

Three days after Godric's man had left, and when she had ensured her father had taken drink and was mellow, Elvina launched her stealthy attack.

"Papa?"

"Mmm, yes sunbeam?"

"She's not a witch, you know."

Osmund frowned at his daughter as she filled his beaker with ale.

"How would you know?"

"I heard the maids talking. She sings hymns and used to travel with a monk."

Osmund roused himself and looked suspiciously at his little girl. He watched as she tucked a loose tendril of hair behind her ear, knowing full well it reminded her father of her mother.

"Godric didn't want her, did he, Papa?"

"There's more who do. What are you playing at, young lady?"

"She is a girl, Papa, no different than I. Would you stand by and allow another to treat me like that?"

"If you consorted with pagan gods and the creatures of the forest, yes."

"Yes, I expect that would be the right thing to do," she murmured sweetly before once more pressing home her attack in a manner no man, no matter how valiant, could resist.

"But, Papa, is it not also right to do what Father Alwine preaches; that it is our duty as Christians to try to save the souls of pagans?"

Osmund grunted as his daughter delicately refilled his beaker.

"Have I not always been good and done what you asked of me? Did I not obey when you said I had to be nice to Cerdic?"

Even in his cups Osmund was beginning to see where the conversation was going. His voice turned hard as he spoke.

"I've worked damned hard to arrange your marriage, girl. You will go to his bed when the time is right without argument."

Elvina laid a soothing hand on her father's arm.

"I know, Papa, and I am truly grateful. No girl could have a more wonderful father," she cooed as Osmund's temper slowly settled, and he took a large gulp of ale. "But wouldn't you be happier if I went with a joyous smile on my face, knowing I was truly happy?"

Once he had settled to her satisfaction, Elvina decided to play to his pride.

"I can almost imagine what your peers will say once I train the Dane girl as my maid. Men will gaze upon her in awe, whispering among themselves that only Osmund, the Bloody, could have tamed the red-headed warrior who slew so many."

When Osmund didn't explode, Elvina smiled quietly to herself as she let the thought settle. Then, with a kiss to his cheek, she demurely withdrew to the women's hall.

Æ

It took three more days of gentle wheedling and persuasion from Elvina, and three more days before all his messengers had returned with paltry offers for the girl, before Osmund, at last, gave in to his beloved daughter. He too had heard the reports of the strange Danish girl's singing. Finally, he came to the conclusion that if he was to have any peace in his hall, his daughter would have to be given her way.

"Enough child!" he grumbled. "If you pour more honey in my ears, they will bleed. Take the little pagan and make of her what you will."

Setting aside his feigned anger, Osmund grinned self-consciously as his warriors heard Elvina's squeal of delight and watched as she threw her arms around his neck.

"Be warned though, I will be watching close," he cautioned. "If I think she is a threat to you, or to my honor, then, before that day is out, she will be swinging from a tree. You understand, girl?"

Elvina again hugged her father as she promised faithfully that the girl would learn, and he would be proud before she rushed from the great hall.

Æ

Elvina paused to catch her breath and settle herself before setting off toward the locked byre, her head high and her cheeks glowing with pleasure.

"I've come for the girl. Open the door," she commanded imperiously. "Hurry up! Do you wish to keep my father waiting?"

At that, the men turned hurriedly and dragged the bar from its socket before pulling the door wide.

"Bring her into the light."

A guard ducked into the noisome darkness before returning, dragging the filthy, huddled girl behind. As he crossed the threshold, he pushed her forward making her stumble and sprawl headlong in the mud.

Elvina frowned as she glared at the guard. On the ground, the Dane girl fought back the urge to whimper. Thinking they had come for her execution, Alfhildr drew upon the last of her strength as she prepared to meet her end the way she had lived her life these past few months, with courage and pride.

But, rather than an executioner, it was the Saxon noblewoman who knelt before her.

Ignoring the vile stench, the fair-haired Elvina placed a gentle hand upon Alfhildr's shoulder.

"Hush. It's all right. I'm not going to let anyone hurt you."

Only then did Alfhildr realize the gods had once more reached out and taken her fate in hand. And, while their chosen messenger this time was by far the most curious of all, the red-haired Dane had long ago accepted that they, like her, were following a most curious and unpredictable path.

Chapter Twelve
A PROPHESY REVISTED

Present Day England
"The Dig"

Stepping into the narrow hall of the small bed and breakfast where Professor Bannon's students were staying, Elva hesitated when she saw Sarah standing against the wall, waiting her turn to shower using the only bathroom on their floor. Knowing how painfully shy Elva was, Sarah hastened to keep her from ducking back into her room.

"Oh, please, don't go," she called out. "Simon's in there. He never takes more than a few minutes. Besides, I really need to talk to you," Sarah quickly added.

Though tempted to put one of the only other girls on the team off by telling her she'd catch up with her later at the pub, Elva could not find it in herself to say no. Reluctantly, she closed the door to her room behind her and joined Sarah in the hall.

Dropping her chin a smidge, Sarah studied the winsome redhead a moment before speaking.

"I know I shouldn't be telling you this, but Peter, well, he rather fancies you."

Unable to hide the blush rising in her cheeks, Elva subconsciously brought her hand up to sweep her long, flowing, red hair back behind an ear while dropping her chin.

"Pish posh. Peter is probably just pulling your chain."

"Oh please," Sarah replied dismissively. "Save that rubbish for the professor. Besides being intelligent and drop-dead gorgeous, you exude oodles of confidence. I mean, a boy would have to be a total cretin not to be smitten by you."

Elva was having none of this.

"If he's so infatuated, why hasn't he said anything to me?"

"Because he's intimidated by you."

"Me?"

Sarah snickered, "Yes, you, little miss perfect."

"Oh, rest assured. I'm far from perfect," Elva snorted.

"That's not what Peter thinks," Sarah continued. "You should talk to him. He's a nice boy, nicer than most of the sorry sods I seem to attract."

Embarrassed by what she was hearing, Elva averted her eyes as the color rising in her cheeks threatened to match that of her hair.

"You know this is neither the time nor the place for that sort of thing," Elva muttered without looking over at Sarah. "The last thing any of us need to do is to lose our focus, not now, not when we're so close."

Having come to suspect there was something Elva had been keeping to herself, a sixth sense that allowed her to all but anticipate what they would unearth at the dig, Sarah tilted her head as she looked over at her friend.

"Close? Close to what?"

Peeking up at Sarah through her lashes, Elva was on the verge of telling her but was stopped when the door to the bathroom swung open, revealing a still dripping, wet Simon with nothing but a towel loosely wrapped about his waist. Upon seeing the two girls, a lascivious grin lit up his face.

"Well, well, well! What have we here?"

While Elva snapped her head about in order to avoid looking at the near naked rugger who was behaving like a drunken sailor, Sarah snorted.

"Nothing you're ever going to have the privilege of pawing."

Turning to Elva, Simon sighed in a most exaggerated manner.

"'Tis such a pity, you know," he replied to Sarah while staring at Elva. "If Ginger, here, would only put half the effort into looking more like a female than you do, she'd be quite the looker."

Glancing up into Simon's eyes, Elva met his smug expression with one that told him he had just vaulted way over the safe line, wiping away his smug expression and causing him to beat a hasty retreat without another word. When he was gone, Sarah looked over at Elva.

"How do you do that?" she asked in awe.

While still looking down the hall to where Simon had disappeared, Elva whispered, "It's a gift."

Æ

**England
1012 AD**

"But why would Alfhildr allow herself to be humiliated like that?" the boy asked his grandmother.

"Humiliated? How was she humiliated?" the old woman asked.

"Alfhildr became a slave, a mere serving girl. No warrior could ever allow that to happen to him, not while he still drew breath."

The old woman thought for a minute before answering.

"What do warriors do?" she finally asked.

"They fight."

"For whom do they fight?"

"They fight for their lord," the boy replied warily as he looked out of the corner of his eye at his grandmother, wondering as he did so if she was trying to trick him again.

"Is that all they do?"

Convinced she was leading him into another trap, the boy hesitated.

"What else do they do?"

When he failed to answer her, the grandmother didn't bother looking down at the frail boy next to her as they continued down a path all but hidden beneath dried leaves and fallen branches.

"They serve. They serve both the earth-bound master to whom they owe fealty and the Lord, our Savior," she muttered. "A great warrior, one who cherishes his honor and his duty above all else, never forgets that, even when it demands more of them than they, themselves, think they can bear."

Æ

Alfhildr could not help but recall the way she had felt when the Old Woman who had cared for her first took her in hand when the time had come for her to learn how to tend to the needs unique to women. In a way, the sullen Dane girl longed for the firm, yet gentle, manner with which the Old Woman had dealt with her, for the heavy-set Saxon wench, who served as both cook and maid to Elvina, had a coarse manner that reminded Alfhildr of the way the boys in her village handled cattle.

It was no wonder Elvina was anxious to find a new maid, she thought to herself as the woman who went by the name of Blythe scrubbed her until her skin was raw.

Were it not for the crucifix she refused to set aside least someone steal it as they had everything else, Alfhildr imagined the old maid would have shown her no mercy whatsoever as she cleaned away weeks of filth. When she was done, the frumpy cook stepped away from the tub and pointed to a stool where clothing was stacked.

"I cleaned you only because no one thought you could manage to do so properly on your own," she snapped. "But I see no reason why I should dress you. I'm sure even a creature like you can manage that."

Without another word the woman turned away and left the room, smirking as she passed the two guards who had been watching her bathe Alfhildr. With swords drawn, both stood ready to strike if the Dane witch did anything untoward.

Any thought of trying to stare down the pair of warriors who were watching her every move was quickly forgotten. It wasn't that Alfhildr was intimidated. Rather, she was embarrassed, embarrassed and ashamed of being reduced to such a pitiful state. Alone, naked, and defenseless, she felt a vulnerability unlike anything she had ever experienced before. With her back to the men guarding her, and her arms held tightly across her chest in an effort to cover her small, but very feminine, bosom, Alfhildr slowly rose up from the wooden tub, stepped out of it onto the cold stone floor and eased her way over to where the clothing she was to wear sat. As she took up each item, she paused, holding it out to examine it as if debating what to do next.

The idea of refusing to don the rough-spun gown did cross her mind but only until a cold draft swept across the floor, causing her to shiver. There was no honor to be had in freezing to death, she sadly concluded. With great reluctance, she slowly began to slip the clothing left for her over her head, piece by piece. As she did so, her humiliation continued to mount until, by the time she was finished, it took all her strength to keep from weeping. Only when she was done did she turn to where the armed soldiers stood, guarding the only door to the room. Unable to meet their stares, Alfhildr simply stood there until one of them came over, took her by the arm, and led her away.

Æ

The greeting with which Elvina met Alfhildr was poles apart from the way the cook had dealt with her. The Saxon girl came to her feet as soon as the guards led Alfhildr into the room. With light, springy steps, Elvina rushed toward Alfhildr, grasping her hands when she reached her.

"You are even more beautiful than I had imagined," Elvina murmured delightedly as she inspected a very dispirited Dane girl, who seemed to be unable to pry her eyes off the floor at her feet. Turning to the guards, Elvina dismissed them with a wave of her hand.

"Leave us now," she said in a soft, yet commanding, manner.

"We cannot do that, my lady," the older of the pair replied firmly.

Upon hearing this, Elvina's demeanor darkened.

"You will leave us, and you will do so now! Do I make myself clear?"

The two guards glanced nervously at each other as if wondering what to do. Their lord would surely give them both a vicious tongue-lashing for failing to obey the orders he had personally given them. Of course, if they ignored the winsome young girl who was glaring at them from across the room and did comply with their instructions to keep an eye on the witch, both men suspected they would receive more than a mere rebuke, for no one said "no" to the only person Osmund cherished more than his honor. After a quick peek back at Elvina, the guards sheepishly slunk out of her sight.

When they were gone, Elvina reached up with one hand and lightly touched Alfhildr's chin. Slowly and gently, she tilted the Dane girl's head back until she could look up and into her eyes.

"There's no need to feel ashamed or sad," Elvina whispered softly. "There is no dishonor in serving a noblewoman. Among my people it is considered a privilege."

For the first time that day, the shame Alfhildr had been harboring was replaced by another emotion, one that caused Elvina to blink and draw back slightly as she found herself wondering if her father had been right. Perhaps it was dangerous to allow the Dane girl to roam free.

No, she told herself as she once more pushed that thought aside. *I am right about this girl. She has a gentle soul, one that simply needs to be tamed. But first...* she concluded as she looked up at Alfhildr's wild mane.

"Come," Elvina commanded in the same firm, yet gentle voice she had used when dismissing the guards. "We need to do something with your hair."

Upon hearing this, Alfhildr forgot about the seething rage that had been bubbling up within her as she pulled one of her hands free and brought it up to touch the ends of her long tresses.

"What is wrong with my hair?" she asked in all sincerity.

Unable to help herself, Elvina laughed.

"Everything. I mean, it is lovely and long and very red, but we cannot have you going about looking like the witch everyone seems to think you are," she explained as she set Alfhildr down on a cushioned stool before a large, polished metal plate that reflected all set before it.

Alfhildr had seen such a plate. Her grandmother had a small one, a present given to her by a then young Folkmar when he had roamed the whale road with his father, trading when they could find someone willing to, raiding when the needs of their people demanded it. And while Alfhildr had caught glimpses of herself in the calm surfaces of ponds that she had stopped to drink from during her wanderings, she had never seen herself like this. Mesmerized, Alfhildr stared at her own reflection as Elvina took up a comb and began to run it through her hair.

"I expect my father would be angry if he saw me doing this," the Saxon girl murmured as she gently worked out the tangle of knots from Alfhildr's hair.

"But I don't care. It's his fault really for not letting me play with the girls in the village," she explained while Alfhildr continued to stare at her own reflection as a thousand and one random thoughts tumbled through her mind.

"I love braiding hair," Elvina continued as if talking to herself.

"Unfortunately, there was no one around me with any hair to speak of who was willing to let me play with it, which is why I was reduced to sneaking down to the stables where I braided the tail of my father's horse."

Upon hearing this, Alfhildr blinked, looking up at the Saxon girl's reflection for the first time.

"You did what?"

Stopping, Elvina looked at Alfhildr's eyes in the polished plate that served as a mirror.

"I used to braid the tail of my father's horse," she repeated defensively.

Unable to help herself, Alfhildr sniggered.

"I expect the horse was even less pleased than your father."

"Actually, I think the horse rather liked it, once it was used to me," Elvina replied proudly. "I hope you like having your hair braided as well."

As quickly as it had come, the smile disappeared from Alfhildr's lips. In its place, a sadness darkened her expression as she once more dropped her gaze.

"I wouldn't know," she murmured softly. "I have never had my hair in a braid."

"Well then," Elvina chirped. "Shall we try it and find out?"

After drawing in a deep breath, Alfhildr looked back at her reflection.

My life's journey has taken many strange twists and turns, she thought to herself as she stared at the reflection of her own eyes in the mirror before her. *Perhaps, this is simply another trial, a challenge the gods have set out before me that must be met and overcome. If that is true, then, I must not waver. I must meet it as I have met all of their trials, with the courage my father would have expected me to show.*

With that in mind, Alfhildr drew herself up as she looked at the reflection of the Saxon girl standing behind her, anxiously awaiting an answer.

"Well," Alfhildr announced making a valiant effort to smile, "I expect I will not know if I like braids until I try them, will I?"

Elvina's smile returned, lighting up her expression as she took up her combing where she had left off.

"Oh, you will like them, hopefully better than father's horse."

Æ

Having been raised as the grandson of an aging chieftain with the specter of one day taking his place, provided he managed to survive the challenges his mother had always feared but never spoke of, Alfhildr was familiar with the underlying intrigue that surrounded Elvina and her father. Nothing the young fair-haired girl with eyes the color of bluebells said or did went unnoticed by those around her. Just as it had been true when Alfhildr had been a child, so it was doubly true for Elvina, as Alfhildr quickly learned from the Saxon noblewoman herself. Her father was aggressively pursuing a union between her and Cerdic, the son of the king, to whom Osmund owed fealty.

The subject of her union with a king's son came up rather quickly and for reasons with which Alfhildr was not at all able to cope. Upon learning the Dane girl had no idea how to braid hair, Elvina hit upon the idea of teaching her by using the old tried and true method she had first used when learning herself, her father's horse.

"I thought about having Blythe instruct you, but I do not think she likes you," the Saxon girl explained as she was combing out the tail of her father's favorite mount before starting.

Upon hearing that, Alfhildr could not help but guffaw in a most unladylike manner, causing Elvina to wince.

"I suppose this would be as good a time as any to mention something my father made me promise when he agreed to give you to me as a servant."

Suddenly on guard, Alfhildr held her breath, wondering what new horror she would have to endure.

Sensing the Dane girl's unease, Elvina hastily explained.

"I know you are different and that you have been leading a life that did not prepare you for this."

Though tempted to reaffirm this supposition with another outburst, Alfhildr managed to check herself this time as she paid close attention to what the Saxon girl was saying.

"You need to learn how to behave in a manner expected of a maid in the service of a nobleman's daughter and future queen. Otherwise, he will have no choice but assign you to duties that will not jeopardize his standing in the eyes of his king and peers or..." Elvina concluded as she took to separating the horse's tail into three strands.

When the Saxon girl did not finish her thought, Alfhildr did so for her.

"Or he will ransom me off to the highest bidder as he originally wished."

With head bowed low, as if ashamed by this sad fact, Elvina nodded.

"Well then, you will need to be a good teacher and I an exceptional student," Alfhildr proclaimed with more cheer than she felt.

"Now, show me how to braid before your father discovers you are once more heaping shame upon his mount."

Having expected her pronouncement to bring a smile to the Saxon girl's face, Alfhildr was a bit taken aback when instead, she looked over at her, wearing an expression that told her there were other, more serious matters to be discussed.

"I am more than willing to teach you everything you need to know. In fact, I yearn to do so, provided you make a promise to teach me things I may one day need if my father does manage to arrange a match with the king's son."

"Teach you? What could I possibly teach you?" Alfhildr asked as she wondered what skills she possessed of which a young girl of noble birth could have need.

"I wish to know how to use sword, shield, and spear," Elvina replied with a deadly earnestness that left no doubt in Alfhildr's mind that she was serious.

"These are dangerous times," she continued. "I have been told the man to whom I am to be wed is called 'the Unready' because so many of the king's noble's fear he is unsuitable to take his father's place. That is why my uncle is against this union. He fears for my safety."

As she listened, Alfhildr could not help but compare the circumstances the Saxon girl was describing to the very same ones she had faced in succeeding her grandfather before her brother's sword had literally cut her out of contention. This thought was quickly shoved aside by another, a realization that the gods were, once more, taking a hand in her life's journey. Rather than the Saxon girl being her ally, as Alfhildr had originally assumed, she was to be Elvina's ally, a new role she had not expected. And yet, it was one that suddenly made perfect sense to the red-haired Dane. All the challenges the gods had set out before her to date, all the companions she had come upon and had learned to trust, had never been intended to help her become a great hero. Rather, they had been sent to teach her how to help another who had an important task she was not able to fulfill on her own.

Perhaps, Alfhildr wondered, *it would be through the efforts of the frail fair-haired Saxon girl, standing next to her, that a real peace would be achieved between Saxon and Dane, and not through her bloody wanderings. That had to be it,* Alfhildr finally concluded. *That had to be the reason her path had led her here.*

With this in mind, she reached out and placed her right hand over Elvina's as the Saxon girl stood there, holding a horse's tail, while she anxiously awaited an answer.

"We shall teach each other the skills I expect both of us will need to know if we are to achieve the tasks our gods have assigned to us. But be warned," Alfhildr added even before Elvina had time to absorb the Dane girl's pronouncement, "learning to use sword and shield will not be easy. It is not like learning to braid hair. Often, a warrior sustains more wounds while perfecting his skills than he does in battle."

Upon hearing this, Elvina could not keep from laughing in a most unladylike manner, just as she had seen the Dane girl do.

"And you think learning to braid hair using a horse's tail is not without risks? Hooves hurt too, you know."

Æ

At first, Alfhildr thought the Saxon girl who had befriended her was impetuous, perhaps dangerously so. Only slowly did she come to appreciate that Elvina was simply eager to learn all she could as quickly as she could from her. This ravenous curiosity was not confined to learning how to wield a sword or fend off an enemy's blow with a shield. The young woman, who was supposed to be the mistress, all but pleaded with Alfhildr to tell her everything about her people, the world beyond the walls of the keep and, most especially, her adventures. Having come to the conclusion that it was her mission in life to prepare the fair-haired Saxon girl to accomplish a task that she had once thought had been hers, Alfhildr obliged Elvina, sharing with her all she knew and to which she had been witness, with one exception. As she had done with Osgar and the monk, Alfhildr drew back whenever the subject of her family or past was brought up.

"How it came to be that I took to the forests as I did is of no importance," she informed Elvina the first time the Saxon girl broached the subject.

"I disagree," Elvina replied, unaware of how sensitive the Dane girl was concerning this matter.

"It is our lineage that determines the course our lives will follow. We must all follow the path set out before us by our ancestors: otherwise, we will wander about aimlessly, lost and without purpose."

Unable to help herself, Alfhildr responded with a sharpness that caused Elvina to recoil.

"Only fools and cowards blindly follow in the footsteps of those who have gone before them. Those who fail to learn from the mistakes of their fathers, and their fathers before them, deserve neither mercy or sympathy, only a short miserable life and a shallow grave."

Realizing she had strayed onto a subject that threatened to drive a wedge between herself and the Dane girl, from that day on, Elvina made it a point to tread carefully whenever discussing Alfhildr's past. Instead, she simply pretended the stories of her being raised by a she-wolf were true. It was a notion that not only added to the allure of the Dane girl, it served to make those who knew of her strange choice of servants all the more intimidated by her. After all, if the daughter of Osmund could tame the Dane witch, who had humbled so many great warriors, perhaps she was the perfect match for a boy who was sadly unsuited for a role he was destined to assume.

Æ

"*No, No, No!*" Alfhildr spat as she repeatedly pounded with the flat of her sword on the shield behind which Elvina was crouching every time that she shouted out the word "no." "Do not flinch. Do not draw away. Do not cower like a frightened little girl. Watch my eyes, not my sword. My eyes," Alfhildr thundered as she followed the exhausted Saxon girl who continued to draw away and to her right under the weight of her ceaseless onslaught. "And use your shield. When the shield wall breaks, it becomes as much a weapon as your sword."

Alfhildr ignored the way two of the guards responsible for protecting the daughter of their lord eyed her. They made sure she never forgot that they were always near at hand, warily watching everything she did, while keeping a firm grip with one hand around their spears and the other resting on the pommel of their swords. Alfhildr knew they were no different than many of their brethren, looking for any excuse to put the damnable Dane witch to the sword. It was for this reason Alfhildr was ever so careful how she went about training Elvina, doing so in secret, far from the prying eyes and wagging tongues that surrounded the Saxon noblewoman every waking hour at her father's burh.

Yet, despite the need to proceed with caution lest she accidently draw blood or raise a visible bruise during her mock battles with Elvina, Alfhildr found she was unable to hold back once she had wrapped her hand about the hilt of a sword, even one as dull as that which she was given by her ever attentive Saxon guards. The inbred instincts of a warrior, so carefully nurtured and honed from the moment she was strong enough to lift her first sword, once more came to the fore. With little regard for the consequences, Alfhildr did not hold back when training the Saxon girl, for she knew that, in battle, there was no such thing as compromise or mercy, only victory or a brutal, quick death. It was a lesson she wished to impart to Elvina, one that allowed her to relentlessly press her attack, even as her Saxon guards watched her with a keen eye and a hand tightly wrapped about their weapons.

When she realized that the Dane girl was not going to let up, Elvina hit upon a desperate stratagem, one she often used when dealing with her father. Once more feigning retreat, she waited until Alfhildr was in the process of cocking her sword arm back as she readied herself to strike once more. Lowering her own sword to her side, the Saxon girl drew her upper body back slightly but kept both feet firmly planted on the ground. When Alfhildr leaned forward to close the distance, Elvina shifted ever so slightly to her left, put her shoulder into her shield and lunged forward, aiming the shield's boss at the Dane girl's exposed and vulnerable right flank.

Caught off guard, and in the process of shifting her own weight from one foot to the other, the impact of Elvina's shield against the side of her unprotected chest knocked the wind out of Alfhildr's lungs and threw her backward. With a thud that even caused the men of arms watching the fight to wince, she hit the ground hard. Elvina, who had often pulled back just when she was on the verge of winning, did not hesitate this time. Boldly stepping forward, she placed a foot over Alfhildr's sword arm, pinning it to the ground while bringing her own weapon about and lightly tapping the Dane girl on the head with the flat of her blade.

"Is that how you do it?" she asked mockingly.

Though soundly beaten, Alfhildr was not about to allow herself to be bested by a mere girl. While still peering into Elvina's eyes, she grasped the edge of her own shield and brought it about in a wide, sweeping motion, hitting the back of the Saxon girl's legs behind the kneecaps, sending her to the ground as well.

Angered by what they took to be duplicity, the guards were about to rush forward and restrain the Dane girl but stopped when both Alfhildr and Elvina broke out laughing as they lay side by side on their backs, winded, sweaty and very much pleased with their own performance.

"Never give your foe a chance to strike back," Alfhildr called out between gasps of breath and laughter.

"But you are not my foe," Elvina replied as she struggled to regain her feet with the aid of one of the soldiers. To this, Alfhildr said nothing as she lay there for a moment, looking up at the regal young woman standing before her.

I pray you remember that when you are a queen, Alfhildr thought to herself as she watched the fair-haired Saxon girl brush the dirt from her clothing.

Æ

"We will not have time to do any weaving today," Elvina reminded Alfhildr as they made their way back to the small hovel on the edge of the village where they would shed the tunics and trousers they were wearing, don their female attire, and turn their weapons over to the guards who served as Elvina's escort.

"Father needs to discuss my uncle's visit with me. Uncle Tofi is returning from the king's court where he has been attempting to secure a marriage between myself and Cerdic on my father's behalf."

Alfhildr made no effort to hide her joy when she heard they would not be doing any weaving. It was an activity she had learned to hate with a passion. Unlike combat, spinning and weaving required a keen eye, nimble fingers, and the sort of patience Alfhildr found she did not have. In battle, even when pitted against a determined and skilled foe, the issue was often decided in a matter of minutes, sometimes seconds. That's what Alfhildr excelled at and enjoyed, quick, bold, and decisive action. Sitting about inside all day long, surrounded by chattering women as they spun clumps of wool into thread as her mother and grandmother had, sent a shiver down Alfhildr's spine.

Surely, the gods had not led her to this place simply to punish her in this manner for failing to live up to their expectations as laid out in the Old Woman's prophecy, Alfhildr thought.

There had to be a task more fitting to her nature that they would demand of her, something that would free her from the enslavement the rough-spun gowns she wore had come to represent. That much Alfhildr was sure of. At the moment, it was the only thing she was.

After a long silence, during which Elvina finally managed to screw up her courage, the young Saxon girl glanced back over her shoulder to make sure her escort was maintaining the discreet distance that, before heading back to the keep, she had surreptitiously ordered them to keep. Deciding they would not be able to hear what she was about to say, she chose this moment to bring up a subject she had been wanting to discuss with the Dane girl for a long time.

"What is it like to be with a man?" Elvina asked in a low, hesitant voice.

Having been lost in her own thoughts, Alfhildr blinked as she took a moment to give her head a quick shake.

"I prefer the company of men," Alfhildr replied without giving Elvina's question a whit of thought or taking note of the way the Saxon girl had couched her question.

"If truth be known, I have never spent any time with women or girls."

Shocked, Elvina stopped, causing Alfhildr to do likewise as she looked back at her mistress and friend, wondering why she was behaving so.

"It's true," she admitted. "With one exception, I have spent my entire life in the company of men. Why do you ask?"

Setting aside the thought of being with a girl who would even consider being pleasured by another female, Elvina slowly took up her pace once more before doing her best to explain her reason for asking.

"I have never had a mother, one who could pass onto me the knowledge and wisdom a woman needs," she muttered as a blush began to rise in her cheeks. "And the idea of going to Blythe and asking her about men, well, that is something I would never do, not unless it became necessary. Which is why I need you to tell me what it's like and what will be expected of me."

Confused, Alfhildr looked over at Elvina.

"What do you mean, 'what it is like'?"

Unable to look the Dane girl in the eye, Elvina slowed her pace and turned her head away to hide her crimson cheeks.

"Being with a man, having him take you and, well..."

Elvina found herself unable to explain any further. Not that she needed to as it finally dawned on Alfhildr what her friend was actually talking about. Stopping in her tracks, the Dane girl's eyes flew open as her jaw dropped.

"By the gods!" she exclaimed loudly. "Are you talking about...I mean, do you think I have actually...Oh, no, no! I have never...I would never..."

She was about to say something crude but stopped just in time when she remembered they were not alone.

It was only then that Elvina realized her assumptions about the Dane girl and what she had been told about how pagans lived was in error. Alfhildr's response alone served to prove she was no different than her, a virgin, ignorant of a wife's duty to her husband.

Behind them, the two guards found themselves unable to check their laughter, earning them both a scathing rebuke delivered at the point of two swords being wielded by a pair of blushing young girls.

Æ

Upon returning to her chamber that evening, after spending time with her father discussing the arrangements for which she would be responsible in order to prepare for a pending visit by her uncle and his retainers, Elvina found Alfhildr curled up on the blanket on which she slept in a corner of the room, leafing through a book. Hanging back, the Saxon girl watched as the Dane girl struggled to mouth the words.

"You can read?" Elvina finally called out.

Startled, Alfhildr all but leapt to her feet, attempting to set the book aside and out of view as she did so.

Smiling, Elvina crossed the room to where the Dane girl stood, bent over, and retrieved the book. Looking up into Alfhildr's downcast eyes, Elvina repeated her question.

"Can you read?"

Crimson cheeked, Alfhildr shrugged.

"A little," she whispered. "Not much. A few words, no more."

Taking the Dane girl by the hand, Elvina led her to the side of the bed where she took a seat, pulling Alfhildr down next to her.

"Well, then, we shall have to correct that, won't we?" the daughter of a Saxon noble announced in a commanding manner that came so naturally to her.

When Alfhildr looked up into Elvina's eyes, the Saxon girl could see the hopefulness within them.

"You would teach me to read better?" Alfhildr asked.

Giving the Dane girl's hand a squeeze, Elvina smiled. "Yes, of course I will. It will be nice to find something I can teach you that you will actually enjoy."

After that, they both had a good laugh. Then, Elvina once more turned serious.

"Tell me, how is it you learned to read in the first place?"

Alfhildr's expression clouded over as she looked away, wondering if she should tell the Saxon girl of the time she had spent with the Old Woman. By doing so, Alfhildr feared she might betray something of her past, something she wished to share with no one, not even the girl who had saved her from the cruel fate so many of her fellow Saxons wished to visit upon her. Yet, to hold back from her did not seem to be the honorable thing to do. Without anyone having to tell her, Alfhildr knew the Saxon girl had angered many of her own people by saving her from being burned alive. A balance needed to be struck, one that would satisfy Elvina's curiosity as well as her own need to do what honor demanded.

"There was an old woman," Alfhildr began slowly, speaking in a low voice as she gazed down at her hands. "I believe she was the last of her people, a people who once populated this island long before either Saxon or Dane turned their backs on their homelands and set out upon the whale road."

"I have heard tell of these people, but know nothing about them," Elvina admitted. "What did this old woman tell you about them?"

Once more, Alfhildr could not help but wonder if the gods had always intended her to find her way to this place in order to serve a girl who would one day be a queen. Ever so slowly, Alfhildr looked up into Elvina's eyes, eyes that told her she could be trusted.

"When the Old Woman spoke of her people, she often made mention of a mighty king who once ruled them. He was a just and wise king, a man she called Artorius."

Chapter Thirteen
THE COURT OF SHADOWS

The Saga of the Old King

Shadows and lies the old King surrounded.
Men's smiles hid their teeth from the young queen to be.
The joining of houses a threat to the greedy
Who sought for themselves the throne and the crown.

The promise of plunder and war bound the traitors
Yet Elvina was trapped in the glittering cage.
Alfhildr now fought with guile and with honey
Strange weapons to shield and win friends for a queen.

Yet allies she had, old friends not forgetting.
The love and the debt that they owed the red maid.
Skadi and Hoenir close by to her call
Osgar, the Hunter, his blade hers once more.

Rich was the feast for the Prince and his bride.
Lavish the table and plentiful the ale.
The king supped too hard and choked on a bone.
To the uproar of the nobles, he fell dead on his throne.

Swift struck the traitors. Sharp spears for the son.
The young Queen Elvina, the next prey they sought.
Yet Alfhildr was swifter, from maid to shield maiden
With Durthfang and wolf's fang, she cut through her foes

In the grey mist, she vanished the young queen away.
By secret path and hidden grove, they fled from their foes.
To the one place of safety she had known in her life
She led fair Elvina to prepare for the fight.
Æ

"It's not right, I tell you," the cook grumbled as she took out her frustration on the helpless dough. "I don't know why her father stands for it. I always knew my place, aye, and kept it."

She glanced around at the other servants as they nodded sympathetically to the oft-repeated complaints of the burly woman if for no other reason than to keep her from taking her anger out on them. Once she was sure she had their attention, she lowered her voice.

"I'm not one to gossip but it seems to me the young mistress has come over all strange since *'she'* appeared."

The cook spat out the word *'she'* with poisonous loathing.

"'T'ain't natural, that's all I'm saying."

At that moment *'she'* and Elvina were laughing as Alfhildr tried once more to tease out wool from her distaff, only to once again send the weighted spindle flying across the small women's hall.

"Alfhildr, you have managed to turn even a simple distaff into a warrior's weapon," Elvina exclaimed, wiping the tears of laughter from her eyes while watching as the Dane stormed over to where the errant spindle had come to rest, muttering under her breath as she did. "You have to gently and evenly flick out the spindle."

Then, with easy grace Elvina effortlessly demonstrated by spinning out and twisting a yard of woolen thread.

Alfhildr groused as she retied her spindle.

"It's all right for you. You learned when you were little."

"And didn't your mother and sisters teach you?"

Even as she said it, Elvina realized her mistake. She watched as a quick flicker of pain darkened Alfhildr's expression before it was swiftly replaced by a brittle smile. The young noblewoman could sense the hurt but felt helpless to breach the battlements Alfhildr had built around her childhood.

Perhaps one day, Elvina thought sadly. *Perhaps one day, she will let someone in who can let her know they care.*

Abruptly she set her spinning aside.

"Come, I want you to show me how to find some of your healing herbs."

"Anything, so long as it's not spinning, least I run someone through with this…" Alfhildr muttered gratefully as she gathered up the tangled mess she had made.

She was about to describe the distaff using a word best left in the stable but managed to catch herself. Instead, she set the offending item aside with relief and headed out into the fresh air with her mistress.

Æ

While the girls headed out of the steading, Lord Osmund sat and idly listened to his steward's report on his holdings.

"…and, of course, my Lord, there has been some talk about the Lady Elvina's new interests."

The man paused uncertainly. He knew full well how sensitive Lord Osmund was to even the slightest criticism of his daughter.

"Nothing wrong with her learning to hold a blade. There's many a man who would be glad if his woman could cover his back. She is, after all, my daughter."

Osmund's words were tinged with pride that, even in a girl child, his warrior's blood came through.

"Indeed, my Lord. However, some believe she has become a little too familiar with her new maid, allowing her to speak too freely and not show the proper respect due to one who will soon be a queen."

Osmund's brow creased at that final comment. Respect was something he understood very well. His fingers drummed on the armrest as he thought. At last, he spoke.

"I'll have words with my daughter."

The steward silently breathed a sigh of relief. The sooner the girl was away and married to Cerdic, the smoother his job would be.

"And now, my Lord, may I mention the new priest down by Ulla's stead? He has started to demand more land for his church and…"

Osmund slumped back in his chair as the trivial arguments and demands of his folk rolled over him again.

Æ

That evening, Osmund surreptitiously watched his daughter and her maid as Elvina dutifully served his meat and ale with her own hands. The young Dane girl stood demurely behind her mistress, handing her the heavy jug and platter as required. As time went on and the ale began to soften his mood, Osmund's concerns about Alfhildr's manner with his daughter faded. It was hard to believe that a scarce five months before, the Dane girl had lain at his feet, a filthy, untamed barbarian. She had certainly blossomed under Elvina's hand.

"More ale, Papa?"

Osmund looked up guiltily from his admiration of Alfhildr's curves into the pretty face of his daughter. With a nod, she delicately filled his beaker, a gentle smile playing across her lips to let him know she had caught him eyeing her maid. With a hint of guilt showing through, Osmund shifted in his seat as he sought to deflect the knowing smirk on his daughter's lips.

"You've done a good job there."

"Thank you, Papa. It's nice to have someone to talk to."

"She's respectful?"

Elvina smiled again. "Yes, Papa. She knows her place."

Having finished her duties, and knowing it was time for her to withdraw, Elvina led Alfhildr from the Great Hall, leaving her father and his warriors to their drinking.

Osmund allowed himself to enjoy the retreating view as the pert little redhead followed her mistress. It was not until the next morning that he considered that there could be another meaning behind Elvina's parting words.

Æ

The vivid, white blossoms of the hawthorns trumpeted the arrival of spring, heralding the time had come to commence the preparations for Elvina's wedding in earnest.

Osmund had spent lavishly to make sure all would see his wealth and power reflected in the gowns and jewels of his daughter. Torcs and bracelets of soft, fat gold, brooches and pins emblazoned with gems and precious amber, fine, woolen cloaks edged with ermine and otter pelts. All these and more were laid at Elvina's feet to be admired, tried on, and, at last, carefully packed for the coming journey.

On the eve of their departure for the royal burgh, Elvina tried hard to sit still and be patient, letting Alfhildr comb out her long, wheat gold hair ready for bed, but her excitement and nerves bubbled up like a mountain spring.

"Papa wants me to wear everything, but I really don't think the amber and the pearls would look well together, especially not with the blue gown. It's all lovely, but, sometimes, I'm sure he thinks I am a pack horse with all the brooches and jewels he wants to show off on me."

Elvina chuckled at the thought while Alfhildr simply smiled as she continued to burnish the girl's golden tresses.

Elvina chattered on about Cerdic, the journey, the King, and the hundred and one other things that whirled through her head until, at last, she fell silent. She reached back to stay the comb, her fingers finding Alfhildr's.

"You know, your hands are softer now."

Alfhildr winced at the compliment.

"It's all the grease in the lambs' wool you've had me spinning."

"No. It's not that. Although your skin *is* softer: it's your touch. It is gentler."

Alfhildr said nothing, unsure if she wanted to hear how much she had changed. With each passing day, she found that she needed to remind herself more and more often that she was a warrior, one with a task the gods themselves had allotted to her. And yet, she found herself now taking a guilty pleasure from the same things Elvina enjoyed, the beauty of a brooch, the softness of a fur.

Was she betraying her gods by doing so? Was she fooling herself?

Elvina noted the way her red-haired maid had withdrawn into herself as she so often did and smiled sadly as she vaguely sensed the hidden turmoil with which the young girl was struggling.

"I almost forgot. With all the gifts from Papa, he included this."

Elvina reached for a small leather scrip and handed it to Alfhildr.

"They're for you."

Hesitantly, Alfhildr pressed her fingers against the soft leather pouch, feeling the odd lumps inside. Taking a seat on one of Elvina's clothes presses, she carefully tipped the contents into the lap of her skirt. A handful of simple brooches fell out in a jumble before her. Unthinkingly, she took up a small black brooch with a bird on it. After setting that aside, her fingers traced out the design of a prettily carved comb decorated with a dragon's head. From where she stood, Elvina held her breath as she watched the young girl touching each simple item carefully, her gaze lost somewhere in the past.

At length, when Alfhildr looked up at her, the girl's eyes were bright with tears.

"Thank you," she whispered in a voice that was little more than a breath. "These are more precious to me than all the gold and jewels in the world."

After she had inspected each and every one of her precious treasures and had carefully replaced the simple items in the scrip, she laid it at the head of her blanket.

Later that night, Elvina thought she heard quiet sobs coming from the foot of her bed where Alfhildr lay. But when she called out, they stopped and there was no answer.

Æ

A spring shower, over as soon as it had begun, turned the enclosure before Osmund's hall into a muddy mess. Men and horses stomped and fretted, all eager to be off to the royal burgh at Sceaftesege. At last, Elvina appeared, trailed by her Dane maid. Clutching the front of their gowns and modestly lifting their hems up, the two carefully skirted the puddles, while doing their best to avoid the fresh droppings left by the horses, as they made their way to where her father waited impatiently. Behind her, Elvina could hear Alfhildr quietly cursing skirts and mud. She smiled to herself at the Dane girl's choice of words.

Some of those oaths, she thought, *were well worth remembering.*

When he saw the two girls emerge, Osmund gestured to a groom, then watched his pride and joy smiling happily as she drew near. His pleasure in her radiance was tinged with sadness, for even though he had striven so long for an alliance with the King, he knew he would be lonely without his daughter near. Osmund shook his head.

Today was a day to be happy, he told himself.

His gaze slipped onwards to the red-headed maid as she walked demurely behind her mistress, her lithe figure sweetly filling a cast-off gown of his daughter's. Osmund snorted. If she were not his daughter's slave, he would be very tempted, very tempted indeed. When he felt himself start to become aroused, Osmund turned quickly to shout at the luckless groom as he returned leading her mount.

"Where's my daughter's horse, you oaf? Hurry up."

A little whinny drew Alfhildr's eyes up from the mud as Dimma was led forth for Elvina. Her joy at seeing the placid little mare again caught in her throat as she realized Dimma was now Elvina's, not hers. As the young noblewoman was helped into the high saddle, Dimma turned to affectionately nuzzle Alfhildr's hair, only to be batted half-heartedly away. It was only when Elvina was settled that she looked down to see her maid almost in tears. Elvina leant down to the girl who had become so much more to her than just a maid.

"Time changes many things. You'll see," she whispered just as her father led the procession out and south toward the royal burgh.

Æ

Sitting easily in the saddle, Lord Osmund rode straight and proud under his banner of the red serpent, its coils writhing fitfully in the warm breeze. Close behind, a dozen mounted huscarls, all dressed in bright mail and iron helms attested to his power and wealth while, further back, twenty spearmen flanked the women, servants, and baggage, their eyes flicking nervously outwards as they guarded the rich treasure of the wedding gifts, a tempting target for Danish reavers despite the strong guard.

It was late afternoon when Osmund called a halt at the edge of a broad glade, deep in the forest. His eye quickly assessed its suitability for defense as he threw up his hand.

"We camp here tonight. I want guards there, there, and there, double posted," he bellowed as his fingers jabbed toward the tree line. "Olwulf, take three riders and sweep deep around. Go out four arrow lengths, no further."

The commander of the escort was about to head off to carry out his orders but was stopped.

"One more thing," Osmund called out before lowering his voice. "The Dane girl. These are her natural elements. Make sure your men keep a sharp eye on what she does and where she goes. And no matter what my daughter says or does, the Dane is not to be allowed near the horses. Understood?"

Olwulf nodded. "Understood, my liege."

Further back in the line of march, where she had endured the indignity of walking alongside the pack animals and among the other servants, Alfhildr snorted to herself at stopping so early in the day. Only after they had did she come to realize she was immensely glad they had. Her legs ached from even this day's undemanding pace. She shook her head and scowled at her own unfitness as she recalled the disdain she had once held for the young monk when he couldn't keep up.

The girls rested while servants swiftly set up camp. A simple linen tent was erected for Elvina and her maid, well apart from the others. Once up, Alfhildr quickly laid out blankets and furs for her mistress then headed toward the trees to relieve herself.

"Hey! Where are you going?" A young spearman called out as he eagerly rushed over to Alfhildr, stumbling over the heavy shield and spear. She noted the sparse downy fluff on his chin and tried to hide a smile as he approached.

"My lady and I need somewhere private."

"But...why?"

Alfhildr looked down at the perplexed youngster and decided to tease him a little.

"Surely you don't expect my lady to pee like a mare in front of you?"

She tilted her head and watched him with interest. The blush alone was worth it. It started with his ears and blossomed like a poppy. Trying hard not to laugh at the poor boy, Alfhildr at last turned and headed out into the trees.

"Be careful," the youngster called out, doing his best to make himself sound manly. "There are wolves and all sorts in the forest. It's not safe."

Alfhildr snorted with laughter.

He's telling me that it's not safe?

She found a peaceful spot and quickly tended to her business before heading back to where the young spearman watched her nervously until she was well within the glade.

Alfhildr reveled in being outdoors again. She pointed out the birds and the flowers to her mistress, who kept looking about nervously. At last, Alfhildr could no longer contain herself.

"Is something wrong?"

Elvina chewed her lip for a moment before replying.

"It's just that I've never slept outside in the forest before."

The look of worry in her eyes stopped Alfhildr from laughing. Instead, she merely reached over and touched Elvina's hand.

"I promise, I'll keep you safe."

Elvina flashed her maid a grateful little smile.

It was full dark when Elvina and Alfhildr retired to the little tent. Unlike her maid, who dropped off almost immediately, Elvina struggled to find a comfortable position on the hard ground. When a lone wolf took to howling at the moon, Elvina's hand shot out from her covers to grab Alfhildr.

"A wolf!"

"Mmmph?" Alfhildr had been fast asleep, enjoying being back in the forest, despite everything.

"There's a wolf out there," Elvina repeated.

"There are lots of wolves out there," Alfhildr muttered groggily. "It's a forest."

"But they might attack us."

"They're more afraid of us than we of them."

"Oh."

Alfhildr rolled over and tried to get back to sleep, but her bladder stopped her.

Grumbling, she struggled out of the tent.

"Where are you going?" Elvina called out anxiously.

"I need to pee."

"But the wolves."

"Don't worry," Alfhildr muttered, still only half awake. "I won't pee on any of them."

The light from the campfire guided Alfhildr back toward the spot she had found earlier.

"Where do you think you're going?" The same youngster who had stopped her before was again on duty.

"To pee," Alfhildr snapped.

"Are you sure you need to? I've heard snuffling and things out there."

Alfhildr started to get annoyed as well as desperate.

"Yes, I am sure. And no, I'm still not a mare. I'll cry out if I need you to protect me from the dark," she replied caustically as she pushed pass him.

It was with a sigh of relief when she finally found the spot and did her business.

Finished, she dropped her skirts and turned. It was only then that she found herself gazing into a pair of eyes staring back at her in the dark. For a moment, the two creatures of the forest stood stock still. Then, the wolf leapt.

Æ

Elvina was relieved when at last she heard Alfhildr pull open the flap of the tent.

"I was getting worried. You were gone so long and with the wolf and all."

As she said it, Elvina could smell a strange musty scent enter the tent.

"Ermm, about the wolf. Do you mind if I bring her in here?"

Elvina squeaked as a cold wet nose found her questing hand.

"This is Skadi. She's my friend," Alfhildr hurriedly explained.

Elvina was about to scream when a rough slobbery tongue started to lick her fingers in the same way her father's hunting dogs often did.

"She's really quite gentle when you get to know her," Alfhildr volunteered. "Brother Plegmund used to tickle her tummy. And she's nice and warm. Please?"

Elvina could hear the pleading note in her maid's voice. Reaching out once more, the Saxon girl cautiously stroked the wolf's ears. She wondered what her father would do if he knew she was sharing her tent with a wolf as her hand caressed the animal's silky fur.

The next morning, Elvina awoke to find herself alone. She stretched and was about to call for Alfhildr when the tent flap was pulled back.

"I have a bowl of water for you to wash in, My Lady. After that, we need to choose the gown and jewels you will wear for your arrival in the royal burgh."

Elvina cocked her head and looked quizzically at her maid.

"Did I dream last night?"

Alfhildr grinned.

"I took her back into the forest before dawn. I didn't think your father would be too pleased if he knew. Skadi's smart. She will keep clear with all these strange men around. But she knows you now."

Elvina wasn't sure if she should be pleased or alarmed at the thought but smiled uncertainly as she reached for the wooden bowl.

Æ

Alfhildr's first sight of the royal burgh shocked her to stillness. She had never seen so many houses in one place, their thatched roofs scattered around four great halls and circled by massive earth ramparts topped with a stout wooden stockade.

"Alfhildr? Why have you stopped?" Elvina frowned at her maid who stood there with her mouth open.

"I…I've never seen anything so big. Did the gods build it?"

Elvina laughed at her maid, although she too was awed by the size of the burgh.

"No, silly, just lots of men on the orders of their king."

Alfhildr scowled at having appeared so unknowing and quickly caught up with her mistress. Yet, as they approached the mighty burgh, her sense of awe only grew. The high earthen ramparts stood three spears tall and the heavy gates were crowned with a massive watchtower. Around them, people swirled, more people than Alfhildr had ever seen before. Warriors, both humble spearmen and mighty huscarls, clad in shimmering mail.

Peddlers, their heavy packs bending them almost double as they stumbled into the burgh, stepped aside to let the wedding party pass. Beggars and jugglers, dumpy matrons and laughing girls, all thronged the muddy streets, while the pervasive stench of night soil and wood smoke lay like a saw across the nose. Then, Alfhildr caught sight of a familiar brown garb.

"Plegmund! Brother Plegmund!" She pushed past two squabbling women to catch the monk's arm.

Surprised to be grabbed by a girl, the old monk turned, his cowl falling back from his bald head.

"Yes, my child?" his brow creased as he waited politely for her to explain herself.

"I'm sorry. I thought you were a friend. He wore exactly the same…"

"So do all who have dedicated their life to the glory of God, child."

Confused and bewildered, Alfhildr let go of the monk's sleeve, stammering her apologies before rejoining Elvina.

Guided by the royal guards, the wedding party wended their way among the noise and bustle until, at last, they reached the royal enclosure where Elvina was ushered into the women's hall. Even as she crossed the threshold behind her mistress, Alfhildr's hackles rose. The hall was airy and light with pretty rugs laid on top of the fresh rushes. Yet, something was not right.

"Lady Elvina, welcome," a statuesque lady declared as she glided across to the flustered Elvina. "We are so glad you have come to join us. We were delighted to hear of your success in wooing Cerdic."

After a slight pause in which neither woman said anything, the statuesque lady realized Elvina did not appreciate who she was.

"My dear child, I am Æmma, the wife of Lord Wilfrid."

Ignoring the red-haired maid, Lady Æmma took the young girl in hand and led her to where the other ladies of importance were awaiting them.

"Let me introduce you to everyone," she declared haughtily. "My lord specifically asked that I look after you while you are with us."

Alfhildr took advantage of this opportunity to look around, trying to spot the cause of her anxiety. Ladies and their maids were gathered in little clumps around the hall, looking sidelong at the fair-haired noblewoman, while outside Alfhildr could see a small knot of men idly watching Elvina as she was whisked away by Lady Æmma. With nothing more she needed to do there, Alfhildr turned to set out and find her mistress's quarters, trying hard to ignore the ominous itch between her shoulder blades.

Æ

The sun had set when Elvina was at last summoned to the King's Hall so the King could inspect the future bride of his son and heir. The negotiations of the *handgeld* and *morgengifu* were long since completed, and he was at last content that, with the mighty Osmund tied to the throne by blood, his son would be secure.

In the dim mists of his failing sight, the aged King spotted the approaching girl.

"Closer girl, closer. I don't bite," he chortled weakly at his own joke as Elvina came close enough for him to at last see clearly. "A pretty young thing, eh, Osmund? Good childbearing hips. I approve." He laughed again, then coughed and spluttered. A servant stepped forward to wipe the dribble from his lips but was irritably batted away.

"So, what do you think, young Cerdic?"

Standing behind Elvina, Alfhildr watched as a slim, young man nervously approached his father.

"I'm sure we shall be very happy."

"Happy? What's happy got to do with it?" The King wheezed angrily and gulped at a beaker of ale before continuing. "You're to breed boys, sons, and lots of them, understand?"

The young man glanced apologetically across at Elvina even as she was nodding demurely in response to the King's response.

"Of course, Sire."

As she watched, Alfhildr struggled to keep her face clear of the anxiety she was feeling. She stole a sidelong glance at her mistress before considering the scrawny young Cerdic again. If she had found him in the shield wall beside her, she would have been very worried indeed.

After she had been inspected, Elvina was dismissed in order to allow the men to continue their business. She and Alfhildr made their way through the crowded hall, back toward the women's quarters. It was then that Alfhildr realized what was wrong. She had expected people to watch Elvina, to steal sidelong glances at their future queen. What she was not prepared for were the looks on their faces. Some watched the girl with a sad gaze before hiding their expression. Many others made little effort to disguise a sly calculating smile before glancing across to a noisy party in the corner of the hall. Near its centre, Alfhildr spotted the Lady Æmma, her hand resting lightly on the sleeve of a powerfully built man, his eyes fixed on Elvina's slim form.

Æ

As they left the Great Hall, Alfhildr sucked down a deep breath. Even the nighttime stench of the burgh was better than the smoky claustrophobic fug of the hall. Although it was dark, people were still moving about the royal enclosure. They had not gone far when a warrior loomed out of the shadows toward them.

"My Lady?" The bulky figure called out as he stopped and addressed Elvina. Alfhildr frowned as she tried to place the familiar voice.

"I saw you briefly when I came on business to your father from Lord Godric."

"Bowdyn!" Alfhildr blurted out as she recognized the tall huscarl. She winced and turned apologetically to Elvina.

"I'm sorry, My Lady. He's a friend, I think."

Bowdyn chuckled. "Have no fear on that score. My Lord's ire should no longer cause you concern."

Having said that, he turned to the bewildered Elvina.

"My Lady, I am glad to see you arrived here safely."

Something in his words caused Alfhildr to stare sharply at the warrior.

"My Lord Godric sends his *loyal* greetings my Lady."

Alfhildr started to frown as she picked up the slight stress on the word 'loyal.'

Elvina smiled uncertainly.

"His greetings are most welcome, Bowdyn. Now, if you will excuse us, I must retire."

With that she started again toward their quarters. After Elvina had made her way past him, Alfhildr nodded to the huscarl, flicking him a hunting sign to wait here.

Once in her mistress's quarters, Alfhildr fretted that the events of the day would cause Elvina to hold her there, chattering incessantly as she often did when excited. Instead, the young noblewoman sat quietly, mulling over in her head what had occurred during the day while Alfhildr prepared her for bed. When at last Elvina did speak, Alfhildr could not miss the concern her tone betrayed.

"You're going to speak with him." It was a statement, not a question.

Alfhildr blushed. "Would you rather I didn't?"

"No." Elvina declared sharply as she reached back and seized Alfhildr's hand. "Find out what's happening, what's really happening. I can feel something's not right, and it scares me."

Alfhildr looked down into Elvina's face and saw the fear in her eyes. Without thinking she reached out and hugged the young girl tight before realizing what she was doing. Suddenly, she jerked back in confusion.

"My Lady, I shouldn't have."

The two girls stared at each other, shocked. Then, Elvina reached out and pulled Alfhildr close.

"I'm scared Alfhildr. I want to be brave like you, but I'm scared," Elvina whispered in her ear as she desperately clung to her startled maid. "Now go. Go and find out what I need to fear."

Æ

Bowdyn was still waiting in the shadowy enclosure when Alfhildr returned. He looked around as she approached before suddenly reaching out and wrapping an arm around her waist.

"Don't struggle, they're watching." His hissed warning stopped her punch in midair. "We need to talk," he muttered.

Without saying another word, he started to weave unsteadily toward the shadows, pulling a very confused Alfhildr beside him.

Once beside the inner stockade, Bowdyn released his grip. Alfhildr could see his white teeth grinning in the dark. Flustered and unsure at the sensation of his hands on her waist, she hid her feelings behind an angry growl.

"Why shouldn't I cut your balls off for that?"

"Because if you did, your lady's enemies would make sure you were hanging from a gibbet by sunrise."

Alfhildr stopped cold at Bowdyn's brutal comment. All her disquiet came flooding back like an icy wave as she stared into the shadowed face of the huscarl.

"Who are my enemies?"

Bowdyn smiled to himself as Alfhildr immediately took the unknown foes upon herself.

"Lord Wilfrid and his supporters are circling around the dying old wolf like red kites. The burgh is flooded with their men ready to 'defend' against the Danes they say."

He shook his head sadly.

"That young puppy, Cerdic, won't be able to hold them, not even with my Lord's and Osmund's spears at his back."

"And My Lady?"

"It depends. A pawn. A prize perhaps. Maybe even a problem."

Bowdyn left his words hanging in the air between them as he watched the young girl before him. Even in the shadows, her coppery hair gleamed, framing her elfin face as his hand still itched where it had tasted the loveliness of her waist. Bowdyn would have smiled at the attractive young girl had it not been for her eyes, green as emeralds, but as hard and cold as steel. The eyes staring thoughtfully back at him were those of a warrior.

"How many men can you muster when I call?"

Æ

With her eyes cast demurely down from the bright morning sun, Alfhildr carefully followed her mistress across the royal enclosure as they went in search of breakfast. Servants now flocked in droves toward the great kitchens preparing for tomorrow's wedding feast. By the gate, a burly hunter staggered into the compound, the carcass of a full-grown stag draped across his shoulders. Elvina laughed as the man tottered forward under the burden.

"It seems that every huntsman for leagues has been scouring the forest for tomorrow."

But no echoing laugh came from her maid as Alfhildr stared dumbfounded as Osgar staggered theatrically onwards to the amusement of the watching crowd.

"My Lady, perhaps it would be better if you broke your fast in your chamber this morning," Alfhildr murmured quietly as she recovered her wits.

Elvina picked up the hidden message at once and glanced questioningly at her maid. A tiny nod confirmed it. She paused for barely an instant before turning back with a grimace and loudly berating her maid.

"I don't have time, you silly girl. Go and fetch me something from the kitchens, then help me with my gowns. Now, be off with you!"

"Yes, My Lady. Sorry, My Lady," Alfhildr muttered, bobbing her head, before hurrying after Osgar into the cavernous kitchens.

The flames from the roasting pits cast flickering red shadows across the walls while cooks and servants shouted and bustled in noisy confusion. Alfhildr stood unsure in the midst of the mayhem, searching for the brawny huntsman. At last, she spotted him arguing with a butcher before he at last turned back toward the massive doors.

"Alfhildr!" The shock on Osgar's face would have made her laugh in other circumstances, but now she shook her head urgently to warn him to keep his teeth together as she flicked a signal to follow. Without another word, Alfhildr turned and quickly slipped outside toward the stalls that had sprung up to lure the unwary wedding guests to part with their silver.

She stood admiring a pretty belt when a figure loomed nearby. Keeping her eyes on the stallholder's wares, she spoke quietly.

"I have need of your sword arm once more."

They both stared vacantly at the belts and buckles as Osgar struggled to understand.

"You're wearing a gown."

Alfhildr was about to snap at the man for his idiocy when she heard the shock in his voice. She took a breath to calm herself. She needed all the allies she could get.

"It's a long tale, neither pleasant nor glorious, but now is not the time. Can I count on you?"

Osgar shook his head and grinned. Alfhildr never used a dozen words when one would do, and he owed this girl.

"My blade is yours. What would you have of me?"

Æ

Half an hour later, Alfhildr made her way swiftly back toward the women's hall. She suddenly stopped and cursed, causing a nearby spearman to grin at such a ripe phrase from the pretty, little redhead as he watched her head back to the kitchens to grab a loaf and a small beaker of beer for Elvina.

From the shadows, one of Lord Wilfrid's huscarls was also watching the young girl on her errand, admiring her trim figure as she headed back to the women's hall. If he had seen her face, he would not have been smiling. Alfhildr now had an enemy, and her expression was one that many enemies had seen, but few had lived long to recall.

Chapter Fourteen
THE REIGNS OF KINGS

Present Day England
"The Dig"

Looking up from what he had been doing, Peter picked up the conversation he had been having with Sarah where he had left off.

"I know one thing for sure, my sister would not have been at all pleased had Dad dragged a team of oxen into the reception hall at her wedding as a gift. Though, that's about the only thing that was missing at the reception," he added after pretending to give the matter a moment of serious thought.

"Don't be such a dolt," Sarah groaned. "They didn't actually bring the livestock that was being offered up as gifts to the wedding. The families simply pledged to hand things like that over to the newlyweds later."

"I knew that," Peter huffed. "I was just making a little joke."

Sarah snorted. "Yes, a very little one."

Several minutes later, Peter once more looked up.

"I wonder if Osmund bothered to gift wrap them?" he chirped.

"Gift wrap what?" Sarah asked.

"The oxen."

Grabbing a clump of clay, Sarah tossed it at Peter. "Will you shut up?"

Grinning, Peter winked. "And who's going to make me?"

Looking over her shoulder, Elva's expression instantly subdued the boisterous Peter.

"I will."

Æ

The Saga of Two Kings

Rich was the feast for the Prince and his bride
Lavish the table and plentiful the ale.
The old king supped hard and choked on a bone.
To the uproar of the nobles he fell dead on his throne.

Swift struck the traitors. Sharp spears for the son.
The young Queen Elvina, the next prey they sought.
Yet Alfhildr was swifter, from maid to shield maiden
With Durthfang and wolf's fang, she cut through her foes

In the grey mist, she vanished the young queen away.
By secret path and hidden grove, they fled from their foes.
To the one place of safety she had known in her life
She led fair Elvina to prepare for the fight.
Æ

Between sniffles, Bishop Beorhtred peeked up at the sullen sky. Disheartened by what he saw, the Bishop bowed his head and whispered a little prayer to the Lord, imploring Him to hold off the threatened rain a bit longer as the bridal couple approached his makeshift altar. First to come was a little girl, the bastard daughter of the king by one of his slaves, scattering foxglove and honeysuckle in Elvina and Cerdic's path across the muddy royal enclosure. Sneezing, the Bishop wiped his nose on the sleeve of his alb before huddling deeper within his heavy vestments like a turtle seeking shelter.

From within the crowd of servants gathered off to one side near the kitchen hall, Alfhildr watched the two small figures approach the chief Christ priest who was flanked by lesser priests and a throng of the brown robed brothers. Elvina's gown of royal blue wool stood out, a rare bright bloom of color under the overcast sky and an otherwise drab setting. A garland of hawthorn blossoms, dog violets, and forget-me-nots was woven into the braids of her hair, causing the serving girls near Alfhildr to sigh wistfully at the sight of the lovely young noblewoman. At Elvina's side, Cerdic shuffled uncertainly, almost hesitantly, ducking his head as if dodging invisible blows, while glancing out of the corners of his eyes at the surrounding crowd of nobles, warriors, thegns, and servants. At length, the young couple reached Bishop Beorhtred where they knelt before the old man, side by side on rugs laid upon the wet earth.

The Bishop held out his amethyst ring for the couple to kiss, then raised his staff for silence.

"*Ecce conuenimus huc fratres coram Deo, Angelis, et omnibus Sanctis eius in facie Ecclesiæ, ad coniugendum duo corpora...*"

As the strange language echoed around the enclosure, Alfhildr shifted about uneasily. She wondered if the high priest was summoning the White Christ and his angels. This, in turn, left her to ponder over what they would do if they discovered a follower of the true gods at the ceremony, a thought that caused her to snort with amusement. It would be thrilling to see the God to whom Plegmund paid homage do battle with Odin if he chose to ride to her aide, though Alfhildr quickly realized it would not be much of a fight at all if what the pious monk said of his God were true.

As the Bishop prattled on and on, Alfhildr set aside all thoughts of the gods as she turned her attention to studying the gathered nobles and servants more closely, sensing they were just as bored with the ceremony as she. On the far side of the enclosure, Alfhildr caught sight of the way Lord Wilfrid was ignoring the handfasting of the royal couple, laughing instead at a joke one of his huscarls had shared with him. She searched further among the restless crowd until she spotted Bowdyn. At least, he appeared to be following the service, bringing Alfhildr a sense of relief to see one man present who was not belittling her mistress's great day.

Eventually, the interminable droning in the strange tongue came to a halting end.

"Benedicat vos Pater, Filius, et Spiritus Sanctus, qui trinus est in numero et unus in numine. Amen," the high priest intoned loudly while making a mystical gesture in the air above the couple.

Following this, the couple once more kissed the high priest's hand before rising to their feet.

Having concluded the religious portion of the ceremony, the King and Lord Osmund boldly sallied forth from the great hall leading a procession of servants, each of whom was weighed down with heavy chests and armfuls of precious cloths. Upon seeing this, the crowd of servants around her came to life, pushing forward in an effort to get a better look. Grabbing the sleeve of a skinny kitchen boy who was doing his best to squeeze past her, Alfhildr asked him what the two Saxon lords were doing. The boy stared at her quizzically.

"Gifts," he chirped. "It's all the rich stuff that gets given, see? They all want to show off."

With that he pulled himself free and continued squirming his way toward the front of the crowd.

And the gifts presented by both parents were magnificent indeed. A scribe read aloud the list of estates and the number of horses, oxen, and slaves each family had brought to the wedding bed. The *morgengifu* and *brýdgifu* being offered up caused both nobles and servants to gasp at the scale of the alliance, causing them to look thoughtfully to where Lord Osmund proudly stood beside the aged King. When the scribe was finished enumerating the list of lands, titles, and livestock, chests of jewels and bolts of rare cloths were presented and displayed. There were so many that Elvina and Cerdic had little time to do more than nod their heads in thanks and acknowledgement before a fresh marvel was presented.

The final item presented was a sword. When Alfhildr saw it, she felt the blood drain from her face. As if in a trance, she watched Lord Osmund place Durthfang in the hands of his daughter. Elvina smiled uncertainly before turning to Cerdic while he unbuckled his own blade and held it out to his fair-haired bride.

"I give you this sword to save for our sons to have and to use," he stammered as he passed the heavy blade across.

Clumsily Elvina accepted his sword before offering Durthfang in its place.

"To keep us safe, you must bear a blade. With this sword, keep safe our home."

Elvina's words, clearly heard within the enclosure, pierced Alfhildr to the heart. Her sword, a sword gifted to her by the gods themselves, was now lost to her forever.

Alfhildr's shoulders slumped at the finality of the gesture as unbidden tears welled up. Yet, even as her despair began to engulf her, a raucous caw pierced the air. Perched atop the great hall, a crow preened itself, then croaked loudly once more before taking wing above the royal couple.

A muttering started at once among the watching crowd. "'S not good, that," a large cook whispered excitedly to a nearby friend. "'Tis a bad omen, you know. 'A crow on the thatch, soon death lifts the latch' is what they say."

Alfhildr paid no attention to what others around her were whispering. Her eyes were fixed on the crow, avidly following Hoenir eastwards until the bird became a little more than a tiny black speck in the troubled grey sky. The message Hoenir had brought might well be one of death and violence, but that was something for which Alfhildr was ready, allowing the forlorn Dane to take comfort in the knowledge that her gods had not deserted her.

Across the enclosure, the wedding party, at last, retreated into the great hall, alerting Alfhildr that she needed to follow in order to serve her mistress.

Æ

There was a happy confusion and much laughter inside of the great hall as lords and thegns, who sat haphazardly crowded together at the long tables, took to toasting the newlyweds. In the distance, Alfhildr could see Elvina and Cerdic being ushered to the high table. She started to duck and weave through the milling rowdy bodies, ignoring the demands for ale while avoiding, as best she could, a sea of groping hands until a slim arm, laden with bracelets, barred her way.

"She has no need of *you*…you vile little wretch," Lady Æmma proclaimed brusquely as she addressed Alfhildr in the haughty, nasal tones she used out of habit. "It is now my responsibility to see that Princess Elvina is served by proper servants, Saxon ladies and girls, not a filthy barbarous Dane like you."

The viciousness of the woman's words struck Alfhildr like a slap in the face. She looked up to see that the soft smile on Lady Æmma's lips did not reach her eyes, which glittered challengingly at the fiery redhead.

"Go. Run back to your little huscarl, *slut*. Perhaps, if you are lucky, you can sneak out and let him take you again tonight."

Alfhildr seethed as the Saxon noblewoman taunted her through tight, smiling lips.

With clenched fists she readied herself to smash the smirk from the woman's face when, from the corner of her eye, she noticed two huscarls watching the exchange closely while a flash of satisfaction appeared on Lady Æmma's face. With icy certainty, Alfhildr realized she was being led into a trap, that even here, on this day, her enemies were seeking to isolate and humiliate Elvina. With a monstrous effort, Alfhildr bowed her head for a moment as her thoughts raced ahead. Only when she was ready did the Dane girl look up at the tall Saxon lady with a warm smile on her lips.

"Lady Æmma, it is so kind of you to offer," Alfhildr stated in a voice dripping with honey that was loud enough to carry to all the nearby tables. "But it wouldn't be right for a high-born lady such as yourself to clean up My Lady's sick. She's got a very delicate stomach, you know. She's especially prone to sudden bouts of violent sickness whenever something nasty comes close, spewing uncontrollably without the slightest warning. I dare say it would be best for you and your lovely gown if it were spared that awful fate, My Lady. But fear not. I'll be sure to let My Lady know of your kind words and concerns."

Without waiting, Alfhildr swiftly backed away from the vile woman, turned, and cut sharply between the tables in search of another route to her mistress, leaving a fuming and frustrated Lady Æmma in her wake.

Æ

Elvina flashed a brief look of relief when she saw Alfhildr appear behind her before turning her attention once more to Cerdic as the King hammered his fist on the table. Slowly the gathered throng quieted.

"My friends. Today, you have seen two houses join. United, they will support the kingdom of the East Saxons. Together, they will rain death upon our foes."

Men cheered the old King's words and pounded the heavy tables with their fists. Smiling broadly, the King held his hand up once more until they settled.

"Lord Osmund, Osmund the Bloody, has made his name slaughtering Danish filth. By this alliance, he will have the chance to do even more, for I name him my high marshal and leader of the Fyrd. Long may his blade run red with Dane blood!"

Again, the assembled lords and warriors gave voice to their approval, hammering and shouting, "Osmund! Osmund!"

Behind the new Princess, Alfhildr kept her eyes cast down at the beaten earth floor as she listened to the raucous mob. When she did steal a glance at the high table, she was surprised to see Lord Osmund himself frowning slightly at the King's decree. Having finished, the King nodded to a servant who stepped forward to hand him a small silver cup chased in gold with intricate designs inscribed around its rim. With a shaking hand, he held it up for a moment.

The watching throng cheered as he presented it to his son.

"The bryd-ale," they shouted as one. "Drink, drink, drink!"

Cerdic took the cup from his father's hand and raised it high for all to see, then sipped from it before passing it onto his new bride. Elvina smiled uncertainly at her husband as she received the delicate cup and carefully sipped from it to deafening applause. When the throng had finished cheering itself hoarse, servants who had been waiting off to the side hurried through the great hall laden with heaping platters and foaming jugs of ale.

Æ

As the wedding feast began in earnest, the leading lords presented themselves at the high table to pay their respects to the Prince and his new bride. Alfhildr watched like a hawk as Lord Wilfrid came forward and knelt before the King. After paying homage to his liege, Wilfrid turned to Elvina, leaning forward to murmur something in her ear.

Whatever he said to her caused Elvina to blush and shake her head rapidly before the Saxon lord withdrew with a satisfied smirk on his face. Behind Wilfrid came a procession of lesser lords and nobles to offer their obeisance to their king before cautiously greeting Elvina and Cerdic. The young Princess smiled uncertainly at all the well-wishers until one with a grey beard approached, causing her face to light up.

"Uncle Tofi!"

"Did you think I would miss this day, Your Highness?" the Saxon lord replied while gracing his niece with a smile. "Your father would never have forgiven me."

After leaning over the table and planting a quick peck on his niece's cheek, Lord Tofi stepped away from the table.

"Unfortunately, my dear, you must forgive me. I'm afraid I must leave now. The Ængles to the north are getting restless. The King wants me back there keeping an eye on them."

With that, the grizzled, old warrior bowed and headed swiftly from the hall followed by his retainers.

Next came Bowdyn, carefully picking his way forward until he too knelt before the King. The old man frowned as he looked down at the young huscarl.

"Tell me, Bowdyn, does the absence of Lord Godric tell me he is among those who oppose this union?"

Bowdyn's eyes snapped wide in shock.

"No, Sire! My Lord is, and always will be, loyal to his oath. He warmly welcomes this union, Sire."

"Then, why isn't he here?" The King's question was quiet but none who heard it could mistake the hidden menace.

Bowdyn looked up. For a moment, his eyes rested apologetically on Alfhildr before turning once more to answer his King.

"It is the Dane girl, Sire. While Godric has found it within his heart to forgive her, he could not set aside the memory of what she did. It would not sit well with his kinsmen if it became known he sat under the same roof with the woman who killed his brother."

"And you, Bowdyn?" the king asked. "You have no problem being in the same hall?"

"I owe her a life, Sire. And," he added as he rose from his knees, "I am grateful she so loyally serves your son's new bride. Only Lord Osmund's daughter could have tamed a Dane she-wolf as vicious as that one."

The King threw back his head and guffawed.

"Perhaps we should all send our daughters to trap Danish wolves."

Around him, his lords joined in his amusement while Alfhildr stared hard at the ground, her cheeks burned beet red as she willed herself to stay calm. Bowdyn had better have a damned good explanation for his words or she really would have his balls this time for sure, she swore to herself.

Æ

At length, the last of the nobles had presented his compliments, leaving them to enjoy the ale flowing freely in the hall. At the high table, Elvina sat uncomfortably between her father and Cerdic while the King made crude jokes about the wedding night. All was merry until a drunken roar and the clash of steel rang out from the back of the hall. Even as a servant rushed to the King's side, Lord Osmund was coming to his feet.

"My apologies, Sire. It looks as if one of my men has gotten into a fight. With your permission...?" Osmund paused as he waited for the King's approval.

"Indeed, Osmund, go. Lord Wilfrid's men do seem overly boisterous this evening.

Perhaps, a swift raid on the Danes would quell their thirst for battle, eh?"

The King laughed again and grabbed a chicken leg smothered in gravy as Osmund hastened to stop the fight. Still laughing, he rammed the leg in his mouth, ripped the flesh from the bone and swallowed. At first, no one noticed. All eyes were on Osmund at the far end of the hall. Then, Cerdic glanced nervously back to his father.

"Sire? Father? What's wrong?"

More turned their heads toward the King as his face mottled and his eyes stared desperately around. Alfhildr watched the old man in horror as he threw himself back in his chair, frantically rocking back and forward. Around him, servants and lords started to shout. One slave tried to offer his master a beaker of ale, but it was dashed from his hand by the struggling king. Another tried to thump the old man on his back only to be pulled away by Lord Wilfrid as he thrust his way to the king's side.

"Stand back! The king needs air. Stand clear," Wilfrid shouted, pushing another servant away from the king's side.

Even as she watched, Alfhildr saw the old man grasp pitifully at his son's tunic while Wilfrid stood by and did nothing. Then, with a final convulsive heave, he slumped forward, sending silver beakers and greasy platters crashing to the floor.

No one moved as a shocked silence fell like a shroud on the great hall. Lord Wilfrid once more bulled his way forward to lay his hand on the Old King's neck. He paused for a long moment, his eyes searching the throng before him. Alfhildr noted a tiny nod toward two huscarls: then, he raised his hand.

"The King is dead."

In the twinkling of an eye, pandemonium erupted as benches were pushed back and men began to shout as they pushed their way forward. When Alfhildr tried to spot the two men Wilfrid had signaled, both had vanished.

Æ

Thegns and lords jostled and snarled in the great hall. Some rushed to the high table to confirm the truth with their own eyes while others sought out friends and allies. Old grudges resurfaced as warriors recalled slights and insults and eyed old adversaries across the hall. Within this maelstrom, Elvina and Alfhildr were swiftly shoved to the side without regard for the Princess's rank or family. From the shadowed edge of the hall, Alfhildr took in everything as her eyes darted about seeking out friends and watching enemies. She sought out exits from the great hall and studied the guards posted at them.

She noted who fled and who stood his ground with his hand tightly clasped about the grip of his sword. But most of all, she watched Lord Wilfrid.

At the high table, Cerdic stood in a daze, staring down at the corpse of his father.

How could death turn such a great bear of a man into a pathetically crumpled heap? he wondered as someone tugged at his arm.

Cerdic ignored it until they tugged again.

"Sire? Sire, we must take the King's body from the hall," Lord Wilfrid implored as he stared into the shocked young man's eyes while tightly grasping his arm. "You must accompany your father."

Without tearing his eyes from his father's corpse, Cerdic nodded uncertainly. He had always accompanied his father. His father would know what to do. He stumbled forward with Wilfrid's hand still tight on his elbow.

Alfhildr turned her eyes away from the drama around the King's body once more. She searched in vain for Lord Osmund or Bowdyn. Then, she saw one of Wilfrid's huscarls returning, a man she had heard someone call Sigeberht. Behind him, a file of grim-faced spearmen followed, their shields clutched tight in their fists while the freshly whetted blades of their spears glistened bright in the smoky hall. Alfhildr's high voice pierced the din of the hall.

"King Cerdic, 'ware the spears!"

The shrill warning pierced the fog of confusion that left the young King bewildered.

His head jerked up at the sound of the woman's voice, one he mistook for his wife's.

"Elvina! I can't leave…"

As he turned back, he caught a spasm of rage on Lord Wilfrid's face.

"Lord Wilfrid, what are you…"

Wilfrid shoved the young King away from him as he growled to his advancing men.

"Kill me this puppy."

Æ

The first bright spear point thrust toward the young King as a snarling spearman lunged forward, hungry for the glory and reward from his liege. Without thought, Cerdic threw himself back, frantically scrambling for the wonderful new blade Elvina had presented him. Yet, even as he wrenched it clear of its scabbard, a young huscarl, by the name of Ædelric, threw himself forward with reckless abandon. With a quick thrust Cerdic had no hope of parrying, Ædelric's razor sharp sword sliced clean through Cerdic's chest, pinning the young king hard against one of the hall's wooden pillars. His upraised arm flew back, sending Durthfang flying from his nerveless fingers in a glittering arc through the smoky air. Deserted by his sword, the savage butchery of the young King began in earnest.

Alfhildr heard the shocked gasp and turned to see the ashen face of Elvina staring at the massacre.

"My Lady, we must flee. *Now!*"

Yet, even as she reached out to grasp her mistress, another hand snatched hold of Elvina's arm.

"My Lord, she's here!" Lady Æmma cried out in triumph as her nails bit deep into Elvina's flesh. "She's here with her witch."

Instinctively, Alfhildr's fist shot out, snapping the tall woman's head back with a sickening crunch. But Alfhildr didn't stop, for the bitter lessons of her childhood had taught her to hit and hit and hit until your foe could do nothing more than lie groaning senseless on the floor. She punched again, driving her fist deep into the belly of the arrogant spiteful cow. With a whoosh, Lady Æmma doubled over, at last letting go of Elvina's arm. Still, Alfhildr wasn't done with her. Reaching out, she grasped the coiled braids of the helpless noblewoman before jerking her knee up into the bitch's face. Only when she heard the crackle of cartilage did Alfhildr allow the bloodied and battered Saxon cow to fall away unconscious to the ground.

Unfortunately, Æmma's shout had done its damage. From the far side of the hall, a yell went up.

"There! Kill them. Kill the brood mare and her witch!"

Three of Wilfrid's spearmen took up their lord's challenge and sprang forward, making their way toward Elvina and Alfhildr, each eager to be the one who claimed the witch's head.

Osmund, too, had heard the shout and, with a roar, kicked aside the brawling warriors who had trapped him so far from his daughter. His sword sang from his sheath as he charged desperately toward the high table where Wilfrid's yelling spearmen closed on the two helpless girls. Yet, even as he ran, he knew he would be too late.

Æ

As the warriors closed on them, Alfhildr's eyes darted about in desperation for something, anything, she could use as a weapon. Then, in the shadows under the high table she spotted a glimmer of steel. Without hesitation, she threw herself forward.

The leading spearman grinned as he saw the red-headed witch scramble under the table. Hiding wasn't going to protect her.

"Come out little mouse," he called out jocularly. "Time to play."

But what emerged was no timid little mouse ready for the slaughter. What he found himself facing was a spitting, yelling vixen wielding a shining blade. The spearman thrust desperately, only to have his spear turned aside. Before he could recover from his surprise, Durthfang bit deep into his leg, slicing through his hamstrings and dropping him crippled to the floor. The last sight he beheld was that of a beautiful savage smile behind the glittering, bloody sword.

Having dispatched the first spearman, Alfhildr spun round to force back the remaining two, weaving a deadly, shimmering pattern with Durthfang in a desperate effort to keep their long spears at bay. Yet, even as the eager spearmen pressed forward, a piercing war cry went up as a sword buried itself deep in the nearest spearman's brain. After yanking his blade free of his first mark, Lord Osmund swung about, laying open the throat of the remaining attacker with the tip of his sword. Only then did he turn to the blood-spattered Alfhildr.

"Keep her safe, girl," was all he had time to shout before turning back to face the embattled hall.

Æ

In the turmoil of the old King's death, Bowdyn had been one of a number to slip from the hall. Swiftly, he had found his lieutenant, loitering as ordered near the inner gate to the royal enclosure.

"Guthric, muster the men here fast, full armed and ready. The old King is dead and Cerdic will need our blades if I'm not mistaken."

Without waiting for a reply, Bowdyn turned and quickly headed back toward the great hall. Yet, even as he approached, the first clash of steel on steel rang out. He drew his sword and started to run when a cry went up that turned his blood to ice.

"Kill the brood mare and her witch!"

In desperation, Bowdyn barged past the fleeing guests and sprinted to where he had last seen the Dane girl, determined to repay his debt of honor or die in the effort.

In the chaos of the hall, Bowdyn pushed and shoved his way toward the high table. One spearman tried to challenge his way, only to take a vicious cut across his arm that sent him mewling to the ground. Then, Bowdyn saw her. The defiant redhead was standing side by side with Lord Osmund protecting the Princess Elvina, Alfhildr's bloodied sword incongruous with the gown she wore.

When Bowdyn finally reached the embattled party, Osmund growled as he drew back his blade, causing Godric's loyal huscarl to swiftly draw back and throw opened his arms wide.

"Hold, My Lord. I mean no harm to you or yours. I have come to repay my debt to Alfhildr and keep my lord's pledge to the King."

Osmund stared suspiciously at the young huscarl for a moment before briefly raising his sword in acknowledgement.

"If your word is true, then join us, though I fear death will be your reward."

Then, his eyes darted back to the hall, assessing the chaos that had, moments before, been an occasion to celebrate his daughter's wedding and the crowning achievement of his life. He shook his head to clear such useless thoughts and gestured with his sword.

"Retreat. We must make for the doors."

Æ

Twice more lone spearmen spotted the small party and twice more blood flowed across the floor of the great hall. The first fell to Bowdyn, who savagely hacked the man's arm clean off at the shoulder. The second made the mistake of ignoring the young girl clutching a man's sword.

As they carefully backed toward the great doors, Alfhildr called out to Bowdyn.

"Can you get us to the gate of the burgh? I have a friend with horses waiting there."

Bowdyn laughed.

"My men are gathering at the inner gate even as we speak. With my brutes, I can cut you a path to the gates of hell."

Behind them, Osmund shook his head and stole a glance at his beloved daughter. He silently cursed himself for being so blind to the danger and failing to prepare for Wilfrid's treachery. Even in the midst of the chaos unfolding around him, he could not keep a deep sense of sorrow and bitterness from welling within as he realized he had failed his child, the one person he worshipped above all others, even over his own life.

At last, they reached the great doors and stood highlighted in the dying rays of the sunset. From within the hall, a desperate shout went up.

"Stop them! Kill them all."

In response, a dozen spearman sped to cut them down. Ahead, the enclosure was clear all the way to the open gate. Even so, Osmund knew they had no chance to reach its safety, not with Wilfrid's men nipping at their heels. In desperation, he grabbed Alfhildr by the arm and swung her toward him.

"Your word!"

"My Lord?"

"Your word as a warrior! Will you protect my daughter?"

When Alfhildr stared at the hardened old warrior's eyes and saw them filled with tears, she understood what he was about to do.

"To the death, My Lord. I swear to you before all the gods of Middle Earth, no harm will come to her."

Osmund smiled briefly at the flame-haired shield maiden.

"Then go. And let her know I loved her to the end."

Without another word, he turned, bellowed his war cry at the approaching warriors as he threw himself against them with his bloody sword held high above his head.

Æ

In the dying rays of the sun, Bowdyn and Alfhildr pulled Elvina along as they raced for the gate and the safety of Bowdyn's spears, while in the gathering mist beyond the burgh's ramparts, Osgar waited.

PART FOUR

SWORD ARM OF THE GODS

Chapter Fifteen
THE QUEST FOR SANCTUARY

Present Day England
"The Dig"

After spending a day with her grandmother, Elva was, as usual, at the dig site bright and early. Sarah found her friend humming to herself while she carefully scraped away at the heavy clay.

"I see at least one of us enjoyed their weekend," Sarah muttered as she took up a trowel and prepared for another long day.

"I did," the red-haired, graduate student murmured pleasantly as she concentrated on gently clearing away an awkward stone. Elva didn't bother telling her friend the reason she had enjoyed herself was because it had been quiet and peaceful with the others gone.

"Peter was disappointed that you didn't join us in London," Sarah informed Elva. "He spent the entire day Saturday moping about like a little boy whose mother has dragged him to the mall."

"If he knew he wasn't going to enjoy it, why did he go?"

"He thought you were going to come along for a change."

Stopping, Elva settled back onto her haunches and stared at her friend. "And what made him think that?"

Sarah shrugged. "Maybe someone told him you were thinking about it."

"And would that someone be you?"

Without looking over at her friend, Sarah once more responded with a shrug.

"Maybe."

Sighing, Elva shook her head.

"You know I'm not interested in that sort of thing."

Easing back on her heels as well, Sarah looked over at her friend.

"What sort of thing?"

Unable to meet Sarah's penetrating gaze, Elva averted her eyes.

"Dating boys," she muttered softly.

"And why not? What's wrong with boys?"

"Nothing, I guess."

"You guess?" Sarah asked cocking an eyebrow. "Don't you know?"

Having grown very uncomfortable with this conversation, Elva took up her digging where she'd left off.

"No, I don't. I've never found the time."

Had anyone else said that Sarah would have laughed. But coming from the shy redhead next to her, she suspected she was being sincere. Deciding to drop the subject, Sarah asked Elva what she'd done at her grandmother's.

"I asked her to tell me stories," came the reply.

"About?"
Once more Elva hesitated.
"Alfhildr," she finally muttered.
"Oh? Anything interesting?"
Before she was able to answer, Elva looked over at her fair-haired friend, once more wondering just how much she should share with her.

Æ

The Saga of the Quest for Sanctuary

In the flight from the burgh, her wings spread once more
Queen's maid to shield maiden, Alfhildr now soared,
Still dire to her foes with blade and with bow,
The sword arm of Justice, Alfhildr now rode.

With her God-given blade, Alfhildr regained,
And on horses and armor hidden nearby by cunning Osgar,
The fiery shield maiden led the lamb from the slaughter,
To where her skill and cunning could be unleashed.

Swift hunters now sought the queen and her friends
Traitors knew well the risk that she posed,
Whilst the crown was still slippery with the blood of the King
As she rode free in the forest, little sleep did they find.

Yet, the hunters soon found their soft royal prey
Had a hide of fine mail and a sting of sharp steel.
Shield maiden and hunter and huscarl made three,
The loyal companions of the future's bright queen.

Twisting and turning by brook and by track
To Osmund's strong holding they sought to return
Yet, foes were before them, home now was a trap,
So, onwards they struggled, no rest from their flight.

Deep into the forest Alfhildr now turned,
'Tween Saxon and Danelaw, the wild lands remained
As shield maiden led Elvina to her last safe domain,
The home of her birthing as Alfhildr the maid.

Hunters pressed close on the heels of the queen,
Cunning ambush, hard fighting the sole prize that they found.
Scarce few made it home, the rest in the woods
Were corpses left rotting for wolf and for crow.

Weary and wounded, the royal party did come,
To the home of the Old Woman, the last of her kind.
Succor and healing at last they had found
Yet, the Seeress foretold of the challenges ahead.

Æ

From her perch overlooking the well-trodden trail, Alfhildr counted six riders. As she did so, her heart sank. Like Bowdyn, she had hoped his men at arms would have been able to fight their way through Wilfrid's men and follow them. Failing that, they had counted on the chaos they had escaped from the night before to delay a determined and organized pursuit by those loyal to Wilfrid, the usurper. Both assumptions seemed to have been a serious miscalculation on their part, for the troop of six well-armed Saxons were riding hard on the same trail her own little party had used just hours before. Leading them was Sigeberht, a man Alfhildr recognized as being one of the old King's huscarl's who had rallied to Wilfrid's side during the massacre in the great hall. The only thing she could take any comfort in was that neither Sigeberht nor the men riding with him were wearing mail. No doubt, they either wanted to lessen their load in order to keep from tiring their mounts or they saw no need.

"We shall soon put that foolish notion to rest," Alfhildr snickered to herself.

Easing back from her concealed position, Alfhildr made her way back to where Dimma and Skadi were patiently awaiting her. Upon seeing her, the she-wolf came to her feet and wagged her tail by way of greeting. Though time was important, Alfhildr paused long enough to kneel down before her faithful companion and gently knead the wolf's neck with the tips of her fingers.

"Once more, we are going to need to make the hunters the hunted," she announced to the she-wolf. "Only this time don't you go running off," she mockingly admonished the wolf as it licked her face.

With that, the red-haired Dane mounted the grey mare, dug her heels into Dimma's flanks and took off at a gallop along a little-known path back to where she'd left the rest of her small party of fugitives, who were anything but helpless.

Æ

The sight of someone on the road ahead, kneeling behind a shield and holding a spear with nothing but the top of their helmet showing, caused Sigeberht to bring his horse to a sudden stop. Behind him, his troop of warriors struggled to rein in their own mounts in order to keep from colliding with their leader. Taking a moment to study the lone figure, the huscarl quickly determined it could only be the Dane witch.

Only a girl could hide her entire body behind a shield of that size, Sigeberht told himself.

Doing his best to keep his men from becoming aware of his own nervousness, he drew his sword before bringing his mount about in order to address his skittish followers who had come to the same conclusion he had.

"Today, you will have the honor of joining me in putting an end to the witch," he thundered in an effort to steel the others for the task at hand.

"Put your faith in God and follow me."

From off to one side, the sound of a crisp *twang* was the only warning Sigeberht had that they had blundered into an ambush. With an arrow in his side, the overconfident Saxon noble tumbled out of his saddle and onto the ground, out of the fight before it had even begun in earnest. Stunned, the others ignored their grievously wounded leader as they took to frantically looking about in a vain effort to see from which direction the attack was coming. When a second member of their party howled out in agony upon being pierced with an arrow, what little enthusiasm the remaining warriors had for their allotted task evaporated as they turned to flee. None of them were able to get very far as they discovered their line of retreat blocked by a pair of warriors attired in mail and standing astride the road behind them. Between them stood a snarling she-wolf, baring her teeth as the fur along her spine stood on end.

Once more, the Saxons reined in their mounts, turning this way and that, in an effort to find some way of avoiding the trap into which their leader had led them. It wasn't until a third member of their rapidly shrinking band was knocked from his saddle by an arrow that those who still could threw down their weapons and cried out for quarter.

Upon seeing Alfhildr emerge from where she had launched her attack, Elvina rose up from behind the shield. Though none of Sigeberht's men had gotten close enough to strike a single blow, the young queen shook from the same nervous excitement most novices experience at the conclusion of their first battle. That, as well as the weight of the mail that Alfhildr had insisted she wear, left her exhausted. Leaning heavily on the spear with which the Saxon huntsman named Osgar had armed her, Elvina watched as her three traveling companions and protectors herded together the men who had survived the ambush that Alfhildr had so skillfully laid. Only when she saw that Sigeberht was stirring did she gather herself up and make for where he had fallen, carefully watching her step least she trip over the mud splattered hem of her blue wedding gown.

Bowdyn was already there when Elvina reached the spot where the stricken huscarl lay on his back.

"What of my father," she demanded, looking down at the man who had led the charge in the great hall the night before.

Ignoring the pain caused by Alfhildr's arrow, a vicious grin lit up Sigeberht's face as he gazed up at a girl who would never be his queen.

"Your dog of a father died yelping and howling like the pathetic shit he was," he snarled. "He was always worthless when it came to fighting real men in a fair fight."

What Elvina did next shocked Alfhildr, stunned Bowdyn and Osgar, and caused the Saxons who had surrendered to wail. Before anyone could lift a hand to stop her, the enraged Saxon girl grasped her spear in both hands, twirled it about, and with all her might drove the spear's tip into Sigeberht's groin. Ignoring his high-pitched shriek, Elvina withdrew the spear, holding it over the writhing nobleman for but a moment.

"Scream, you bastard! *Scream!*" she howled viciously as she once more drove the spear into the prostrate huscarl.

Amid howls that were anything but human, Sigeberht desperately grasped the end of the spear with both hands while thrashing in agony.

"Scream like the swine you are," Elvina yelled once more as she gave the spear a violent twist, first to the left, then right.

Only when she withdrew the bloody tip a second time and was preparing to strike again did someone finally stop her. Stepping up, Bowdyn grasped the spear's shaft, staying the young queen's next thrust. When Elvina looked over her shoulder at him, he ignored the anger in her eyes.

"Your highness. He has suffered enough."

For the briefest of moments, Elvina glared at the huscarl. Then, without warning, her fury gave way to tears. Releasing her grip on the spear, she pivoted about and fled to where their horses were tethered. After tossing aside the spear, Bowdyn began to follow but was stopped by Alfhildr.

"Leave her go," the Dane girl murmured. "A queen should be allowed to weep in private."

Having come to trust Alfhildr's judgment, Bowdyn turned instead to dispatching the still whimpering Sigeberht before walking over to where Osgar and Skadi were guarding the pair who had surrendered. Any doubts that he had entertained about following the Dane girl or pledging his allegiance to what he had once mistaken to be a frail, young girl, who had been denied her throne before she had been afforded an opportunity to be seated upon it, had been erased by what he had just witnessed. Though he did not yet know how Godric would go, Bowdyn had little doubt he would follow Elvina to the very gates of hell itself, provided Alfhildr was at his side.

Æ

It wasn't until early evening, just as the light was beginning to fade, that Alfhildr decided she had given Elvina ample time to grieve in private. Leaving Bowdyn and Osgar to finish preparing camp, Alfhildr went over to where the Saxon girl sat alone under an old oak with her back to the others. With her arms wrapped tightly about her drawn up legs, Elvina was gazing down at the ground before her. Without a word, Alfhildr knelt down in front of her. Reaching out, she placed a hand over one of Elvina's.

"It's getting dark and you're cold. You need to come over to the fire."

Looking up, the young Saxon queen gazed searchingly into Alfhildr's eyes.

"Do you suppose what the priests say is true?" she asked. "Is there a place in heaven for a man like my father?"

While she was familiar with some aspects of the Christian faith, Alfhildr wasn't confident enough to answer Elvina's question, not directly. Instead, she drew upon what she knew best in an effort to put her friend and mistress' mind at ease.

"I have been taught to believe that when a warrior, such as your father, dies an honorable death, the Valkyrie collect him up from the battlefield and take him to Valhalla. There he sits with Odin himself and other worthy warriors to await *Ragnarök*, the final struggle, one I expect is no different than what your priests call judgment day. So yes," Alfhildr concluded, trying to be as positive as she could be, "I expect your father is in heaven."

Suddenly, Elvina reached out with both of her hands and grasped the one Alfhildr had placed upon hers. Despite the gathering darkness, the young Dane girl could see the desperation in the young queen's eyes.

"You don't think he died as Sigeberht said he did, do you?"

Having seen far too many good men die, Alfhildr knew even the strongest and most valiant warrior sometimes found his death wound too painful to endure in a becoming manner. For all his defiance and pride, even Sigeberht could not keep from crying out like a wounded animal. Still, the truth did not matter at the moment. All that was important was comforting the young girl who had saved her from a horrible end, a girl who Alfhildr had come to believe was the key to fulfilling the task her gods had allotted to her. So, she returned Elvina's desperate gaze with a brave little smile as she clutched the girl's hands tightly.

"Your father died a valiant and noble death, sacrificing his life to ensure your safety."

Then, rising up off the ground without letting go of Elvina's hands, Alfhildr pulled the Saxon queen to her feet.

"His task here in Middle Earth is finished.

Yours is only beginning. I expect there are many challenges ahead for which we must be ready. But before we can tend to them, we must first eat and rest."

When Alfhildr went to pull her hands away, Elvina refused to let them go.

"Tonight, when we lay down to sleep, will you sleep with your wolf?" she asked hesitantly.

"Yes, of course. As a guard, Skadi is better than a troop of huscarls," Alfhildr replied with a hint of pride in her voice. "She is warm as well."

Looking down, Elvina shrugged.

"Do you think she would mind if maybe, perhaps…"

The Saxon girl made no effort to hide the fact that she was frightened. Alfhildr knew she had good reason to be. While she was able to take everything that was happening in her stride, from being pursued by armed soldiers and riding hard all day to living off the land, this was all new to the fair-haired young girl who had been bred to be a queen. She needed time as well as a gentle hand to guide her through the coming days.

Once more, the red-haired Dane girl found herself in the position of protecting a servant of a god different than hers. As she had once done for a monk, Alfhildr would now do for a queen. Smiling, she gently squeezed the hands of her Saxon friend.

"I am sure the two of us can share a blanket as well as a wolf."

Æ

In the morning, when Alfhildr was satisfied that Elvina was over the worst of her grieving, she took the young Saxon girl down to a nearby stream while Bowdyn and Osgar prepared the animals for the day's ride. It would be a difficult one since she and the Saxon huscarl had decided it would be best if they stayed off of the main roads and trails and instead took to the hidden paths that she and Osgar had often used.

"Few know these forests as well as Osgar," Alfhildr assured Bowdyn. "Besides being hesitant to follow us along paths with which they are unfamiliar, after yesterday's ambush and the wild stories I expect those who survived will surely spread, anyone else sent after us will be cautious."

Finding no grounds upon which to disagree, Bowdyn gave his assent.

At the stream, after helping Elvina wash away the last of Sigeberht's dried blood from her hands and face, Alfhildr handed her trousers and a tunic.

"Where did these come from?" Elvina asked as she held the trousers out at arms-length in order to examine them. "Did Osgar pack them away as well?"

Alfhildr chuckled. "No. I am sorry to say I never thought we would have to flee as we did. Some of Sigeberht's men were kind enough to offer their clothing to your cause."

"They what?"

"They gave up their clothing," Alfhildr replied as she took to pulling her own mud-stained gown up over her head in order to don the trousers and tunic she would wear for the rest of their journey.

"They were quite willing to part with them seeing as how our two stalwart companions were holding a sword at their throats when I insisted that they strip."

Unable to help herself, Elvina's eyes grew large.

"Did you watch as they undressed?"

Alfhildr had turned her back while the Saxons had been shedding their clothing, behavior that gave both Bowdyn and Osgar something to laugh about. Naturally, Alfhildr didn't tell Elvina this, taking advantage of this opportunity to give her friend something to laugh about as well. Furrowing her brow, Alfhildr regarded Elvina as if she had just heard the silliest question imaginable.

"Of course I did. Why?"

Flummoxed, Elvina just stared at the Dane girl. Unable to think of anything appropriate to say, she quickly changed the subject by asking if she could go without wearing Alfhildr's mail.

"No, you may not," Alfhildr replied in a mockingly haughty tone.

"But it is heavy," Elvina whined. "Besides, should we run into more of Wilfrid's men, you will need it more than I do."

When she saw Alfhildr about to object, Elvina drew herself up and addressed her in a manner she had often used when ordering about her father's servants.

"I insist *you* wear it."

Having expected the young queen to eventually resort to her well-honed methods of dealing with people, Alfhildr patiently explained it would be a great hindrance if she did.

"I will be scouting all day. Should I run into trouble, speed will be my armor. Even if Skadi and I do not see anything, the burden of carrying the mail about all day will wear my poor mount out, a horse that will have to travel twice as far as yours. Besides," Alfhildr added with a twinkle in her eye, "you are no longer my queen, or mistress, so save your regal manner of dealing with people for those who care about such things."

"Oh? If I am not your queen, or mistress, what am I to you?" Elvina replied, doing her best to sound as if she were offended, but failing miserably.

"You are my friend, now and until my dying breath."

Æ

Before splitting off with Skadi and doubling back to a point from which she could watch to see if they were being followed, Alfhildr took Bowdyn aside.

"As you ride with Elvina today tell her stories."

Frowning, the huscarl looked at Alfhildr as if she were mad. Ignoring his expression, she explained.

"Though she is a queen, she is still very much a young girl, one who has not only lost her father but is facing an uncertain future filled with challenges that would give pause to the wisest king. It would not be wise to allow her to dwell upon what lies ahead."

When she saw a glimmer of understanding in Bowdyn's eyes, Alfhildr smiled, but only for a second as she tried to make it appear as if she were being deadly serious.

"Do not let anything happen to my friend while I am gone, Saxon. Otherwise, I will deal with you as I should have for what you said the other night in the King's great hall."

"You will find you will have a more difficult task if you try," Bowdyn replied before stepping back and looking down at his long mail shirt that came down to mid-calf.

"As you can see, I took your advice."

Æ

It quickly became clear to Alfhildr that Sigeberht's troop had not been the only one Wilfrid had dispatched to hunt down Elvina and snuff out the only person who could rally those nobles who were opposed to his claim to the crown. Riding hard all day, she made a wide sweep around the path along which Osgar was taking the balance of her small party of fugitives, going from behind to well out in front of it. Though she did not see any of Wilfrid's men, the signs of many well-shod horses being ridden hard and in the direction that they would need to head were enough to tell Alfhildr that their hope of making it without a fight to Osmund's keep or that belonging to Elvina's Uncle Tofi were nil. Wishing to avoid battle if possible, Alfhildr decided it would be best if they took Elvina to a safe haven where she could stay while the rest of them scattered in search of allies, a place Wilfrid would never think of looking for her. With that thought in mind, Alfhildr tugged at Dimma's reins and turned her mount toward the spot where she and Osgar had agreed to spend the night.

Æ

It was dark before Alfhildr finally reached the hidden dell she and Osgar had often used in the past for a camp. Ever so quietly, she made her way to where she could see her traveling companions while remaining hidden among the trees. A self-satisfied smile crept across Alfhildr's face when she saw Elvina sitting next to Bowdyn, listening with rapt attention as he told her of his adventures with Godric. Alfhildr was about to advance into the camp when Skadi began to growl.

While doing her best to act as if she had not been taken by surprise, Alfhildr turned to face Osgar who was standing several feet behind her with his sword drawn.

"That cursed wolf of yours is better than a troop of guards," he muttered as he sheathed his sword before coming up next to her. "How is it that miserable lout who took you managed to get past her?" Osgar asked.

Embarrassed, Alfhildr looked down at the ground.

"Perhaps, one day, when we are both old and very drunk, I will tell you. At the moment, we have much we need to discuss."

Osgar drew himself up as he stretched out his hand to allow Skadi to lick the grease of a recently slain and roasted stag from it.

"First, you and this pet of yours will eat. Then, we talk," the Saxon huntsman announced in a manner that told Alfhildr he would tolerate no argument from her.

Suddenly realizing she had not eaten all day and suspecting Skadi was just as famished as she was, Alfhildr offered no resistance. With Osgar at her side and to the joyous shrieks of a friend who was glad to see she had returned safely, Alfhildr made her way toward the warm and inviting fire.

Æ

Too hungry to care about the way Elvina stared at her disapprovingly, Alfhildr continued to use her teeth to tear off great chunks of meat from the portion Osgar had handed her. It was the face Bowdyn kept making as she spoke of what she had come across during her day's ride that concerned her. She could tell he was worried. She just couldn't tell what it was that was bothering him. It wasn't until Alfhildr had concluded that he spoke, after taking a few minutes to mull over what he had just heard. As he did so, he continuously glanced over to where Elvina was seated.

"It is as we feared. Wilfrid believes those who disapprove of what he did will rise up against him, provided they find someone around whom they can rally, either someone who they respect or…"

When he didn't continue, Elvina looked away, knowing full well what the huscarl was hinting at. Alfhildr, never having fully grasped the intricacies of Saxon politics, looked back and forth between Bowdyn and Elvina.

"Or what?" she finally asked.

Drawing herself up, Elvina took a deep breath.

"Or they find someone with a legitimate claim to the throne," she whispered.

"That would be you," Alfhildr blurted out.

"Perhaps," Bowdyn interjected.

"But she was married to Cerdic, your king's only son and the rightful heir to the throne," Alfhildr stated as she tried to verbally navigate her way through the confusing discussion.

"Married, yes," Bowdyn murmured. "But it was not consummated. Because it wasn't, Wilfrid will be able to argue that Elvina has no legitimate claim to the throne."

"But neither does he. Or does he?" Alfhildr asked as she became even more confused.

"He does not. However, since the old king's line has been wiped out, the throne goes to whoever can grab it and keep it. At the moment, that's Wilfrid. To ensure no one challenges him, he needs to eliminate anyone who could be used to rally around by those of us who despise him."

Turning, Alfhildr regarded Elvina. For her part, the young Saxon girl had been listening to this exchange in silence. Though she was doing her best to keep up a brave front, Alfhildr knew her well enough to appreciate that she was barely holding herself together. Still reeling from the loss of her father, Elvina now had to deal with the burden of being hunted like an animal. Alfhildr knew what she would need to do. She simply did not know how to go about it.

When it came to dealing with people, she was out of her depths. There was no need to be subtle or circumspect when hunting or fighting. One simply waded into their enemy or gave chase to the prey they had set their sights on until they had run it to ground. Dealing with an emotionally distraught young girl, caught up in a web of politics that she didn't quite understand, was something entirely different. It required a careful balance of straight-forward, no nonsense solutions tempered by the same delicate touch she had seen Elvina use when embroidering an intricate pattern on a garment. Whether she would be up to this unfamiliar challenge was something about which Alfhildr was unsure.

Glancing over at Bowdyn, she stared into his eyes before speaking.

"It might not be a bad idea if you and Osgar gather up some more wood for the fire before we turn in," she stated in a manner that made it clear her suggestion was more than a suggestion.

Understanding what the Dane girl was saying, Bowdyn came to his feet as did Osgar.

"I believe you are right. We will be back soon."

When she knew they were well out of earshot, Elvina looked over at Alfhildr.

"I can't do this," the Saxon queen stated flatly.

"You have no choice," Alfhildr shot back. "To turn your back on this challenge without even trying would waste your father's sacrifice. He died not only protecting you, he died defending what he thought was right and proper."

Though Alfhildr had no idea if the last part of her statement was true, it didn't matter. In order to rally the young Saxon girl to the task she believed had been handed down to them by the gods, Alfhildr needed to make it sound as if it was.

"It is now up to you to find the strength and courage to make his sacrifice something more than a heroic gesture. You need to be the queen he spent a lifetime preparing you to be."

"But how?"

The quiver in Elvina's voice when she asked that question told Alfhildr this was not the time to go into details. Instead, the Dane girl brought her arms above her head and stretched, cat-like.

"First, we settle in for the night and rest. In the morning, when our heads are clear, perhaps we will be better able to see our way forward."

Then, coming to her feet, she looked down at the woman who she believed held the key to fulfilling the Old Woman's prophecy, a woman who, at the moment, was a queen in name only.

"While I tend to my horse, it would help if you make yourself useful by rolling out our bedding."

Glad to have something to do, Elvina took up her assigned task as Alfhildr wandered over to where Dimma was waiting, pleased with herself for managing to sidestep an awkward moment while keeping her friend from losing hope.

Æ

Over the next few days, Wilfrid proved he was no fool as Alfhildr came across clear signs that told her groups of mounted men were prowling the disputed region separating Saxon lands from Dane holdings. For the most part, the little party of fugitives managed to steer clear of their pursuers by guile, deception, and hard riding. When that proved impossible, Alfhildr would hang back, using her skills with the bow to empty Saxon saddles and give those who survived a good reason to continue on with greater care.

While doing so, the Dane girl would always single out the leader of these small bands of hunters, not only to provide those who were nothing more than followers an excellent excuse for turning back but also as a means of thinning the ranks of men qualified to serve as lieutenant's in Wilfrid's army when it came time to raise their own and seek battle. Whether the young Saxon queen would be able to find enough nobles loyal to her or at least displeased with Wilfrid was a question Bowdyn could not answer. At the moment, such things were of little importance. Reaching a safe haven where they could hide Elvina was all that mattered.

Throughout their quest for sanctuary, Godric's most trusted huscarl made sure he was never far from Elvina, something for which Alfhildr was thankful. Not only would he need to protect the young queen if they found themselves unable to avoid Wilfrid's patrols, the stories with which he regaled the young Saxon queen kept her mind off the challenges that awaited her in the not so distant future. It was only when she sidled up next to Alfhildr, while they were watering their horses, and opened a whispered conversation with her that she became aware there was more on Elvina's mind than the crisis at hand.

"What do you think of Bowdyn?" she asked doing her best to make her question sound innocent.

Looking up from the stream from which Dimma was drinking, Alfhildr glanced over her shoulder to where the Saxon huscarl was tending to his mount while Osgar stood watch.

"Bowdyn is a good fighter."

"Yes," Elvina agreed shyly. "I can see that. But what do you think of him as a man?"

"He is an honorable man, one whose word can be trusted. He is the sort of man I would want to have on my right in a shield wall."

Becoming somewhat exasperated that her friend was not quite understanding what she was asking, Elvina sighed.

"Yes, yes. I expect that is all true. But what do you think of him as, well, as someone a woman would wish to be with, to marry?"

Finally realizing what the young Saxon girl was asking, Alfhildr once more looked over at Bowdyn to study him. After a long pause, she replied without looking back at her friend.

"I expect if I were a woman, I would want just such a man."

Only when the young Dane turned back and saw the confusion on Elvina's face did Alfhildr realize what she had just said.

Æ

When she saw the other three halted just short of the ford, as if they were waiting for her, Alfhildr dug her heels into Dimma's flanks.

"What are you holding back for?" she shouted as she closed on them. "Wilfrid's men are not far behind me."

Bowdyn brought his mount about.

"They hold the ford," he snapped. "The other party you were tracking yesterday has doubled back."

Reining in Dimma, Alfhildr peered ahead as if trying to see what the Saxon huscarl was talking about before looking back over her shoulder.

"There were only six of them, far less than the band to our rear," she announced. "We stand a better chance of fighting our way across the ford than waiting to be caught between the two."

Bowdyn nodded. "Agreed. I will stay here and hold off those behind us for as long as I can. You and Osgar take the queen across the ford."

When Alfhildr saw Elvina's concerned expression, she shook her head.

"No! You stay with your queen. She will be in need of your services when it comes time to rally the Saxon nobles. I will hold back those coming on."

Before Bowdyn could object, Alfhildr brought Dimma about and dug her heels into the horse's flanks, calling out over her shoulder as she galloped off.

"No more talk! Go!"

There was no time to scout about for a place to hide. There was barely enough time to dismount and settle herself down for the task at hand before the lead rider came around the bend in the trail not more than a spear's throw from where she stood. The man barely had enough time to appreciate that he was in trouble before an arrow struck him square in the chest, sending him backward out of the saddle. The two men behind him attempted to rein in their mounts but were also unhorsed with an arrow before they could do much of anything.

There followed a momentary lull during which Alfhildr imagined those who had yet to round the bend arguing over what to do. While they hesitated, Alfhildr found herself debating how long she should stay where she was. Waiting too long would allow them to dismount and circle around her by going through the woods. She had just about decided that she had waited long enough when she heard a voice call out, followed by a chorus of cheering. They were going to charge her.

As the feeling of pounding hoofs shook the ground beneath her feet, Alfhildr took in deep, well-measured breaths as she struggled to steady herself. With deadly deliberateness, she brought her bow up, drew back the bowstring, and waited. In those few seconds, she imagined she could hear her own heart beating as she focused her entire attention on where the tip of her arrow was aimed.

Then, he was there, a mounted thegn, standing upright in his stirrups as he rounded the bend. As she had done to his companions, Alfhildr knocked him from his saddle with a well-aimed shot. Behind him, his companions ignored his fate, pressing forward as the riderless horse continued on with the others, dragging its stricken master behind it.

Another arrow sent a second Saxon down, then a third. And still they came on.

Tossing aside her bow, Alfhildr drew her sword, bringing it up to the high guard. She waited until the very last second before stepping back off the trail, dropping to a knee, and bringing her sword around in a great sweeping arch just above the ground, striking the front legs of the lead rider's horse just below its knees. With an ear shattering shriek, the horse went down, violently throwing its rider over its head. Without rising up, Alfhildr thrust her sword up into the exposed flank of the next horse as it galloped by.

With two riders and their mounts down and flailing madly in their death throes, the remaining Saxons milled about, trying to make sense of what was happening. In this confusion, Alfhildr sprang to her feet, letting out a battle cry that sent a shiver down the spines of the surviving Saxons. Having had their fill of this carnage and, having no stomach for dealing with the vicious Dane witch on their own, they wheeled their mounts about and fled.

Alfhildr wasted no time dispatching the wounded Saxons. Content to leave their fates in the merciful hands of their beloved Christ, she snatched up her bow, ran to where Dimma was, and quickly pulled herself up into her saddle. Driving hard, she splashed across the ford ignoring the sight of a dead Saxon floating face down in the river. Upon leaving the river, she heard the ring of steel on steel just ahead. The others were still engaged. Once more, Alfhildr dug her heels into Dimma's flanks as she rushed to the sound of a desperate struggle.

The scene Alfhildr burst onto caused her heart to leap up into her throat. Bowdyn was doing his best to hold back one opponent while desperately trying to come to the aid of Elvina who was struggling to keep a second Saxon warrior at bay. Osgar had his hands full dealing with two men, both of whom were proving to be more than a match for her old companion. Even Skadi was doing what she could, snapping wildly at a fifth Saxon who was being prevented from coming to the aid of his companions by his fear of the she-wolf. Alfhildr didn't waste any time debating which way to turn. Without having to think about it, she made for Elvina.

Once more, the young Dane girl let out a war cry that cut through animal and human alike, causing everyone to all but stop what they had been doing and turn toward its source. The Saxon, who had been pressing home his attacks on Elvina, looked up at the enraged, red-haired fury as she rode him down. He had no opportunity to react before a single, quick swing of Alfhildr's fearsome blade laid open his exposed back.

Osgar also took advantage of the way his foes' attention had been diverted, dispatching one of his tormentors with a quick thrust of his spear before turning his full attention to the other. Bowdyn was not so lucky. The warrior, who he had been keeping at arm's length while turning from time to time to assist Elvina, recovered quicker than he did. Before Bowdyn could pull back and clear of the Saxon's blade, its tip sliced neatly along the huscarl's exposed calf just below the point where his mail shirt ended.

Leaping down from her saddle, Alfhildr rushed to Bowdyn's aid, forgetting about the Saxon Skadi had been keeping at bay. That oversight cost her dearly as she felt the sting of a blade slice across her upper arm. Instinctively, she pulled away before turning to parry a follow-on strike from her new foe.

The Saxon, who had been facing Bowdyn, was not about to let his momentary advantage slip away. Stepping up, he brought his sword up over his head in preparation to deliver a killing blow, stopping only when the air once more reverberated with the shrilled cry of a female voice. Only this time, it was not Alfhildr's.

"*Nooooo!*" was all Elvina sang out as she all but leapt over Bowdyn in order to thrust her sword into the Saxon's chest. Enraged, she held nothing back, running Wilfrid's man through until the sword's guard was resting against his ribs.

Upon seeing this, the Saxon facing Osgar threw down his sword and dropped to his knees, crying out for quarter. Osgar gave him none. By the time Alfhildr had managed to fend off her attacker and rush to Elvina's side, the bloody clearing had all but fallen silent. Only the sound of Skadi's vicious snarling, as she ripped out the throat of the Saxon who had wounded her mistress, could be heard.

Æ

Osgar stared at the blade of the dagger he held in the fire, watching as it began to glow red. Alfhildr was watching it as well, knowing full well what was coming.

Neither said a word. Across from them, Bowdyn was laying on his stomach with his wounded leg resting on Elvina's lap. Try as she might, the Saxon queen found she could not abide by Bowdyn's advice and look upon what she was doing as no different than mending a tear in an article of clothing. She knew her attempts to stitch up the wound on his calf was hurting the valiant huscarl who had put himself in harm's way to protect her, an effort that had nearly cost him his life. Only this thought and the need to be as strong as her companions had allowed Elvina to set aside any reservations she had and do everything she could for a man who was everything Cerdic could never have been.

When he judged the dagger's blade to be hot enough, Osgar looked over at Alfhildr.

"Are you ready?"

Unable to speak due to the strip of leather she held clamped between her teeth, Alfhildr merely nodded.

Withdrawing the dagger from the fire, Osgar shifted about until he was facing her.

"Place your hand in my armpit."

Upon doing so, Osgar clamped his arm down tightly, locking Alfhildr's outstretched arm securely against the side of his chest. Reaching up with the hand of the arm he was using to steady Alfhildr's wounded arm, he grasped her elbow.

"Are you ready?" he quietly asked once more looking up into her face.

After screwing her eyes shut tight, Alfhildr again nodded. With that, Osgar laid the dagger's glowing blade across the gash in Alfhildr's upper arm.

From where she sat, Elvina watched as her friend's body stiffened and her face betrayed the agony she felt as the huntsman attempted to cauterize Alfhildr's wound. The hiss of hot steel on skin and the smell of burning flesh mingled with the blood from Bowdyn's wound that left her fingers sticky, causing the young Saxon queen's stomach to turn. Only the courage her companions had shown earlier that day and, again, as they were having their wounds tended, kept her from breaking down in tears.

Across from her, Alfhildr found that she was unable to do the same. When he was satisfied that he had succeeded in sealing up the wound, Osgar removed the dagger's blade from the young Dane girl's arm and looked up into her face. As necessary as it had been, it still broke the grizzled huntsman's heart to know he had been the cause of so much pain to a girl he had come to cherish as if she were his own daughter. Tossing aside the dagger, he drew Alfhildr into his arms. Placing her head against his chest, he softly stroked her long, red hair as he cooed reassuringly.

"It's done, little one. Cry. Cry and let your tears wash away your pain. You have no need to be brave with us. You are among friends."

For the first time in a very long time, Alfhildr let herself go. Weeping, she allowed herself to be cuddled in Osgar's arms. And though she knew there were still many challenges ahead, for a brief moment, there in the arms of a man, she relished a sense of security she had never felt before.

Æ

Long before they came into sight, the Old Woman knew they were approaching. Looking up from the goats she had been feeding, she watched as the exhausted and bloodied fugitives silently rode into the clearing before her hovel. Gazing up into Alfhildr's eyes, she smiled.

"I have been expecting you."

Chapter Sixteen
A PAUSE, A SECRET, A PLEDGE

Present Day England
"The Dig"

The sound of Professor Bannon's battered old Land Rover caused Elva to look up from what she had been doing. While wiping the sweat from her brow, she watched as he climbed out, grasping a folder in his hand. Upon spotting Elva, he waved for her to join him.

"We've got something of a mystery here," Bannon called out, while holding the folder up, once she was close enough to hear him.

"The analyses of the bits of clothing we were able to recover from the garment our little warrior was wearing under her amour left the lads back home scratching their heads," Bannon confessed as he cast a wary eye at Elva.

By now, the young, red-haired graduate student was used to the circumspect manner with which Bannon sounded her out whenever he or any of the other students stumbled upon something that puzzled them. She followed her professor into the shade of the tarpaulin that they used for shelter and where samples recovered from the dig were initially brought to be cleaned, sorted, and catalogued. Elva had a hunch that she already knew what was bothering her mentor.

"The clothing worn under the rather ornate armor turns out to have been wool, undyed, and quite coarse," Bannon informed Elva as he opened the file and showed her.

"It's not the sort of garment in which one would expect a personage who had been honored with an elaborate funeral to be buried."

Elva shrugged before taking a long sip of bottled water.

"Perhaps, the garment had a particular significance to Alfhildr," she ventured when she was done drinking. "It might have been a gift given to her by a humble kinsman, a grateful ceorl she had once saved or something Alfhildr owned before she became a legend."

Looking at his prized student over his glasses, Bannon grunted.

"Elva, you know we have yet to establish with any degree of certainty that this is Alfhildr."

Having gone over this same argument time and time again, Elva made no effort to contain the frustration she felt every time she heard it.

"Well, just who in the bloody hell else could it be?"

After a moment of silence, during which the professor stared at his student while she caught herself, he returned to the matter at hand.

"Based on the amount of material we were able to recover as well as where it was located when we did, it would seem the tunic she wore was rather long."

"Perhaps it wasn't a tunic," Elva muttered as she set aside her bottle of water and took the report from Bannon's hands to study it more closely. "Perhaps it was something of far greater significance to Alfhildr."

Rather than attempting to point out, once more, to his protégé that they had no conclusive evidence that the remains they had unearthed were those of the legendary warrior, Bannon held back, for even he was beginning to suspect, as many of his students were, that the shy, red-haired graduate student they'd all come to rely on just might be right.

Æ

England
1012 AD

"Do you know why an oath is so important to us and why those who break them are shunned as they are?" the grandmother asked the boy at her side.

"Because God hates oath breakers," the boy replied without hesitation.

"Yes, yes, that is true," the old woman nodded as they continued on their weary journey.

"But that is only one of the reasons. The real reason is that a pledge made by one person to another is the glue that holds them together. It is like the oath a man and a woman exchange when they marry. With nothing more than their words, they bind themselves, one to the other, here and forever. To break an oath is to betray the other."

"Like the usurper did," the boy intoned.

The grandmother nodded. "Yes, like the usurper. A person who breaks their oath cannot be trusted. Would you wish to stand in the shield wall next to a kinsman who had not honored the oaths he gave in the past?"

The boys shook his head. "No, never."

"Why not?"

Once more the boy hesitated as he wondered why his grandmother was asking him such an obvious question.

"Well, if a man broke his word bond once, he could very well do so again. In battle, a warrior who cannot be trusted is dangerous."

"Our village and families are no different than a linked shield wall," the old woman explained. "Warriors derive their strength not only from their weapons and armor, but from the trust they place in the man to their left and right. For if we do not trust those around us, even the slightest challenge will undo us all."

As the boy took all this in, a thought occurred to him. "Grandma?"

"Yes?"

"When we get to where we are going, promise me you will stay with me."

The boy's request, as simple as it was innocent, brought a tear to the old woman's eye.

"Yes," she whispered as she gave her grandchild's hand a squeeze. "I will not leave your side. I promise."

Æ

When the Old Woman woke just after dawn and saw Alfhildr's bedroll was empty, she knew exactly where the young Dane girl was. After adding fresh wood to the fire in the hearth, she pulled a cloak about her shoulders and made her way toward the door, taking care not to wake any of the Saxons. Just outside the entrance, the Old Woman paused to take in a lungful of crisp, clean, morning air before going any further.

As expected, she found Alfhildr standing in the center of the small enclosure where the goats were kept. What did surprise the Old Woman was the girl was wearing the rough spun gown she had once so stridently refused. Any thought of mentioning this was dismissed out of hand as the Old Woman suspected there were other, more important matters the two needed to discuss in private.

Familiar with the Old Woman's footfalls, Alfhildr didn't need to look about to know who was coming up behind her.

"I see the old billy is gone," she muttered softly.

"Yes," the Old Woman replied nodding her head sadly as she reached out and greeted her beloved goats by patting them on their heads.

"He left us this past winter, but not before ensuring his line would go on."

A smile brightened Alfhildr's face as she looked up from what she was doing at a pair of young goats who were new to her.

"The grey male looks like his father."

"And what of you, child?"

Unsure what she was asking, Alfhildr glanced over her shoulder. "What about me?"

"Have you any issue?"

Wide-eyed, the young, red-haired girl spun about and stared at the Old Woman.

"You mean have I given birth? No! Of course not!"

"Why of course not? Both of the Saxon males who have been traveling with you seem to treat you as if you were kin. Either would be a suitable match for a girl such as yourself."

In a vain effort to hide her crimson cheeks, Alfhildr went back to feeding the goats.

"How can there be a match for someone like me when even I don't know what I am," she muttered.

"So, you still refuse to accept your lot in life."

"But I have," Alfhildr countered without looking back. "It was because I have willingly given myself over to the will of the gods that I am here with three Saxons, the sworn enemies of my kinsmen."

Laughing, the Old Woman shook her head as she went over to where Alfhildr was standing. Taking the red-haired girl in hand, she led her back to the hovel.

"You cannot allow your entire life to be ruled by the gods, child. Even the Fates who weave the thread of life need an occasional nudge this way or that if we are to live full and meaningful lives."

Upon hearing this, Alfhildr snorted.

"At the moment, if my life becomes any fuller, I fear I will need a packhorse to help me carry the burden I have taken upon myself."

Pleased that the girl had not lost her sense of humor, the Old Woman smiled as she led her to a bench adjacent to the hut's entrance.

"Come, let me look at your wound now that we have the light. I need to see it clearly while we talk before the others begin to stir."

"I will not allow you to put any maggots on it," Alfhildr replied haughtily.

"I will if need be," the Old Woman informed her former charge in a tone that left no doubt she would not tolerate any cheek.

"You may be the bane of Saxon brigands and Dane raiders: but, at the moment, you are a girl in need of help."

Rather than being offended by what the Old Woman had said, Alfhildr took comfort in knowing someone cared for her, not because of what she had done or could do for them, but simply because they liked her for who she was.

Æ

The manner in which Alfhildr was dressed wasn't the only change the Old Woman noted with more than a little pride. After allowing each member of her little party an opportunity to collect themselves and ease into the day, to wash off the filth of the trail with water Alfhildr herself had drawn from the well, and have something to eat, she took to assigning them tasks that needed tending to.

By midmorning, Osgar had been dispatched to hunt down enough fresh game for several days.

"Though she would never say a word, it would be rude to deplete the food the Old Woman has stored for her own use," Alfhildr explained. "While we are here, we must look after our own needs. Besides," she added in a hushed voice no one else could hear, "I want you to ride a wide circuit, sniffing about as you go for any signs of our pursuers."

Convinced the Old Woman really was a witch, Osgar was glad to be away from the hovel, if only for a while.

With his leg wound in danger of festering, Bowdyn had little choice but to stay close by. That did not mean Alfhildr did not find gainful employment for him. In addition to tending to their horses, she suggested he take the whetstone to their weapons as well as rummage through the collection of odds and ends the Old Woman had inherited from warriors to whom she had tended in the past. While Bowdyn also entertained doubts about their hostess, he was more prudent in how he expressed his concerns on that matter.

Despite Alfhildr's plea for her not to dip into her stock of food, the Old Woman took to baking bread and making goat cheese. She asked Elvina if she would care to help her but Alfhildr explained that would not be possible.

"I shall need her to assist me in foraging for suitable material so I can fashion arrows for my empty quiver."

Suspecting the Saxon girl would be more of a hindrance to Alfhildr in this effort, the Old Woman correctly guessed the real reason her former charge was taking Elvina along was to allow the two of them an opportunity to talk in private, as well as give the would-be queen the feeling that she was being useful. As she watched them disappear into the forest, trailed closely by the she-wolf, the Old Woman smiled to herself. Though the red-haired Dane still found herself unable to accept what was so plain to all, the child who she had pulled back from the brink of death was more than ready for the tasks the Fates had allotted her.

Now, the Old Woman told herself, as she went back to her own chores, *came an even greater challenge, preparing Alfhildr for what would follow when the day came for her to lay aside her warrior ways and take up her rightful place with people as a wife and mother, whether they be Danes or Saxons.*

Æ

"No, that piece will not do either," Alfhildr informed Elvina while trying to keep her exasperation in check. "Look, it's curved. We need to find branches that are straight, otherwise the arrow will not fly true."

Upon seeing the pained expression on the young queen's face, Alfhildr selected a good sample of what she was looking for from the bundle they had already collected.

"Take this. We're looking for pieces that match this. It's not a problem if they're longer. When it comes to working with wood, it's much like hacking off limbs. Taking a bit off here or there is easy. Putting it back to how it was is well-nigh impossible. Trust me," she snickered as she took up her search once more. "That is something I know a great deal about."

While Alfhildr was able to laugh at her own little joke, Elvina found nothing funny at all in her friend's comment. It did, however, serve to remind her of something that had been on her mind for some time, something their flight from the royal burgh had brought into sharp focus. Deciding this would be as good an opportunity as any to ask Alfhildr questions about her past, Elvina tried to find a way of doing so without causing her friend to hold back as she often had whenever she had tried to bring up the subject in the past.

Not long after they had resumed their search for wood from which to fashion arrows, Elvina asked Alfhildr if all Dane girls were taught to hunt and fight as well as she had been. With her attention focused on the immediate task at hand, Alfhildr was blissfully unaware that she was being skillfully led into an ambush by a girl who had learned the art of guile and politics from a master.

"No, not at all," Alfhildr replied off-handedly. "The girls of our village spent much of their days learning to spin, weave, cook, and tend to the inside chores that fill a woman's day."

Pausing, Alfhildr stopped before a tree that had a number of promising branches. With her small axe at the ready, she took to inspecting those branches that caught her eye, lopping off only those she deemed to be suitable.

"Are many Dane girls taught to fight?"

Without looking away from what she was doing, Alfhildr shrugged.

"I suppose some are. That doesn't mean our women are defenseless. Most can handle an axe, dagger, or a knife to defend themselves if need be, just as some of the Saxon women I have come across are able. But serious weapons training? That was something only the boys did."

"Then, how is it you are so proficient with sword and bow?"

Just like that, Alfhildr suddenly realized what she had said and what Elvina's questions had been leading up to. Trying hard to pretend she hadn't been rattled by her questions, Alfhildr scrambled to fashion a believable answer.

"My grandfather taught me, as did some of my father's friends," she muttered.

"Why were you taught to use sword and bow and yet none of the other girls were? I mean, I find it strange that you would be trained as you were while your mother neglected to teach you how to spin and weave."

Unnerved by Elvina's statement and more than a bit irritated with herself over how careless she had been with her answers, when Alfhildr turned to face Elvina, she made no effort to check her anger.

"You would be wise not to bring up the subject of my mother, ever."

In addition to being thrown off guard by such a vicious response to what she had thought was an innocent question, Elvina found herself frightened by the look in her friend's eyes. They were filled with hatred; the sort of hatred Elvina had seldom seen. Dropping the branches that she had collected, the Saxon queen retreated several steps, apologizing profusely as she took to wringing her hands.

"I'm sorry, Alfhildr. I didn't mean to upset you. I'm... I'm sorry. Please don't be upset."

The fear Alfhildr saw in Elvina's eyes checked her anger. Turning away, she silently took to cursing herself for upsetting one of the few people she could trust.

"No," she muttered mournfully without looking back. "You have no need to apologize. I am the one who should be sorry for behaving as I did. It's just that…"

Unable to continue and unsure what to say, with her head hung low, Alfhildr moved away from Elvina.

Setting aside her apprehensions, Elvina drew herself up. It was clear to her that Alfhildr was troubled, troubled by an unseen wound that had never healed. Determined to do something to help, Elvina moved to where Alfhildr stood hunched over, supporting herself with an outstretched arm on the tree from which she had been taking branches. Placing a gentle hand upon the Dane girl's shoulder, Elvina cooed sympathetically.

"You have taken far too many burdens upon yourself, dear friend. Over the past few days, you have been strong and brave for me, placing your life at risk time and time again. Allow me to repay that kindness by sharing your burdens no matter what they are."

Glancing back at the young Saxon girl, Alfhildr hesitated. Trust had become a commodity that was not easily given. Having been betrayed by her own kinsmen, the red-haired Dane girl had learned to trust only those who earned it as Osgar, Bowdyn, and Skadi had. That was when it occurred to Alfhildr that of all the people she had come across, no one had taken a greater risk by befriending her as had Elvina, a girl whom she could have easily dispatched on numerous occasions while she slept. Even more compelling was the realization that the young Saxon queen had placed more than her life at risk when she had taken her by the hand and led her from the dank cell in which she had been rotting. At a time when so many powerful Saxon lords had been baying for her blood, Elvina had placed her honor, as well as that of her father in jeopardy by the mere act of befriending her.

With a sigh, Alfhildr straightened up and drew in a deep breath before turning to face Elvina.

"Come, sit," she whispered, indicating a log lying on the ground with a sweep of her hand. "You of all people deserve to know the truth."

"About?" Elvina asked hesitantly as she swept aside the hem of her skirt and took a seat.

"About a boy named Gunnvor and the strange fate the Norns have woven for him."

Æ

When afternoon began to fade into early evening and the two girls had not returned, both Bowdyn and Osgar set off to find them. It was not hard to track their footsteps, littered as it was by discarded branches and hack marks on trees. The two Saxons found Alfhildr and Elvina seated on a log. Both were staring off in different directions as if each were thinking of something neither wished to share with the other. Cautiously approaching, Bowdyn cleared his throat to get their attention.

"My Lady," he muttered to Elvina. "It will soon be dark. We should return to the Old Woman's hut."

When she looked up into the huscarl's eyes, he could not help but see there was something bothering her. Yet, she said nothing as she came to her feet and walked past him without uttering a single word or looking back at Alfhildr. Taking note of this strange behavior and the long faces both girls made no effort to hide, the two men exchanged glances. With no need to say a word, Bowdyn nodded before following Elvina while Osgar ambled over to Alfhildr where he settled down beside her.

"What troubles you, little one?"

For the longest time, Alfhildr said nothing. When she did speak, Osgar could not help but notice the mournful tone in her voice.

"I did something I should not have done, something I fear may well put an end to our friendship."

"Did you argue?"

"No, something even more damaging than that. I told Elvina the truth."

Æ

Their meal that night passed in silence, with Bowdyn hovering near Elvina and Osgar staying close to Alfhildr. As they ate, neither girl looked over to where the other sat, both wearing long faces and lost in deep, unfathomable thought. Only when it came time to settle in their bedrolls was this strained silence broken when Osgar noticed Alfhildr gathering up her things before heading for the entrance.

"Where are you going?" he asked.

"I, um, I'm, going to sleep outside with Skadi in the lee of the shelter where the wood for the hearth is kept."

Having grown used to her ways, Osgar did not offer to go with her.

She wishes to be alone, he thought, *if only to give the young queen an opportunity to mull over whatever it was that was troubling her without Alfhildr underfoot.*

That explanation was quickly proven wrong when Elvina began to gather up the blankets off the small bed a young boy named Gunnvor had once lain on as he hovered near death. This time Bowdyn spoke.

"Where are you going, My Lady?"

"I am going to sleep outside as well," she replied while looking over at Alfhildr.

The two girls stared at each other for several long seconds before Alfhildr spoke.

"I am afraid if you do that, My Lady, Bowdyn will insist on sleeping outside as well," she murmured. "We are still not safe from danger."

Before the huscarl could gather up his bedroll, Elvina turned to where he had been watching the two girls.

"While I appreciate the gesture and do not wish to disparage your courage or skill as a warrior, that will not be necessary," Elvina stated in the clear, firm voice of a noblewoman speaking to a loyal underling.

Then, turning once more to Alfhildr, she smiled.

"I will be with someone I trust above all others. Someone I am proud to call friend."

Æ

Neither Bowdyn nor Osgar ever found out what had transpired between the diminutive Dane warrior and their exiled queen. All they knew for sure was that whatever had come between them while searching for arrow shafts was now in the past. When they joined the huscarl and huntsman for an early morning meal of bread and goat cheese, they were ready to move forward.

"So long as Elvina lives, the usurper's position will be in danger," Alfhildr stated as she chewed with her mouth half full.

Rather than being rattled by this blunt, though factual, assessment, Bowdyn noticed his young queen nod in agreement without betraying a whit of fear.

"As I see it, we have but two choices. Either we can continue to hide, or we can find a way of challenging Wilfrid and those who murdered Osmund."

"There is only one course open to us," Bowdyn replied with a certainty that afforded no room for debate. "There is more at stake here than honor or settling a blood feud. Wilfrid on the throne is as much a danger to the people he wishes to rule as he is to the neighboring kingdoms and the Danes. While I profess to have no great love for the Danes, the war he will bring on between them and our people is one he will never be able to win," Bowdyn admitted as he glanced over at Alfhildr.

"Your father knew that," Bowdyn continued as he turned once more to Elvina.

"So long as he and your uncle stood united behind the king, they were able to keep Wilfrid's ambitions in check. That's why your marriage to Cerdic was so important. Now, with Osmund gone and the old king dead, Wilfrid will be able to isolate Tofi."

"We must not allow that to happen," Elvina announced with more conviction than she felt. "Wilfrid has no legal claim to the throne."

"Neither do you, My Lady," Bowdyn quickly pointed out.

When Elvina saw the puzzled look on Alfhildr's face, she leaned over in order to whisper in her friend's ear.

"Cerdic did not consummate the marriage."

Still confused, Alfhildr pulled away and stared at Elvina.

"But I saw you kiss the high priest's ring, twice. And you drank from the sacred cup as well."

Before answering, Elvina sheepishly glanced over at the two men, both of whom were struggling mightily to keep a straight face. Turning back to Alfhildr, she once more whispered in Alfhildr's ear. When Bowdyn and Osgar saw the red-haired Dane's eyes grow to the size of hen's eggs and her cheeks glow bright, neither could hold back, earning both a withering glare from the painfully naïve young girl.

In an effort to turn attention away from Alfhildr's embarrassment, Elvina tossed her head back and cleared her throat.

"We must move quickly before Wilfrid can sway those eorls who had helped my father keep his dangerous ambitions in check."

"My Lady, even if we do manage to hold all of them to the obligation they made to your father, without the king's levy, which Wilfrid will be able to call upon, we will have no chance," Bowdyn explained.

"You will if the Danes join with you to unseat the usurper," Alfhildr announced.

As one, the three Saxons turned to Alfhildr.

"The Danes? Marching side by side with Saxons?" Osgar snorted. "We will see the second coming of our blessed Lord Jesus before that happens."

"They will join if the price is right." Alfhildr countered.

Turning to face Alfhildr, Elvina dropped her gaze.

"My father put everything he had into securing an alliance between our house and the old King's," Elvina explained quietly.

"Even if some of my father's huscarls managed to escape the massacre at the royal burgh, rally the *fyrd*, and secure all my father's holdings, there is nothing left with which to pay a mercenary force. And I seriously doubt if my Uncle Tofi or any other Saxon lord, who had once stood with my father and the king against Wilfrid, would be willing to risk their fortunes to purchase the services of Dane mercenaries. If anything, word of such a deal would strengthen Wilfrid's hand."

In the silence that followed, Bowdyn looked over at Alfhildr who was lost in thought.

"She's right, you know," he murmured.

"There is something she can offer them no other Saxon is willing to offer," Alfhildr stated calmly when she finally did look up at Bowdyn.

"What would cause Danes to fight for a Saxon queen other than the promise of silver and plunder?" Bowdyn asked incredulously.

Alfhildr ignored Bowdyn's unintended slight to her kinsmen, meeting his steady gaze instead with a calm, almost placid expression.

"Something far more valuable than gold, coin, or jewels."

"And what's that?" Osgar asked.

"Something both Dane and Saxon crave, though few are willing to openly admit it," Alfhildr replied as she looked into the eyes of the three Saxons.

"Peace."

Æ

Suspecting the Saxons would need some time alone in which to freely discuss and debate how best to go forward, Alfhildr accepted the Old Woman's invitation to help her as she gathered honey from a nearby hive and hunted for the herbs that she would need to create fresh potions.

"I expect, in the coming days even if you will not be in need of them, others with you will," the Old Woman explained as they set out.

Alfhildr suspected there was more to her desire to spend time away from the others with her. Not long after they'd set out this was confirmed.

They had not gone far from the hovel when the Old Woman let slip the real reason that she had asked Alfhildr to join her.

"Soon you will face a new challenge, a trial that will demand you call upon skills far different than those you have relied upon in the past."

Having come to trust the Old Woman's ability to see into the future, Alfhildr regarded her warily out of the corner of her eye.

"What sort of challenge?"

Looking over at the waif of a girl walking along side of her, the Old Woman smiled.

"It will be one more in line with your true nature."

Furrowing her brow, Alfhildr tried to discern what the Old Woman was talking about.

Understanding what the young Dane's expression meant, the Old Woman's eyes fell to the rough spun gown Alfhildr had been wearing since she'd arrived. As her cheeks reddened, Alfhildr averted her eyes as she searched for an excuse to explain away her choice of clothing.

"The tunic and trousers I wore when we arrived needed to be cleaned and mended."

"I did that the day after you arrived," the Old Woman volunteered.

"They weren't completely dry yesterday," Alfhildr countered.

"They were dry this morning."

Having had each of her excuses rebuffed thus far, Alfhildr took to looking about the forest as she scrambled to find another reason.

"When I'm wearing women's clothes it's easier to pee," she finally muttered in a last desperate bid to explain away why she still wore the gown.

The Old Woman laughed as she shook her head.

"Child, have you forgotten who you are talking to? While you may be able to fool the huscarl and that wily huntsman by the way you are able to hold your own when dealing with worldly matters, I imagine even you have come to suspect your days of wandering about as if you were apart from the people who populate Middle Earth and their ways are nearing an end."

Looking down at the ground before her, Alfhildr kicked a clump of dirt with the tip of her toe.

"But I am apart from them."

"Only if you choose to be, child."

"But where would someone like me fit?" Alfhildr asked plaintively.

Once more, the Old Woman smiled as she studied the diminutive Dane, making it clear to Alfhildr with her eyes that she was looking at the rough spun gown.

Æ

There was no great or elaborate ceremony to mark the event. No kissing of rings, chanting of sacred oaths, or exchange of tokens. Such trappings were not needed, for all who witnessed the exchange of pledges between a Saxon queen and a Dane warrior understood the significance of what the two girls were doing and the depth of commitment each had for the cause they championed. Elvina gazed intently into Alfhildr's eyes as she grasped the Dane's forearms.

"Before God and these witnesses, I swear to you and all your people, when I have assumed my rightful place upon the throne, I shall not rest until there is peace between my people and yours."

After a brief pause, Alfhildr spoke.

"Alone, or with my people, I shall stand at your side until the murder of your kinsmen has been avenged and all that is rightfully yours has been restored," she intoned. "This pledge I make freely and without reservation."

After a moment's silence, the two girls embraced and exchanged quick, light kisses on each other's cheeks before stepping back while still clasping hands.

Bowdyn broke the silence. "It is done," he solemnly announced.

"Aye," Osgar murmured as he nodded. "Now comes the hard part."

Chapter Seventeen
UNHEALED WOUNDS

Present Day England
"The Dig"

Upon returning to her room, after an exhausting day of teasing away another layer of sunbaked clay that stubbornly clung to the treasures it had held captive for centuries, Elva threw herself down onto her bed. The temptation to cuddle up about the threadbare stuffed wolf her grandmother had given her when she had been a child and give in to sleep was almost too strong to resist. But resist she did.

With more effort than such a simple task should have demanded, Elva sat up and gave her head a quick shake before pulling her filthy Arsenal Club Tee off over her head.

Pausing, she looked about the room, wondering where she'd thrown her robe. That was when she caught sight of her mobile phone laying in the corner where she'd tossed it the previous night after she'd ended a particularly sharp conversation with her mother in mid-sentence.

The idea of calling her back and apologizing never entered Elva's mind. As far as she was concerned, she had no reason to apologize. Yet, simply leaving the matter that had resulted in another contentious spat to fester, without some sort of resolution, would only make an already strained relationship even more insufferable. After drawing in a deep breath, Elva slowly let it out, knowing the only solution to this current impasse was to call her grandmother and see what she could do to smooth her own daughter's ruffled feathers. She always had in the past, just as the old woman always knew just what to say to cheer Elva up whenever she found herself in a serious funk.

Æ

The Saga of the Heartless Homecoming

The old woman's hut the queen did it shelter,
Wounds knitted, hearts rested within its scant walls
Now, they looked forward to defeat the usurper
No longer behind but ahead did they seek.

Dread purposed, heavy hearted, the friends went their ways
Saxon and Dane to their own folk did go.
An army from each to defeat the usurper,
To honour their oaths and for peace between foes.

Hard was the road that Alfhildr now took,
The ghosts of her past pressed close as she rode.
To the home that was no home,
To the kin who were lost.

Red-haired and bright armoured, the shield maiden came,
With she-wolf and raven, her people she called.
"The gods have sent me," Alfhildr proclaimed,
"Fight now for a peace for your children and halls."

The chieftain, Snurre, Alfhildr's brother, scoffed when he heard
Though he knew not the blood that they shared.
How can you win what no man has before?
What makes you so certain of the victory you claim?

Long ran the argument, amongst the Dane men
While Alfhildr waited in the house that was no home.
Only one saw the child behind the dire shield maiden
The grandmother's sharp eyes saw more than the rest.

The arguments raged four long days in the hall
Whilst Alfhildr waited nearby for their call
As she tarried, the grandmother came to her camp
And, at last, the shield maiden laid bare her sad tale

After four weary days, brave Sigmund arrived.
His blood debt to the shield maiden he honored that night.
Peace does she offer and peace we shall have.
For our children and future, I will march at her side.

Æ

    Bowdyn set off just after dawn, promising Elvina, before he left, that he would rally to her cause those nobles who had been aligned with her father, starting with his own liege, Godric. Alfhildr could tell by his response to Elvina's plea to return safely that he didn't understand what was behind her concern for his welfare. Not yet anyway. Given time, she was certain the young Saxon queen would find a suitable way of ensuring that he became aware that her interests in him went well beyond political intrigue and military necessity. Of that Alfhildr was sure. At the moment, it was the only thing about which she was.
    For her part, the red- haired Dane girl tarried, finding excuse after excuse to delay her own departure. Elvina was pleased to spend a little more time with

her friend, convincing Alfhildr that she should have her hair braided before she rode off.

"You need to look your best when you face your people," the Saxon queen admonished. "Oftentimes, men find themselves unable to refuse the pleas of a pretty girl when common sense and logic dictates that they do otherwise."

Although Alfhildr knew she would need to do more than smile and murmur sweet supplications in order to win the support of the Danish chieftains she would soon be facing, she saw no harm in giving into the elaborate grooming ritual upon which Elvina insisted. Alfhildr would need every advantage she could muster if she were to convince her kinsmen to fight for a Saxon queen. If braided hair helped her achieve this goal, so be it.

Osgar, who had been adopted by Elvina as her personal bodyguard, would be staying with the young queen at the Old Woman's until Bowdyn returned to fetch them. The Saxon huntsman could tell the young girl he had come to love as a daughter was apprehensive, perhaps even a little scared of her coming ordeal. At one point, while Alfhildr was feeding the Old Woman's goats for a second time that morning, he asked if she wished him to ride with her. Without bothering to look up from what she was doing, she shook her head.

"No," she muttered making no effort to hide her mounting anxiety. "Things will be difficult enough without showing up with a Saxon by my side."

In an effort to bring a smile to the girl's face, Osgar grunted.

"Oh, and I suppose strolling into your village with a snarling she-wolf at your side and a squawking crow perched on your shoulder is going to be taken in stride by your people."

Rather than laughing, Alfhildr looked over at her Saxon companion out of the corner of her eye.

"My people are very superstitious. They believe the gods have the ability to assume the shapes of animals, even people. I am counting on Skadi and Hoenir to give me an advantage in the coming days, one I will need if anyone is to take me seriously."

As a God-fearing Christian, who tended to respect some of the old traditions of his own people, Osgar found he could not fault the girl's argument. If truth be known, he still looked upon the she-wolf and crow as being more than simple creatures of the forest, just as he suspected there was more to the Dane girl they followed.

Eventually, when the sun was approaching its zenith, Alfhildr discovered she had run out of excuses for putting off her departure. Having said her farewells to the Old Woman, who chose to remain inside, and with a heavy heart, Alfhildr pulled herself up into the saddle as Elvina and Osgar watched.

"Do be careful," Elvina called out.

Unable to trust her own voice, Alfhildr simply gave her friend a weak smile before looking over at Osgar. The two hunting companions simply nodded. With that, Alfhildr gave Dimma's reins a tug to one side, turning her back once more on the Old Woman's hut as she rode off to a place she had once called home.

Æ

The village Alfhildr had known as a child was on the edge of Danelaw, leaving it vulnerable to sudden and frequent incursions by Saxon raiders. Her grandfather's people also had to be on guard to fend off rival Dane chieftains who wished to expand their own holdings or protect one of their own from a revenge killing brought on by a blood feud to which they had foolishly become a party. So, it came as no surprise to Alfhildr that, by the time she reached the fortified little village at the heart of Folkmar's holdings, a crowd had gathered about its entrance, an entrance blocked by a lone figure leaning on an upturned battleax. Wearing a conical helmet reflecting the sun's bright rays and with his shield slung over his back, the young warrior stood ready to either greet or challenge Alfhildr. Not far behind him was a brute of a man who was bigger and older than the first, prepared to assist him if need be. Alfhildr recognized the second warrior, recalling he was a particularly nasty lout named Hrolf, a man for whom few of her kinsmen cared. His presence there at the entrance to the village was ominous. Easing Dimma to a halt, she carefully motioned with her right hand for Skadi to hold, for like her mistress, the she-wolf was wary of the warriors barring their way.

There followed a strained silence, broken only by the sound of Hoenir's shrilled squawk as the crow leisurely circled about just overhead. Try as he might, the young warrior at the gate could not help but glance up at the bird as it fluttered about, swooping down low just behind Alfhildr before soaring up over her right shoulder. Once past her, it turned sharply to begin another tight circuit. When the warrior blocking her path finally did speak, Alfhildr could not help but be pleased to note a twinge of apprehension in his voice.

"Who are you, and what do you want?"

With as much flair as she could manage, Alfhildr threw her grey cloak back over her left shoulder, revealing her bright mail and Durthfang's glittering hilt.

"I am Alfhildr, sword arm of the gods and guardian of the innocent," she announced in a clear, crisp tone that betrayed none of the apprehensions she harbored.

Ignoring the gasps and muted mutterings that rippled through the crowd that had assembled atop the walls of the stockade and behind him, the lone warrior took a deep breath as if mustering up his courage. "What is your business here?"

Satisfied that she had managed to establish her identity without having to endure a rigorous challenge, Alfhildr tightened up her reins, causing Dimma to prance about before answering. When she did, she spoke with all the confidence she could muster.

"I have come to speak with the mighty Folkmar, chieftain of your tribe as well as all the chieftains who wish to put an end to the bloody fighting between Saxon and Dane, senseless bloodshed that deprives our kinsmen of the freedom to enjoy their life's journey in peace."

Once more, a ripple of muttering and hushed exchanges could be heard from the crowd. Though he tried to hide his growing apprehensions, the warrior blocking the entrance couldn't help but nervously glance about at his kinsmen in an effort to gauge their reaction to Alfhildr's bold proclamation. Realizing he had no choice but to hear the red-haired female out, the warrior again drew himself up as best he could.

"I speak for Folkmar," he announced doing his best to impress Alfhildr while keeping his uncertainty in check.

For her part, Alfhildr found it difficult to suppress a smile from spoiling her stern, uncompromising expression, that was until the warrior responded to her request to identify himself. In the twinkling of an eye, her smugness turned into something entirely different.

"I am Snurre, son of Gunnar. On behalf of Folkmar, I will hear your argument and judge its merits."

Æ

Try as hard as she could, Alfhildr could not keep from glancing over at her brother out of the corner of her eye as the two walked side by side through the village toward the great hall where the freemen who were not following them were already gathering. He was very nearly a man now in stature and carriage. His beard, though still in its infancy, promised to be as full and impressive as her father's had been. In many ways, Snurre reminded her of Gunnar, at least what she could recall of him. Whether he had inherited their father's gentle manner and wisdom was something that remained to be seen.

Upon entering the great hall, the emotions Alfhildr had been struggling to keep in check once more threatened to undo her resolute demeanor as fond memories of the place came to the fore. As a child, she had spent many an hour in this very hall, hidden beneath one of the tables. From there, she would listen to the heroic stories with which her kinsmen regaled their companions or their debates as they discussed grave matters. Her grandfather always knew that she was there. Sometimes, he even slipped food from his own plate to her as she crouched at his feet. Both had enjoyed the little game they played.

Of course, she had been someone else then, a child who was no more. Standing where she should have been was her brother, the very boy whose sword had cut her loose from her moorings and had left her adrift on a sea of uncertainty. As she stood there, to his left, waiting for the freemen to finish assembling and settling, Alfhildr found herself struggling to hold back an avalanche of emotions ranging from anger and resentment to confusion and, oddly enough, relief; relief over the fact that she did not have to stand before her assembled kinsmen wondering, as Elvina did, if they would stand by her side or raise their swords against her in an effort to strike her down. Glancing over at a very concerned Snurre, Alfhildr imagined her brother was facing his first challenge of this magnitude, leaving her to wonder how she would have handled this crisis had the mantle of leadership he now wore been hers.

A call by Snurre for silence caused Alfhildr to set aside her wandering thoughts and turn her attention back to the issue that had brought her to this place. With an ease that belied the nervousness she felt, Alfhildr stepped out into the middle of the room, carefully presenting to her kinsmen the agreement Elvina was willing to enter into if they were willing to help her regain her crown.

"We will not be serving as mercenaries but as free Danes, fighting to achieve something our people have not known these many years—freedom," Alfhildr took great pains to point out.

The same heavyset warrior with dark hair and a massive mustache, who had stood just behind Snurre at the gate and was now seated to the right of him, snorted.

"We are already free, girl."

Snapping her head about, she regarded Hrolf. He had never made a secret of his desire to take Folkmar's place when the old man passed on, no doubt looking upon the chieftain's grandsons in much the same way Wilfrid had viewed Cerdic. To be fair, Alfhildr remembered all the men said he was a good man to have at your side during a fight if things were going their way. Few, however, trusted him. She'd often heard her grandfather whisper to his supporters when he thought no one else was listening that when he passed on, Hrolf was to be watched.

"He will make his move only when I am gone," he warned his confidantes. "It is a challenge, I fear, that my grandson will not be able to handle. I am counting on you to stand by Gunnvor."

Gunnvor, of course, was no more. Whether her grandfather had asked those same men to transfer their allegiance to Snurre was something Alfhildr did not know. The only thing she was sure of at the moment was that Hrolf's seat, next to her brother, was no mere luck of the draw. Snurre needed him to help prop up his position. Either that or the man still had his eye on taking her brother's place and was only waiting until he could dispose of Snurre without incurring a blood feud. Not that any of that made a difference to the matter being discussed. Hrolf was someone who Alfhildr expected she would need to watch. First, she had to meet the challenge he had presented to her head on.

"Yes, you are free," she replied crisply. "Free to watch your kinsmen be slaughtered by marauding Saxon's sent out by their nobles year after year in an effort to roll back the gains our ancestors made."

Slowly, Alfhildr took to looking about the room, casting her gaze from one man to the next as she spoke.

"The freedom I speak of is the freedom all people crave, the freedom to harvest the crops they planted in the spring when summer has passed. The freedom to watch their children grow until they are ready to strike out on their own or take up the plow and distaff passed on to them by living parents who will be free to enjoy the autumn of their lives in peace."

"For this, you ask us to pledge our fealty to a Saxon?" Hrolf all but spat making no effort to hide his distaste for such a thought.

"No!" Alfhildr shot back without hesitation. "We go forth together, a Danish army under Danish command."

"And who will lead this army?" Snurre asked tentatively as he tried to regain some semblance of control over the assembly.

"I will," Alfhildr announced with far more confidence than she felt.

Upon hearing this, some of the assembled freemen openly scoffed at the idea while others took to muttering with their neighbors. The moment she had expected and prepared for had arrived. After letting this chatter go on unabated for several seconds, Alfhildr drew herself up. Placing her left hand upon the pommel of her sword, she thundered out a clear, unwavering challenge to the assembled freeman.

"If there is a man here among you who believes he is better suited to do so, step forward now. But be warned, I am Alfhildr, the sword arm of the gods," she proclaimed boldly. "Though many a valiant warrior has tried to put me in the ground, the gods themselves have assured me there is no man here on Middle Earth who is able to defeat me in battle."

"What assurance do you have that we can trust the Saxons," Hrolf asked disdainfully.

To everyone's surprise, she replied she had none.

"I have the word of a queen who has yet to sit on her throne, but that is all. The only thing of which I can assure you is that if we do nothing, if we refuse to risk all in this endeavor, nothing will change. Come summer, the Saxons will return and raid our farmsteads and villages. We will, then, have no choice but to repay their deprivations in kind, which will demand they come back once more to settle the blood debt we have incurred. Only by taking a bold move can we stop this insanity. Besides," she added as she slyly lowered her voice and let a hint of a smile dance across her lips, "even if we do fail, we will not lose, for those of you who have the courage to follow me into battle and fall will be whisked away by the Valkyrie to Valhalla where you will sit at Odin's table, side by side with your ancestors. Can any of you think of a greater reward?"

Æ

Having stated her case, Snurre made it clear he needed to discuss the issue with his kinsmen. In order to do so freely, he called upon his young wife, a girl who had been waiting patiently off to one side to escort Alfhildr to the home of his mother. As surprising as it was to discover that her brother was already married, Alfhildr was stunned to find out that his wife was Halla, a pleasant girl who had once been the object of Gunnvor's affections.

For her part, Halla made no effort to hide the awe with which she regarded Alfhildr. Though legends spoke of shield maidens and their deeds in battle, the shy, young woman had never met one before, a fact to which she quickly admitted.

"I had expected something very different."

Alfhildr ignored the irony of Halla's confession. Instead, she asked about her grandfather, doing her best to make her question come across as if it were little more than idle curiosity.

"Folkmar has grown old and infirm in body and mind," Halla muttered sadly. "They say he was never able to set aside his grief for the death of his oldest grandson, a boy known as Gunnvor."

Halla's words pierced Alfhildr's heart like an arrow. Unable to keep from noticing the strange girl's reaction to this news, Halla glanced over at Alfhildr out of the corner of her eye. Eager to stop Halla from staring at her, Alfhildr fixed her in a steady, unflinching gaze.

"Is there something wrong?"

After giving her head a quick shake, Halla smiled apologetically.

"Oh no. It's just that Gunnvor had hair like yours. And his eyes were green as well. I expect if he were here, next to you, people would mistake you for sister and brother."

"Well, we're not," Alfhildr snapped without thinking.

Thrown by the sharpness of her response, Halla drew back. Unsure what she had said to offend the strange girl, she said nothing more as they continued on to a home where an even greater challenge than the one Alfhildr had already faced in the great hall awaited her.

Æ

With great trepidation, Alfhildr crossed a threshold that was painfully familiar to her. Following Halla into the smoky mud and lattice hut, Alfhildr stood off to one side as Snurre's wife announced her.

"Mama, Grandmother, this is the shield maiden known as Alfhildr."

The two older women stopped what they had been doing and stared past Halla at Alfhildr. Both stood stock still, shocked at seeing the red-haired warrior standing before them, though the reason for their reactions were poles apart. As Halla had been, Ragna, the mother to Snurre was awe-struck by the sight of the notorious shield maiden, attired in fine mail and armed to the teeth.

After wiping her hands on her apron, the woman who had given birth to a child named Gunnvor stuttered as she motioned to a seat and invited Alfhildr to sit.

It was the glint of recognition in her grandmother's eye that worried Alfhildr. Doing her best to ignore the old woman's expression, she shed her heavy woolen cloak and accepted the cup of spring water Halla offered her, which she rapidly gulped down in an effort to do something, anything, to mask her nervousness.

The awkward silence that followed was broken when a weak voice called out to Alfhildr, one she hardly recognized. Turning toward its source, she saw a frail old man, one who bore little resemblance to her grandfather, seated in a corner on the far side of the room. Yet, that was who it was. The two eyed each other in silence before he spoke out again.

"Mother?"

Furrowing her brow, Alfhildr stared at her grandfather.

"Excuse me?"

"Your name," the old man mumbled. "Is it not Thorgerd, the wife of Kraki, my father?"

While Ragna looked at her father-in-law as if he were mad, the expression on Urthr's face told Alfhildr her grandmother knew the truth. Coming to her feet, she thrust the cup toward Halla.

"I must tend to my horse," she stammered before turning to rush out the door.

"When the freemen have reached a decision, have Snurre send someone to find me," she called out over her shoulder as she went. "I will be encamped where the rune stones stand."

Behind her Alfhildr left a very confused and bewildered group of people who had once been her family but were now nothing more than strangers.

Æ

It came as no surprise that it was her grandmother who brought news of the decision upon which the men of her village had settled as well as a warm pot of soup, fresh bread, and beer.

At first, neither said anything other than to exchange muted pleasantries and an admonishment by Urthr to eat while the soup was still warm. Only when her grandchild had finished did the old woman speak.

"All this time, I thought your mother had been wrong leaving you as she did."

Seeing little point in pretending she was anything other than who she was, Alfhildr made no effort to hold back the anger she had so carefully kept in check earlier in the day.

"And now? You believe she was right in turning her back on her oldest child, just as you did?"

Undaunted by the sharpness of her grandchild's tone, Urthr nodded.

"Yes. What she did was the only thing she could have done. And if you give the matter the thought it calls for, you will agree."

Having done that very thing many times before, and having come to the same conclusion, Alfhildr dropped her gaze, staring into her campfire as she let her pent-up anger melt away.

"While that may be true, the pain I felt when I discovered I had been abandoned by everyone I knew is a wound that has never fully healed," Alfhildr muttered without looking back up into her grandmother's eyes.

"You must be alive to feel pain," Urthr stated calmly. "Had you returned to the village, there is no way of knowing if you would have survived for very long. And, even if you had, where would you have fit?"

As difficult as it was for her to accept, Alfhildr knew full well that she would have been an outcast, no different than the Old Woman in the forest. Finally, looking up at her grandmother, she asked who else knew the truth.

"To the best of my knowledge, only I do. Everyone else is either too awestruck or fearful of you to see past the mail and sword you wear with such ease."

"And the freemen? What of their debate?" Alfhildr asked as she set aside her personal concerns for the moment.

"Though Hrolf tried to persuade your brother and the other men to reject your call to join you, they were soundly shouted down," Urthr informed her grandchild.

"Messengers have already been sent out to the other chieftains calling them in for a council to be held six days hence to discuss the matter."

A wave of relief swept over Alfhildr. Though the issue was far from decided in her favor, the balance seemed to be going her way.

"Will you return home with me?" Urthr asked as she prepared to leave.

Alfhildr had no need to give this question a second's thought. Looking up at the old woman, Alfhildr smiled as she settled back against her saddle and took to gently kneading the soft folds of skin about Skadi's neck with her fingertips.

"I *am* home."

Æ

Over the next few days, Alfhildr did not bother venturing into a village that was neither home nor welcoming like the glade where she camped among the rune stones erected by her people. For her, the village was filled with ghosts and nothing more. Her own family and the people with whom she had grown up were now as indecipherable to her as the writing chiseled into the monuments to the departed. While it was true that her kinsmen had all changed to some degree or another, there was no escaping the fact that the path she had been following had reshaped her into an entirely new being, one all but divorced from the frail child who had once been known as Gunnvor. It had taken a journey to the place of his birth to appreciate that there were no paths leading back to what had been. The only roads that lay open to Alfhildr were those shrouded in the grey mist of an uncertain future.

Choosing which of those roads she would follow, once she had fulfilled the prophecy, was the challenge to which the Old Woman had alluded, one Alfhildr did her best to ignore, at least for the moment.

Only one person made the effort to visit Alfhildr each day. In addition to bringing her food and news of the gathering that would soon take place, Urthr was interested in learning the truth about her grandchild.

"I have heard many strange and curious tales about your adventures and deeds," she informed Alfhildr. "Some believe you are a *seiðr*. A few think you are one of the goddesses come to Middle Earth to protect our people. Many of the women are fearful for the lives of their husbands and sons, claiming you are Valkyrie, sent by Odin himself to snatch their men off to Valhalla."

"I am none of those things," Alfhildr sighed. "I am simply me, Alfhildr."

"I know that," Urthr replied. "But who is Alfhildr?" she asked pointedly.

The red-haired girl did not answer at first, gazing off toward the distant horizon as if searching for the answer to that question. When she did speak, the sadness in her voice brought a tear to her grandmother's eyes.

"I do not know. I fear I never will."

Æ

On the agreed upon day, Alfhildr took her time preparing to address the gathering of chieftains. Unlike the first day, when she had worn her hair tightly bound in a braid, Alfhildr carefully combed out her hair, draping it about her shoulders. While Elvina looked upon her golden tresses as something of a crown to be worn proudly, Alfhildr had come to appreciate that her red hair was as much a weapon as her sword or bow. She had seen the look of terror in men's eyes when they realized they were in the presence of the dreaded Dane witch. Besides, her uncovered head and flowing hair told all who saw her that she was a free woman, unbound and independent, beholden to no man. Having been in the service of another, Alfhildr had come to cherish her freedom above all else.

Taking her time, Alfhildr made her way to the longhouse where the chieftains were already assembled. Besides allowing her an opportunity to make something of a grand entrance, her leisurely ride through the assembled crowd gave those who had accompanied their chieftain to this council an opportunity to see her for themselves, just as Osmund had when he had paraded Elvina through the King's Burh at Sceaftesege.

On entering the hall, the room went silent. With Skadi at her side, she slowly made her way to the head table where she skillfully inserted herself between her brother and Hrolf. His efforts to browbeat her there, in the presence of the assembled chieftains was met with the same icy stare she used when facing down a foe in battle. When it became clear that the man, who had the ear of Snurre and an eye on his position, was not about to back down, Alfhildr reached across with her right hand and grasped the hilt of her sword without ever breaking eye contact. For an instant, everyone in the room held their breath, waiting to see what Hrolf would do. As much as he would have loved to have put an end to what he considered her foolishness, he realized this was neither the time nor the place for that. With his anger all but palpable, he stepped back and away from the head table.

Having succeeded in meeting her first challenge of the day, Alfhildr turned to deal with the next, rallying the Dane chieftains to Elvina's cause. She started by using the same approach that she had before her brother and his freemen by carefully putting forth, to the assembled chieftains, all the reasons they should fight Wilfrid.

"There can be no peace between this man and our people," she carefully explained, placing more emphasis upon the threat all Danes would face if Wilfrid were allowed to remain upon the throne.

"If that man is allowed to consolidate his tenuous hold on the crown he has usurped, he will wage an unending war against us. I have been among them: I know this to be so. Only by striking now, while the Saxons are still divided, can we hope to forestall a long and bloody struggle, one in which both sides will suffer, leaving us weak and vulnerable to the Kingdom of Westseaxna as well as other Dane chieftains from across the whale road who covet our lands."

When she had finished, Alfhildr stepped back, but remained in the great hall as an animated debate unfolded. On one side, there were those who saw the value of an alliance with Elvina and the peace it would bring. Against them were men who saw such an alliance as little more than a ploy by a Saxon queen to have someone else do their fighting for them in order to avoid a blood feud with their own kind while weakening the Danes.

The debate dragged on for hours as those who had holdings bordering Saxon lands argued in favor, and others, who had little to fear from Saxon raids, opposed the idea. Mixed in with this argument, from time to time, was an oft-expressed opinion that it would be the height of folly to follow a mere girl into battle, even one who all believed was just as capable with a sword as rumors of her feats claimed she was.

Just when it appeared the scales were beginning to tip inexorably against the venture, the sound of loud voices outside the crowded great hall caused everyone in the room to go silent as all eyes turned toward the door. With a shove, it was forced open, revealing a man who filled the void.

Stepping forward, the enormous red-bearded newcomer looked about the room until he spotted Alfhildr standing at the head of the table. Upon seeing her, he called out over his shoulder to his companions who had crowded in behind him.

"It's true," he thundered. "The little elf who denied us our fun is here."

For the briefest of moments, Alfhildr held her breath as she waited to see what the newcomer would do. She didn't have long to wait, for Sigmund bounded across the room toward her with a grace at odds with his massive frame. Upon reaching her, he swept the red-haired girl up into his arms, all but crushing her in a hug as he twirled her about as if she were a child of ten.

"By the gods, I am happy to see you once more, little elf, alive and in good health."

Overwhelmed by his enthusiasm, Alfhildr ignored the pain his embrace was causing her still healing wound as she regarded him with mock severity.

"I would say it was a joy to see you once again, as well, if you didn't smell like a dead goat."

Sigmund threw back his head as he let out a mighty roar. "*Ha!* As feisty and sharp-tongued as ever." Grinning, he gazed into Alfhildr's eyes.

"I would give you a kiss, but I cherish my manhood too much to risk it."

The men belonging to Sigmund's warband, who had managed to crowd into the room, joined their chieftain in a round of laughter as Alfhildr's cheeks turned beet red.

"Put me down you great oaf," she demanded as she made a great show of beating on his chest with a clenched fist that caused him no harm.

Once on the floor, as Alfhildr took a moment to collect herself, Sigmund spoke.

"I hear you are calling for us to march with you to fight the Saxons," Sigmund stated loudly as he took up the matter that had brought him to this place.

"We march to join a Saxon army to fight a Saxon king who usurped the crown from its rightful heir," Alfhildr informed Sigmund.

"And what do we get in return? Silver? Slaves? Land?"

With an earnestness that left no doubt in Sigmund's mind of her sincerity, Alfhildr replied.

"Peace between our peoples, now and for as long as we have the courage and wisdom to set aside our petty grievances and live life as the gods intended."

While still resting his hands on her shoulders, Sigmund stared into the green, unflinching eyes of the diminutive female before him. Ever so slowly, a grin began to turn up the corners of his lips as he gave Alfhildr a wink.

"So, it is still peace that you seek. This time for all. Well, if that is the way it is to be, then Sigmund, the Just, will follow this girl to Hel if necessary," he announced loudly as he looked past Alfhildr at the assembled chieftains.

The cheers of his men, who had pushed their way into the room or were standing just outside, served to drown out the last of the opposition Alfhildr had been facing, for no man in the longhouse had the courage to stand against Sigmund.

Sensing that he had carried the day for her, Sigmund looked down at Alfhildr.

"I have ridden long and hard to stand by your side, little one. Now, are you going to tell me where you hide your mead, or will I have to squeeze you until you confess?"

The only squeezing that followed was done by Alfhildr as she wrapped her arms about the great oak of a man before her as best she could and hugged him as she had never hugged another before.

Chapter Eighteen
THE SPIDER'S WEBS

The Saga of the Three Armies

Three armies stood, each enemy to the twain.
Saxon watched Saxon, and Saxon watched Dane.
The oaths of two girls had scant strength to bind them
All alert for betrayal, unsure of their gain.

The sharp-eyed usurper, his name I'll not speak,
Cunning traps for his foes that spider did weave.
Gold for the Dane and lands for the Lord,
To set friend against friend, sly plans had he wrought.

Secret messengers he sent to seek cowards and oath breakers,
Honeyed words did they use to sweeten his lies.
In the camps of his enemies, harsh words were soon spoken
With suspicion and greed, he sought their defeat.

Two days and two nights the armies did stand.
No battle cry raised: no banner advanced.
In the midst of their camps, men sought their own gain
Over honour with peace that the shield maiden sought.
Æ

The damp log spluttered on the small hearth, throwing out a shower of sparks onto the rotting rushes. As he listened morosely to the report of the young huscarl, King Wilfrid prodded the barely smoldering fire with his toe.

A stinking little fire in a stinking little peasant's hovel, He thought. *If those idiots hadn't let a stupid girl child get away, he would still be warming himself in his great hall.*

"Sire, we have had reports from our spies in the traitor's camp. The banners of Godric and Tofi have been joined by those of Aldhelm, Oeric, Wulfhere, and Redwald."

Wilfrid grunted at the news. None of the names surprised him. At least now his enemies had come together to offer him a single neck to cut.

"How many spears?" he demanded.

"Sire?"

"It's a simple question. How many spears?"

"Perhaps three hundred, Sire."

"And the Danes?"

"The scouts spotted three large warbands, maybe two hundred in all, before they were forced to draw back."

Ædelric watched as his lord and king, lost in thought, stared into the fire. After screwing up his nerve, he leaned closer.

"Perhaps, we should draw back apace, Sire. If we were not here to tempt them, like as not they would fight each other."

"Fool!" Wilfrid's vicious snarl caused the young huscarl to draw back in shock.

"Did you not think those two little tarts will keep them apart? Or perhaps you have no stomach for a fight? Is that it? Are you lily-livered as well as stupid?"

Ædelric flushed as the King's anger poured over him.

"Sire, I merely thought to..."

"You didn't think! Get out!"

Seething with fury at the King's insults, the proud warrior sketched a stiff bow before storming out of the dark hovel. Wilfrid ignored the man's antics as he returned to staring into the sputtering smoky fire.

How dare he think that I would run?

Hunching forward closer to the flames, he turned his thoughts back to deciding what to do, mourning the loss of so many of his best men, like Sigeberht, during their futile pursuit of Osmund's little bitch and the red-haired Dane as he did so. He now had little choice but to depend on impetuous young fools like Ædelric, making an already trying situation all the more difficult.

A little while later, a woman's soft steps intruded on his solitude. Assuming it to be some servant girl, Wilfrid was about to curse her roundly for entering without his permission when firm hands grasped his shoulders. He tensed for an instant until strong fingers pressed deep, kneading and pulling his muscles. He relaxed and stretched his back as the fingers started to ease his stiffness. Wilfrid closed his eyes as he spoke.

"The stupid little shit was afraid. It's as if the numbers are all that matter."

Tendrils of fine hair tickled his cheekbone, joined by the smell of lavender and musk as Æmma leant close.

"Unlike you, my beloved," Æmma murmured in his ear, knowing her scent was teasing him.

"No other man would have had the courage to seize the moment and do what was needed. Now, you have been afforded an opportunity to finish the job and be rid of all your foes with a single stroke."

For a while, she allowed her fingers to work, unknotting her lord's tension and easing his stress. When she judged he was ready, Æmma leant forward once more.

"Perhaps the stupid boy did have one useful idea."

Under her fingers, she felt Wilfrid's shoulders tense once more, causing her to hurriedly continue.

"Not to withdraw a yard, never that," she murmured.

Only when she felt his shoulders ease did she again whisper sweetly in his ear.

"But, perhaps, we could sow discord and distrust among those who dare oppose you. After all, the pagan Danes are greedy and faithless. When have they ever turned down gold? Equally, there is little love among those who have rallied behind Cerdic's little tart. Long have Tofi and Godric bickered on their borders. Why not pass a message to Tofi informing him that Godric has it in mind to marry the tart himself and take your crown?"

Wilfrid laughed sourly. "You would have me fight with women's weapons?"

"Only to ready them for the slaughter, my beloved."

Æmma hid a secret smile, knowing her seeds were well planted.

"Then, your blade can drink until it is sated."

Wilfrid grunted. "But Tofi will want vengeance for his brother, that bastard Osmund."

"If gold works for the Danes, why not *weregild* for Osmund? And perhaps...." Æmma paused slyly, waiting for her lord.

She smiled to herself as he demanded gruffly, "Perhaps what?"

"What if the *weregild* were also to be a *morgengifu*, the bride price for Cerdic's tart? Betroth her to our son. Then, I could keep her in my hall and under our control."

"The lad's only eleven summers."

"Then, she will have time to learn patience and obedience, won't she?"

Wilfrid guffawed at the viciously sweet tone of his wife. If the little bitch were under Æmma's control, he had no doubt she would take her time extracting a slow and painful revenge for the bitter injuries the red-haired maid had inflicted. He turned to look at his wife in the gloomy hut. Her eyes glittered with malicious glee from within the purpling bruises surrounding them while, below, the crusted, bloody mess of her flattened nose showed stark against the whiteness of her cheeks.

"And the Dane witch?"

"She's a witch. Burn her," Æmma declared before pausing to savor the thought. "Burn her slowly."

After Æmma retired from her lord's presence, something of a smile began to tug at the corners of Wilfrid's lips. At length, he came to his feet and shouted from the door of the hovel.

"Ædelric, I have work for you."

Æ

Out of the corner of his eye, Lord Tofi watched his niece closely. Gone was the meek little thing he had seen in the King's great hall or the child who had run to hug him when he visited his brother. Now, he watched as the young queen spoke animatedly and with passion to Godric's huscarl and friend, the young Bowdyn. She reached out and touched the man's arm before the two shared a smile. Tofi kept his face clear of his thoughts at that simple gesture. He had not credited the words of the scruffy little urchin who had tugged at his sleeve the previous night. Yet, in the light of the morning, his doubts began to rise. Across the camp, Elvina and Godric's man laughed again.

There was no love lost between Tofi and Godric. More than one blood feud had cost both *weregild* for the actions of their men. Now, Tofi found himself wondering if Godric was seeking to displace him by worming his way into the young queen's good graces just as Wilfrid's messenger had hinted in the gloom of the night.

"My Lord Tofi, one who wishes you no ill has a message," the boy had started. "Like you, he does not trust the Danes, faithless pagans who will turn on all honest, God-fearing Saxons at the first sniff of weakness."

At first, Tofi was going to hang the little spy from the nearest tree, but as the words tumbled out of the urchin's mouth, he started to listen. Wilfrid was offering him both *weregild* for Osmund and a place of honor. His messenger had hinted that his spies had discovered a plot by Godric to take the girl and the kingdom for himself should Wilfrid be defeated. It wasn't until he had gone out into the morning and seen his niece and Godric's friend laughing that Tofi realized there could very well be more truth to Wilfrid's warning then he had first imagined. By mid-morning, he had the urchin brought to him once more.

"Tell your master these are my terms and return with his answer tonight."

Æ

By midday, when all was ready, Tofi sought out his niece.

"Elvina, my dear, I have arranged for your aunt and her maids to join us. It is unseemly that you should not be attended, and I'm sure that after your adventures you will wish for more gentle company."

Elvina smiled with her eyes, but her tone was sharp.

"Dear uncle, you are too kind. But I intend to stay here until my father and husband are avenged and my oath to the Danes fulfilled."

"And so you must, my dear. But I would be more at ease if you were properly attended as your honor and status demands. It is no less than your father would expect."

Tofi paused as he let the barb about Osmund sink in.

"Despite the troubling times we are passing through, you must not allow yourself to forget what he taught you or who you are."

Elvina blushed at the reproof and bowed her head.

"You are right, uncle," she murmured sheepishly.

Still, a spark of defiance did remain.

"But be warned," she announced after drawing herself up. "I shall not leave here until his murderer is brought to justice and my pledge to the Danes has been fulfilled."

Tofi smiled and arranged for a trusted escort of his own men to replace the scruffy huntsman his niece had been relying on as a bodyguard before ordering them to take her to her aunt. With that taken care of, he rode out to check the camp's guards and waited for Wilfrid's reply.

Later that afternoon, when Bowdyn sought out the young queen, he was politely, but firmly, turned away from the makeshift women's hall.

"The queen is resting and being tended by her ladies," the huscarl guarding it declared curtly. "Perhaps, she will be able to see you later."

By the evening, after two more failed efforts to get past Tofi's guards, Bowdyn turned to Godric, his Lord.

"My Lord, why should she not see me when only this morning she asked me to join her for dinner?"

Godric rubbed his chin reflectively as he frowned at his disquieted friend.

"Did she say that or another?"

"It was always one of Lord Tofi's huscarls."

Godric sat still in the gathering gloom as he mulled over this unexpected development.

"It seems our friend Tofi does not approve of her freedom. Or, perhaps, it is our company to which he objects," he added upon further reflection.

After giving the matter much thought, a broad grin slowly appeared.

"There is one who even he can't stop from speaking with our queen." Godric sprung to his feet and grabbed Bowdyn's arm.

"Take that huntsman the queen is so fond of and ride at once to Elmham. Return with Bishop Beorhtred. Tofi dare not deny him access to the queen and Beorhtred owes me for his elevation to his See."

Æ

The scrawny herbalist shuffled into the Danish camp with the dawn, bowed under the weight of his pack. A sentry had grabbed him by the scruff of the neck and was dragging him to his chieftain when Hrolf intercepted him.

"What's he doing here?"

"Claims he's an herbalist, but like as not he's a spy."

Hrolf stared at the scared little man for a long instant, then turned to the guard.

"I'll take him to Snurre. You get back and make sure no more are sniffing about."

Once the sentry had headed back to his post, Hrolf leant down until his face was inches from the terrified eyes of the herbalist.

"So little spy, give me one good reason why I shouldn't gut you and leave you for the dogs."

A trembling hand inched forward and opened between the two men revealing a trio of gleaming yellow coins.

"There's lots more where that came from," the herbalist murmured. "More than a witch can offer."

Hrolf grinned before leading the man deep into the Danish camp.

Æ

Snurre had been drinking his courage since mid-morning and was already unsteady on the bench as Hrolf crouched close beside him, murmuring in his ear.

Snurre's eyebrows shot up.

"And he offered gold?"

"A thousand pieces."

"What for?"

"To go home and let Saxon fight Saxon."

Snurre peered blearily at the single gold coin in his palm.

"Would we have to share it?"

"If we march away home, then who's to know?"

"But the witch and that big bastard Sigmund who is never far from her side said we had to fight."

"Sigmund's a fool whose head has been turned by a pretty girl, a witch no less, who probably spreads her legs for him. Why should we fight? For peace? Is that what you want? No plunder? No glory? No chance of reaching Valhalla?"

As Snurre continued to stare at the single coin, Hrolf pressed his advantage.

"Even if we do fight, you should be leading us, not her. Do you really want to go into battle behind a woman's skirt? Would Folkmar have done it?"

By midday rumors and gossip began to swirl slowly around the Danish camp.

The witch has spelled us. Why else are we here with no promise of plunder? Didn't she attack our kinsmen when they sought revenge on Saxon scum? She spent time amongst the Saxons, a slave they say... Isn't she still their slave bringing us to our doom?

As the warriors muttered and drank, no one took notice of Hrolf taking the little herbalist out into the forest.

Æ

It was mid-morning as Tofi made his way to the makeshift women's hall at the center of their camp. He nodded to the huscarl standing guard and pushed past the rotting blanket that served as a door. Within, he found Elvina sitting impatiently as her aunt finished braiding her long tresses.

Elvina's face lit up when she saw him. "Are we about to attack?"

Tofi laughed. "My dear girl, warfare is rather more complex than that. We are still waiting for the levies and the Danes are still gathering their strength. We will deal with Wilfrid in good time, I assure you."

"Alfhildr never waited. She used to charge straight in before her foes had a chance to brace for her attack."

Tofi's smile grew broader. "Indeed, but I have to care for my men, our men now. I'm sure you would not wish to see men die due to lack of thought and proper preparations?"

Elvina frowned. "So, we wait? But what of Wilfrid?" Her voice rose at that thought. "I want, no, I *demand*, justice for Cerdic and my father."

"And justice we shall have." Tofi's voice rose to match that of his niece.

"But if it is at the cost of good men slain for no reason and Danish warbands running amok on our borders, then the price is too high. You are a queen now. As such, you are obliged to put the good of your folk before yourself."

Elvina's shoulders slumped as her uncle's reproof bit home.

"You are right. I must learn to put my people first and be patient."

She paused for a moment in thought.

"But what of the Danes? What of my oath to Alfhildr?"

"They want peace? Then, peace we shall give them. I daresay many of their warriors will be glad if it can be won without shedding blood."

Tofi watched in satisfaction as Elvina reluctantly accepted his argument.

"I will take my leave now. There is still much to arrange."

And with that, he turned and pushed his way out past the mildewed blanket and into the bright sunshine.

"Ah, my Lord Tofi."

Tofi's head snapped up to see a man in a richly embroidered gown standing before him.

"Bishop Beorhtred. What brings you to our camp? I would have thought a church would be more appropriate than a battlefield."

"That is so. But we must also minister to our flock when they are most in need," the portly bishop smiled as he gestured to his companions.

"Lord Godric here felt your forces and your niece would be in need of spiritual guidance and asked if I would come. Indeed, I came so swiftly that I have only one scribe to attend me."

Beside him a young monk in a rough brown robe bowed his head.

"Young Plegmund here, apparently has travelled widely in these lands as well as having a fine neat hand."

The young monk blushed, keeping his eyes on the ground as Beorhtred sketched a blessing in the air above Lord Tofi before making his way into the women's hovel. As he passed within, Tofi and Godric exchanged polite nods, their faces carefully blank.

Æ

Throughout the bright morning, as the three armies continued to watch each other's camp across the water meadows, the bishop scurried between Godric, Tofi, and the women's hut.

"My dear Godric, can't you see that any war would be ill-advised. What Tofi proposes is both prudent and safe. Surely, you of all people have no love for the Danes after what they did to your brother?"

"I gave my solemn oath to the old King. Would you have me break an oath made before God?"

"Of course not, my son. But we must look to the future. The law is plain. If Wilfrid offers *weregild*, then it is only Christian, as well as wise, to accept it."

"And Elvina?"

The bishop gently smiled. "She is a young girl. In time, her grief will fade. A union with Wilfrid's house will not only hurry that, it will protect both our people and the holy mother church."

"I don't trust Wilfrid."

"But can you trust the Danes? Young Plegmund here knows as much of them as any man. He even met their witch."

Godric's eyes narrowed as he stared at the hesitant young monk.

"Perhaps, there is something in what you say, Your Grace. You have given me much on which to think."

Satisfied that he succeeded in his self-appointed task, Bishop Beorhtred pushed himself to his feet.

"Then, I shall leave you to your thoughts with my blessings."

As the bishop turned to go, Godric cleared his throat. "Your Grace? If you have no objection, could Brother Plegmund remain and pray with me? I fear I shall need the Lord's guidance as well as His wisdom during my deliberations."

A smile tugged at the corners of the bishop's lips.

"Of course, my son, of course. I shall leave you to your thoughts and prayers with my blessings. When you have reached your decision, one I am sure the Lord will smile upon, send Brother Plegmund to me with your answer."

After carefully straightening his robes, the Bishop made his way back toward the women's hut.

Brother Plegmund sat uncomfortably as Godric watched him in silence. He felt like a mouse in the presence of a playful cat. At last, he could stand the silence no longer.

"My Lord, you would pray?"

Godric watched him for a moment longer before replying.

"No. I wish to talk. Is what the Bishop said true? Have you met the Dane witch?"

Surprised by the question, Plegmund once more answered with more honesty than tact.

"My Lord, she is no witch. The Dane who goes by the name Alfhildr is just a young girl with a skill for war who carries with her a wound in her heart I fear may never heal."

"But the wolf?"

"Skadi? She likes having her tummy scratched."

Godric found himself taken aback by the casual, off-handed manner with which the monk answered this question, causing him to pause before continuing.

There is a child-like innocence about this monk, Godric told himself, a naïveté that told him he could be trusted.

"They say the girl has a wolf's dugs and the wings of a bat hidden under her clothes."

Plegmund grinned. "No, she's just a girl."

"How would you know? Have you seen her naked?" Godric watched as the young monk blushed beet red, causing the Saxon noble to laugh.

"So, you have. I will not ask how that came to pass," he muttered in jest before once more turning to the matter at hand. "Is she pretty?"

This time, it was Godric who waited uncomfortably under Plegmund's gaze. At last, the monk answered, but his gaze had now shifted to the landscape of his memory.

"Yes, My Lord, she is pretty," he admitted softly. "But it is her voice and her spirit that are truly beautiful," he continued as he looked up at the Saxon lord.

"Though she may pay homage to pagan gods, I have never met another who has a soul as pure or as honest as hers. On that, I swear before our Lord."

"Tell me about her." Godric meant it as a command, but Plegmund heard the wistful plea in the warrior's voice and smiled.

Æ

As the shadows began to lengthen, Plegmund made his way toward the women's hut. He had seen his Lord Bishop in close counsel with Lord Tofi and knew he would not have a better chance. The huscarl on duty looked at him quizzically as he approached but bowed his head and stood aside as the young monk sketched a blessing in the air before entering the hut.

As he stood just inside the hut, while his eyes adjusted to the dark within, Elvina stared disconsolately at the skinny young man. Inside, she felt a leaden weight as the hints and suggestions of her uncle and the Bishop had coalesced into the awful truth of their plans while Godric and Bowdyn stayed away as if she were unfit to be even be seen with. Her uncle and the Bishop both wanted her to betray her father, her husband, her oath, and her friend, a betrayal dressed up in pretty words designed to make it appear as if it was her duty to do so. Now, they had sent yet another churchman to plead and twist her conscience.

"My Lady, may I speak?" His voice was diffident and unsure.

"Why not? Everyone else has hammered my ears to remind me of my duty." Elvina's tone had a bitter edge.

Plegmund came closer and knelt as if in prayer beside the distraught young queen. On the far side of the hut, her Aunt nodded approvingly before turning back to her maids.

"I bring a message from a friend and news of another." His words were pitched low and Elvina had to strain to hear.

"Does Skadi still like to have her tummy tickled?"

In that instant, Elvina's heart soared. She was no longer alone.

Æ

The sun was finally setting when Plegmund picked his way between the lean-tos and shelters of the Saxon camp to where Godric waited. As he ducked under the lintel, a grin was plastered from ear to ear despite his disobedience to his Lord, the Bishop.

"I have a letter from the queen for both you and Alfhildr. She remains determined, despite her uncle and my Lord. Can you see it safe delivered to the Danish camp?"

Within minutes, Bowdyn and a handful of companions were riding east toward the cluster of Danish banners.

Æ

Throughout the afternoon, the sour rumors and arguments about the red-headed witch had washed across the Danish camp. As the dark gathered and men supped more mead, isolated fights broke out. They were quickly stopped by their chieftains, but even they began to look suspiciously toward the small lean-to shelter the girl had set up in the midst of Sigmund's warband. As Alfhildr and the bearlike Sigmund had walked around the camp perimeter, conversations stilled at their approach as men took to watching the two with an appraising eye. When they reached Snurre's section of the line, the looks were more hostile, and men did not lower their voices.

A shout went up from a nearby sentry, "Saxon riders," causing men to toss aside whatever they had been doing and quickly take up shields and spears. Sigmund and Alfhildr hurried toward the shout, along with a score of half-drunken warriors. When Alfhildr reached the guard, she could see four riders warily approaching, their shields slung across their backs to show they came in peace. Behind her, men watched suspiciously as the lead rider reined to a halt a spear's throw away.

"I have word from the queen for her Danish allies and the warrior Alfhildr."

Alfhildr smiled as she recognized the muscular huscarl and shouted back a heartfelt greeting.

"Approach, friend, and bring me your queen's message."

Bowdyn slipped from his horse and came forward on foot. He grinned when he saw the small red-headed warrior, then paused at the sight of the burly giant fingering his axe beside her.

When Alfhildr caught the suspicious glances between the two men, she stepped between them.

"Peace, Bowdyn. You are safe here. I would have you and Sigmund as friends, as both are warriors I would trust on my right side."

At her words both men looked back at her sheepishly.

"This peace business will take some learning," Bowdyn muttered as he shook his head while Sigmund snorted in amusement at sharing the same thought.

"You have word from the Queen?"

Bowdyn stepped forward, but before he could speak, a loud voice shouted from the watching Danish warriors.

"Fresh orders from your Saxon masters? What do they want now? To harness us like oxen to the yokes of their ploughs?"

Alfhildr spun round in fury to see Snurre pushing his way toward her with his grinning shadow, Hrolf, close behind. Snurre planted his feet belligerently in front of the huscarl.

"So, what's your message, Saxon? We all want to hear. There are no secrets amongst us." He turned and looked sideways at Alfhildr. "Or are there?"

Alfhildr's hand leapt for Durthfang, only to feel a tight grasp on her wrist. In her rage, she glared up at her captor to see Sigmund shaking his head slowly.

"My Lady, the Queen, has no secrets from her valiant allies. Her message is simple and for all to hear. She stands by her oath to fight alongside you and to live in peace with you."

Bowdyn glanced across at the young warrior girl and the suspicious throng around her as he considered if it was safe to give her the letter with which his Lord had entrusted him.

"Is that all?" Snurre demanded with a sneer.

"What else is there to say? An oath was made. An oath will be kept."

Then, regretfully, Bowdyn turned away and returned to his waiting companions.

Behind him, Snurre turned to the waiting warriors.

"Well, I have something to say. We have wasted enough time on this foolishness. I do not care for some girl's oath. I call for a council to be held tonight, where I will demand we put an end to this childish dream. We will never live in peace with Saxon scum for their oaths are worth less than my piss."

A growl of agreement echoed from many throats until Sigmund stepped forward.

"A council is it? Well, you have the right, as do we all. But not when half-stewed in mead. If there is to be a council, then it shall be in the morning. Only fools and halfwits spout prattle when sotted."

His gaze swept across the watching warriors, daring any to challenge his word. At last, he stared at Snurre until the young chieftain's eyes slipped away from his angry glare.

"No one disagrees? Good! Tomorrow it is."

Æ

Alfhildr's knuckles were white as she followed Sigmund back to his camp, wishing as she did so that her blade had not missed her brother during her battle with him, the one which had set this long journey of hers in motion.

"That slimy little toad spawn. That little dog turd. I'll slice his guts out and feed them to him. I'll...."

"Wait and see what happens." Sigmund interjected.

Alfhildr gawped in shock at the burly warrior as he grinned in the gathering dusk.

"Now hold your peace, little elf," Sigmund whispered as his eyes darted about. "The dark has long ears."

Though she tried to pry more from him, he just grinned. Infuriated, Alfhildr rolled herself in her blanket and hugged the bemused Skadi close.

Despite her certainty that she wouldn't sleep, many hours passed until a shout dragged Alfhildr from her dreams. Startled, her eyes flew open to the sight of Sigmund standing over her in the dark.

"Come, little sister. Come and see what mice we have found scurrying in the woods."

With that he turned and headed to the campfire.

Rubbing her eyes, Alfhildr unrolled herself from her blankets and away from a complaining Skadi before stumbling across to the fire. In its light, she could see a scrawny ferret of a man, his eyes wide with fear, being held tight between two of Sigmund's warriors. Skadi padded over and sniffed at his groin. The man moaned as his bladder let loose to the amusement of the watching men while Skadi quickly backed away to escape the unexpected torrent.

Sigmund stalked over to the helpless captive and lowered his face so he could stare into the man's terrified eyes.

"So, little mouse, why were you scurrying around in these woods?"

As he spoke, his hands were deftly running over the man's clothes and pouch. He smiled as he opened the pouch and thrust his hand within.

"You're a wealthy little mouse, aren't you?"

When he pulled his hand out, men gasped at the fistful of gold glittering in the firelight.

"What's going on here?" Snurre called out as he pushed his way through the spellbound circle with an ever-present Hrolf pressing close behind.

Alfhildr could hear the desperation in her brother's tone.

Sigmund didn't bother to turn round.

"We caught ourselves a little spy, creeping around with gold to spare."

He looked up and cast his eye around the watching warriors.

"Has anyone seen this man before?"

His gaze settled on Snurre and Hrolf, but another voice called out.

"He claimed he was an herbalist. But I handed him over to one of Snurre's men and went back to my post."

Sigmund grinned, his eyes not leaving Snurre.

"And is that man here?"

"Aye, he's the big bugger behind Snurre."

Hrolf sauntered close to the fire.

"He seemed harmless enough and he had herbs, so I sent him on his way. What of it? If he's a spy, kill him and have done with it."

Without stopping, Hrolf whipped out his dagger and lunged for the pinioned man. Alfhildr leapt forward, ripping Durthfang from its scabbard as she did to block the desperate Hrolf.

Caught totally off guard by the girl's speed and the feeling of sharp, cold steel being pressed against his throat, he shuddered to a halt.

"Why so eager to kill him, Hrolf?" Alfhildr murmured while sporting a sly little smile. "I want to hear what he can tell us. Don't you?"

When Hrolf did not answer, she turned toward her brother. It was only then, as she looked deep into his frantic eyes that she knew he had been bought. Despite her best efforts, the red mist of her rage began to well up within her, leaving her struggling to keep it under control. She stepped back and spoke to the watching warriors.

"Go! All of you," she snapped. "This will be dealt with in the light of day, not hidden in the dark."

She watched as her brother winced at her words. At length, and to the sound of muttered grumbling, the men reluctantly began to disperse until she called out once more.

"Snurre. I would have words with you."

The young chieftain unwillingly turned to face the angry shield maiden, the flames of the fire turning her loose tresses blood red.

"You called for a council in the morning. Well, know this. If there is a council, then before we discuss anything concerning the future actions of this army, I will demand that this spy is put to the test in front of everyone. Do you understand?"

She paused to watch as guilt crawled across her brother's face.

"Of course," Alfhildr continued with a smugness that warned Snurre she knew he was guilty. "Should we need to march off into battle before the chieftains can be gathered, there will be no time to put the spy to the test, will there? If that proves to be the case, then I see no need to bother ourselves with this sad matter. We will simply hang him and be done with it."

She smiled coldly at the nervous young chieftain.

"I shall look forward to hearing your decision."

With that, she turned her back dismissively and returned to her lean-to without another word.

Æ

The fires were also bright in the camp of the young queen's army. Not far from the women's hut, Lord Tofi had gathered together the other lords and their huscarls. With Bishop Beorhtred at his side and an eye on Godric, Tofi cleared his throat, causing the crowd to fall silent.

"My friends, I have momentous news. None of us wish for our realm to be torn asunder and for that reason..."

"No, none of us wish to see our realm torn asunder." Elvina's high voice cut across Tofi's carefully planned words. "None of us wish for brother to turn against brother and families to turn against themselves."

Having made her presence known, Elvina stepped into the circle of light being thrown off by the fire. All eyes turned toward the young queen who, but a few scant weeks before, had been thought of as little more than an empty-headed girl of little use other than to breed. The stern-faced figure before them, casting her sharp gaze from man to man, made all who saw her suddenly aware of a strength she had hidden well. With her hair tightly braided and pinned, and attired in a flowing red gown trimmed with otter pelt, she took her place in the center of the gathering. In one hand, she grasped a heavy war spear, its tip still dripping with the blood of a freshly slain goat. In the other, she held the shield Bowdyn had given her after escaping from the King's great hall. It too was splattered with blood, the blood of her kinsmen.

"There are those among you who feel that any king is better than strife. There are those here who crave a strong arm above a just one."

She turned and looked coolly at Bishop Beorhtred before she went on.

"There are those who seek the safety of the Holy Church above what is right."

Elvina paused as her gaze once more swept the assembled warriors.

"Do any of you believe Wilfrid is a just man? Does anyone here believe a man who murdered the rightful heir to the throne is an honorable man? Would you trust him on your right in the shield wall?" She paused again. "Any of you?"

Behind her, Elvina heard her uncle stir, causing her to whirl around and face him.

"Lord Tofi, *you* have the right to accept *weregild* for my father's death. But as a widow, I too have rights. I can accept or refuse *weregild* for my husband. I alone will choose if I wed again. That is the law!"

Only when she saw he wasn't going to contest her point did she turn once more to address the assembled nobles and their retainers.

"Before God, I give you my oath: I shall never accept *weregild* for the murder of Cerdic. I shall never marry into the house of the usurper. I will stand on this field and face the man who murdered my father and my husband."

Elvina's eyes flashed as she thundered out her pledge before her warriors.

"And I...will...have...peace...with...the Danes!"

Then, before a man could move, she held the spear high above her head and twirled it about with stunning ease before driving its blade deep into the turf before her astonished uncle. With that, she turned and haughtily stalked through the silent, awestruck crowd to return to the women's hut, tightly clutching the shield that was, for her, the last link she had to her father.

Chapter Nineteen
THE BOAR SNOUT

Present Day England
"The Dig"

Like everyone else, Sarah ignored the way Elva groused when Professor Bannon announced that they were taking a day off from toiling at the dig in order to visit Daneford Meadows, the site where local legend held that the battle between Godric's army and the usurper to Cerdic's throne had taken place. Though she would never admit it, Sarah could tell Elva was looking forward to the little excursion.

As was her way, upon disembarking from the minivan, the winsome red-haired graduate student wandered off from the group. Sarah followed close behind, crossing a small stream, before drawing up next to Elva on a small rise that looked back over the empty meadow they had just crossed.

Without looking over at her friend, Elva began to speak in a hushed, almost reverend tone.

"Can you imagine what it must have been like?" she whispered as her eyes scanned off to the left where Professor Bannon told them the army loyal to the old king had mustered.

"Shield wall smashing into shield wall. It began there, at the edge of the small stream when the usurper's army fell upon the outnumbered Danes," Elva recounted as her voice took on an edge.

"From their commanding position, Elvina's nobles held back at first, content to watch the Danes bloody and wear down the usurper's army."

Cocking her head to one side, Sarah glanced quizzically over at her friend.

"I thought it was Godric's army?"

Out of the corner of her eye, Elva regarded Sarah.

"That may have been what was recorded in the Saxon chronicles, but it's not the way things were."

"And you know this how?" Sarah asked incredulously.

Elva did not answer. Instead, she went back to studying the lay of the land, easily piecing together in her mind how the events of that long-ago day had played out when a red-haired Dane girl and a wolf led an army into battle.

Æ

England
1012 AD

No longer able to contain his excitement now that they had finally reached the part of the story that he had been anxiously awaiting, the young boy all but tugged at his grandmother's hand.

"Yes, yes, you have already explained how the nobles who had rallied to Queen Elvina's standard were reluctant to fight the usurper's army. I can tell you: I wouldn't have held back, not for a moment. I would have pitched into them the moment I spotted their encampment."

The boy's comment caused the grandmother to glance over at the willowy, red-haired child.

Yes, she told herself, *he probably would have, just as his impetuous ancestor had.*

Æ

The Saga of the Boar Snout

No trumpet was needed, no cautious plea heeded.
Red hair was their standard, a she-wolf their guide,
Boldly, the Danes advanced behind the shield maiden,
Yet, quiet Saxon lords stayed their young queen's hand.

Ahead of her army, the lone shield maiden strode,
As cowards and worms, her foes did she goad.
At length, a brave huscarl accepted her challenge,
Yet, Durthfang bit deep, and he fell to the ground.

In fury, the Saxons swept down off their hill.
The crash of the shield walls like thunder did roll.
With Sigmund beside her, and Skadi close by,
Beneath the raven banner, Alfhildr stood her ground.

Holding back from the fight, the queen's army did watch,
As the Danes fought their battle and blunted their spears
The young queen cried out for her oath to be honoured,
And brave Godric stepped forth to answer her call.

The shield walls drew back, both sodden with blood,
As the queen's men advanced, come fresh to the fray.
Their spears bit home hard, but the shield wall stood firm
The usurper's brave warriors two armies did hold.

Lord Godric knew then that apart they were beaten
Only as one could the battle be won.
He looked to his left and saw the Danes' banner,
The bright raven showed proud above their grim ranks.

> *Below that brave raven, red hair drew him close.*
> *Bloodied but unbowed, the shield maiden called.*
> *"With me, a boar's snout," she demanded with glee*
> *"Together," he answered as their shields married tight.*
>
> Æ

All hope that the indecision staying the hand of those who had rallied around Elvina's red serpent banner had been overcome by persuasion or guile disappeared when Alfhildr rose from her bedroll on the third morning. She saw no indication that the young queen's forces were making any preparations to assemble. Disheartened by this, as well as the prospect of facing a contentious council of her own later that day, Alfhildr wandered out beyond the edge of the Dane camp facing the two Saxon encampments where she could be alone and think. There, she sank to the ground with Skadi at her side. Together, the two looked out across the open meadow at the ridge where Wilfrid's army sat, waiting patiently for distrust and internal strife to tear his foes apart.

At first, all of Alfhildr's thoughts were squarely focused on what she would do if it came to pass that a confrontation between her and Snurre could not be avoided. Ever so slowly, her concerns began to fade as her eyes kept being drawn to a line of scrubby gorse that lay between where she was sitting and the usurper's camp. The low-lying vegetation continued on around and through the shallow dip that separated Wilfrid's ridge and the one Elvina's forces occupied. There was a stream there. Alfhildr was sure of it. Small by any measure, one she imagined anyone would be able to ford with ease. Moving a formed body of warriors across it, however, was an entirely different matter. It would break up the cohesion of any shield wall, no matter how slowly it advanced. No commander would willingly take it on with an enemy within striking distance, not if he could avoid it. As Alfhildr saw it, the problem she needed to solve was how to convince Wilfrid it was to his advantage to come down off his commanding heights, cross the meandering little stream, and attack her.

Provided of course, she thought to herself as she glanced over her shoulder at the small knots of Dane chieftains who were gathering behind her to talk among themselves, *she had a force with her for Wilfrid to attack.*

"They're arguing again," Alfhildr sadly muttered to Skadi as she kneaded the loose skin about the wolf's neck.

"They are asking themselves the same questions Elvina's nobles are. 'Why should we fight for a mere girl?', 'Can we trust a people who are our blood enemies?', and," she concluded with a hint of bitter cynicism, "'What's in this for me?'"

Coming to her feet, Alfhildr once more looked out over the field before her.

"I expect if I were them, I would be asking the same questions," she sighed.

"But I am not them. I am Alfhildr," the young red-haired girl concluded. Drawing herself up, she took in a deep breath, which she slowly let out.

"Come, Skadi," she called out as she turned to head back to her shelter. "Let's see if this Dane witch can conjure up some magic."

Æ

When Sigmund saw Alfhildr arming herself, he called to his men to do likewise before going over to find out what she was up to.

"Off to pay our Saxon friends a visit?" he asked jokingly.

"Yes," she replied looking up at him. "Would you care to join me?"

Alfhildr's determined expression and the look in her eye told the red-bearded chieftain she was deadly serious. Having come to expect the unexpected from the diminutive female warrior, Sigmund wasted no time calling for his men to form up at the double-quick even as he raced back to retrieve his own axe and helm.

The sudden flurry of activity around Alfhildr's raven banner caught the attention of the other Dane warriors by surprise, causing them to assume they had somehow missed an order to take their place in the line of battle. Without waiting for any word from their own chieftains, they took to arming themselves as well before rushing over to form up on either side of Sigmund's warband. Those chieftains who attempted to hold their men back until they found out what was going on were hooted down and jeered as their own men pushed them aside. One of Snurre's fiercest warriors, who had been grabbed by Snurre, pulled his arm away from the young chieftain and glared at him with unveiled contempt.

"Stay if you like and hide in Hrolf's shadow, but I and the rest of your kinsmen go forward."

At the center of the rapidly expanding line of animated men was Alfhildr, waiting under a banner bearing the image of a bird that Sigmund claimed was a raven, but the diminutive red-haired Dane insisted was a crow. Unable to see over the heads of her own warriors, she turned to Sigmund.

"Well?"

After taking a quick look around, Sigmund grunted.

"All those who will be coming are here. We are ready."

"Does everyone know the agreed upon signals?"

Sigmund nodded.

"All know one blast from Eirik's horn means advance. Two will bring the line to a stop."

"And should we need to go back?" Alfhildr asked.

The towering warrior's expression darkened.

"Sigmund, the Just, never retreats," he muttered contemptuously.

"You will if I so order it," the winsome young girl attired in mail glowered as she stared down the massive chieftain before her.

"A long, steady tune will cause the shield wall to back off, maybe," Sigmund added.

"Fine," Alfhildr snapped. "Now, are you ready?"

"Ready for what?"

That was a good question, Alfhildr thought as she took her place next to Sigmund.

What had begun as nothing more than an impulse now demanded a deliberate act, one of a magnitude unlike any Alfhildr had ever undertaken. Sigmund must have understood what was going through her mind, for he placed a gentle hand on her shoulder and whispered in her ear.

"We are with you."

Thus reassured, Alfhildr once more took in a deep breath before she slowly drew Durthfang from its sheath, raised it briefly above her head and then lowered it until its tip was pointed at the center of Wilfrid's camp.

"Forward!"

Æ

The sight of the Dane shield wall moving across the open meadow toward Wilfrid's ridge caused both Saxon camps to spring to life. The nobles who had followed the usurper gathered about him. With unabashed glee, he watched but for a second before ordering them to form their men and prepare to give battle. That the Danes would be foolish enough to attack his position without waiting for the young queen's army to join them was an unexpected stroke of luck, one on which he had not counted. Perhaps, he thought to himself, if he routed the Danes, the nobles who had rallied to Elvina's standard would see the error of their way and desert the girl who was queen in name only.

From the other ridge where Elvina and her army were encamped, the young Saxon queen watched the advancing Danes for but a moment before turning to her uncle who had rushed to her side.

"Form the army," she commanded.

Tofi took a moment to study the jumbled Dane formation as it slowly lurched across the meadow below them as well as Wilfrid's response to it. His keen military eye told him all he needed to know. Despite their fearsome reputation as warriors, the outnumbered Danes stood little chance of prevailing over Wilfrid's superior numbers and his commanding position, a fact of which Tofi suspected many a Dane warrior was well aware. Even the manner in which both flanks bowed back from the center marked by the raven banner, especially the Dane left, told him that the majority of the warriors down there did not have their hearts in the little witch's enterprise.

"I will form your army, but I advise we hold," he informed the girl who he viewed more as a niece than his queen.

At first, Elvina was confused as she glanced back and forth between the advancing Danes and her uncle. She had listened to what he and her nobles had said in their war councils. She had gleaned enough from those long, drawn out, and pointless debates to understand that the Danes could not hope to overcome Wilfrid's army so long as the usurper held firmly to the high ground upon which he stood.

"Hold?" she asked incredulously as she watched the raven banner that marked where her friend continued to boldly advance.

"Hold for what?"

"To see what happens," Tofi explained as if he were speaking to a child. "If the Danes are routed, then there will be no point in our risking battle. If they do manage to break Wilfrid's army, then we will wait until both armies are scattered and exhausted."

"But you know the Danes cannot break Wilfrid's shield wall where it stands. You yourself said as much," Elvina asserted, hoping as she did so there was something she still did not understand about war and strategy, but suspecting otherwise. "What then?"

When Tofi did not answer, Elvina found she had no choice but to make a statement, one none of those who had flocked to her father's red serpent banner could ignore. Without another word, she pivoted about on her heels and stormed off to the women's hut.

Ignoring the antics of his naïve niece, Tofi smiled to himself as he watched the Danes continue.

Æ

Unable to stay at her mistress' side as the tight packed ranks of the Dane shield wall advanced, Skadi raced out before Alfhildr. To the men standing in the front ranks of both Saxon armies, it seemed as if the Danes were being led by a wolf, causing more than a few to mutter to their neighbor as an uncomfortable feeling slowly wove its way up their spines. Though they were all good men, ready to fulfill their obligation to their lord, most were farmers and tradesmen called from their hearth to fight when needed. Few had anything more than a spear, shield, and helmet. To them, the Danes were monsters, vicious creatures from another world. The sight of a wolf leading them into battle and rumors that they had a witch in their midst only added to the apprehension all men feel when battle is at hand.

Æ

Just before they reached the line of scrub she had been eyeing, Alfhildr brought the Dane shield wall to a stop. Beyond the small stream and atop the gentle rise beyond it, Wilfrid's forces had formed their own shield wall. After pausing just long enough to muster up the courage for what she would need to do next, Alfhildr stepped out of line. Turning to Sigmund, she removed her helmet. As she was handing it to him, she issued her final instructions.

"Whatever happens, do not advance. Have some of your men quietly spread the word for all archers to drop back and form a line behind the rear rank."

"So, little one, are you going to tell me what you intend to do?" Sigmund asked as he took to leaning on the handle of his upturned battleax.

Alfhildr managed to muster up a brave little smile as she looked up at the massive red-bearded warrior.

"I thought I would go out there and invite Wilfrid's army to come off their ridge and join us here for a little friendly blood-letting."

Sigmund snorted. "If anyone can charm them off that hill, it's you."

"It's not charm I intend to use," she replied, giving the red-bearded Dane a sly little smile and wink.

"I'm counting on male vanity, Saxon pride, and the arrogance of a man who thinks he is fit to be a king."

After signaling Skadi to stay, Alfhildr made her way to the little stream that she forded with ease.

Once across, she gave her head a quick shake, causing her flowing, red hair to cascade about her shoulders. Ready, she rested the flat of her sword on her shoulder as she took to slowly strolling back and forth along the length of the stream, looking up at Wilfrid's shield wall.

"I am Alfhildr," she bellowed, "sword arm of the gods and protector of Saxon and Dane. I have come to watch you pledge your allegiance to Elvina, your queen."

Up until then, the Saxon shield wall had stood silent. Now, a chorus of laughter and jeers erupted all along its length. Alfhildr waited until it died down. When it did, she stopped and swung Durthfang off her shoulder in a wide, dramatic sweep before planting its tip in the ground and placing both of her hands upon its pommel.

"So, it has come to this," she proclaimed. "I shall have to beat you into submission."

"You will die trying, witch," a lone voice called out, just as Alfhildr had hoped.

"And who will do this valiant deed?" she shouted. "Which of you brave warriors, defender of a man who murdered his own king has the courage to come down here and strike me down?"

The silence that followed was broken only by the sound of nervous shuffling within the ranks of Wilfrid's army as kinsmen surreptitiously eyed their neighbors. Behind Alfhildr, Sigmund turned to his own men who were all exchanging broad grins as they realized what she was up to.

When she had waited long enough, Alfhildr grasped her sword by its hilt and once more took to pacing, only this time she was animated, feigning rage as she glared at the ranks above her.

"I would piss on your so-called Saxon honor and courage, but first I would need to find it," she spat. "Are there any men quivering behind your shields who has the courage to face a mere girl?" Alfhildr thundered. "Are there any men among you at all?" Stopping, she threw her arms out to her side. "Are there? One! Find one, just one who has the balls to come down here, to me, and take me on."

"You are a witch," a voice called out.

"And you are a coward, hiding among cowards," she growled as she thrust the tip of her sword at Wilfrid's assembled army.

Ædelric found himself unable to tolerate the taunts being hurled at them by a waif of a girl. That, coming in the wake of the insults Wilfrid had heaped upon him when he had brought news of the Dane army proved to be too much for the proud warrior to endure.

Determined to show his new king and fellow huscarls that he was someone who could not be trifled with, Ædelric pushed his way through the linked shields of his kinsmen. As he boldly marched down the slope to where Alfhildr stood, a cheer rose up from Wilfrid's army, drowning out the usurper's desperate shouts for the impetuous fool to hold his position. At the foot of the hill, Alfhildr ignored the cheers of the Saxons as she watched him approach.

"So, it begins," she whispered as a grin slowly crept across her face.

As the Saxon huscarl made his way to where she was waiting, Alfhildr sized up her foe. Ædelric was a well-built man, not nearly as tall or broad in the shoulder as Sigmund but a stout, imposing warrior, nonetheless. Drawing upon every ounce of courage she could muster, Alfhildr tossed aside her shield before bringing her sword up and resting it upon her shoulder once more.

When he was within a rod of her, the Saxon stopped. For her part, Alfhildr took up a slow, leisurely pace as she circled about him, looking her opponent over from head to toe as if inspecting a horse that she wished to buy.

"So, you are going to do what so many men who have gone before you have failed to do," she stated calmly as she continued to slowly circle about the Saxon.

"May I see the face of the valiant warrior who will be remembered for all times as the man who slew the red-haired Dane witch?"

Without a moment's hesitation, the huscarl threw off his helmet and pulled back the mail hood that had been protecting his head and neck.

"I am Ædelric, son of Hunuald, defender of my King and humble servant to our blessed Lord Jesus. I have no need of mail or helm to protect me from a common pagan whore," he proudly proclaimed. "God is with me," the huscarl thundered.

Turning her head, Alfhildr spat on the ground. "That is what I think of you and your god."

No longer able to contain the rage Ædelric had managed to keep in check up until that moment, the young huscarl brought his sword up high, drew his bulky shield tightly against his chest, and let out a fearsome war cry as he lunged at Alfhildr with all the finesse of a wild boar. Unburdened by a shield and far quicker on her feet, Alfhildr danced about to her right, just as she had done when she had faced Sigmund. Ædelric, caught off-guard by the Dane's speed, attempted to follow her movements by twisting his torso about, bringing his sword arm around and craning his neck in an effort to keep his eye on the fleeting target. Taking advantage of the opportunity this awkward stance presented her, Alfhildr grasped the hilt of her sword with both hands, swung it about in a wide, sweeping arch and with all her might, brought it down upon the back of the Saxon's outstretched neck.

Durthfang's razor sharp blade hardly slowed as it sliced cleanly through the Saxon's neck, sending the head flying off and showering Alfhildr in a misty haze of blood. An audible gasp rose up from the ranks of Wilfrid's army as it drew back in horror. Behind her, Sigmund led a low, guttural chant that echoed across the field to the accompaniment of shields being beaten by swords and spears.

"Alfhildr! Alfhildr! Alfhildr!"

Ignoring the adoration of her own troops, Alfhildr made her way to where Ædelric's head had landed. Picking it up by its hair, she held it at arm's length and spat into the lifeless eyes of the slain warrior before tossing it back up the hill toward Wilfrid's shield wall. With the taste of her foe's blood on her lips and her pulse racing, Alfhildr once more threw her arms out at her side as she faced the assembled host before her.

"Is that the best of you?" she thundered. "Is there not a man among you who can hold his own against me?"

By this time, the dead Saxon's head had rolled back down the hill to where Alfhildr stood. With as much effort as she could, she kicked it aside once more spitting on it as it rolled away.

The insults and abuse being heaped upon Ædelric's mortal remains by the vile Dane witch proved too much for his kinsmen. Following a mighty roar, they broke ranks and surged forward, vowing vengeance and hurling insults at Alfhildr for the manner in which she had disrespected their slain brother, friend, and comrade. Behind them, Wilfrid, hoarse from his efforts to keep his army in check, found he had little choice but to follow the jumbled mass of warriors he no longer commanded. With cohesion lost, and, with it his ability to control his army, all now depended upon his superior numbers and Tofi's ability to keep his young queen in check.

Alfhildr allowed herself a self-satisfied smile as she watched Wilfrid's shield wall disintegrate before her eyes. Having accomplished what she had set out to do, the red-haired girl retrieved her shield before leisurely making her way back across the stream to rejoin her own army, pausing only long enough to give the Saxon's head one more boot with her foot.

Æ

Try as he might, Wilfrid could not stop the headlong charge his army had taken up. The best he could manage to do was to find a piece of high ground at the foot of the ridge that his army had once occupied and watch as his warriors rushed forward.

Ignoring the arrows that pelted them and led by enraged huscarls who had been sprinkled about among the common thegns to stiffen their resolve, the Saxons stormed across the stream and valiantly pressed on. All who could manage to do so pushed their way forward to where the witch stood side by side with a monstrous Dane made even more frightening by his wild, red beard.

For their part, Alfhildr and Sigmund greeted the teaming mass before them with something akin to glee. In their rush to be the first to extract vengeance, the Saxons pressed against one another, denying their neighbor as well as themselves the room they needed to properly wield their weapons. With brutal efficiency, Alfhildr and Sigmund worked together. Swinging his doubled-handed axe high above his head, Sigmund rained down killing blow after killing blow upon the jumbled mass before them. Crouching low, with her shield held above her head to protect both herself and Sigmund's exposed torso, Alfhildr hacked at the unprotected ankles and calves of her foes or thrust upwards under the mail shirts and shields of the Saxon's before them, disemboweling them with brutal efficiency. Even Skadi managed to join this bloody mayhem, darting out from between the red-bearded warrior and her mistress to snap, grab, and rip away at any exposed flesh into which she could sink her teeth.

And so, it went on, up and down the length of the Dane shield wall. With his advantage of position forfeited by a frenzied quest for vengeance and his superiority in numbers of little use because of the haphazard manner in which his army had fallen upon the Dane shield wall, all Wilfrid could do was watch from the small mound that he shared with his standard bearer and a few chosen huscarls and hope in time numbers would prevail.

Æ

At first, Elvina's aunt said nothing as she watched her niece strip off her gown and replace it with a pair of worn trousers and a blood-stained tunic that she pulled from her camp chest. Though Merica did not know it, those articles of male clothing were the very same ones Alfhildr had given her after their flight from the King's great hall. Only when the older woman saw the young queen take up a mail shirt did she realize what was afoot.

"Just what do you think you are doing?" Merica demanded imperiously.

"I made a pledge to a friend that I am obliged to fulfill," Elvina replied without bothering to look over at her aunt as she struggled to pull the mail shirt down about her.

"I will not allow you to leave this hut dressed like a common ceorl," Merica stated in a tone meant to inform the young girl in no uncertain terms that though she may have been a queen, she was not at liberty to do as she pleased.

When this approach did nothing to stop Elvina, as she took to fastening a sword about her waist, Merica decided to take matters in hand. Drawing herself up, she made for her niece as Elvina was adjusting her panoply.

"I will not stand by idly and watch you make a fool of yourself," she thundered.

Satisfied all was fitted about her just as Alfhildr had shown her, Elvina once more reached down into her camp chest to retrieve her helmet. That was when she felt her aunt's hand on her arm.

"Are you listening to me, girl?" Merica demanded.

Naturally, Merica expected some sort of show of defiance from her headstrong niece, perhaps a sharp rebuke or maybe even an effort to pull away or push her aside. Elvina's actual response was not at all what the older woman had expected, leaving her stunned and fearing for her life.

Never having had a dagger's point pricking the soft skin on the underside of her chin, Merica found herself at a loss for words. Upon seeing this, Elvina filled the silence.

"You may be my aunt, but there are times when family ties mean nothing," Elvina hissed as Merica carefully backed away, doing her best to escape the dagger her niece continued to hold at her throat.

"Be warned, old woman, I have gutted a man whose only sin was to insult my father's good name. So, believe me when I tell you, I will slit your throat from ear to ear without giving the matter a second thought if you dare to interfere with my obligations as a queen. Now, go, go to your corner and stay there until you are called."

Wide-eyed and shaking, Merica fled as far from her niece as the small hut permitted, watching the fearsome young girl, who she thought she had known, take up shield and spear before storming out of the hut.

Æ

In the wake of her childish antics the previous night at the council fire and the look in the young girl's eyes, Tofi realized what Elvina was up to the second he saw her emerge from the women's hut dressed for battle.

"We have waited long enough," she thundered as she approached him. "I order you to lead our army forward, or I shall do so myself."

With the same patronizing smile, he always used when dealing with his niece, Tofi brushed aside her order.

"There is no need to rush into this," he murmured, satisfied things were working out for him as well as they were. "The battle is still in the balance. We can afford to wait a little longer."

Realizing, at last, that her uncle had no intention of doing anything until both armies were fought out and, then, sally forth and pick upon the remains of both like a scavenger, Elvina turned to where her nobles had been watching and listening as this little drama played out. Though the thought of going down and joining the maelstrom taking place at the foot of the ridge where her army stood idle caused her stomach to knot up, the idea of doing nothing as Alfhildr and her Danes struggled against overwhelming odds overrode any trepidation the young queen felt. Drawing herself up, she took a moment to steady herself least her assembled nobles hear the fear she felt in her voice.

"I made a pledge to the Dane known as Alfhildr, a pledge I intend to keep. If I must go forth and honor that pledge alone, then so be it. But forward I will go, with or without you."

Deciding he had allowed his niece to go on long enough, making a fool of herself and of him, Tofi decided the time had come to take her in hand before she did something that could not be undone. His attempt to do so, however, was checked by Osgar, who stepped before the Saxon nobleman. Drawing himself up, Tofi glared at the huntsman as his hand grasped the hilt of his sword. Osgar was unmoved. Leaning forward until he was nose to nose with Tofi, Osgar muttered under his breath so that only Tofi could hear him.

"You'll be dead before your sword is halfway out."

Deciding there was little point in pushing his luck, the nobleman relaxed and backed away, content instead to rely on the secret agreement he had forged with the other nobles.

Godric paid no attention to the confrontation between Tofi and Osgar. His thoughts were on other, more personal, matters as he found himself once more wondering if he could bring himself to come to the aid of a Dane who had killed his brother. Looking to where Bowdyn was standing with his other huscarls, he stared into his friend's eyes.

They were all but imploring Godric to step forward and take up their queen's challenge. Deciding he had already made his choice when he had first pledged his loyalty to Elvina, Godric gave his most trusted warrior, advisor, and life-long friend a nod before stepping out from among the gathered nobles.

"Just as you pledged to stand with the Danes, a proud people who have more than kept their word, I pledged to defend both your honor and your life," he announced boldly as he drew his sword.

"To that end, I will go forth, alone if need be, provided," Godric added as he lowered his voice so that only Elvina could hear him, "Your Highness, remain here with Osgar, your faithful guardian."

Relieved, Elvina did not trust her voice to thank Godric. Instead, she turned to where the other nobles had been gathered to implore them to join him. When she did, she found she had no need to say a thing, for, as she watched, every nobleman who had flocked to her father's banner was drawing his sword and rushing forward to take his place behind Godric. As he was preparing to lead them off, Elvina reached out to Godric and placed a hand upon his cheek.

"Go, my noble Lord," she whispered. "Go with my blessing and prayers to save both my crown and my friend."

Æ

With a suddenness that caught both Alfhildr and Sigmund by surprise, the Saxons before them pulled back. Pausing only long enough to catch their breath, both looked about to see what had caused the sudden drawing away of their foes. Only when they heard the cry, "The other Saxon army is advancing," coming from somewhere off to their right did Alfhildr realize what was afoot. Like the Saxons who made up the left of Wilfrid's line, she wasn't sure who Elvina's army intended to attack.

The urge to go forward, to close with Wilfrid's army before it could organize a shield wall on the far side of the stream was tempered by the realization that Elvina's uncle just might have managed to push her aside as she had feared and joined forces with Wilfrid. Had it just been her own life in the balance, Alfhildr would not have hesitated to press the attack on Wilfrid's wavering line. But it wasn't. If she went forward, Sigmund's men would go with her, just as those to their right would. Unwilling to needlessly risk the lives of her kinsmen, Alfhildr shouted out for her line to hold before ordering Sigmund to send a few picked men down along the rear of their army's right with the message that it was to draw back.

"They will pivot on us," she shouted out once the runners were on their way. "If the Saxon's advancing upon us attack Wilfrid, we will join them."

"And if they don't?" Sigmund whispered in her ear.

"Well, at least one of us will have the honor of dining in Valhalla tonight," Alfhildr replied grinning as she used this unexpected pause to catch her breath.

Æ

With a thunderous clash, the Saxons defending Wilfrid's standard absorbed the shock when those following Elvina's closed with them. Any hope Godric had had of catching Wilfrid's right on its back foot before it had a chance to collect itself disappeared, as his initial charge was rebuffed. Even worse, there was a wide gap between the two armies fighting for his queen. Having failed to roll up Wilfrid's right, Godric turned his attention to linking his left with the Dane right. After instructing Bowdyn to hold their center together, and with the huscarl carrying Elvina's standard at his side, Godric made his way to the left of his line.

Æ

"They've hit the Saxons on the left," Sigmund bellowed.

With a thousand and one things racing through her mind as she desperately tried to restore some semblance of order to the jumble of confused warriors about her, Alfhildr at first thought Sigmund was trying to tell her the Dane right had gone forward and hit Wilfrid's line instead of backing away.

"No! No!" she shouted in desperation. "They must go back. Send someone to the right and order the chieftains to swing their line back before it is too late."

Now, Sigmund was confused. "But they did."

Realizing there was something going on that she did not quite understand, Alfhildr stepped out of line in order to look off to the right to see what was going on there. That was when she saw Elvina's red serpent banner bobbing up and down in the midst of warriors pressed up against Wilfrid's left.

"They are with us!" she shouted.

"That's what I have been telling you," Sigmund shot back. Ignoring his exasperated tone of voice, Alfhildr ordered him to sound the advance.

"There will be confusion if we go forward while some are still backing away," he warned.

The fiery, red-haired girl took a moment to look about.

"Our center is holding and Snurre is pressing the Saxon right," she shouted above the din of battle. "We must rally our right and close up on the queen's left. On me!"

Before Sigmund could say a word, she was gone. Turning to the standard bearer, Sigmund growled.

"Well, come on. We can't let her win this all on her own."

Æ

Godric had no time to wonder how Wilfrid had been able to absorb the shock of his charge and still maintain a shield wall after having fought the Danes as long as they had. With the Danes on the far left still pressing against Wilfrid's right and those closest to his men milling about in what was now the center of the combined Dane-Saxon line, he was momentarily at a loss as to what he could do to bring order out of chaos.

That was when he heard it, a clear, high-pitched voice singing out above the din of battle. *"On me! On me!"*

Turning, Godric caught sight of the raven banner, the one that marked where the Dane girl would be. With his own men to his right finally coalescing into something resembling a shield wall, he raised his own sword high and cried out to his men,

"To the left! On me and to the left!" Without waiting to feel the man to his right push in upon him, Godric made for the raven banner, closely followed by the huscarl carrying the queen's red serpent standard.

He was not more than a few feet from the Dane standard when the warrior who had been calling out to her kinsmen to rally turned. In an instant, he knew it could be no one else save the Dane named Alfhildr. With her flaming red hair flowing from beneath the bright silver helm, dented on both sides and her face streaked with the blood of many a vanquished foe, Godric stared into eyes that shone like bright emeralds. Excited, yet in complete control of her senses, the Dane girl thrust her sword in the direction of Wilfrid's shield wall.

"We must break it," she roared to Godric without waiting for him to speak. "Form a boar's snout with your men to the right. Mine will close up on the left."

To attempt such a thing in the midst of this chaos with soldiers from two armies who had never fought together was unthinkable. And yet, as Godric watched, he could see the girl, ably assisted by a huge Dane sporting a red beard and wielding a massive axe pulling her warriors together into a tight wedge. Without further hesitation, he turned to his own men and began to issue orders, using his sword to push, prod, beat, and point them into something resembling a wedge. Only when he saw the other nobles and huscarls taking up his orders and echoing them down the line did he turn back toward the Dane girl.

Once more, their eyes met. This time she was grinning like a fiend.

"Will you go forward with me?" she shouted out above the clash and clatter, screams, and cries of battle.

Caught up in the exhilaration of combat, a feeling unlike any other, Godric leveled his sword toward Wilfrid's line.

"We will go forward together," he cried out in a clear, unwavering voice. With that, the two commanders pushed their shoulders together, locked shields and advanced.

As was his habit, Godric focused on the man he would slam into as he was closing, seeking to lock eyes with him in an effort to determine how he would attempt to parry his blow. To his surprise, the dark-haired warrior directly in his path was paying no attention to him. Instead, like the man to his left and right as well as every other rebel Saxon who were part of the shield wall near its center, he was watching the diminutive, red-haired Dane on Godric's left. The Saxon noble could see fear in their eyes, a wild and unfathomable terror inspired by the sight of Alfhildr's flaming red hair, her steady, unflinching gaze, and the sight of a sword some claimed had been forged by pagan gods.

It was this fear, and not the weight of the advancing wedge, that neatly cleaved Wilfrid's shield wall in two. Drawing back, the rebel Saxons, who had been defending the line where Alfhildr and Godric had been boring down, backed away. When they found their way blocked, some turned to flee, pushing their way through the tightly packed ranks of warriors behind them. Others threw away shields and weapons before dropping to their knees and clasping their hands in prayer as they begged for mercy from warriors caught up in the frenzy of battle, fierce men who were in no mood to grant any. The few who attempted to resist did not last long, struck down either by Alfhildr or Godric, leaving little for Sigmund and Bowdyn to do other than follow closely behind, ready to protect their respective commanders with sword, axe, and shield.

Step by step, Alfhildr and Godric advanced, climbing over the bodies of the dead and dying who littered the trampled grass now glistening bright red with the blood of the slain. The wedge of sweating, grunting warriors following in their wake slowly drove the two halves of Wilfrid's army further and further apart until the tip of this human spear broke through the final rank of the usurper's line of battle. With a suddenness that caught both Alfhildr and Godric by surprise, they found themselves in the open with no one other than Wilfrid and a half dozen or so rebel warriors huddled about their standard on a small rise to the rear of the disintegrating shield wall.

Without any thought for their personal safety, both Alfhildr and Godric surged forward. Determined to be in on the kill, Sigmund and Bowdyn swung out from behind, the red-bearded Dane to Alfhildr's left, and the loyal huscarl to Godric's right. Each took up his or her own particular battle cry as they charged.

Only Wilfrid and his standard bearer stood their ground. Though both knew the day was lost, neither was willing to dishonor the good names of their fathers by dying with their backs to the enemy. When she was within striking distance, Alfhildr brought her sword high above her head. To parry her blow, Wilfrid instinctively raised his shield up over his head. In doing so, he exposed the left side of his body to Godric, a mistake of which Elvina's general took full advantage. While his liege was thus engaged, Bowdyn ran the standard bearer through. Sigmund, finding no rebels within striking distance was left with nothing better to do but curse his luck as his eyes darted about in search of someone to attack.

What followed was always the bloodiest part of battle. It is during this final, terrible frenzy when most who die are struck down, for there is no longer any cohesion, no one to watch a comrade's back, or protect the man next to him from a blow with his shield. The warriors belonging to the defeated army who seek salvation in flight are not concerned about what is happening to those foolish enough to stand their ground. Their only concern is escape, tossing aside anything that might hinder their efforts to find sanctuary as the victors, caught up in an all-consuming bloodlust snap at their heels. They are driven forward by a desire to seek vengeance for a friend or kinsmen who has just been slain, mete out punishment for a wrong to their people, their king, their honor, or simply to strike one final blow to work off the frenzy that the sickly, sweet smell of warm blood brings out in human and animal alike. In the end, it is exhaustion and the desire to liberate the dead of valuables they will no longer need that brings the battle to a close and not a sudden onset of mercy or regret for what they have done.

Neither Alfhildr nor Godric took part in this final frenzy of bloodletting or looting.

The diminutive Dane girl remained on the small rise where Wilfrid had once stood, watching as a victorious army, her army, swept all before it. In that moment, she realized that she would never again behold such a sight, for the task the gods had allotted to her had been achieved, her prophecy had been fulfilled.

No one needed to tell Alfhildr that her days of blood, battle, and adventure were at an end. She simply knew it. What lay ahead for her was a mystery, one she would ponder later. For now, she was content to revel in the sound of her name ringing in her ears as her fellow Danes and more than a few Saxons, took to shouting out over and over and over again.

"Alfhildr! Alfhildr! Alfhildr!"

Godric had no need to quest after the rich booty that littered the battlefield around him either, for the prize he inexplicably found himself longing for was standing there before him, basking in the glory that was rightfully hers.

PART FIVE
THE PEACE WEAVER

Chapter Twenty
THE GOLD-CHASED ARMOR

Present Day England
"The Dig"

Sarah looked up, once more, from the sifting screen she was holding steady while Elva picked through the shards of pottery in its tray. She made a face as she watched their professor, seated in the shade of a tarpaulin chatting with a journalist from *Current Archaeology,* the UK's premier magazine for news and events in the field of archaeology.

"You should be over there," the fair-haired undergrad muttered making no effort to hide her bitterness over how news and information concerning their discovery was being handled.

Elva didn't bother to look up from what she was doing.

"I'm sure in time, we'll all get credit for what we've done, if not in some boring magazine article no one ever reads unless they're stuck in the loo, then when final grades are posted."

Sarah shifted her gaze from Bannon to Elva.

"It's not right, you know. We would never have gotten as far as we have if it weren't for your suggestions and insights into what we've been finding here."

Tired of listening to her friend, Elva sighed.

"Right or wrong has nothing to do with what we are doing. We're archaeologists, concerned with unearthing the story of our past so we can ferret out the truth. The last thing I want is to kick up a fuss over who gets the credit for what we've accomplished. I've worked too long and hard on this project to throw it away over a petty little squabble."

With that, Elva went back to her sifting.

Though the idea that her friend intended to do nothing to claim credit for her contributions to the dig offended Sarah's sense of fairness, she said nothing. By now, she'd come to appreciate there was something more going on here than Elva let on. Just what was driving her friend was a mystery she was determined to unravel, just as Elva was struggling to unearth the evidence that she would need to prove that the story behind a warrior, once thought to be little more than a legend, was so much more than that.

Æ

"I've been told there are a number of your students who believe the remains you found are those of the legendary Viking warrior named Alfhildr," the journalist casually stated as he watched Professor Bannon for his reaction.

"What are your thoughts on the subject? Do *you* think you're on the verge of putting a face on an age-old myth?"

Having expected this question to crop up at some point during the interview, Bannon paused as he looked out from under the tarpaulin he and the journalist were seated under and over to where Elva and another student were sifting through soil from the site.

"I'm a scientist, Neal," Bannon slowly replied. "I cannot afford to allow my student's enthusiasm or emotions get in the way of the facts; facts based squarely on what we are unearthing here."

"So, you don't believe what you're finding here has anything to do with that legend?"

Looking back at the journalist, Bannon gave the journalist a thin, tight lipped smile as he shook his head.

"No, of course not."

England
1012 AD

"But there is no more to the story," the boy declared.

Looking over at him, out of the corner of her eye, the grandmother smirked.

"There's always more to the story. It's just that sometimes people forget bits and pieces of it, or they don't bother passing them on."

Confused, the boy gazed up at his grandmother.

"Why would they do that?"

"There are many reasons, not all of them honorable. In the case of Alfhildr, I imagine it would have been awkward for some of her kinsmen and politically inconvenient to her allies if she had been given too much credit for their victory over the usurper."

"But that's dishonest," the boy exclaimed.

"That, child, is history."

Æ

The Saga of the Gold-chased Armor

Red ran the brook with the blood of the slain.
Together victorious, the Saxons and Danes
The usurper's army scattered like chaff
Before queen's and shield maiden's ravening host.

Rich was the plunder, silver and gold,
But richer for many the tales that were told.
The deeds of brave warriors acclaimed by their friends,
Sung by the bards by campfire and hearths.

The rarest of prizes Alfhildr did find,
Sure Falissar she saved from the usurper's camp.
Richer still the armor that all warriors claimed
Fine wrought and gold-chased, men lusted for the mail.

A challenge was issued to settle the claims
For the golden-chased armor 'tween Saxon and Dane
A contest was offered to shoot for the prize
And Danes soon were betting on Alfhildr's sharp eyes.

A feast was declared to cement new-found trust
'Tween Saxon and Dane, a future to build.
Shield maiden appeared—now modestly gowned,
And all men looked longingly at the girl with the blade.

As the gods now discarded her strong arm and sword,
In a new battle, the shield maiden soon found herself caught
'Tween her heart and her past, she struggled to find,
A place and a future for the girl left behind.
Æ

The tide of battle slowly ebbed, then faded as warriors turned their hands from slaughtering their broken foe to pillaging the usurper's camp. In their wake, they left Alfhildr and Godric where the two had ended the battle, catching their breath as their rage ever so slowly leached away. Godric used this opportunity to glance, out of the corner of his eye, at the young girl beside him as she cast aside her iron helm.

Paying no heed to him, or what was going on around her, Alfhildr closed her eyes and lifted her chin ever so slightly before giving her head a quick shake. A soft breeze caught her hair, causing it to flutter about wild and free like a flaming, red banner.

Mesmerized by this unexpected image of unadorned beauty so at odds with their surroundings, Godric felt a sudden urge to tell her she was beautiful. Inexplicably, he found himself wanting to tell her she had stolen his heart, that he wished nothing more than to have her at his side, then and ever more. But the words would not come. Instead, he simply stood there mesmerized and tongue-tied, watching the red-haired Dane in stunned silence.

Lost in her own thoughts, Alfhildr felt the joy of victory give way to a numbing uneasiness. With her great battle won, she suddenly felt rudderless and adrift on a sea of uncertainty, wondering as a gentle breeze washed over her face if this was how the gods always treated their chosen instruments, discarding them like spoiled children the moment they were no longer needed or useful. Ignoring the yells and hollers of Saxon's and Danes celebrating the plunder they took from the dead or discovered in the abandoned camp that was now theirs, cheerful voices that mingled with the pitiful cries of the wounded, Alfhildr cast aside her troubling thoughts for the moment as she turned her attention to caring for her weapons. Taking up Wilfrid's cloak, she used it to wipe Durthfang's sticky blade clean before examining its edge for nicks. It was only when she held the blade up to catch the light that she caught sight of the intent stare with which Godric was regarding her.

"Lord Godric?"

Dumbstruck, Godric found himself struggling mightily to respond.

Not knowing what was troubling the Saxon, Alfhildr turned ever so slowly to face him.

Thoughts and words knotted themselves hopelessly on his tongue by a sudden, unquenchable desire for the red-haired Dane before him, a yearning that warred with the memory of his brother's death and the demands of his family's honor. Only when he saw her rising concern reflected in her face did he push aside his confusion and blurt out the first thing that came to mind.

"You...you fight well."

Even as those words slipped from his lips, he mentally kicked himself for uttering such an inane comment until he saw a genuine smile light up her face. But, before she could answer, a harsh shout went up from the usurper's camp.

"Lord Godric! Alfhildr! Come now!" Bowdyn cried out as he frantically waved to them from the edge of the camp while behind him Alfhildr could see Sigmund dragging two warriors apart by the scruff of their necks. She let out a heavy sigh as she set aside her concerns and made her way toward the spot where a crowd of Saxons and Danes was gathering. Behind her, Godric allowed himself a sad smile before he followed closely on the heels of the captivating shield maiden.

When they reached a cluster of peasant hovels, they were greeted by a chorus of vile words and insults being traded freely back and forth by two snarling mobs that Sigmund was barely holding at bay by threatening both with his axe.

"We were here first," a Saxon bellowed. "It's ours!"

"You could only run fast because you were skulking behind the skirts of your queen while real men did your fighting!" a Dane replied scornfully.

"If you want to fight, then..."

"Enough!" Godric's roar quieted the two groups. "If there's plunder to be had, it shall be shared fairly."

He scowled at the Saxon warriors until they lowered their swords, though they continued to glare menacingly at the Danes.

Snurre grinned at their discomfort. "Good dogs, listen to your mast..."

The sensation of Durthfang's tip pricking his throat cut his words short.

"Before you say another word, you might remember we have yet to hang the spy." Alfhildr murmured.

Snurre deflated as he realized the power the red-haired bitch held over him. Ever so cautiously, he stepped back and away from her blade. Still, he remained unbowed.

"What is found here shall be shared equally," he declared loudly once he had managed to regain the use of his voice.

"I demand every penny be shown before all as the share is made. Of course, if that's all right with you?" he added sardonically while eyeing the suspicious Saxons.

Having barely avoided a disastrous rift between the two armies, Godric and Alfhildr selected a few trusted men who took to emptying the three small hovels under the watchful eyes of both Saxons and Danes. Chests of coins and precious ornaments, bundles of richly embroidered clothes, and weapons were laid out for all to see and count. In the middle of this effort, Alfhildr thrust out her arm.

"That's mine."

Tumbled behind a bundle of spears men could just make out a deeply curved bow. A Saxon huscarl who had already spotted the curious bow and longed to take it for himself challenged the imperious young girl.

"It's plunder. All have an equal right to claim it."

"Not if it bears my mark," Alfhildr shot back even as she squatted and took to scratching in the dirt. "On the belly of the bow you will find these letters. Wilfrid stole it from me, and I claim it back."

This, of course, was not true. The bow had been taken from her when she had been captured by one of Osmund's men. Alfhildr, however, had no wish to disparage the name of Elvina's father in any way, so she laid the blame on a man who was both reviled and very dead.

The huscarl picked up the bow and inspected it carefully for the marks Alfhildr had made. With a grunt, he grudgingly handed it across before he went back to staring like a hawk at the new treasures that were being added to the pile to see what else he would demand as his when the plunder was finally divided. In contrast, Alfhildr paid no heed to what the others around her were doing as she ran her fingers lovingly over Falissar, checking for any hurt the usurper had done to her gift from the gods.

A shared gasp rising from the men pressing the growing mound of booty dragged Alfhildr's attention away from the bow. When, once more, she looked over at the entrance of the hovel, she saw two men were carefully bringing out a shirt of fine-wrought mail.

At its collar and sleeves, the iron rings gave way to glittering gold. Even from a distance, Alfhildr could see it was truly the armor of a mighty warrior.

Drawn to its unrivaled beauty, a jostling crowd quickly formed around it.

Once more, Godric and Sigmund had to shout in order to calm Saxons and Danes who had become consumed with a lust for the gold-chased armor.

Last to be brought forth was a terrified but still proud Æmma, pushed unceremoniously from the smaller hut with a weeping maid clinging to her skirt. As Alfhildr watched, Dane and Saxon warriors grabbed the two women. She was tempted to intervene until the memory of how Æmma had tried to trap Elvina for the spearmen on the night the old King died stayed her hand.

For their part, the Saxon's took to squabbling over the maid, wanting nothing to do with Æmma, mostly because no one wanted their fellow warriors to suspect they were sympathetic to the usurper's cause. That, and her disfigured nose proved to be too much for many a man as one Saxon warrior muttered loud enough for Alfhildr to hear.

"Only a Dane would take pleasure in a woman as ugly as that."

While the thought of what the men who took the women would soon be doing caused Alfhildr to shudder, she consoled herself with the bitter thought that at least when they were finished with Æmma and the others they found, they would still be alive.

Upon seeing Alfhildr's expression, Sigmund guessed what was going through her mind.

"It would be best if you stayed clear of such matters," he muttered quietly. "You may be favored by the gods, but even they know there are times when it is best not to interfere with the affairs of men."

Nodding sadly, Alfhildr turned away, slapping her thigh with her hand to signal Skadi to follow. Together, the two wandered off in search of someplace far from the moans of the wounded and the screams of the women who had been dragged from Wilfrid's camp.

Æ

As the shadows lengthened, Alfhildr found herself back in Sigmund's part of the Dane camp where she finally gave into her exhaustion. Around her, men were already drinking heavily, some to celebrate their victory, others in their relief at still being alive. As she sat idly scratching Skadi's belly, she listened to men boasting of their exploits to friends and laughing at the death of their foes. Nearby, Sigmund looked up from running a whetstone down his axe and grinned at the girl.

"Don't mind them, little one. It's all just piss and wind. Most of them have never been in a shield wall before today."

Alfhildr smiled self-consciously and shook her head.

"I don't mind. Let them have their fun. They've earned it."

Yet, even as she spoke a new voice, louder than the rest took to bragging drunkenly.

"All men know we owe our victory to Snurre, son of Gunnar, son of

Folkmar. He held his ground until the lazy Saxons got off their arses."

A ragged cheer followed, egging Hrolf on as he praised the young chieftain whose position he coveted.

"Women in battle? They're there to please the winners, nothing more."

Sigmund growled and started to pull himself up onto his feet until Alfhildr raised her hand tiredly and stopped him.

"No! I'll have no more fighting tonight. What does it matter what a drunken sot shouts? You and I know the truth."

"But he's a snot-filled little toad who was ready to turn tail for gold."

"So? He fought. We won. As you said, everything else is just piss and wind."

Grumbling, Sigmund reluctantly settled back down and returned to smoothing out a nick in his axe's blade. Every so often, he glared across at Snurre's fire. For her part, Alfhildr turned away and wrapped herself close in a blanket. Within minutes, she slipped into a sound, dreamless sleep with one hand resting on Skadi's neck and the other wrapped tightly about her sword's hilt.

Æ

In the queen's camp, the scenes of drunken celebration and bragging were little different from those Alfhildr had tried to ignore. Yet, in a corner a man and a woman sat quietly and talked.

"She served you for months," Godric stated questioningly. "Did she tell you nothing of her childhood? Surely you asked?"

Elvina looked away from Godric's imploring gaze. She owed this man so much, yet she could not betray Alfhildr's trust.

"Alfhildr's upbringing is a far country with well-guarded borders. I am sorry, Lord Godric, but it is not for me to tell you her story."

He shook his head in frustration.

"I feel like I'm torn in two. My honor demands that I take vengeance for my brother. I should hate her but…" He lapsed into painful silence.

"But what?" Elvina gently prompted the confused man.

"Ever since I set eyes on her, I can imagine being with no one else. All I can think of is her flaming hair. All I see are her eyes sparkling like emeralds. It's as if she has put a spell on me."

Godric's eyes suddenly sprang wide in shock as he stared at his queen.

"Is she a witch? Could she have put a spell on me?"

Elvina was about to laugh, but the earnest expression on Godric's face warned her not to mock her most loyal general. Instead, she carefully shook her head and looked him straight in the eye.

"Alfhildr is many things, but I promise you, a witch is not one of them. The magic you speak of is all of your own making, My Lord."

Still, Godric frowned as he battled with his thoughts and emotions.

"But what of my brother? I must not, I cannot, leave him unavenged. How can I feel this way when my duty demands blood?" His voice rose as he argued bitterly with himself. "Even though it would cost me dearly, my forefathers' ghosts demand no less than her death."

"Perhaps there is another way." Elvina's voice was hesitant as an idea began to form.

"What? Tell me." Godric's tone was brusque until he realized to whom he was speaking. "I'm sorry, My Lady. That was rude of me. What do you suggest?"

Elvina hesitated for a moment as she put her thoughts in order.

"You must have justice for your brother, yet wish no harm, just as I wish no harm to Alfhildr." Godric nodded eagerly at Elvina's words. "Will you accept the *weregild* for your brother?"

The simplicity of the idea hit Godric like a thunderbolt. It was some time before he could speak.

"Can she pay?"

"You forget, she was my servant. Thus, the obligation falls to me," Elvina smiled at the thought of giving something back to the girl who had so little yet had already given her so much. "Be assured that the price demanded by law will be met, My Lord."

Even in the dark of the night, it was as if the sun had risen for Godric. He tipped his head back and laughed for joy. Yet Elvina had not finished, her voice now stern as she cut across his laughter.

"One more thing, My Lord. Alfhildr is never to know of this. I have your word?"

Still laughing, Godric reached out and grabbed his young queen's hand as he slid off his camp stool and took a knee before her.

"My Lady, you have my solemn oath before God. I am your man to death and beyond, for never has a man been better rewarded by their ruler."

On the far side of the battlefield, Alfhildr slept on as Urðr, Verðandi, and Skuld took to reweaving the thread of life to create a new tapestry for a diminutive, red-haired Dane.

Æ

It was mid-morning before the warriors and their lords were in a fit state to attend the council where the plunder would be divided. Danes and Saxons met warily in the meadow between their two camps, though most considered the stunningly, bright sun to be a crueler enemy that morning than Wilfrid's army had been the previous day. Saxon lords and Danish chieftains gathered in a loose circle, their men clustered behind, all staring hungrily at the treasure piled before them, yet uncertain how to start.

Before any could speak, a young girl approached. Clad in a rich gown and walking with regal assurance, Elvina stepped carefully into the circle to stand beside the jumbled wealth. For the first time, the Danish warriors saw the Saxon queen whose word they had been persuaded to trust and whose fight had led them to this place. Many found themselves wondering what she had that made Saxon's fight and die for her. Yet, if Elvina noted their curiosity, she did not show it. Instead, she looked around the gathering, making eye contact with as many as she could see before speaking.

"My friends, a simple oath in a forest glade was made. It swore to a peace between Saxon and Dane and the defeat of those who wished for the slaughter of our men, both Saxon and Dane, the rape of our women, both Saxon and Dane, and the enslavement of our children, both Saxon and Dane."

Elvina paused to gather the warriors' attention still more closely.

"You came, both Saxon and Dane, and, thus, I greet you as friends, with no thought to your blood, and stand foursquare by my oath that all shall share of the peace equally for as long as it is within my power to uphold it. And, in proof of that oath, I say that this wealth shall be shared equally, to the last penny, among those who fought for that peace."

Elvina turned toward the wary Danish chieftains.

"Who amongst you shall speak for all? To judge what is fair?"

Men turned and looked at each other, unsure if they should step forth until Snurre arrogantly pushed his way forward.

"I speak for the Danes."

Unnoticed, Alfhildr laid a warning hand on Sigmund's arm as he was about to voice his protest.

Elvina turned to her Saxon lords and spoke again.

"And who amongst you shall speak for the Saxons? To judge what is fair?"

This time, there was no uncertainty as Bowdyn quickly came forward, causing Elvina to quickly look away as she struggled to conceal a smile the mere sight of the young warrior brought to her lips. She turned once more to the Danes.

"While two can argue just as well as two hundred, there must be one to make the final judgment. Who here would all trust to act with honor and fairness?"

Suddenly, Sigmund felt a firm shove in the back, pushing him forward and causing him to grunt in surprise. It wasn't much of a sound, but one loud enough to break the awkward silence and cause all eyes to turn toward the towering red-bearded Dane.

Behind him, one of his men shouted out, "Sigmund. We trust Sigmund."

From the Saxon half circle, Godric too raised his voice.

"I have fought beside Sigmund, a man I am told is considered to be just by his own kinsmen. I, therefore, choose him to stand before Saxon and Dane to judge the claims made by each."

Elvina held her hand out in welcome to the confused bear of a man who was looking suspiciously at the red-haired girl beside him.

"Then, Sigmund it shall be, and tonight, once this is done, I ask that you all join my table that we may feast to the sharing of wealth and peace for all."

Behind the Danish half circle, one of Sigmund's warriors grinned and winked at Alfhildr, who was trying very hard to look innocent of the morning chat she had had with Elvina while the men were still deep in drink-sodden slumber.

Æ

Once the arbiters had been chosen, the sharing of the plunder went swiftly and with little rancor. The central pile quickly dwindled as it was precisely split in two. Slowly men's eyes began to focus on the gold-chased armor, ignoring silver chased mead horns and rare, blue glass goblets. Tension grew as all watched and waited to see who would win the beautiful mail shirt. At last, when it was the only item left, a silence gripped the crowd while Bowdyn and Snurre each eyed the other warily, marshaling their arguments as to why they should take the prize. Understanding what was afoot and wishing to avoid a contentious argument, Sigmund raised his arm before either could speak.

"One shirt cannot be worn on two backs. Nor can it be cut in half without destroying it. Another way must be found. This is the armor fit for a great warrior. Therefore, to a great warrior it must go. Yesterday, the enemy's shield wall was broken by two such warriors, one Saxon," he grinned at Godric, "one Dane," a nod toward the suddenly blushing Alfhildr.

Around the circle, a hum of whispered conversation erupted, causing Sigmund to raise his voice.

"We know they can fight with blade. But can they shoot?" The hum became a buzz as he pressed on.

"I rule that tomorrow the two who broke the shield wall must prove their skill with bow as they have with blade, the winner to take the armor, for its wearer will indeed be a great warrior worthy to own it."

A shout of approval went up from the gathered warriors. Within moments, both sides had clustered around their chosen champion, offering advice and encouragement before wandering back to their own camps in small groups. There, they would share their new-found wealth among their warriors as they celebrated with mead. And, while Saxon lords called upon bards, Dane chieftains summoned their skalds, setting them to the all-important task of weaving a heroic legend that would recount their deeds and courage so nothing would be forgotten by those who had not been there, as well as their ancestors yet unborn.

Æ

As the sun slowly slipped toward its rest, a young warrior accompanied by a she-wolf stormed through the Saxon camp. Knowing better than to try and stop the red-haired Dane, the pair of guards posted at the entrance of Elvina's tent quickly stepped aside as Alfhildr pushed past them and burst in, catching the young queen as she was rising from her bath. Thinking nothing of her friend's intemperate manner, Elvina turned toward Alfhildr.

"What now?" she asked doing her best to make her question sound as if she were being serious as she took the towel from Diera, a young girl who was being trained to be her maid.

"Has someone made a disparaging remark about your skills with a bow and you wish to slay them?"

"He came to our camp," Alfhildr muttered as if in shock. "He came up to me and said he wished to have speech with me."

"And?"

"He wants to wed me!" Alfhildr exclaimed in wide-eyed shock.

"Godric?"

"No," Alfhildr snorted as she folded her arms tightly across her chest and took to nervously pacing back and forth. "His horse."

Ignoring her friend's sarcastic remark, Elvina turned to her maid and asked for her robe. While she was able to take Alfhildr's behavior in her stride, the young Saxon maid stood staring at the Dane as if she were waiting to be struck down.

"Diera, my robe," Elvina called out once more.

Without taking her eyes off the fiery shield maiden, who was still attired in chainmail and trousers, Diera retrieved the robe and passed it to her mistress as if in a trance.

"You may go, Diera," Elvina announced before going over to Alfhildr, taking her in hand and settling her animated friend down on a camp stool.

"So, Godric has expressed an interest in you," Elvina murmured, making no effort to hold back the joy she felt for her dear friend.

Giving her head a quick shake, Alfhildr regarded the Saxon queen with furrowed brow.

"Yes, that's what I said."

Then, in the twinkling of an eye, her expression changed from barely concealed rage to the forlorn look a child wears when faced with a problem they have no idea how to solve.

"And why is this a problem?" Elvina asked. "Godric is a noble and honorable man, one any woman would be proud to wed."

"But I cannot marry him!" Alfhildr exclaimed.

"Why not?"

"Because I'm..."

Just like that, the question that had haunted her since waking up in the Old Woman's hovel leapt to the fore once more, stopping Alfhildr in midsentence. Just what was she? Alfhildr turned away from Elvina's expectant gaze. If what the Old Woman said was true, and if the blood that flowed with each moon was the way of things for women, then she had never really been a boy. Nor was she a true warrior, at least not in the eyes of those who she admired and had so long tried to emulate. Odin chose only the fittest and bravest male warriors to join him in Valhalla to await Ragnarök with him. Even in her wildest dreams, Alfhildr had never imagined being able to take her place there next to her father.

Now, with the Old Woman's prophecy fulfilled and the gods no longer in need of her, Alfhildr found herself at a loss. When she finally did look back up at her friend, she reached out in desperation and grabbed Elvina's hand, making no effort to hold back the tears of despair that were now streaming down her cheeks.

"What should I do?"

Chapter Twenty-one
"HER FINAL VICTORY…"

Present Day England
"The Dig"

Ever so carefully, Sarah balanced the two pints of cider she was carrying as she made her way through the crowded pub back to the table where Elva sat alone. Upon reaching it, the red-haired graduate student looked up at her and grunted as she took hers.

"Where in bloody hell did you go for these, Cornwall?"

Unfazed by her friend's comment, Sarah smiled as she took her seat.

"Peter was at the bar. He was asking about you again."

Shaking her head, Elva looked up at the ceiling and sighed.

"What in God's name do I have to do to convince him that I have no interest in dating? Smack him up the side of the head with a shovel?"

Before answering, Sarah took a moment to study the winsome young girl across from her. As much as she admired her intelligence as well as her ability to organize things at the dig, a skill Bannon was sadly lacking, to say that Elva was socially awkward would be a major understatement. She got on well enough with everyone when they were at the dig, but once the day was done and it came time to enjoy a well-deserved break from scraping away at clay or sifting soil, Elva withdrew into a shell that prying her out of defied Sarah's best efforts. "I do hate to be a nag, but what harm would it do if you were at least a *little* polite to Peter?" she murmured as she looked down at her glass of cider.

In disbelief, Elva stared at her friend. "You can't be serious."

"I am."

"And what good would it do if I pretended that I fancied Peter? By being polite, as you put it, I would only be encouraging him. And what then? When we got back to the university, he'd try to continue seeing me, leaving me no other choice but to tell him to sod off," Elva patiently explained.

Undeterred, Sarah smiled. "Oh, I think not. I think you're just trying to live up to your reputation as the Wicked Witch of the Midlands, one that does not suit you at all, that is, once you allow someone to get to know you."

"Oh, and who would that be?"

Sarah lifted her glass, but before taking a drink, she peered into Elva's eyes and winked.

"Oh, I know you better than you think, dear girl."

A chill ran down Elva's spine as she found herself wondering just how much the fair-haired girl across from her did know. It was a thought that was to haunt Elva for the balance of the night and well into the next day.

Æ

England
1012 AD

As the two rested on opposite ends of a fallen tree trunk that had seen the passing of many a generation of Saxon and Dane, the boy said nothing, content to gnaw away at the sweet cake his grandmother had brought along for their journey. She could tell he was thinking about something, something that was bothering him but that he did not know quite how to put into words. Finally, she asked him what was on his mind.

At first, the boy did not speak as his thoughts, his feelings, and his fears warred with each other. When he finally spoke, he found he could not look up at his grandmother. Instead, he turned his head and faced away from her as if embarrassed by his very thoughts.

"What's it like to be with someone?" he finally whispered.

"To be with someone?" the grandmother repeated. "As in a marriage?"

Finding it impossible to answer, at least verbally, the boy simply gave his head a quick nod while keeping his worried expression hidden from her.

Æ

The Saga of Alfhildr's Final Victory

Close fought was the contest 'tween maiden and lord
Alfhildr was leading 'til above a crow cawed.
Her last arrow sped wide, away from the mark,
And Godric the prize took, to the cheers of his folk.

Yet, the lord was not finished, for he picked up the armour
To lay before Alfhildr in proof of his ardour.
"My desire is not mail but a hand and a wife.
I would have thee beside me for the rest of my life."

"My Lord, I have nothing but my blade and my bow,
No bride gift can I bring to honor your hall."
Yet Godric refused to be moved from his aim.
"Your treasure is peace 'twixt Saxon and Dane."

The prophecy completed, her victory to yield,
To a man strong and noble, the girl at last healed.
Thus, shield maiden turned peace weaver, fiery warrior to fair bride,
Safe lands did she make, no enemy at her side.

Æ

Elvina reached out and drew the crying girl toward her. As she wrapped her arms about the distraught Alfhildr, she felt as if her world had come full circle. She recalled reaching down to a bedraggled waif, crouching in the mud of her father's holding.

Elvina's eye's teared as she too felt overwhelmed by a journey that had started with that single, simple act. So many sacrifices, so much suffering, so many dead. Yet, here, in her arms, was one who had sacrificed more than any. With that thought in mind, the young Saxon queen took a moment to gather the strength she would require to do what she knew was needed.

Ever so gently, Elvina whispered in her sobbing friend's ear. "Your gods know who you are. Your friends know who you are. And I know who you are. The time has come for you to search your own heart and accept who you are. Only then will you be able to embrace the destiny that awaits you."

In her arms, the racking heaves of the forlorn girl's sobs eased as Alfhildr tried to make sense of what Elvina was saying.

"Together, we have won the chance of peace, yet it is only a chance. In their infinite wisdom, your gods have given you a weapon that you have long turned your back on, one as beautiful as Durthfang and as piercing as Falissar with which to seize this chance and forge it into the peace for which we both long."

Confused and bewildered, Alfhildr frowned. Her prophecy had been fulfilled. She was sure of that, just as sure as she was that the gods had no further need of her. The Old Woman's prophecy said as much. What more could they want? What more did she have to offer them? Slowly, she lifted her head from Elvina's shoulder as she took to regarding her friend with a quizzical stare.

"Tell me, Alfhildr, do you know of the legends of Hildeburh or Wealhtheow?"

Alfhildr's eyes sprang open in surprise as Elvina continued.

"The calling of a peace weaver is both honored and honorable. It is a role no man can undertake, and few women have the strength to bear. Yet, without someone trusted and admired by all, what chance has our fledgling peace? Now, do you understand the final weapon your gods have presented you with? Your beauty."

"They haven't deserted me?" Alfhildr's voice was childlike in her wonder as Elvina's words at last sank home. "They still need me?"

The Saxon queen once more pulled her friend tight.

"All the days of your life, just as I will always need you as my dearest friend."

She watched as Alfhildr's face came alive once more, not with the fury of battle, but with jubilation, as they laughed as one in the sheer joy of the moment.

When at last they broke apart, Elvina sniffed, wrinkling her nose as she did so.

"We had better set to sharpening your new weapons," she advised as she nodded at the still warm bath behind her. "I have just the thing."

Æ

The early summer evening settled gently upon the queen's camp as the Danish chieftains nervously arrived to join the Saxons to celebrate their victory. At their head, Sigmund swiftly made for the one Saxon he knew and trusted, a worried frown on his face.

"Bowdyn. I can't find Alfhildr. She went off with her wolf after your man Godric spoke to her and none have seen her since."

Bowdyn grinned self-consciously.

"I am told a certain fiery warrior stormed into the queen's tent several hours ago. Apparently, neither has emerged since."

"But what duty could possibly demand she remain shut up so long with..."

The words died on Sigmund's lips as the flap of Elvina's tent was pulled aside to allow a very nervous Dane girl to emerge, side by side, with a Saxon queen, who embraced her as a friend and equal.

Elvina wore a simple gown of pale blue wool, its edges trimmed with silver thread and a golden torc at her throat. But Sigmund's eyes and those belonging to every man present were glued on the fearsome shield maiden. Her slight frame was accentuated by a figure-hugging gown of sea green, richly embroidered with fine golden thread. Her fiery hair had been tamed into two lustrous ropes of plaited, red gold, revealing her elfin face and startling emerald eyes while at her throat an amber pendant set in gold emphasized the delicate curve of her neck. But not every trace of the old Alfhildr had been banished. At her side, Durthfang hung from a richly tooled sword belt that encircled her slim hips while, by her side, Skadi gamboled playfully around her skirts, glad to be free at last from the confines of the tent.

A stunned hush fell across the throng of warrior chieftains and Saxon nobles as the two beauties carefully negotiated their way toward them. Alfhildr craned her neck to look up at Sigmund, an apologetic grin gracing her lips.

"Please forgive my not sending word: but, as you can see, I had things to attend to."

She waited as the great bear of a man tried to fashion a reply, but no sound came until at length he managed to blurt out a phrase for which he would be teased for years to come as his closest friends took to calling him Sigmund, the Observant.

"You...you're...you're a girl!"

With that, the spell was broken as Saxons and Danes guffawed at the stunned Sigmund's powers of observation. The earlier wariness between the two parties was dispelled by shared mirth, allowing the men to begin to mingle with their former foes. Yet, to one side, a single warrior remained alone, standing still in frozen awe. If the mighty Sigmund had been poleaxed by the beauty of the diminutive girl, then Lord Godric had been pierced clean through to the heart.

Æ

As the servants laid out the trestles and benches, Elvina mingled among the warriors, chatting easily with all she met, captivating both Saxon and Dane as she went. Yet, not all were enamored by the young queen as Alfhildr quickly noted. Off to the side, standing aloof and apart, was the woman the Dane had been told was the queen's aunt. At the moment, she was staring malevolently at her friend. Recalling what Elvina had told her of Merica's behavior on the morning of the battle, Alfhildr decided to strike while the opportunity was there.

In a manner that would have made her fair-haired Saxon friend proud, had she known about it, Alfhildr managed to maneuver the young queen's aunt to where the two could share a word in private. Holding the noble woman's arm in a manner that seemed natural to the casual observer but alerted Merica that she'd best not try to pull away, Alfhildr leaned forward and whispered in her ear.

"At this very moment, there is a flat-nosed woman who thought she would be queen being passed from warrior to warrior in one of our camps. No doubt, it would not please your niece to know her aunt shared that fate, provided, of course, Elvina somehow managed to find out what I did with you," Alfhildr added as she pulled back, tilting her head to one side as she gave Merica a sweet little smile.

"So, I suggest that you find a way of coming to terms with accepting what will be," she concluded as she dug the tips of her sword hardened fingers into the soft flesh of Merica's arm.

Pulling away ever so slightly, Merica gazed in horror into the Dane girl's piercing, green eyes. Had she been anyone else, the noblewoman would have brushed aside the threat as little more than drivel. But this was Alfhildr, the red-haired witch, a girl raised by wolves, who was gazing back at her with an intensity that caused the noble woman's blood to run cold. Swallowing hard, Merica slowly backed away, fleeing as quickly as decorum permitted once Alfhildr released her arm.

Elvina, who had been watching this private exchange out of the corner of her eye, later asked her friend what they had been discussing. The young Dane girl replied in an affected lyrical tone as she gazed down at the amber pendant Elvina had given her.

"Oh, I was asking your aunt what the proper form of address is for a queen." Then, looking up, while giving Elvina a beguiling smile, Alfhildr lightly placed her hand on Elvina's forearm. "You know how I am when it comes to such things. I haven't a clue."

Giving her dearest friend a knowing look, Elvina smiled in a manner that told Alfhildr she was on to her.

"Yes, I do know you, far better than you suspect."

With that the young queen dropped the matter and returned to the quiet conversation she had been having with Bowdyn.

Æ

When the feast was ready and the guests were called to the tables, Elvina ensured the warriors who had broken Wilfrid's shield wall were given seats of honor. At the high table, Alfhildr found herself tightly wedged between Lord Godric and Elvina's uncle, Lord Tofi, leaving Elvina to entertain Sigmund and Bowdyn with equal measure.

At first, Lord Tofi was confused by the pretty, little thing seated beside him. Before they had been seated, his wife had muttered something about a vicious witch, leaving him to expect some hulking brute of a woman with manners to match. But, as the ale and mead flowed, he found himself inexplicably falling under the spell of the charming, young girl next to him, causing his mind to wander.

Perhaps, he thought with a quiet smile, *through her, he could continue to wield some influence over his confused and wayward niece.*

Yet, even as Tofi set about complimenting Alfhildr, in a new campaign designed to achieve what he failed to gain on the field of battle, she paid little heed to his words as she became incredibly aware of the closeness of Lord Godric. The normally decisive, young warlord sat tongue-tied and nervous beside her, saying little as they both picked tentatively at their food. Yet not a moment passed when she did not feel his eyes on her every gesture, causing her to become anxious and shy at the attention Godric seemed incapable of withholding. Tofi never caught on that his sly flattery washed over the young Dane without making purchase, for Alfhildr simply sat there as if in a trance, her head slightly bowed as her eyes remained fixed on the food before her like a startled fawn until, at last, she could contain her anxiety no more.

Unused to the strong drink and the proximity of a man whose mere presence quickened her pulse, Alfhildr suddenly jumped to her feet.

"Air!" she blurted out as she grasped the edge of the table to steady herself. "I need fresh air."

With that she stumbled and weaved her way unsteadily between the other revelers and out into the dark night as strange and unfamiliar thoughts and feelings whirled about in her head. Behind her, a troubled Godric started to rise in order to follow until Elvina laid a restraining hand on his arm.

"Gently, My Lord, gently. If you would win her, you must learn to give her space."

Reluctantly, Godric heeded his queen's advice and settled back, turning his thoughts instead to what he would do on the morrow when he faced her in their contest for the armor.

Once outside the queen's camp, Alfhildr found herself confronted by two figures.

Alarmed, she stepped back, her hand flying to Durthfang's hilt. Her fears, however, were quickly put to rest as Sigmund spoke up.

"Come, little one, it is long past time we had a word with you."

"About?" Alfhildr asked as she struggled to focus on Sigmund and Osgar while swaying to and fro like a young sapling in the wind.

Taking her by the arm, Osgar easily swung the unsteady Dane about.

"It is time we talked to you about life and what lies ahead."

"Bed," Alfhildr muttered, doing her best to keep from slurring her words while making her druthers clear to two men who had stood by her when no one else would.

"I don't want to talk any more. I have had enough of talk for one day. First, Elvina talked one ear off. Then, Godric stared at the other all evening. No more talk, please. It's my bed I want."

"In time," the Saxon who had come to view the red-haired Dane as a daughter replied. "But first, we talk."

Æ

With her companions on either side, the trio made their way to a fire Osgar had prepared in the forest between the two camps. There, the men took a seat on a log, gently pulling the diminutive red-haired girl down between them.

"Your days of wandering the forests accompanied by a she-wolf and a squawking crow are at an end, little one," Sigmund announced in a firm, almost fatherly manner that told Alfhildr he would brook no argument from her. "It is time you look to your future."

A sudden wave of sadness swept over Alfhildr as two men who had become the closest thing that she had ever had to a father listened to her laments.

"I have done nothing but think of the future these past few days," Alfhildr muttered mournfully.

When she looked up at each man in turn, both Osgar and Sigmund could see the makings of tears welling up in her eyes and she, in turn, could see the compassion in theirs.

With that the dam burst as Alfhildr took to pouring out her heart, unable to hold anything back as she told of her loss and her despair, all her hopes, dreams, and fears in a manner Elvina could never have understood. Most of all, she spoke of a boy named Gunnvor and the strange journey that led him to become the sword arm of the gods known to all as Alfhildr. She spoke long into the night until there were no words left unsaid. At last, she fell silent, staring anxiously back and forth at the Saxon hunter and the Dane chieftain, fearful of their scorn and disgust at what she had been and what she had become.

After a long pause, it was Osgar who broke the silence. His voice wavered as he strove to contain his emotion.

"I never knew. Before God, I never guessed or thought that anyone, even the hardiest warrior, could survive what you have been through. And now, you are afraid that we would forsake you? That your gods would turn from you?"

He choked in bitter remorse as he recalled his intent that first morning in the forest.

"Forgive me, Alfhildr, you are braver and stronger than I will ever be."

With that, he lapsed into silence as Sigmund took up the conversation.

"You stunned me with your blade and skill in the forest. I knew then that you were special. You stunned me again this evening when I saw you leave the Saxon queen's tent."

He let out a snorting laugh.

"Me! Sigmund, the Just, ring giver, and warlord for three score warriors rendered speechless by a slip of a girl."

His voice grew quiet once more as he shook his head in wonder.

"I always thought that there was something familiar about you, but I never guessed. I was a shield brother of Gunnar, son of Folkmar. I fought beside him more than once and got drunk with him more times than I can remember. A better man, I never knew."

He turned his head slowly to stare intently into Alfhildr's glittering eyes.

"I *know* he will be sitting in Valhalla among all the fabled dead of our people, bragging to all who will listen of the deeds and beauty of his daughter until Odin himself has no choice but to cry out for Freyja, demanding to know why you are not already amongst her Valkyrie."

Upon hearing his words, relief washed over Alfhildr like a cool, flowing stream.

Though still anxious and uncertain of her future, she knew then that the poisonous burden of her past had at last been cut from her troubled soul. Reaching out, she hugged both men tight, allowing her tears to wash away the last vestiges of her shame onto Sigmund's broad shoulder. In time, when sleep came upon her like a gentle summer breeze, Sigmund swept the troubled young girl up into his arms with ease, cradling her like a child as he carried her back to her lean-to where he gently wrapped her in her grey cloak.

Stepping back, he watched as Skadi snuggled close beside her mistress. Upon feeling the she-wolf, Alfhildr draped an arm about her neck.

"Sleep well, child," Sigmund whispered as a tear took to racing down his cheek where it was lost in his bushy moustache.

"Tomorrow, you will be challenged as never before. When the time comes, may the gods smile upon you."

Æ

The dawn broke bright and sharp, bringing with it a flurry of activity as both Saxon and Dane prepared to break camp and head back to their homes as soon as the contest was finished. Within the Danish camp, men stared wherever Alfhildr went, still garbed in the sea-green gown with braided hair. Even with her sword and wolf, few could see the fiery shield maiden who had stood alone before their lines and shouted her defiance at the usurper's army. Alfhildr barely noted the attention. Her mind and spirit were awhirl with all she had heard, said, and seen since the battle, while she prepared mechanically for the challenge.

She thought of Sigmund's words and what he had said about her father. Would he be looking down upon her from Valhalla with pride? She thought of Elvina and the weapons she told her the gods had gifted her with as she touched the warm amber pendant that rested against her bare skin just below her throat. But, above all else, her thoughts darted back again and again to Lord Godric. Godric, a Saxon warrior, advancing shoulder to shoulder with her as they broke the shield wall. Godric, standing nervously before her like a lovesick puppy as he stammered clumsily over his words while asking for her hand. Godric sitting beside her, so close that she could feel his eyes watching her every move. And, with each thought, Alfhildr felt her heart and stomach fluttering within.

In the queen's camp, Godric too was trying to quiet his anxious thoughts as he prepared. When a shadow fell across him as he examined the fletching of an arrow, he glanced up to find Bowdyn nervously hovering before him.

"My Lord, there is something I must discuss with you that is, well, it is important, a matter I have been reluctant to broach with you before," Godric's childhood friend and loyal huscarl stammered.

Setting aside the arrow, Godric eased back in his chair.

"Since we were boys sparring with wooden swords, we have never held any secrets back from the other. What is so terrible that causes you to do so now?"

"My Lord, last night, at the queen's table, she expressed a desire to, ah, well, she and I, ah…"

A broad smile lit up Godric's face.

"By God's good grace, you have finally found a match that suits you."

Stunned, Bowdyn blinked.

"But, my Lord, I would have to leave your service. And, though I would not be king, but merely a queen's consort, I would still find myself in the awkward position of being elevated to a station above yours."

With a smile that grew, Godric came to his feet, reached out, and clasped

Bowdyn's hand.

"There is no station higher than that of friend and shield brother. You have both my blessing and heartfelt congratulations!"

At length, when Bowdyn took leave of his friend and former lord, Godric stood there watching with pleasure as his former huscarl all but ran toward Elvina's tent. A thought occurred to him. Perhaps this news was a portent. Just as his friend had found his soul mate, this day could very well bring him his. With that thought in mind and a smile on his lips, Godric returned to his preparations.

Æ

At the appointed hour, the two hosts gathered in the meadow. This time, there were no shield walls surging toward a common foe. Instead, two mobs of boisterous warriors were milling about, chatting, laughing, and mingling freely as they eagerly awaited some sport. They aligned themselves in no discernable fashion on either side of a lane a hundred paces in length. At one end, were two banners, the red dragon of the Saxon queen and the raven standard that the Danes had followed into battle. At the other, was a single target supported by three poles, a circle neatly sawn from the trunk of a thick oak, two spread handbreadths wide, at its center, a mark in blue, the size of a fist, showed dark against the fresh-cut wood. Fifty paces beyond the target, a thin wand had been placed, no thicker than a man's thumb, shivering ever so slightly in the light breeze.

At last, a raucous horn demanded the attention of the throng as Sigmund stepped out between the lines.

"You all know why we are here," the bear of a man announced. "A mail shirt fit for a mighty warrior demands its owner should prove their worth. Two warriors broke the dead bastard's shield wall, so we need to see what more they can do, don't we?"

A good-natured roar went up from the assembled warriors.

"Each will have three arrows with which to attack yonder target. The three closest to the mark shall take the prize."

Again, the crowd cheered until Sigmund raised his arm once more.

"But, if after three arrows both are close, there is a final test. See the wand beyond the target? The first to split the wand will be our victor."

Men looked at the distant wand and muttered to themselves doubtfully. Surely, even a master of the bow would be hard pressed to hit such a mark. Sigmund ignored the muttering as he called forth the contestants.

"Lord Godric, stand forth."

The tall, muscular warrior strode out from the waiting lines, his fair hair pulled back from his face and his beard freshly trimmed. In his hand, he held a great yew bow as tall as himself. He turned toward the watching Saxons and punched the long stave into the air to a resounding cheer.

"Alfhildr, stand forth."

Men watched in silence as the girl stepped to where Godric and Sigmund waited with a grace few who had followed her into battle could have imagined. Beside the two large men she appeared petite and dainty, attired in a gown befitting a queen. Yet, none laughed, for all had witnessed for themselves her ferocity, skill, and courage. In her hand, the deep curve of the fabled Falissar drew many eyes away from the girl's face as both sides weighed the skill and weapons of the unlikely duo.

"Godric will shoot first, then each in turn."

With that final pronouncement Sigmund stepped back as a hush descended on the eager warriors.

Godric hefted his bow as he squinted at the sun and tried to judge the strength and direction of the breeze on his cheek. Then, with his heart in his mouth, he nocked his first arrow and drew. He held the heavy bow at full stretch for a moment, then loosed.

The shaft speared the target halfway between the mark and the edge. A quick cheer went up from the watching Saxons until Alfhildr stepped up to the line. At her feet, Skadi sat eagerly as if waiting for her friend to bring down a deer. Alfhildr paused as she watched the breeze ruffling the fur on Skadi's back. When she did act, she did so with a single, graceful motion, drawing as she brought Falissar up in a flowing curve, releasing without pause. A shout went up from the Danes as the arrow clipped the edge of the blue mark.

Godric frowned and bit his lip as he eyed the distant target. Once more he drew, paused, then loosed. Once more the Saxon warriors cheered as his second shaft bit deep in the center of the blue mark.

Alfhildr could feel her heart beating fast when she stepped forward a second time. With great effort, she pushed her feelings down until she was focused upon the task at hand once more, conscious only of a small flurry of wind that suddenly sprung up, causing her to wait with her eyes fixed on Skadi's neck. Then, once more, the fluid raise, draw, and loose. Godric watched entranced as the girl slowly lowered her bow before looking up to see his shaft split in two in the distant mark as the Danish warriors went wild.

At last silence settled. The gentle breeze dropped to nothing as if the watching warriors had stilled it with their indrawn breath. Godric raised his bow a third time.

As he loosed, a tiny breath of wind sprung up. His arrow slipped a fraction in its flight as it sped toward the mark. A groan erupted from the watching Saxons as they saw he had once more clipped the edge of the blue.

By now, Alfhildr's heart was beating faster than a sparrow's wing. Still unsure if she wanted to defeat the noble lord who stood beside her, the red-haired girl hesitated, struggling once again to set aside all other thoughts and feelings save one; winning the gold-chased armor. Only when she had settled herself did she look down at her first and most faithful ally to watch how the wind blew through the fur on Skadi's neck.

It was then, in the silence of that moment that she heard it. High above the assembled Saxons and Danes, a bird was lazily wheeling about. Its harsh croak pierced the stillness, sending a sudden chill down Alfhildr's spine. Shocked, she raised her eyes upward as the call was repeated. In that instant, the final words of the old woman's prophecy splashed like fire in her mind.

> *No man shall defeat her, but her final victory will be to yield,*
> *Safe lands shall she make with an enemy at her side.*

Only after Hoenir had turned and flown off into the sun did Alfhildr draw and loose with a strange smile on her lips and peace in her heart.

For a long moment, nothing happened as a stunned silence followed when the gathered Saxons and Danes saw she had missed the blue mark, had missed the wooden target altogether. In shock, they searched for Alfhildr's third arrow, until a Dane noted the distant wand.

It was split clean in two.

Æ

Men stood dumbfounded, unsure what this meant until Sigmund lifted up the gold-chased armor and held it out to the stunned Godric. The Saxon lord at last tore his eyes from the young girl, who still stood serenely gazing down toward the distant mark, to stare up in shock at the burly Dane. No words were spoken as the two men shared a look.

In silent reverence, Godric at last accepted the heavy mail, causing the Saxon warriors to break into a wild cheer. Yet, their joy was short-lived, quickly fading in surprise as their champion turned swiftly and placed the beautiful mail at Alfhildr's feet. Having done so, Godric stood there before the diminutive, red-haired Dane, nervously gazing into her eyes, waiting patiently for the noise to subside. For her part, Alfhildr found she could do nothing but quizzically stare into his deep, blue eyes, eyes that reached out to hers and touched her very soul.

"Alfhildr, I offer this as my *morgengyfu*, if you would consent to be my wife."

Slowly, like the crashing of waves, a storm erupted in the still meadow as men yelled themselves hoarse. Saxon and Dane alike shouted out their approval and laughed uproariously in relief of the tension. Yet, at its heart, a man and a girl stood quiet, each staring uncertainly at the other.

At last, Alfhildr summoned the courage to speak. Her words whispered so only Godric could hear.

"My Lord, you honor me. But before I can accept, I must tell you my story that you may know exactly who I am."

Godric watched in confusion as tears gathered in the corners of Alfhildr's eyes and heard the tremor in her voice. Elvina, who had been watching her friend closely, came up next to her, took her by the hand, and led the overwrought girl gently away to her tent, motioning Godric to follow.

Æ

Alfhildr paced nervously as she recounted her tale a third time. She relived the bitterness of her wound and the desertion of her mother, the harshness of the forest and her capture and imprisonment. The words spilled out, once more, of how she had tried to protect the weak and helpless only to become hunted herself. Then, her tone softened as she looked across at Elvina and spoke of her miraculous delivery and Elvina's gentle world until that too was torn asunder, setting them all on the path that led to this field and this tent.

When she had finished her story, one even she found difficult to accept as true, Alfhildr looked into Godric's eyes. In them, she saw nothing of the hatred, disgust, or shock she had expected. Instead, the Saxon noble continued to stare at her with a longing that was unsettling to a young girl unschooled in the ways Elvina took for granted.

In a final half-hearted and desperate attempt to avoid something she knew was meant to be, yet feared giving into, Alfhildr sighed.

"I can bring nothing to such a union other than the poor, wretched body and troubled soul you see before you."

A warm, inviting smile lit Godric's face as he crossed the tent to where Alfhildr stood watching, wearing an expression that reminded him of a lost child. Upon reaching her, he gently took her in his arms.

"All that I wish, all that I need, is right here before me."

Upon hearing that, a shiver ran through Alfhildr, one Godric felt.

"Shhh, do not be afraid my shield maiden," he whispered as he leaned forward and kissed a very anxious, yet willing, young girl.

Æ

By mid-afternoon both camps began to melt away as men turned their faces toward their scattered and distant homes. Alfhildr stood close beside Godric, his arm around her waist as she watched her brother lead his men into the darkening forest. A sudden chill caused Alfhildr to shiver. In a way she could not possibly understand, she suddenly realized that Snurre would not live out the year. His youthful arrogance, fueled by the manner in which he had taken to lording over his kinsmen, all but ensured someone would challenge him. And while she had no doubt that he was a capable warrior, he now carried the burden of having to prove himself superior to all contenders. It was a task Alfhildr did not think he was up to.

Alfhildr gazed up at the skies as if searching for some solace.

"So be it," she finally muttered, content to leave her brother's fate to the gods, just as her mother had done with her.

When the warband she had once thought she would lead was no longer in sight, Alfhildr reached down and ruffled Skadi's ears. She had her own fate to deal with, one that would be just as daunting as the one that her brother would face. Then, she smiled as the arm round her waist tightened. At least in her shield wall, there was someone beside her who she knew she could count on.

Æ

Fall arrived late that year, allowing men to rejoice at the bountiful harvest and the peace that accompanied it. A queen ruled the land of the East Saxons and no raids or feuds spoiled her justice, her borders at peace with her Danish neighbors. In a distant monastery, a monk sat at a high desk, his fingers stained black with ink.

Pleased with his efforts, Brother Plegmund anxiously watched as the bishop read through the recorded account of the events leading up to the battle between their new queen's army and that of the usurper's, a man whose name was already being expunged from living memory. The monk's joy quickly turned to confusion, then to shock, when the bishop began to frown as he continued to read. Finally, when he was unable to go any further, he looked up at Plegmund.

"This will never do," the bishop grumbled.

"I'm sorry, your Grace, but what will never do?" Plegmund asked.

"This, what you have written," the bishop thundered as he swept his hand across the offending document. "You heap glory upon a pagan while barely mentioning the valiant deeds of our queen or the brave nobles who rallied to her side."

"Your Grace, I only recorded the truth of what I saw."

When the bishop realized the naïve young monk did not understand what was at stake, he glared at him.

"You are either a fool or an idiot," the bishop muttered. "Bring me quill and ink."

Obediently, the shaken young monk did so. He remained but a while longer, watching as his bishop took to crossing out entire passages of his account or scribbling quick notes in the margin.

During a pause, as he was dipping the end of the quill into the inkpot, the bishop looked up at Plegmund.

"This entire account will need to be recopied before I send it off to the cardinal. Go and fetch Brother Eamon. His hand may not be as steady as yours, but, at least, he has the good sense to be careful as to what he commits to parchment."

Plegmund was about to leave when the bishop once more called out.

"And you, you are to keep this to yourself. Understood?"

Though he didn't, Plegmund nodded before slipping from the scriptorium and into the cloister. He didn't quite know what he would do at the moment. Even though Alfhildr was a pagan, the young monk knew he was obligated to do right by her and what she had accomplished. If that meant defying his earthly masters, then so be it. Alfhildr had taught him courage was more than a word that warriors used to burnish their deeds and achievements. The red-haired Dane, who he had followed and in whom he had put his trust, had shown courage in the face of trials very different from those the saints he and his brothers revered and the warriors she had led into battle had faced: yet, they were no less daunting. The least he could do was have the courage to preserve the truth, if not for the Church and the nobles it served, then for those who, like Alfhildr, found themselves lost, alone, and in need of a guiding light, a beacon to guide them to a brighter, happier dawn.

Chapter Twenty-two
PASSING INTO LEGEND

Present Day England
"The Dig"

With the end of the season fast approaching and Professor Bannon eager to wrap things up at the dig in order to return to his lectern and lecture hall, Elva became more erratic as the days passed without her finding the final piece of evidence that she would need to prove the diminutive warrior they had unearthed was Alfhildr. Abandoning the methodical approach that had served her so well up until then, she took to roaming about the perimeter of the dig in ever-increasing circles. A few days before they were due to leave, when he could stand it no longer, Bannon followed her.

"What in God's name has you so distracted, Elva?" he asked when he managed to catch up to her as she stood in the middle of a field adjoining the dig, looking about as if trying to decide where to look next.

"You've been running about like a headless chicken these past few days."

"I can't find it," she muttered without looking back at the professor as she flapped her hands at her sides in frustration.

"Found what?" Bannon asked.

"The rune stone. The legend speaks of a rune stone that was erected in memory of Alfhildr."

Having indulged his star protégé up to now, Bannon decided the time had come to put an end to her wild claims that the remains they had found belonged to a mythical figure, one that could not possibly be related to Godric, the man credited with establishing a community straddling what had once been Saxon lands and Danelaw.

"Elva, as much as I cherish your enthusiasm for this quest of yours, need I remind you that we are archeologists, dedicated to the scientific study of cultures through the examination of their material remains, artifacts, and historical records, records that can be validated," he informed the red-haired grad student in the tone he often used to put a student on notice that he would brook no argument.

"I've not come across any mention of a rune stone in any of the written accounts of the legend or records associated with Godric or this community, and, believe me, after we found those remains, I've gone through them all."

Coming to a halt, Elva folded her arms across her chest, wondering if she should say anything or simply let the matter drop. Finally, with a sigh she turned to face Bannon.

"That's because there's another."

Having found himself wondering from time to time if she had been working from a source of which he had no knowledge, Bannon thought for a moment.

"Setting aside the fact that if there is such a document, which for some odd reason you've kept to yourself, does it by any chance mention where this rune stone might be?" he asked making no effort to hide the incredulity in his voice.

"No. I thought it would be here, where the funeral took place," she muttered as she once more took to looking about.

A smile began to creep across Bannon's lips as he realized Elva just may have handed him the means with which he could put the girl's foolish notions about Alfhildr to rest.

So, he decided to pander to her wild fantasy this one last time.

"Well, if such a stone did exist, did you ever consider that it would be someplace else, someplace where memorials to the dead are normally kept?"

"A cemetery?" Elva asked making no effort to disguise her incredulity as she gazed up into her professor's eyes.

"Why not?

"Alfhildr never converted to the Christian faith."

"But, according to the legend, she married a Christian."

"Yes."

"I expect you know what *prima signatio* means," Bannon stated.

In the twinkling of an eye, Elva's frown disappeared.

"Prime signing, making the sign of the cross over a pagan, the first step to conversion."

"It allowed non-Christians to live among Christians and do business with them," Bannon explained. "They were even admitted to a special part of the mass, the *primsigndra messa*."

"So, the rune stone just might be…"

Without finishing her thought, Elva took off for the village church whose foundation was said to have been laid down when the Great Keep was built. There she wandered about from stone to stone, looking for anything that even remotely looked as if it might be a rune stone. Bannon followed her as she did so, sporting a self-satisfied smile as the young graduate student's frustration grew when she could find nothing that even remotely resembled a rune stone.

In time, they were joined by the vicar who asked them if he could be of help. At her wit's end, Elva explained what they were looking for.

"Oh, you'll not find anything like that here," the elderly vicar replied happily, unaware of the effect his words were having on the red-haired graduate student.

"I suppose if there were something like that it would be where Godric's chapel once stood."

Bannon and Elva stared at each other before both turned to the vicar and almost shouted in unison, "What chapel?"

"There's not much there anymore," the vicar explained nervously as he wilted under the hungry stares of the two archeologists. "It's almost impossible to find unless you know what you're looking for. It was built deep in the forest at the end of a foot path that's quite difficult to follow even in the best of times."

Æ

England
1012 AD

As they neared the place where the path came to an abrupt end in a small glade, the young child sensed his grandmother's nervousness.

"What is it?" he asked as he took to looking about the forest.

Realizing her behavior was frightening the red-haired child at her side, the old woman forced herself to set aside her apprehensions and, instead, finish the story she had started, one she hoped would give the child entrusted to her care the courage he would need to see him through the coming ordeal.

"As I was saying, in time, Alfhildr did willingly yield to Godric," the grandmother stated as she picked up the story where she had left it off.

"But until her death and even beyond she remained faithful to the ways of her people."

Æ

Looking up from her own careful efforts, the daughter-in-law of a Saxon noble and his Danish lady frowned as she watched her daughter harshly yank a ragged clump of wool from her distaff. "Kendra! What are you doing?"

The red-haired girl made a face as if wondering why her mother would ask such a silly question.

"I am spinning wool into thread."

"Is that the way I showed you?" the mother asked.

"It is the way grandmother does it," the young girl replied haughtily.

Making no effort to hide her displeasure with the way her daughter had answered, Swefred set aside her own distaff.

"How many times have I told you it is not wise for you to do what your grandmother does?"

"You allow Leofric to do what she does." Kendra shot back without hesitation.

"Leofric is a boy. There are things a boy must know, just as there are certain things necessary for a girl to learn."

Confused, the red-haired girl thought for a moment before looking over at her mother.

"How is it, then, that Grandma Alfhildr is able to do both?"

Wincing, Swefred did her best to find a suitable answer. Just how much she wished to share with others of what she knew of her mother-in-law, especially her own children, was something with which she had always been unable to come to terms. Even she had difficulty wrapping her head around something that was almost too fantastic to believe.

"Well?" the impatient little girl asked.

Looking over at her daughter, Swefred regarded the girl while wearing a cunning little smile.

"Perhaps that is a question best answered by your grandmother herself."

"Can I go ask her now?" Kendra asked, all but bouncing up and down in her seat.

Sensing the child would be insufferable until she had, Swefred nodded.

"Yes, yes. Go and find her and see if she will share her story with you."

"Do you know where Grandma Alfhildr is?" the girl asked as she tossed her tangled distaff aside without giving any thought to where it landed.

Swefred sniffed, making no effort to mask the revulsion she felt over the way her mother-in-law carried on.

"You'll probably find her in the stable dragging her skirts through the manure or out on the edge of the woods where the men practice with the bow."

Before Swefred could remind her daughter to be careful and not get dirty, as she often did whenever she spent time with her grandmother, the winsome young girl with flowing red hair was gone.

Æ

Having grown bored with listening to the tired old stories he had heard all too often, Godric rose from his chair. He quickly raised his hand, signaling his gathered huscarls and thegns that they were to remain seated.

"It has been a long and tiring day," he explained apologetically. "I expect tomorrow will be even more demanding, so you must excuse me."

With that, he withdrew from the great hall flanked on either side by his two sons, young men who had inherited their father's features and robust stature.

"There is still much we must do if we are to be ready to receive the queen and her consort," Godric informed his sons. "There is a larder that needs restocking."

Upon hearing this both boys grinned knowingly. Gunnar, the older of the two, could hardly contain his excitement.

"A hunt. Will mother be joining us?"

Oswin, the younger of Godric's sons guffawed.

"Of course, she will. Even with eyesight that is not as keen as it once was, she can still outshoot any of us on our best day."

While Oswin had not intended his comment to be cruel, Godric could not help but feel a pang of sadness at the thought that his beloved wife was growing old. Though she tried valiantly to keep him from noticing, she was finding it more and more difficult to keep up with him whenever he indulged her lifelong passion for the hunt. There had been a time when the opposite was true, when she would ride rings around him and leave him red-faced at the end of the day when their catch was paraded before the rest of the hunting party. Those days were gone now, and it saddened the Saxon lord.

"Father? Is something troubling you?"

With a shake of his head, Godric looked over at Gunnar.

"Sorry," he muttered apologetically. "As I said, it has been a long day. Now, if you will excuse me."

With that, he wandered off alone to where his beloved Alfhildr was waiting for him.

Æ

He found the Danish girl who had captured his heart so many years before quietly seated by the window, staring out at the bright full moon. He often found her there watching, listening. Crossing the room, he placed his hands on her shoulders as he too took to gazing out over the moonlit forest off in the distance.

"I thought I heard her again earlier this evening," Alfhildr whispered as she reached up and placed a gentle hand on one of Godric's. "I know it's foolish. Skadi has been gone now these many years. Still…"

The sadness in Alfhildr's voice caused Godric's vision to blur as his heart went out to her. She seldom allowed herself to dwell on what was no more, focusing all her considerable energy and determination on her family and the people entrusted to Godric's care. In an effort to shake her free of her melancholy mood, he informed Alfhildr that he would be taking their sons out on a hunt in the next few days.

"Gunnar wished to know if you will be accompanying us," he announced, hiding a sly grin behind her back as he did so.

As he had expected, Alfhildr snapped her head about and looked up into his eyes.

"And what did you tell him?"

Godric shrugged. "I told him I would have to see if you would be able to. I mean, with so much to do around here in order to prepare for Elvina and Bowdyn's visit, I didn't know if you would need to stay behind and see to it that the household staff had everything in hand."

After slapping the hand that hers had been resting on, Alfhildr rose to her feet and headed over to the table where her personal items were tossed about in a rather haphazard fashion.

"Oh please!" she snorted. "Swefred and that other prissy girl Oswin married would have a fit if I tried to interfere with the way they run the household."

As he watched his wife take a seat before her mirror and undo the braid she often wore, Godric chuckled.

"Can you blame them? When you are left in charge you try to run the household staff as if it were a warband. I fear if you had your way, the queen would find herself being greeted by a shield wall."

Alfhildr smirked as she took to combing out her still flowing, red hair using an old comb decorated with the carving of a dragon's head.

"I expect neither she nor Bowdyn would be a bit surprised."

Joining her laughter, Godric shook his head. "No, I expect they would not."

"Kendra came to me today," Alfhildr announced suddenly in a voice that caused Godric to be on guard.

"Oh?" Was all he asked, wary as to where their conversation was now taking them.

"She asked about me," Alfhildr replied flatly.

"What about you?"

Turning, Alfhildr looked over at Godric as he sat on the edge of the bed wearing an expression of cautious attention.

"She wants to know everything. She is curious about my childhood. She asked how it came to be that I am better at hitting the mark with an arrow than spinning yarn. And she all but demanded to know if the stories people tell about me are true."

"What did you tell her?"

Looking back at the mirror, Alfhildr took a moment to study her reflection. Though she could not see him, Gunnvor, son of Gunnar was there. So, too, was a young and untamed Alfhildr, sword arm of the gods. Even the faint image of a maid to a timid young Saxon girl could be seen peeking back at her. With a sigh, Alfhildr looked away.

"I have been told there are many stories concerning my past. Kendra is old enough to hear the truth. Besides," Alfhildr added as her gaze dropped to the floor, "I think it is important for someone to know the truth in case, well…"

Leaping to his feet, Godric rushed over to Alfhildr. Dropping to one knee, he gathered her up in his arms, resting her head on his shoulder as her tears began to flow.

"All our children and their children have been healthy and grew as God meant them to," he murmured reassuringly. "There is nothing to fear."

Pulling back, Alfhildr looked into Godric's eyes.

"And what if my gods, or yours, decide one day they are in need of someone different, someone like me?"

Unable to answer her question, Godric asked what she intended to do.

"I shall tell Kendra the true story of my life, if for no other reason than to ensure there is someone who will always be there ready to help if the gods decide to once more take one of our line in hand and set them upon a path different from that of their kinsmen."

Coming to his feet, Godric looked down at his beloved Dane girl and smiled before bending over and planting a gentle kiss on her upturned lips.

"You are as wise as you are beautiful."

Setting aside her sadness, Alfhildr smiled.

"And you, Sire, are a shameless flatterer.

Now," she announced crisply as she turned once more to face the mirror. "If we are to be off on the hunt in the next few days, there is much to do. First, we need our rest."

"Who said I was planning on allowing you to rest tonight?" Godric muttered as he made his way back to their bed.

Upon turning about, he could see a twinkling in Alfhildr's eyes and a mischievous grin as she regarded his reflection in the mirror.

Æ

The second day of the hunt turned out to be as frustrating for Alfhildr as the first had been. Twice she had been on the verge of skewering a boar and twice the beast she had been pursuing was killed by another. The first animal had fallen to Oswin, who made a point of looking over at his mother and smirking as Godric heaped praise upon his youngest son for his achievement.

The second was run to ground by a huscarl who later tried to apologize to Alfhildr but was swiftly told he had nothing for which to be sorry.

"It was a good, clean kill," she admitted amiably. "Your skill and courage as well as your humility do you great credit."

Determined she would not be denied again, it was just after dawn of the final day of the hunt when Alfhildr set off with only Gunnar at her side. Of her children, she had always felt the closest to him, an unspoken bond that they shared. Much of the day was spent in a futile search for a suitable mark. It wasn't until late afternoon when Gunnar caught sight of a massive beast.

"There!" he shouted as he thrust his arm out in the direction where he had spotted a monstrous boar scurrying back into the undergrowth.

"If we manage to run that to ground, tonight Oswin will dine on his own boastful words."

Before he could take up the chase, Alfhildr brought her mount about and spurred it on, shouting out as she flew past her startled son.

"There will be no '*we*' today, boy."

With more than blood in common with his mother, a grin lit up Gunnar's face as he took up the chase as well, catching up to her with ease. Together, they galloped side by side through the forest, hurling taunts and lighthearted insults at each other as they rode hard after their prey. Upon reaching a thicket, they separated, each going around it a different way. Alfhildr caught sight of the boar scurrying through a clump of bushes first. Determined not to lose sight of it again, she dug her heels into the flanks of the wretched nag she was riding.

Dimma would have never allowed her to fall behind her intended prize like this, Alfhildr told herself as she strained her eyes in an effort to see where the boar had gone.

With her heart set on being the first to spear the beast, she crashed through a clump of bushes, hoping to find the boar on the other side. To her surprise, the brute had come about and was waiting for her. The skittish mare reared as Alfhildr threw herself from the saddle, landing clumsily as she struggled to pull the broad-bladed boar spear from its holster. But before Alfhildr was able to free the spear, the mare dragged herself free and turned, whinnying in panic to flee the snarling boar.

For a moment, the boar stared angrily at the diminutive hunter, its breath steaming the air. Then, with a vicious squeal, it charged. Standing her ground, Alfhildr drew her beloved Durthfang and crouched, the sword held low, ready to gut the massive brute. She was grinning when the enraged beast hit.

Æ

After making yet another circuit of the campfire, Godric stopped to peer off into the gathering darkness. When he saw or heard nothing, he muttered more to himself, but loud enough to be heard by the rest of the hunting party who had been watching him.

"They should have been back by now."

From where he sat propped up against his saddle, Oswin dismissed his father's concerns.

"It's your fault for letting those two ride off together. You know how they get once they've set their sights on some hapless creature."

Godric did not reply as he prepared to resume his incessant pacing. He was kept from doing so, however, when a guard sang out a warning.

"Rider coming into camp."

All ears perked up as they listened to the guard's challenge.

When no response came from the newcomer, those who had settled about the fire came to their feet, some reaching for their swords as they did so. After a second challenge went unheeded a cold, and invisible, hand reached into Godric's chest and wrapped itself about his heart. When the guard next called out, it was to announce Gunnar was coming in.

What relief Godric felt was short-lived, for when his oldest son finally did advance into the firelight, he could see tears streaming down his cheeks as the young man's chest heaved uncontrollably. Behind him, he led two horses. Across one lay the carcass of a massive boar, blood still dripping from the gaping slash in its belly. Across the other was a motionless bundle wrapped in an old grey cloak from which long, flowing, red hair spilled in an unruly cascade.

Æ

Kendra entered the Great Hall where she was told her grandfather sat alone. The fire was unlit and, despite the warm sunshine outside, the hall was cold and dark. A single figure sat stiffly upright by the hearth, still and silent, staring sightlessly toward the open window. Kendra bit her lip and paused uncertainly for a moment.

"Grandfather?"

Godric started as he returned from his reverie. He glanced over his shoulder to where the girl stood but a second before quickly turning his head away as she resumed marching toward him with her head held high. A swift hand wiped a tear from his face before he came around to greet the red-haired girl who carried herself with such purpose.

"What is it I can do for you, child?"

"I have come to help you as you prepare Grandmother for her last voyage," the girl stated in an even tone that took the grieving lord by surprise.

Upon seeing the confused look on her grandfather's face, Kendra explained.

"Grandmother Alfhildr told me of her adventures. She often spoke of the gods her ancestors once revered and how she could never find it in her heart to cast them aside as she had been. She showed me all her great treasures, things mother would never understand, but which meant the world to Grandmother. So, I thought it might be best if I helped by picking out those items that she would wish to take with her."

In silence, Godric looked upon the diminutive red-haired girl before him, standing proud and resolved, just as his beloved Alfhildr had on the first day he had laid eyes on her. Making no effort to hold back his tears, he smiled.

"Your grandmother would be pleased."

Pushing himself up from the chair, Godric took the young girl by the hand and led her up to their private chamber.

Æ

As Kendra looked around, she saw that nothing had changed since she had last sat with her grandmother. The table was still cluttered with parchment and saddlery, brooches, and knives. The lid of the clothespress remained ajar as it had been, a cloak draped untidily across one corner.

"There is your grandmother's chest and, there, her table," Godric whispered as he gazed around as if seeing it all for the first time.

"She used to sit and watch from the window as she combed her hair, her beautiful red hair…"

Unable to continue, he stopped. Suddenly, without another word he spun about on his heel and pushed his way from the chamber.

For a moment Kendra gazed sadly after her grandfather. After drawing herself up, she turned and started to sort through the jumble before her. From the table she picked up a simple comb decorated with the carved head of a dragon. This she laid beside a golden brooch, the gifts of an old woman who, Grandma had said, had been the last of her kind. From the wall, Kendra lifted a strangely curved bow and ran her fingers over its belly, touching the letters, FLSR, cut deep into the bone. This, too, she set aside, along with its quiver and a simple bracer well-worn and scuffed from frequent use.

Kendra turned to the chest. She lifted out armfuls of richly embroidered gowns and underskirts until at last, near the bottom, she found what she sought. A simple homespun gown, as rough as any a serf would wear was wrapped tight around a carved and inlaid box. Kendra laid the dress beside the bow before delicately opening the little box. Inside was a collection of unremarkable brooches, all tangled together, roughly carved from wood and bone. Kendra pulled out one at random and held it up to the light to admire the simple black brooch that was carved like a crow.

"Every one a life," Alfhildr had told Kendra on the day she had shown the box to her, explaining how she had come to be in possession of each and every item in it.

"Every one a gift from those who had little but from whom the raiders demanded more. When I touch them, I promise it will never happen again while I have breath to draw a blade."

With a sigh, Kendra replaced the brooch and closed the box. In the corner, two stout hooks had been driven between the tight-fitting stones. From them, Kendra lifted down their burdens with difficulty. First, Durthfang, freshly cleaned from the boar's blood and whetted sharp once more by a disconsolate Gunnar. Next, an old linden shield, the painting of two ravens on a blue background now peeling with age. Finally, there was the shirt of close-wrought mail trimmed with gold links, still bright and freshly polished even though it had hung unused for many years.

As she struggled with the heavy mail, the door banged open. Lord Godric smiled sadly as he saw the things Kendra had laid out before adding a small chest to the pile. His granddaughter frowned questioningly until he opened the chest and stood back to let her see within.

"They're Skadi's bones."

Her frown deepened.

"I thought Skadi went into the forest to raise her own pups and run free. Grandma told me. She said that when Oswin was born Skadi knew it was time for her to go off and raise her own pups."

"That is what I told your Grandma. The truth …"

Godric was forced to pause as he struggled to rein in the sorrow that threatened to overwhelm him once more. Only when he was ready did he continue.

"The truth is I woke one morning and found her curled up peacefully, dead in her sleep. Alfhildr was near her time with Oswin and I couldn't bear to tell her."

Godric paused in melancholy recollection.

"I took Skadi into the forest and buried her quietly, but now..."

Godric took a mighty, shuddering breath, then again forced himself to go on.

"Many a night, these two old friends lay snuggled together. I think it only fitting that they do so for eternity."

With the same courage her grandmother had drawn upon to face many a challenge during her life's journey, young Kendra nodded dry-eyed as she took the box and added it to the things she had collected.

"Grandma Alfhildr would like that."

Æ

Kendra stood beside her mother on the hill as her father, uncle, and the men who had once fought at her grandmother's side placed the litter bearing her mortal remains within the stone ship. Swefred sniffed and glowered at the pagan rites, glad that she had kept her children away. She had railed at Gunnar when he had told her of his father's plans for the funeral.

"We are Christian! Would you have me risk my immortal soul, as well as our children's, in this heathen practice? Remember who you are, Gunnar son of Godric."

But Gunnar had glowered at his fiery-tempered wife as she stormed off to complain to their priest, dragging an unwilling Leofric and Kendra in her wake.

"I remember well, woman," he thundered after her. "I remember that I am also Gunnar, son of Alfhildr, sword arm of the gods."

With that he had turned to join the waiting warriors, Saxon and Dane, as they prepared to honor his mother in a fitting manner.

On the hillside, Kendra's mind took to drifting as the last of the heavy stones were being carefully set in place. She thought of all the wondrous tales Grandmother Alfhildr was so fond of telling her, tales of strange gods and mighty adventures. Tales of a lost soul and her many challenges and adventures. Tales of a legend.

Just then, the squawk of a bird distracted the red-haired girl. Looking up, Kendra spotted a crow circling about, way above the gathering of Saxons and Danes. It was a message, she told herself as a small smile graced her lips, a message sent to her by her grandmother and her pagan gods.

"So, it shall be," Kandra whispered.

Not hearing clearly what his sister had said, Leofric leaned over and whispered in her ear. "What did you say?"

Glancing out of the corner of her eyes, Kendra took a moment to pull back a few strands of her flaming, red hair and tuck them behind her ear, but said nothing. This would be her secret: one she would make sure only those of their line who understood and believed would be entrusted to preserve.

Æ

At last, the somber procession returned to the Great Keep. Lord Godric stood tall and proud as he watched the last of the saddened mourners leave. Kendra finally broke free from her mother and went to stand beside him in the gathering dusk. As the sun was setting, the young red-haired girl looked up at her grandfather.

"We should honor Grandmother as her ancestors once did with a rune stone, Grandfather."

The thought caught Godric's imagination, causing a brief smile to brighten his face. Then, just as quickly, it faded.

"I am afraid the good bishop would frown upon such an honor, though it is one justly deserved."

"They have no need to know of it," Kendra volunteered.

"You cannot hide something like that, child."

"Not hide, Grandfather. Just put it where it belongs, in the woods Grandmother so loved and where her soul still resides, free and happy with Skadi, Hoenir, and all the others who loved her, and she loved them."

And so, it came to pass that Godric built a chapel not far from where it was said Alfhildr had begun her journey. And beside that chapel, he had a monument erected. Cut deep in its rough surface ancient marks were made.

Godric raised this stone in memory of Alfhildr,
Warrior, wife, peace weaver

EPILOGUE

England
1012 AD

The more the boy's pace slowed, the faster his grandmother spoke, for she realized he had finally come to understand how their strange journey would end, for he knew he was different from the other boys. It was only now, upon hearing his grandmother's story that he finally understood just how different he was.

When she did finish, the two lapsed into an uncomfortable silence. Eventually, the boy spoke. With a voice as downcast as his moist eyes, he asked if her story were true, if he really was related to Alfhildr through blood, and if so, then, why did his family live in the village and not the keep Godric had built.

Before answering, the grandmother raised her eyes to the heavens to thank the saints, to whom she had prayed to so long and hard, for being afforded an opportunity to forge the final link between what had been and what was.

"A family's fortunes ebbs and flows like the tides," the old woman carefully explained. "Not everyone in our line met the challenges they faced as Alfhildr did. Some held back, unable to summon the courage to take the final step necessary to live as God had intended. I expect there were those who feared what their kinsmen would say or think of them, just as Alfhildr's mother did. Others refused to see the truth for what it was, brushing aside Alfhildr's achievements as little more than a childish story."

With furrowed brow, the boy cocked his head to one side as if trying to work out why his ancestors had behaved so foolishly before glancing up at his grandmother out of the corner of his eyes.

"What made them act like that?" he finally asked.

"Nothing made them do anything. From time to time, everyone is confronted by an opportunity to do what is right or what needs to be done if they are to take advantage of those gifts God and our ancestors bestowed upon us. Not everyone has the courage to reach out and seize the moment. You see, even the most humble man and woman is free to choose which path they will follow and how far they are willing to travel along it. No one, not even the mightiest king, can take that away from us. The only thing in this life that is pre-ordained is death. And while it is true others do have an impact on our lives, such as your parents and the lord who lives in the keep, in the end, we must take responsibility for our own lives and what we do with them."

Once more, the two lapsed into silence. Only when thin ribbons of smoke could be seen just ahead, rising lazily from a small hovel did the grandmother feel the boy's grip on her hand tighten as he slowed his pace, then stopped.

"Will it be painful?" he asked in a small voice as he struggled to hold back his tears.

"Bringing forth a new life is always painful," she murmured as she recalled how she had screamed when she had endured the rigors of childbirth.

The boy stood there for the longest time, wavering between going on and turning back. The desire to flee, to return to his village and the only life he had known was tempting. His grandmother would not try to stop him. He knew that. The only thing that kept him from doing so was one question: what then? What would become of him if he did not go forward? He had no way of knowing if he would finally be able to overcome the handicaps that kept him apart from the other boys, just as it was impossible for him to imagine what his life would be like if he did embark on the strange journey that lay before him.

Of course, neither had Alfhildr, the boy suddenly realized. While her legend told of a child torn loose, by chance, from the only world she had known, she too had stood at a crossroads, facing a decision no different than his. She had to choose between remaining with the Old Woman who had healed her or face all the trials she would have to endure once she had taken up the challenge of which her prophecy spoke.

It must have demanded both courage and determination to do so, the boy thought, *courage to go on when common sense dictated otherwise, and a determination to live her life as her pagan gods had intended. Could he meet the sort of trails his storied ancestor had faced just as she had?* the boy wondered.

And if he did accept the life fate was dangling before him, what would his purpose here on Middle Earth be? Alfhildr had united a people at a time when the idea of Saxon and Dane sharing this island in peace was unimaginable. What great quest would the ordeal he was about to undergo serve? How would his prophecy read?

Then, in the twinkling of an eye, the boy knew what he would do. He would do more than simply keep the true story of a legendary warrior alive just as his grandmother had. He would do all he could to make sure the truth of her story saw the light of day so that her kinsmen, a people who had once turned their back on her, would come to see Alfhildr was more than a mythical figure, conjured up by clever storytellers and endowed with supernatural powers and gifts. He would make his people understand that she was, in truth, no different than they were, a simple soul struggling to make sense of her life, to live it as nature and her pagan gods intended. How he would do so, or even if he could make his own people believe a tale that was even more fantastic than the legend with which they had grown up, would be a true challenge, one he suddenly found he could not turn his back on.

Thus resolved, the frail, red-haired child let go of his grandmother's hand, drew himself up, and went forward on his own. Upon stepping out into the small glade before the modest hovel, he saw an old woman feeding goats. Turning toward him, she gazed into his eyes and smiled.

"I have been expecting you."

Æ

Present Day England
"The Dig"

With her mobile phone pressed against one ear and a finger jammed into the other, Elva struggled to make herself heard over the rousing celebration going on in the high street pub overshadowed by The Great Keep.

"I said it was just as you told me, Grandma. Everything, every detail was exactly how you said it would be," Elva all but shouted.

In the pause that followed, the young graduate student imagined she could see the warm, knowing smile her grandmother often wore whenever she spoke of the legends of which she was so fond.

"Listen Grandma Godric, I really must go. I'll call tomorrow after things have calmed down some. Okay?"

Upon ending that call, Elva scrolled through the list of contacts on her mobile phone's directory. When she found the number she was looking for, she hesitated as her fingers hovered uncertainly for a moment before she hit speed dial.

"Dr. Gibson's office, please. Thank you. Mr. Gibson? It's Elva Gunnorson. Could we arrange a consultation? Yes, I know I delayed doing so for far too long, but there was something I had to do first. Yes, it's complete, so, at last, I'm free to go forward. No, not my parents. My grandmother will be with me. Is that all right? Yes, I'm certain it's what I want."

When she was finished and had tucked her mobile into the pocket of her jeans, Elva hesitated. Even out on the street, she could hear Professor Bannon and her fellow students celebrating the success of the dig as well as the stunning discovery of a hitherto unknown copy of *The Saga of Alfhildr*, written in Plegmund's own hand. Whether she would keep the priceless document that had been handed down from grandmother to granddaughter for generations or donate it to the university was a matter that did not need to be decided that night. At the moment, there was another, more pressing duty to which she needed to attend.

Before she could get on with her own life, one that had always been something of a puzzle to her, the red-haired descendant of the fabled Viking shield maiden needed to pay homage to an ancestor. Turning her back on the pub where her professor and friends were anxiously awaiting her return, Elva took up the unopened bottle of champagne she'd spirited out of the party and headed off into the forest to a place where one journey had ended and another had begun.

Æ

Easing back on her haunches, Elva studied the inscription that she had lovingly traced out with a finger wet with champagne.

"Godric raised this stone in memory of Alfhildr, warrior, wife, peace weaver," she murmured.

As the evening shadows fell upon the pagan memorial, causing the wet runic characters to glisten in the late afternoon sun, Elva pulled a few strands of her flaming red hair back behind her ear as she found herself wondering if she would ever find a love as deep and enduring as the one Godric had had for Alfhildr. She hoped so, just as she had once hoped that the stories her grandmother had told her were true.

The squawk of a bird circling somewhere overhead caused Elva to look up. Try as she might, she could no more see the bird, lost from sight in the bright summer sun, than she could see what lay ahead for her as she prepared to embark on her own long-delayed journey. At that moment, the only thing that she could be certain of was that what she had once thought of as a curse was a blessing, one that had been lovingly passed down to her by a young girl who, in truth, had been no different than her.

AFTERWORD
Historical Background, Setting, Factual Data, and Inspirations
H.W. Coyle

Alfhildr

There is an Alfhild in Norse legend, a maiden who disguised herself as a warrior in order to avoid marriage to King Alf. Her life was perhaps based on that of a real 9th-century Viking pirate.

There is also a story titled *Alfhild and the Dragon-Sword* by Thorskegga Thorn that is a modern tale based on old myths.

The poetic sagas that precede each major section of *The Legend of Alfhildr* are original creations written by Jennifer Ellis using Icelandic sagas as examples.

The history, reflected in this story as far as customs, culture, medical treatment, beliefs, and conduct, is based on historical research. The underlying medical condition described in this story is addressed separately.

Dark Ages vs Middle Ages & Contemporary English Histories of the Time

Today most historians divide the period between the fall of the Western Roman Empire in the 5th to 16th Century into three periods: The Early Middle Ages (5th-10th Century), the High Middle Ages, (11th-13th Century) and the Late Middle Ages, (14th-16th Century).

The Early Middle Ages have also been referred to as the Dark Ages. The concept of a Dark Age originated with the Italian scholar Petrarch (Francesco Petrarca) in the 1330s and was originally intended as a sweeping criticism of the character of Late Latin literature. Petrarch regarded the centuries since the fall of Rome as "dark" compared to the "light" of classical antiquity. Later historians expanded the term to refer to the transitional period between Roman times and the High Middle Ages, including not only the lack of Latin literature, but also a lack of contemporary written history, general demographic decline, limited building activity, and material cultural achievements in general. Popular culture has further expanded on the term as a vehicle to depict the Middle Ages as a time of backwardness, extending its pejorative use and expanding its scope.

Histories written in England by natives of England during the Early Middle Ages are pretty much confined to the following:

The first known history of England written after the Romans was written by a monk named Gildas. His three volume *De Excidio et Conquestu Britanniae* (*The Loss of Britain*), was written about 540. It was, for the most part, polemic and heavy on religion.

The five volumes of Bede's *Historia Ecclesiastica Gentis Anglorum*,

(*The Ecclesiastical History of the English People*) completed in 731 AD covered the history of England from 55 BC, (Caesar's invasion) to 730 AD, earning him the title, "The Father of English History."

In 893, a monk named Asser wrote a biography of Alfred, called *The Life of King Alfred*. The biography is now the main source of information about Alfred's life, and provides far more information about Alfred than is known about any other early English ruler.

The Anglo-Saxon Chronicle is a collection of annals that were written in Old English and initially started late in the 9th century, probably in Wessex, during the reign of Alfred, the Great, and completed in 1116. Almost all of the material in the chronicle is in the form of annals, by year. The earliest are dated 60 BC, and historical material follows up to the year in which the chronicle was written, at which point contemporary records begin.

In 1086, the first full accounting of England was recorded in what was known as the *Doomsday Book*, which was an extensive survey of England ordered by William, the Bastard.

Intersex Conditions[12]

This story revolves around a child who is intersex,[13] an intermediate or atypical combination of physical features that usually distinguishes male and female. This is usually congenital, involving chromosomal, morphologic, genital, and/or gonadal anomalies, such as diversion from typical XX-female or XY-male presentations. In the past, people suffering from this condition were known as "hermaphrodites."[14]

Although not common, these conditions are also not rare. They are among the most commonly seen intersex conditions and have a prevalence of 2 or 3 cases per 1000 population. These conditions present instances of undermasculinization and both syndromes can occur in the same individual.

A result of potentially hundreds of genetic mutations to the androgen receptor gene, androgen insensitivity syndrome (AIS) manifests in a notable inability of an individual who has XY sex chromosomes to respond to

---

[12] *Adapted from* Quigley CA, DeBellis A, Marschke KB, El-Awady MK, Wilson EM, French FS. Androgen receptor defects: historical, clinical, and molecular perspectives. Endocrine Rev 1995; 16(3):282).
[13] See also Editor's Comment.
[14] Today the use of this term is considered to be stigmatizing and misleading and, as such, inappropriate, see https://isna.org/faq/hermaphrodite/.

androgens. This inability occurs despite the presence of testes and typical testosterone production, transport, and metabolism. Of particular consequence is the relative or complete failure of the individual to respond to testosterone or dihydrotestosterone.[15] Schematic representation of a grading scheme for clinical classification of AIS includes grades numbered 1 through 7 in order of increasing severity.

> Grade 1: normal masculinization in utero,
> Grade 2: male phenotype with mild defect in masculinization (eg, isolated hypospadias),
> Grade 3: male phenotype with severe defect in masculinization—small penis, perineoscrotal hypospadias, bifid scrotum or cryptorchidism,
> Grade 4: severe genital ambiguity—clitoral-like phallus, labioscrotal folds, single perineal orifice,
> Grade 5: female phenotype with posterior labial fusion and clitoromegaly,
> Grade 6/7: female phenotype (grade 6 if pubic hair present in adulthood, grade 7 if no pubic hair in adulthood).

Storytelling: Viking and Saxon Traditions

Storytelling is the conveying of events in words, images, and sounds often by improvisation or embellishment. Stories or narratives have been shared in every culture and in every land as a means of entertainment, education, preservation of culture, and to instill moral values. Crucial elements of stories and storytelling include plot and characters, as well as the narrative point of view.

Folklorists sometimes divide oral tales into two main groups: *märchen* and *sagen*. These are German terms for which there are no exact English equivalents. The first one is both singular and plural.

Märchen loosely translates as "fairy tale(s)" (though fairies are rare in them) and take place in a kind of separate "once-upon-a-time" world of nowhere-in-particular. They are clearly not intended to be understood as true. The stories are full of clearly defined incidents and peopled by rather flat characters with little or no interior life. When the supernatural occurs, it is presented matter-of-factly, without surprise. Indeed, there is very little affect generally: bloodcurdling events may take place, but with little call for emotional response from the listener.

Sagen is best translated as "legends" that are supposed to have actually happened, very often at a particular time and place and draw much of their

---

[15] An endogenous androgen sex steroid and hormone.

power from this fact. When the supernatural intrudes (as it often does), it does so in an emotionally fraught manner. Ghost and lover's leap stories belong in this category, as do many UFO-stories, and stories of supernatural beings and events.

The Vikings had professional poet/storytellers, known as *skalds*. They composed and recited poems in a fairly simple verse form that relied heavily on alliteration and also the use of kennings.[16] Most skaldic poetry was written for a particular occasion and often praised heroic virtues. The Vikings also had stories known as *sagas*. These sagas often recounted the lives of famous people and great heroes, although others were about more everyday types.

In Saxon England, there were also professional storytellers, called *scops*, who traveled from village to village telling tales in return for food, lodging, and money. A good *scop* was a respected member of the community and could be well rewarded for his skill. A *scop* might also use music to emphasize parts of the story or as "background music." Indeed, another word for a poet or storyteller was *hearpere* (harper), implying the use of this instrument (or the lyre from which it developed) by this person.

The one thing they all had in common was that they almost always tried to make some point about society or demonstrate how people should or should not behave, much as Aesop's moralistic fables did.

Medical Treatment (Chapter 2)

Many people believe that techniques of reconstructive surgery and infection management are largely an invention of the last 300 years. Cosmetic surgery, however, was practiced during the height of the Roman Empire since 200AD.

The word "plastic surgery" is derived from the Greek word *plastikos*, which means to mold or shape. Greeks preformed minor procedures such as otoplasty—the repairing of damaged ears—and more complicated procedures like scar removal. The Romans performed plastic surgery for reconstructive purposes on wounded soldiers and cosmetic purposes for freed slaves and rich upper classmen. Cataract operations became almost routine in ancient Rome. Branding or scar removal was a pricey, yet sought after, procedure that many freed slaves pursued to reduce the stigma of having been a slave. Some women received otoplasty because their ear lobes had stretched from wearing heavy earrings.

There are three big names that came out of Rome during the practice of

---

[16] A kenning is a figure of speech in which two words are combined in order to form a poetic expression that refers to a person or a thing. For example, "whale-road" is a kenning for the sea. Kennings are most commonly found in Old Norse and Old English poetry, see https://www.litcharts.com/literary-devices-and-terms/kenning.

medieval surgery. A Greek physician, Galen, a Roman physician, Aulus Cornelius Celsus, and a Greek surgeon, Paul of Aegina. These three laid the grounds for major developments in plastic surgery. Galen wrote best-selling books on human anatomy and Celsus wrote a book entitled *De re medicina* that mentions the reconstructive surgery of a man's face and a primitive nose job. Celsus's book was so good it was used for more than 1,700 years. From the Byzantine and Arabian empires, medicine was developed to help foster surgery.

Although there was no anesthesia available, surgeons used opium poppy capsules (morphine), henbane seeds (scopolamine), and alcohol for minor pain relief. Romans knew little about germs and how they related to disease, but they did use techniques to kill germs before and during surgery like boiling their tools and washing wounds with acetum, a mild acetic acid solution.

The Saxons and Danes had numerous options when it came to the treatment of infection and the management of blood loss. The most common were:

Honey was widely available at the time and well-known as an antibacterial since Egyptian times. Honey is primarily a saturated mixture of two monosaccharides. This mixture has a low water activity. Most of the water molecules are associated with the sugars and few remain available for microorganisms, so it is a poor environment for their growth. If water is mixed with honey, it loses its low water activity, and therefore no longer possesses this antimicrobial property.

Hydrogen peroxide is formed in a slow-release manner by the enzyme glucose oxidase present in honey. It becomes active only when honey is diluted, requires oxygen to be available for the reaction (thus it may not work under wound dressings, in wound cavities, or in the gut), is active only when the acidity of honey is neutralized by body fluids, can be destroyed by the protein-digesting enzymes present in wound fluids, and is destroyed when honey is exposed to heat and light. Honey chelates and deactivates free iron, which would otherwise catalyze the formation of oxygen free radicals from hydrogen peroxide, leading to inflammation. Also, the antioxidant constituents in honey help clean up oxygen free radicals present.

When honey is used topically (as, for example, in a wound dressing), hydrogen peroxide is produced by dilution of the honey with body fluids. As a result, hydrogen peroxide is released slowly and acts as an antiseptic.

Maggots are an ancient and well-understood mechanism for wound disinfection and debridement that have made something of a comeback in recent years. Maggot therapy (also known as maggot debridement therapy or MDT, larval therapy, larva therapy, larvae therapy, biodebridement, or biosurgery) is a type of biotherapy involving the intentional introduction of live, disinfected maggots (fly larvae) into the non-healing skin and soft tissue wounds of a human or animal for the purposes of selectively cleaning out only the necrotic tissue within a wound (debridement), disinfection, and promotion of wound healing.

Herbal options include thyme, sage, and radish, all of which have antiseptic properties. Best of all is yarrow (also known as soldier's friend). Yarrow was often borne on the helmets of Saxon warriors as a charm and has been mentioned in the *Illiad* as a secret herb that Achilles used to treat his wounded men. It is still used in veterinary practices to this day.

Mystical elements of both Danish and Anglo-Saxon society (Chapter 3)

In Norse culture, the practice of magic—with the exception of runic magic—was almost exclusively a female art. When men did become practitioners, they were frequently seen as effeminate and cowardly. Magic as described in the Norse sagas was not a single art: rather, there was *seiðr*, *spá* (*spae*), *galdr*, and runic magic.

Seiðr was the darkest art, encompassing what, today, we would refer to as witchcraft. It included powers of illusion and prophecy, the ability to affect men's minds, and control the weather or animals.

Spá is primarily focused on prophecy and the understanding of men's *wyrd* or fate. There is some mention of *spá-kona* being used for healing magic—both of the mind, as well as the body—although such mentions are rare in the sagas. Equally, the laying on of hands, linked to runic magic, was occasionally mentioned for healing purposes.

Galdr refers to the chanting of magical songs and incantations.

Runic magic involved the casting of the runes and was more a masculine activity, although the sagas do mention *seiðr* witches also using them. One of the earliest descriptions of a rune casting comes from Tacitus in Chapter 10 of his treatise *Germania*, a translation of which is below.

Augury and divination by lot no people practice more diligently. The use of the lots is simple. A little bough is lopped off a fruit-bearing tree and cut into small pieces: these are distinguished by certain marks and thrown carelessly and at random over a white garment. In public questions, the priest of the particular state, in private, the father of the family, invokes the gods and, with his eyes toward heaven, takes up each piece three times and finds in them a meaning according to the mark previously impressed on them.

Finally, there is the perceived magical powers of menstrual blood. Throughout all cultures and religions, significance has been placed on menses, either positive or negative. In Norse mythology, the god, Thor, reached the magic land of enlightenment and eternal life by bathing in a river filled with the menstrual blood of "giantesses," that is, of the primal matriarchs, the "Powerful Ones" who governed the elder gods before Odin brought his *Asians* (*Aesir*) out of the East.

Creatures of the Night (Chapter 4)
Old Norse folklore, as depicted in *The Legend of Alfhildr*, is linked to Germanic folklore. This is clearly evident in the manner in which both Old Norse and Germanic folklore dealt with the supernatural. *Vættir* is an old Norse term that literally mean "beings." These nature spirits were divided up into "families" that included:

Álfar (elves, both light elves and dark elves)
Dvergar (dwarves),
Jötnar (giants) and
Gods, (the *Æsir* and *Vanir*).

Like the Germans, the Norsemen believed *Vættir* wandered about in the forests of Middle Earth, the home of humans. Middle Earth, or *Mittgard*, was in today's vernacular, the place between heaven and hell. It was believed *Vættir* had the power to bring either mischief to the people of Middle Earth or help them. As the Angles, Saxons, and Jutes, who crossed the whale road to the island that later became known as England, were also a Germanic people, they shared these same beliefs, though they gave their supernatural beings other names. Even after the conversion to Christianity, belief in the creatures that lurked in the dark forests did not disappear.

J. R. R. Tolkien based his mythology on that of the Norsemen, Germans, and Saxons as they believed it during the early medieval period, which is when *The Legend of Alfhildr* takes place. Even Tolkien's "Orcs" have their origins in Old English (Anglo-Saxon) folklore. The word *orc* is Old English for foreigner, monster, or demon. It was the term used to refer to the Normans who invaded England in 1066, which suggests that Tolkien probably didn't celebrate William, the Bastard's, birthday, unless he marked it by hanging an animal hide out the window of his home.

Wealth, Arms, and Armor (Chapter 5)

In the early medieval period, where everything was laboriously handcrafted, and even winning iron ore from the ground was a manual process, the rarity and cost of such items is difficult to comprehend.

First, it is necessary to understand the value of money. The "exchange rate" offered below isn't perfect but will provide an idea. As an interesting aside, the reason the UK still uses the currency of "pounds" comes from the Anglo-Saxon period when a pound referred to a Troy pound, that is, 373 grams of silver.

For example, a Saxon silver penny (d) equals £20 today; 1 shilling (s) equals £100 today; 1 pound equals £4800 today.

Research from across Europe gives the following rough values to our Saxon warrior's horse, weapons, and armor.

A mail shirt or *byrnie* at 529d is worth approximately £10,000 ($12,900 USD) in today's money. A sword and scabbard from 308d to 240s, or £6,000 to £24,000 ($8000-$30,000 USD). A horse would cost 193d or £3,800 ($5,000 USD).

Even stirrups were rare and expensive at 81d (£1,600, $2000 USD).

To put all this in context a male slave in Anglo Saxon times cost about 240d (£4,000, $5100 USD), which made his life worth approximately the same as a horse.

Armor

At the time, a short chain mail shirt or *byrnie* was the principal form of protective armor for those who could afford it. It generally had short sleeves and reached to the waist.

Swords

The cost of swords made them relatively rare on the battlefield, with poorer warriors bearing a spear and dagger as their offensive weapons. As a result, swords were cherished possessions, being passed down in families for generations. By the eighth century, the typical sword had a blade about 30 inches long and about 3 inches wide, tapering to a point. The grip was protected by a narrow iron guard with a large iron pommel, often decorated. Swords were considered to have a greater value if they had a history or had belonged to a famous warrior, perhaps because they were seen to have been imbued with the previous owner's bravery.

The Concept of Sin (Chapter 9)

Sin, as understood by the Christian faiths, did not exist as such in the Old Norse religious belief system before conversion to Christianity. The word *synd* (sin) does not appear in Viking literature until 1030 and only in connection with the Norwegian saint-king, Olav Haraldson.

Viking Age ethics were based on the concept of shame and honor. The distinction between crimes committed openly and those in secret made all the difference to Vikings. For example, the law required a person who killed another to report the deed to the first person they met. An exception was made if the first two houses across which the killer came were owned by relatives of the person killed. The third house, however, could not be bypassed. If the individual adhered to the law in this manner, the deed was considered manslaughter and the punishment was often compensation to the family of the dead person.

Murder, on the other hand, was a killing that was done in secret and not reported. A person caught committing murder brought shame to himself and his family.

Breaking an oath given in public was also a crime that brought great shame to the oath breaker. In many ways, this was seen as worse than murder, for oaths and loyalty were the glue that bound Viking society and was the chief underpinning of their legal system.

Even more telling is the Christian concept that humans are born in a state of sin, due to the original sin committed by Adam and Eve. This was a concept that befuddled pagans. St. Augustine's concept that unbaptized infants go to hell as a consequence of original sin, confirmed by the Council of Orange in 529 AD, among others, was a major sticking point for many pagans when considering converting to Christianity.

My intention here is to provide the reader with a bit of context, for it is impossible to judge the actions of the characters in this story, or any other historical work, using our present-day cultural, social, and religious norms. The characters portrayed in the *Legend of Alfhildr* were different people, raised and living in a culture very different from ours, in a world that bears little resemblance to that which we know today.

White Christ (Chapter 9)

In Norse pagan society during this period, Christ was referred to as "the White Christ" or *Hvítakristr*. There were derogatory connotations in calling a man *Hvitr* (white or fair) as it implied cowardice or effeminacy. The current term "lily livered" stems from this. Thus, the "White Christ" was considered unmanly compared to Red Thor, who was a warrior's god.

Combat and Tactics (Chapter 19)

The *svinfylking*, known as the "swine array" to the Romans (and later the Saxons), and the "Boar Snout" to the Vikings, was a wedge formation used to break a defending line. Sometimes several *svinfylking* formations were grouped side by side creating something like a saw's blade. It is believed this saw-like formation was used by Gaius Suetonius Paulinus, Roman governor of Britain, in order to press and destroy Queen Boudica's numerically superior army at the Battle of Watling Street in 60 or 61 AD.

In one version of it, (such as described in this chapter), two warriors form the tip of the snout. Behind them follow three warriors. The third rank had four, the fourth rank five and so on. Sometimes archers were included, either somewhere in the center or in the very rear of the formation, firing at a high angle just ahead of the formation's tip, thus forcing the warriors who were in the defending shield wall to decide if they were going to hold their shields up over their heads to protect themselves from incoming arrows, or low, to fend off the wedge of spears, two-handed axes and swords coming at them.

Unlike modern military formations in which soldiers stand at arm's length apart, those in a Boar snout stood shoulder-to-shoulder, asshole to bellybutton. It was a difficult formation to form and hold. Today, this formation is still used in rugby.

The shield wall was a well-drilled formation, requiring the warriors who formed it to overlap their shields, thus creating a "linked" cohesion that caused the entire wall to become a single entity rather than a cluster of individual shields.

In a shield wall, the man to the right covered the right side of the warrior next to him with his shield. In this formation, it was the second rankers who did most of the killing either with spears or double handed axes, weapons that did not allow the warrior wielding it to use his own shield. Well-drilled warriors in a shield wall would work in concert, with one man threatening a high attack, causing the defender to hold his shield up to protect his head and upper body while the other attacker would crouch low, using a short sword to hack at exposed ankles or thrust up, disemboweling or gelding the defending warrior.

All other ranks provided weight for the pushing match that always occurred when both sides tried to break the other wall. When a wall did break, for a brief time, the battle turned into a single-combat fight.

The real slaughter in battle normally occurred when one side broke, for a fleeing warrior could not run for his life while protecting himself with his shield, which was usually tossed aside because it was now of no value to him, If anything, it would be a detriment as it could slow his flight. (As the French are so fond of saying; "*Sauve qui peut!*"—"Run for your life!")

The victors, on the other hand, whipped up into a serious killing frenzy, sometimes known as bloodlust, redoubled their efforts to "count coup" (count strokes/blows). After all, no self-respecting Dane or Saxon warrior wished to return home without someone's blood on his weapon. Besides, it was so much easier to collect valuables from a dead or wounded man bleeding out on the ground than from one who was running away from you.

It is believed that the habit of lightening one's load during a rout by tossing shields aside is where the Spartan mothers' admonishment to their sons, "Return with your shield, or upon it," came from, for a warrior who was victorious had no reason to chuck his shield while those who fled did.

Some of you may find this sort of talk to be grim, yucky, disgusting, etc., etc., etc. But that's the way things were back then. The Vikings and Saxons were warrior cultures, raised in a brutal time, a time in which courage, honour, and physical prowess in battle were not only considered to be virtues, but were entirely necessary if one wished to live freely and honour their gods as they saw fit. Those who could not do so were either slaves or corpses.

Rune Stones (Chapter 22)

A rune stone is typically a raised stone with a runic inscription, but the term can also be applied to inscriptions on boulders and bedrock. The tradition began in the 4th century and lasted into the 12th century, but most of the rune stones date from what is sometimes called the late Viking Age. Rune stones have been discovered in locations that were visited by Norsemen, which include England and Ireland.

Rune stones are often memorials to deceased men, but some are dedicated to famous or much-beloved women. One such example is a rune stone called the The Dynna Stone, which was originally located in Gran, Norway and erected to a woman. The inscription reads:

> Gunnor, Thythrik's daughter, made a bridge in memory of her daughter Astrid. She was the most skillful girl in Hade land."[17]

This stone is now located in the Norwegian Museum of Cultural History in Oslo, Norway.

The Women of England, circa 875 AD

The freedoms women enjoyed in the pre-Norman, Anglo-Saxon culture as well as Old Norse society is more akin to that experienced by American women on the frontier of colonial America and later in the United States. These

---

[17] From Wikipedia: A transliteration of the runic inscription reads:
kunuur kirþi bru þririks tutir iftir osriþi tutur sina su uas mar hanarst o haþalanti. Translated to English, the inscription reads: "Gunnvôr, Þryðríkr's daughter, made the bridge in memory of her daughter Ástríðr. She was the handiest maiden in Haðaland," https://wiki2.org/en/Dynna_stone, https://www.khm.uio.no/english/news/norwegian-rune-stones.html.

societies did not have any place for useless mouths that did nothing more than babysit. This was especially true when the men were off hunting, exploring, or defending the community.

The role women played in Norse culture is found in the evidence excavated from the graves of those women. Scales used by merchants in the marketplace spoke of women who ran businesses. Tools and farm implements hint at women wed to their land. And the weapons of war found with the remains of females marked them as true shield maidens who took their places in the shield wall to defend their kinsmen.

The concept of marriage derived from love rather than negotiations is found in the inscriptions left on rune stones.

During the Saxon and Viking periods, women took up the spear and sword and fought alongside men more frequently than history tends to credit. One particular burial records:

> In 1867, a Viking Age grave containing a single skeleton with oval brooches (characteristic of a woman's grave) and a "sword-like item" was discovered in Santon Downham, Norfolk, England.[18]

Of special note is the story of Aethelflaed, daughter of Alfred the Great, also known as the Lady of the Mercians. She combined the role of warrior and peace weaver with great skill, defeating numerous Norse invasions and being renowned as a skilled and ruthless general. She ruled Mercia after her husband's death from 911 to 918 AD.

The coming of the Normans in 1066 not only brought a military and political subjugation of the Saxons: it also imposed the Roman/Latinized concept of a woman's role in society upon all of England.

It is also of interest to note that hair was quite symbolic when it came to announcing a woman's place within Saxon and Dane cultures, both of which have their origins in northern Germany. Young, unmarried girls wore their hair long and oftentimes unbound. When they married, it was covered or worn bound up. By wearing her hair unbound and cascading freely about her shoulders, Alfhildr was proclaiming to all that no man or culture held dominion over her.

Word Choice and Language

In writing this story, I have made the conscious choice to use commonly used English in the narrative as well as the conversations between characters, much in the same way that the people who produced the series *1066* did. To have used Old English, either in its entirety or snippets would have been

---

[18] *Women in the Viking Age*, Judith Jesch, Boydell Press, ISBN 0 85115 278 3.

awkward and cumbersome, making reading something of a challenge. A few examples include:

> **huscarl** instead of *ðegn, hirð, hirðmenn* or 'Hearth Troop'
> **witch** instead of *seiðr*, (Old Norse), which is the practice of witchcraft or *wicce* (Old English)
> **noble** instead of *eorls*
> **army** instead of *here* or *fyrd*
> **king** instead of *cynn*

There are cases where either Old Norse or Old English words have been used, mostly when I felt it would not interfere with the flow of the story. Anyone who wishes to have an idea what *The Legend of Alfhildr* would read like if I had used Old English more often is invited to read the small extract from Beowulf that follows below as it was written in Old English and later translated.

Old English:
Hwæt. We Gardena in gear-dagum, þeodcyninga, þrym gefrunon, hu ða æþelingas, ellen fremedon.

Translation by Seamus Heaney:
So. The Spear-Danes in days gone by and the kings who ruled them had courage and greatness. We have heard of these princes' heroic campaigns.

As you can see, even the modern version does not exactly roll off the tongue. So, in order to keep the story chugging along and keep the readers from rolling their eyes and giving up, I have taken liberties when it comes to word choice. *The Legend of Alfhildr* may be an old story, but one written for modern readers who rely on language with which they are familiar.

The letter 'Æ'
Æ (lower case: æ) is a grapheme formed from the letters "a" and "e." Originally a ligature representing a Latin diphthong, it has been promoted to the full status of a letter in the alphabets of some languages, including Danish and Norwegian. As a letter of the Old English alphabet, it was called *"æsc"* ("ash tree") after the Anglo-Saxon futhorc rune that it transliterated. Its traditional name in English is still "ash."

In English, usage of the ligature varies in different places. In modern typography, and where technological limitations make its use difficult (such as in the use of typewriters), "æ" is often eschewed in favour of the digraph "ae." This is often considered incorrect, especially when rendering foreign words where "æ" is considered to be a letter (e.g. Æsir, Ærø) or brand names that make use of the ligature (e.g. Æon Flux, Encyclopædia Britannica). In the United States, the problem of the ligature is sidestepped in many cases by use of a simplified spelling with "e": compare the common usage, "medieval," with the traditional "mediæval." However, given the long history of such spellings, they are sometimes used to invoke archaism or in literal quotations of historic sources, for words such as dæmon. Often, the graphene will be replaced with a simple "ae" as in archaeology.

The Mystery behind "Hel"
One may wonder why it is that the word "hel" managed to become "hell." I offer two theories on this subject.

The first is that the English, in an effort to make their language even more complex and incomprehensible to those non-English speaking people who have a well-ordered and organized language based on rules and logic, decided to add another 'l' just for the "l"-ell of it.

The second theory concerns my ancestors, the Welsh, always a favorite whipping-boy for the English. I postulate that when the Welsh decided to migrate west when the Saxons, Angles, and Jutes ruined London's neighborhoods, the second "l" in hell was one of those letters they forgot to pack, just like all those vowels that are missing from their language. My guess is, upon taking over the now vacated lands, the Saxons and Angles found the recently abandoned "l" lying about, lost, and forlorn. Rather than waste it, they decided to add it to a word the Danes had left behind, thus turning "hel" into "hell."

Anyway, that's my story and I'm sticking to it.

Artorius
There is much debate over who the legendary king of ancient Britain was. Some believe he was an amalgam of several heroic figures, one or more who might have been named Artorius, Arcturus, Arturus, Arto-uiros, or Arthwr. How and when these various names evolved into the modern Welsh version of the name "Arthur" is not known.

All that is known with any degree of certainty is that the Arthurian legend has been a part of British folklore in one form or another since the end of the Roman occupation.

Michener's *The Source and other touchstones*
For those who dabble in creative writing, you will know that the inspiration for a story often comes from the most unusual sources. Sometimes, it springs forth from a single, unique idea at the oddest times. Other times, it

results from a confluence of different ideas that somehow magically congeal into one scathingly brilliant idea.

The Legend of Alfhildr is the result of the latter. Having found myself impressed by Jenny's writing[19] and story line in *The Frozen Balance*,[20] I thought I would try my hand at a "sword and shield" story (or a "hack and slash" story as I prefer to call them).

My love of the Anglo-Saxon tradition was peeked recently by watching the British miniseries *1066*.

The final leg of this tripod, at least as far as I am concerned, was James A. Michener's 1965 novel *The Source*, which I read not long after it was published. It was the way he told his story, through the eyes of both the archeologists as well as the people who had made the history that gave me the idea of telling the story from both ends. In *The Source*, the present day was called "The Trench." In *The Legend of Alfhildr*, I call it "The Dig." Even after forty years, the enjoyment I found in that story stuck with me until, at last, I was able to have a go at it myself.

Other sources of inspiration, in a roundabout way, have been drawn from Charlton Heston's movie *The Warlord*—a gritty portrayal of life in the "hack and slash" era—as well as *An Army of Angels: A Novel of Joan of Arc* by Pamela Marcantel. I highly recommend this book for those of you who have enjoyed *The Legend of Alfhildr* and wish to read something very similar to it, both as far as style and the way of telling the story of a historical figure through fiction.

Now, why Jenny agreed to join me in the insane, yet immensely enjoyable adventure is something she'll have to tell you. All I know is I enjoyed the ride. I hope you, dear readers, have enjoyed it half as much as Jenny and I have.

---

[19] Co-author Jennifer Ellis.
[20] https://www.goodreads.com/book/show/41833667-the-frozen-balance, https://www.amazon.com/Frozen-Balance-Jennifer-Ellis-ebook/dp/B07HCVHMZJ.

ABOUT THE AUTHORS

H. W. Coyle

As the youngest of three children and the only son of an only son of an only son, I started out in something of a hole. This wasn't helped any by childhood asthma and a total lack of coordination. With handicaps like that, it's no wonder I never developed into the sort of rough and tumble lad that every good blue-collar father wanted. Not that I minded. You see, throughout my childhood, I can honestly say that I always wanted to be a female simply because that was how I saw myself. In an age when men were men and women were Donna Reed, I knew enough to keep certain things to myself. It was my lanky stature and preferences for reading, history, and less manly pursuits that cost me dearly on the playground, not my hidden passions and dreams. From an early age, I found myself dealing with a conundrum, one I could not share with anyone. Physically, I knew I was a male, a rather poor specimen of one, mind you, but male, nonetheless. And yet, I was unable to identify with any of the traditional views and desires associated with being male. Growing up in the late 50's and early '60s meant that I didn't have access to a great deal of information concerning my dilemma. By the time puberty hit, I found I had but two choices, neither of which were very appealing. I could go to New York City and become part of the Stonewall crowd or I could go against my own nature and create a persona that would be acceptable to my family and permit me to survive in the "normal" world in which I had been raised. So, I left home in 1967, when I was 15, and never really looked back. The less said about my life from 1967 to 1970 the better. How I survived those years, despite my best efforts, is something I attribute to a combination of divine intervention and pure dumb Irish luck. That I was afforded the opportunity to start over again was due chiefly to the intervention of a Marine Colonel who served as something of a mentor. With his help, I secured an ROTC scholarship, acceptance at a fine, respected, and very strict southern institution, and even did a term at Oxford. After graduating in 1974, I embarked upon a military career that took me to all sorts of picturesque spots around the world, the sort of which most Americans have never heard. I've stood many a watch, literally on the DMZ between North and South Korea, as well as patrolled the border dividing East and West Germany. I even had an opportunity to jump with the French Foreign Legion, though that is a rather unique story that is somewhat blurred due to cheap French wine. Along the way, I married a person who will always be the love of my life and my best friend. Between us, we had three children, all of whom are adults now. My military career came to something of an abrupt end in 1991 when I had something of an epiphany during the Gulf War. Upon returning home, I began the slow, arduous journey that eventually led to where I had always wanted to go.

Jennifer Ellis

Jennifer Ellis started writing before anyone told her that it was dangerously addictive. By the time she found that out, it was too late.

She graduated from the Royal Military Academy Sandhurst more years ago than she cares to remember before embarking on what she laughingly calls a "diverse and eclectic career path." A path that took her from the jungles of Central America, through the bogs and hedgerows of Northern Ireland, to the mountains of Bosnia and Kosovo; then, onwards, to the sandbox of Iraq (fleetingly) and most recently to the dusty plains of Afghanistan.

Along the way, she has also transitioned from being a regular army officer to becoming a cyber security consultant and, most recently, a computer science teacher.

OTHER PUBLICATIONS

Other Trans Fiction Available from Stephanie Castle Publications
Publishing Transgender Fiction
https://stephaniecastle.ca/new-releases/

Flipping (2020)
It cost him nothing but it cost her everything.
Forest J. Handford
Born on a space station, Samir Zeka was raised Muslim, observes a Halal diet, fasts during Ramadan, and prays 5 times every day. An introvert, he mostly stuck to his work, his home, his family, and his church community, until the day he decided to push beyond his comfort zone and attend a party that would forever change his life. Intending to look his best for the party, Samir searched his neural link "mesh" for random looks until he came across one that suited him. After some fine-tuning, he "flipped" to the persona of Samantha, a late 30s East Asian, cat-eared woman with shoulder-length purple hair. At the party, Samantha meets Anna, someone who will change Samantha's perceptions of herself and transform both of their lives. (https://stephaniecastle.ca/flipping/)

The Elysian Project: A Story of Betrayal and Payback (2019)
D. Axt

The Elysian Project is an expertly written, fast paced action thriller with a twist. It follows US marine scout sniper, Brent chandler, his surviving teammate, Lyle, and his adopted father (the Gunny), as they go after those responsible for betraying Brent's sniper team during a military operation in Haditha, Iraq. Chandler's betrayal didn't just change the lives of his U.S. Marine sniper team forever. It set him on a path of unimaginable discovery. His quest for the truth and revenge quickly goes awry, drawing the attention of billionaire Stanley Tivador and the DOJ-FBI cabal he controls. The chase is on, from northern Minnesota's Superior National Forest to the Canary Islands. With help from the Gunny, his crotchety, retired Marine father, and Staiski, his friend and former sniper teammate, Chandler uncovers a terrorist plot of carnage inconceivable in magnitude and in lives lost. With seconds remaining, they risk everything to stop The Elysian Project.
(https://stephaniecastle.ca/the-elysian-project/)

Partnership: A Novel about Friendship, Love, Family and Gender Transition (2019)
Stephanie Castle
Edited and preface by Margot Wilson

What happens when a lawyer, the son of a prominent Vancouver family, and a baker, the son of a devoted Catholic family who moved from Italy to Montreal following WWII, team up while going through gender reassignment? This humorous, yet serious, depiction of two families coping with gender dysphoria and the challenges of keeping family relationships intact addresses both legal and religious issues, The depiction and commentary on a range of human personalities in the hands of the author are both perceptive and entertaining. The underlying accuracy of this fictional story depends on the author's personal experience as a transgender woman and as a counselor in the transgender community in Vancouver.
(https://stephaniecastle.ca/partnership/)

Far Side of the Moon: A Novel about the Life of a Trans Child (2019)
Stephanie Castle
Edited and preface by Margot Wilson
In Far Side of the Moon, Marjorie Burton and her husband, Jack, demonstrate all the attributes needed to help their child, Jenna, through a successful male to female gender transition. For children raised in an era when the condition of gender dysphoria was unknown, when anything unusual or unexplained was written off as a sexual aberration, it is small wonder that children, like the author, kept their feelings hidden out of shame and fear. Fortunately, that is not what happens with Jenna.
(https://stephaniecastle.ca/far-side-of-the-moon-a-novel-about-the-life-of-a-trans-child/)

**Now Available from
Perceptions Press**
Publishing innovative, avant-garde (and occasionally provocative) transgender fiction and non-fiction
https://perceptionspress.ca/

Demon of Want
Freja Ki Gray
Izumi Yamakawa, a directionless twenty-something, is a part-time employee of the Oh Joy Toy Store. When she witnesses her manager die in a horrific merchandising accident, she discovers that he was a member of a Japanese demon hunting organization and had been eyeing her for recruitment due to her family lineage. Now Izumi, along with her trans girlfriend Maria, and a boisterous sword-for-hire, Rhea, get caught up investigating the various monsters and demons running the Oh Joy Toy company. Demon of Want is an eclectic blend of tongue in cheek urban fantasy, over the top violence, and gratuitous sex. https://perceptionspress.ca/demon-of-want/

Trans Deus
Paul Van Der Spiegel

Paul Van Der Spiegel

In the beginning was the Verb,
the Verb was with God, the Verb was God.
In her was life,
that life was the light for all people.
The Verb was made trans woman
and she lived amongst us, full of grace and truth.
Her light shone in the darkness,
and the consumer-military-technocracy
comprehended it not.
We cast our votes on TV remotes,
crucified her live on Channel Five.
(https://perceptionspress.ca/trans-deus/)

Can't Her Bury Tales: A Transfeminine Coloring Book (2020)
Iona Isabella Rivera

Hail weary traveler! Come closer! I don't bite…hard. You lookit poorly, come take a sit by the fire. Rest and grab yourself some stew I got cookin. Tell me, what brings ya my way? Adventure? Hearsay? Curiosity or plain ol' boredom? Well, no matter whence you came, I surely have a story that will peak your delight. Perhaps a tale of a terrible tragedy? Or a catty, Communist comedy? How about some lore on fallin in love? Or a heroic tale of harrowing a horrible governorship? Or be you one that pines over Power? Maybe a familiar fable of family? Oh! Pardon my rambling. Come tell me your tale, traveler. What colors will you paint with me? Tell, was your way hard, rocky and steep? Show me. Perchance our stories crossed at some point. After all, we have more in common than our differences tell. (https://perceptionspress.ca/cant-her-bury-tales/)

Life Stories Available from TransGender Publishing
Publishing Transgender Life Stories and Non-fiction
https://transgenderpublishing.ca/

TRANScestors: Navigating LGBTQ+ Aging, Illness and End of Life Decisions
Volume I: Generations of Hope
Edited by Jude Patton and Margot Wilson
This volume (and the ones that follow) have been in the works for some time. What finally emerges after many months of assiduous advertising, recruiting, editing, and organizing is a volume of intimate, nuanced, and heartfelt stories that reflect the wide diversity in the ways in which trans, non-binary, and Two-Spirit people have come to recognize, signify, embody, and celebrate their difference as their authentic selves. Moreover, with an increasing emphasis on the experiences of trans youth, elders constitute a routinely overlooked, disregarded, and/or silenced segment of the community. In response, this volume documents the myriad ways in which trans elders are coming to terms with the real-life challenges of aging, illness, and end of life decision-making.

TRANScestors is planned as a series of edited volumes that address the issues of LGBTQ+ aging, illness, and end of life decision-making and will be published by TransGender Publishing. Additional volumes include: Volume II: Generations of Change, Volume III: Generations of Pride, and Volume III: Generations of Challenge.

We are God's Children Too (2020)
Rona Matlow
At the heart of Jewish experience is narrative. Around the dinner table, we tell stories of our families, recalling the quality of a grandmother's cooking, the kindness (or stinginess) of a particular uncle, the ways in which traditions have developed and shifted in our families. In synagogues and Jewish schools, we read the Torah, which is filled with stories of our religious patriarchs and matriarchs. And then there are the stories of Diaspora–the history of Jewish communities existing in exile for over two millennia. There are family stories and history books dedicated to our many wanderings. All of these stories help Jewish people connect to their heritage and lineage. What of the queer Jew? Even as more and more Jewish communities emphasize inclusivity and

find a place for queer congregants, Jewish stories do not. The Bible offers no queer lessons, leaving queer Jews split in two; a Jewish heritage and a queer present. Enter Rabbah Rona Matlow, with hir queer *midrashim*. *Midrashim* are stories which approach Biblical texts from new perspectives, often exploring areas of confusion or possible contradiction within the Bible. Unlike Torah, they are not presented as factual, but as possibilities. Fictions which might yet be possible alternate histories. *Midrashim* bridge gaps. Rona's queer *midrashim* bridge the gap between the contemporary queer Jew and the (seemingly cisgender and straight) Bible, offering a way for us to see ourselves in our Jewish tradition.
(https://transgenderpublishing.ca/we-are-gods-children-too/)

QdQh: Queen of Diamonds, Queen of Hearts, The Life and Journey of Michelle Nastasis, the First Known Transgender Professional Poker Player (2020)
Michelle Nastasis
QdQh: Queen of Diamonds, Queen of Hearts is the life story of Michelle Nastasis, the First Known Transgender Professional Poker Player.™ Michelle is courageous whether going head to head with the best poker players in the world, speaking out on television for LGBTQ+ rights, or marching in parades to celebrate being transgender. She is calm, cool, collected, and absolutely fearless. Possessed of fierce intelligence, Michelle is a beacon for younger transgender people. She shoots straight from the hip. She's blunt, loud, sarcastic, and occasionally irreverent. So, sit back and enjoy the ride.
(https://transgenderpublishing.ca/misunderstood/)

Transgender Heart: Life Stories from the Inside Out (2020)
Bodhi Thompson Gardner
Transgender Heart is a collection of short stories that trace the heart-journey of a small farm kid, youth, and adult, from rural Saskatchewan, across the binary landscapes of life. A deeply grateful soul emerges, while exploring all the hidden nuances of the people, places, and things that held them together. Hidden comforts are revealed from the inside out, an inner harvesting of an authentic self. Their true self searching for somewhere to belong, finds love, acceptance, and authentic connection in the most intriguing and unusual spaces. Black hockey skates not only enrich their game but authenticate their heart. Spaces of unconditional love come from

four-legged wild beasts, two-legged mentors, matriarchs, warriors, and elders. An RCMP officer who saw their struggle and offered a hand instead of handcuffs, gifts of nature, and family support abound: however, the biggest surprise of all is their most cherished treasure, the one thing that kept them alive for over 50 years. Transgender Heart highlights the courage and tenacity of the human spirit to rise up! (https://transgenderpublishing.ca/transgender-heart/)

Dancing the Dialectic: True Tales of a Transgender Trailblazer, Second Edition (2020)
Rupert Raj

Rupert Raj is a trailblazing, Eurasian-Canadian, trans activist, and former psychotherapist, who transitioned from female to male in 1971 as a transsexual teenager. Dancing the dialectic between gender dysphoria and gender euphoria, cynical despair and realistic hope, righteous rage and loving kindness, this Gender Worker tells us all about his lifelong fight for the rights of transgender, intersex, and two-spirit people—and his later-life role as a Rainbow Warrior working to free Mother Earth's enslaved animals. (https://transgenderpublishing.ca/dancing-the-dialectic-true-tales-of-a-transgender-trailblazer-second-edition/)

Glimmerings: Trans Elders Tell Their Stories (2019)
Margot Wilson and Aaron Devor (editors)

Tell us your story. A story about growing up before the age of global communication, at a time when the Internet and worldwide connectivity were still visions of the future; when inflexible, dichotomous categories of male and female, men and women, existed; when heterosexuality was the only sanctioned form of romantic attraction or sexual conduct; and when any expression of interest outside of these strict prescriptions was severely censured. Tell us your story about living in a time when those whose preferences, perspectives, and behaviours contravened the prevailing paradigms and prohibitions, when you had to negotiate dark, prejudicial places where fear, shame, guilt, despair, isolation, and a little bit of hope. Contributing authors include: Stephanie Castle, Joanna Clark, Ms. Bob Davis, Dallas Denny, Jamison Green, Ariadne Kane, Corey Keith, Lili, Ty Nolan, Jude Patton, Virginia Prince, Rupert Raj, Gayle Roberts, Susanna Valenti, and Dawn Angela Wensley.

(https://transgenderpublishing.ca/glimmerings-recognition-authenticity-and-gender-variance/)

My Untrue Past: The Coming of Age of a Trans Man (2019)
Alex Bakker

Born the youngest daughter in a small-town family in the Netherlands, Alex Bakker underwent gender reaffirming transition when he was twenty-eight years old. A new beginning, in the right body, he literally put everything that reminded him of his old life into boxes, never to be opened again. More than fifteen years later, he has finally gathered the courage to face his past. In *My Untrue Past*, Alex goes in search of the painful truth. What does it mean to be betrayed by your body, to be immensely jealous of boys, and to decide that everything needs to be different? (https://transgenderpublishing.ca/my-untrue-past-available-now/)

Girl in the Dream: Stephanie (Sydney) Castle Heal, a Transgender Life (2018)
Margot E. Wilson

Girl in the Dream is the life story of Stephanie (Sydney) Castle Heal, an advocate, activist and elder in the Canadian transgender community. The outcome of an almost four-year collaboration of storytelling, recording, analysis, and writing, *Girl in the Dream* is a first-person narrative that depicts in intimate detail Stephanie's transgender journey. An enthusiastic and accomplished raconteuse, Stephanie tells her story with the verve, passion, and expressiveness of a veteran storyteller. https://transgenderpublishing.ca/girl-in-the-dream/)

Feelings: A Transsexual's Explanation of a Baffling Condition, Second Edition (2018)
Stephanie Castle
Edited and Introduction by Margot E. Wilson

Feelings is written in a style that reveals Stephanie Castle as a woman of great confidence, conviction and humour. It reflects her attitudes toward life in general and transgender issues in particular, and definitively emulates the intricacies of her personality and character. *Feelings* provides a very personal view into one transgender woman's journey, a metamorphosis that is as vital, authentic and significant today as it was when she wrote it. A complementary volume to *Girl in the Dream*, *Feelings* provides a comprehensive and in-depth view into the nature of the transgender experience based on the intimate, challenging, and often poignant experiences and perspectives of one singularly remarkable woman. (https://transgenderpublishing.ca/feelings/)

Coming in 2020/2021 from
Perceptions Press
Publishing innovative, avant-garde (and occasionally provocative) transgender fiction and non-fiction
https://perceptionspress.ca/

PUBLICATION EXPECTED IN 2021
7 Minutes
Paul Van Der Spiegel
At the point of death,
lost to all we've known,
adrift from those we've loved,
what stories do we tell
ourselves?
(https://perceptionspress.ca/7-minutes/)

Coming in 2020/2021 from
TransGender Publishing
Publishing Transgender Life Stories and Non-fiction
https://transgenderpublishing.ca/

PUBLICATION EXPECTED IN 2020/21
Life Trips: Navigating LGBTQ+ Aging, Illness and End of Life Decisions
Edited by Jude Patton and Margot Wilson
Volume One: Generations of Hope
Volume Two: Generations of Change
Volume Three: Generations of Pride
Volume Four: Generations of Challenge

Studies indicate that LGBT+ people are still discriminated against in most health care settings and in long term care facilities despite advances made in the past few years in gaining more rights. Evaluating physical and mental health care needs, facilitating access to health care providers and advocating for clients' right as well as end of life decisions and planning for personal legacy options are important aspects of navigating LGBTQ+ aging. Having served as a health navigator for clients with chronic illness and offering end of life doula services to LGBTQ+ community members, Jude Patton collaborates with and advocates for his clients to successfully manage their health care needs. Jude is a proud, open and out, elder trans man, who has worked with underserved populations for most of his career, including LGBTQ+ folks, geriatric clients, developmentally disabled adults, homeless/chronically mentally ill and drug addicted clients. *Life Trips* is planned as a series of edited volumes that address the issues of LGBTQ+ aging, illness, and end of life decision-making and will be published by TransGender Publishing. Additional volumes include: Volume II: Generations of Change, Volume III: Generations of Pride and Volume IV: Generations of Challenge. (https://transgenderpublishing.ca/life-trips/)

PUBLICATIONS EXPECTED IN 2020
HAG: Here and Genderqueer
It used to mean something else
Nae Whitman
HAG is a love story to my LGBTQ chosen family and the survivors who thrive there. Some better than others. A story which, during its birth, became so much more.
https://transgenderpublishing.ca/hag-here-and-genderqueer/

PUBLICATION EXPECTED IN 2020
Before My Warranty Runs Out: Human, Transgender and Environmental Rights Advocate
Joanna (Sister Mary Elizabeth) Clark and Margot E. Wilson
Joanna (Sister Mary Elizabeth) Clark is an elder trans woman and advocate. During the 1980s and 1990s she was an LGBTQ+ activist and speaker. She was the first person to

serve as a man in the US navy and as a woman in the US army. Later, as Sister Mary Elizabeth, she was the driving force behind the AIDS Education and Global Information System (AEGIS) database. These days, her focus is primarily on environmental activism. *Before My Warranty Runs Out* is a personal narrative that recounts Joanna's life experiences. (https://transgenderpublishing.ca/before-my-warranty-runs-out/)

PUBLICATION EXPECTED IN 2021
From Shame to Freedom: A Gender Variant Woman's Journey of Discovery
M. Gayle Roberts
Born in England during WW II, Gayle Roberts immigrated to Canada in 1951 and is an UVic alumnus with an MSc in Physics. She transitioned in 1996 as her high school's Science Department Head and science teacher. Gayle coauthored the guidebook Supporting Transgender and Transsexual Students in K-12 Schools and is author of *From Shame to Freedom: A Gender-Variant Woman's Journey of Discovery*. Gayle feels strongly that trans individuals should document their life experiences. She utilizes specific literary writing techniques (creative nonfiction) to create factually accurate narratives. *From Shame to Freedom* is one of those narratives.
(https://transgenderpublishing.ca/from-shame-to-freedom/)

PUBLICATION EXPECTED IN 2021
Young Kid, Old Goat: Transgender Journey to Understanding the Man Within
Jude Patton and Margot Wilson
Jude Patton is an elder transman and LGBTQ activist, advocate and educator since before his own transition in 1970. He founded Renaissance Gender Identity Services in the early 1970s and began publishing *Renaissance Newsletter* in the mid-1970s. Jude started one of the first informal support groups for FTM men and incorporated these into The John Augustus Foundation. Joined by Joanna Clark, these became known as J2CP Information Services, taking over Paul Walker's work with Erickson Educational Services. In *Young Kid, Old Goat*, Jude's personal life story and ongoing work is highlighted. (https://transgenderpublishing.ca/young-kid-old-goat/)

PUBLICATION EXPECTED IN 2021
Gender Odyssey: Journey of an Intrepid Androgyne
Ariadne (J. Ari) Kane and Margot Wilson
Ariadne (J. Ari) Kane is a gerontology specialist with Theseus Consulting & Coaching Service. (S)he has developed several workshops focusing on issues of gender, sexuality and health in the latter decades of the lifespan. Many are designed for the LGBT Community. (S)he has been a leading authority on gender diversity in postmodern America and has given presentations at many universities and institutes in the United States and Canada. (S)he is one of the creators of the Gender Attitude Reassessment Program, a workshop on gender for sexologists and healthcare professionals. (S)he co-authored *Crossing Sexual Boundaries* with Professor Vern Bullough. *Gender Odyssey: Journey of an Intrepid Androgyne* is the distillation of 40+ hours of recorded conversation that provide a decadal representation of an intrepid traveler who has forged an idiosyncratic path through gender exploration, variance and expression.
(https://transgenderpublishing.ca/gender-odyssey-journey-of-an-intrepid-androgyne/)

PUBLICATION EXPECTED IN 2021
Unconditional Love: Stories of LGBTQ+ People and Our Emotional Bonds with Companion Animals
Edited by Jude Patton and Margot Wilson
Our experiences with marginalization often affect our feelings of self-worth. While many people in our lives are unable (or unwilling) to provide the emotional support we need before, during and post-coming out, or transition, our companion animals never fail to see us as we truly are and never fail to express their unconditional love for us. No wonder we love them and derive multiple benefits from our relationships with them. They are woven into the fabric of our lives. *Unconditional Love* is planned as an edited reader that tells the stories of how the unconditional love of (and for) our companion animals has supported, encouraged, confirmed, validated, endorsed and sanctioned our authentic selves. Our reading audience includes those in the LGBTQ+ community who have found sanctuary and validation in the love shared with our animal companions as well as those in the broader community who revel in the company of our non-human loved ones.
(https://transgenderpublishing.ca/unconditional-love/)

**Coming in 2020/2021 from
Castle Carrington Publishing**
You have a story. Let us help you tell it.
https://castlecarringtonpublishing.ca/

PUBLICATION EXPECTED IN NOVEMBER 2020
Until I Smile at You
How one girl's heartbreak electrified Frank Sinatra's fame!
Peter Jennings with Tom Sandler

It's 1936. Take Ina Ray Hutton, the "Blonde Bombshell of Rhythm," add 22-year-old Ruth Lowe, who become Ina Ray's pianist. Ruth marries music publicist Harold Cohen, but he dies in the midst of debilitating surgery. Ruth is devastated, full of heartache, a grief-stricken widow far too early. Consumed by anguish, she pours her heartache into a lamenting anthem that becomes an internationally famous song—"I'll Never Smile Again"—destined to electrify the career of 25-year-old vocalist Francis Albert Sinatra. Ruth next composes what becomes Sinatra's theme song, "Put Your Dreams Away." And then, Act Two begins for Ruth Lowe: she withdraws from the limelight to become a caring wife, loving mother, society doyenne, and friend to many. Amazingly, this superstar has escaped the investigation and adoration that her life so richly deserves—until now.
(https://castlecarringtonpublishing.ca/until-i-smile-at-you/)

PUBLICATION EXPECTED IN 2021
Pushing the Boundaries!
How to Get More Out of Life
Peter Jennings

Pushing The Boundaries! How To Get More Out Of Make Life features profiles of 32 people from around the world (many of whom are well known, and featuring many Canadians) who reveal how they triumph in life.

We're talking people who have overcome uneasiness about taking risks, like daredevil Nik Wallenda; doctor-of-change, Patch Adams; intersex supermodel, Hanne Gaby Odielle; international clothing designer, Tommy Hilfiger. Also included are Canadians like Marina Nemat, who defied certain execution in her teens at Evin prison in Tehran; McDonald's of Canada Chair, George Cohon, who persevered through 14 years to break into the Russian market; Rick Hansen, who pushed himself around the world in a wheelchair to raise awareness of people with disabilities; Katie Taylor who's broken the glass ceiling by becoming the first female Chair of a major Canadian Bank; Donald Ziraldo, who put Inniskillin Winery on the map by making Icewine into an immensely popular beverage worldwide; etc. As Jack Canfield, renowned co-author of the *Chicken Soup For The Soul*® series says in the book's Foreword, "Having the conviction to reach beyond your fears and take chances means you're ready to achieve lasting success." (https://castlecarringtonpublishing.ca/pushing-the-boundaries/)

PUBLICATION EXPECTED IN 2021
Being Happy Matters
Peter Jennings

Being Happy Matters is a re-launch of a previously published book *Why Being Happy Matters*. The updated Introduction references COVID-19 and how happiness can be an antidote to the stress and anxiety people are experiencing right now. The original volume presents interviews with people in Canada, the U.S., Asia, Europe and Australia, each of whom reveal what happiness means to them and why it matters. Readers will meet international PhDs who are actively studying the science of positive psychology (i.e. happiness). This book features Peter Jennings in conversation with 37 intriguing individuals, including John Robbins, heir of the Baskin Robbins empire (who tells Peter about turning down his inheritance and then losing his life's savings in the Bernie Madoff scandal, but still exhibiting a positive outlook of happy perseverance to life's reversals); Roko Belic, California-based Oscar-nominated director of the award-winning film "Happy"; Dr. Christine Carter, sociologist and positive psychology specialist at Berkeley University ; Rolling Stones keyboardist Chuck Leavell (who shared with Peter the joy he gets from working with his buddy former President Jimmy Carter on key environmental issues); Major League Baseball legend Shawn Green; celebrated super-model & businesswoman Monika Schnarre; Time magazine humour columnist Joel Stein; 84 year old Playboy cartoonist Doug Sneyd; Leo Bormans from Belgium, author of the respected "World Book of Happiness"(who explains what lies behind his discussions with global experts); and much more. (https://castlecarringtonpublishing.ca/being-happy-matters/)

CPSIA information can be obtained
at www.ICGtesting.com
Printed in the USA
BVHW041914020421
604057BV00016B/747